D1798522

THE OUTER SPHERES

BOOK TWO
OF
DIAMOND ROADS

Andrew Wallace

AC Experiments

Diamond Roads: The Outer Spheres
First Edition 2016

ISBN: 978-1542524575

www.andrewwallace.me
@AndrewWallaceDR

Cover design by Bonnita Moaby
www.facebook.com/bonnitadoodles

Published by AC Experiments Ltd
info@acexperiments.com

The AC Experiments name and logo
are registered trademarks

For Vicky

1

"They're in the chamber with you," 23 says in my head.

I grip the heavy rifle tighter.

"Where?" I say.

"Converging on your position," 23 says.

Her low, husky voice is hard with quiet authority. I narrow my eyes in frustration and peer into the eerie blue half-light of the Outer Spheres. My vantage point on a wide shelf high above the vast, empty diamond plain should be ideal, but…

"I can't see them," I say.

The other seven members of New Form Enterprise Unit 7/10 are suddenly awake and around me.

"Captain, they're two hundred metres from you," 23 says.

"Move back," the Ledge says.

We glide towards the last wall of Diamond City. Beyond the kilometre-thick spherical barrier, solid rock reaches all the way to the burned surface of the Earth.

"Forget it," 23 says. "The subs know you're there."

"But where," the Foster-Blacks says, "are *they*?"

"They're closing on you," 23 says. "I don't understand how you can't see them. There are at least five hundred now."

Our position, chosen for the security of the wall and a good view of the plain below, has become a terrible liability.

"How do they know we're here?" Velasquez says.

"I can see them from one direction but not the other," 23 says.

"Captain, these subs don't look right."

Fear makes the scars through the hacked blonde stubble on my scalp itch.

"Shall I get down there and have a gander?" Razor says.

"Not until we figure this out," the Ledge says.

I point to the far right.

"That archway is shallower now than it was earlier," I say. "It has slowly shrunk, millimetre by millimetre."

They turn to me.

"I think the subs are under the floor," I say.

They consider it.

"If you had that many kilos you'd use a proper assault force-" the Foster-Blacks begins.

"Wait," Iqbal says and no one speaks for a moment. "I hear them."

We listen to a shuffle of feet, sporadic muttering and the myriad frictions of many people on the move.

"But how…?" Khadisha whispers.

"Holo, isn't it?" Krae says.

A rope grows out of the floor beside him and slithers over the edge. We watch as it lowers; ten metres, fifteen, twenty and then its tip penetrates the floor without obstruction. Krae snatches up the rope and it shrinks towards us as he deposits it.

"They're all around you," 23 says.

The Ledge looks at me.

"Get behind us, Charity," he says.

I step back, bump against the wall and watch the unit take up defensive positions. For a while they wait, motionless.

The first subs explode through the floor! Emaciated and barely clothed, they move with jerky, last-ditch speed.

"Get back!" Razor roars at them.

I feel a clench of hopeless compassion. The NFE don't want to open fire on the subs; these tragic wrecks are not sub-human, just very unlucky. However, there are eight of us, five hundred of them and they are hungry.

"We will shoot!"

I lean forward to see how the subs got over twenty metres off the floor to reach us and spot a broad staircase beneath their scrabbling bare feet. I rest back against the wall and grip the rifle with renewed vigour. No starving sub would waste kilos on steps. Someone else has unleashed an army of the desperate on Unit 7/10.

The unit opens fire with predictably devastating results. The subs don't even slow down; they are a scraggy, stinking, barely human wave. Some tear flesh from falling comrades and swallow it before the floor absorbs the corpses. One woman bites into the shoulder of another; the first woman is no older than my twenty-four years but her attack rips out the last of her yellow teeth. She screams in frustration and rushes at the NFE until her toothless head is transformed into fine red mist by a shot from Khadisha. The body is seized; subs gulp the flowing blood and come at us again.

"There's another rec swarm," 23 says. "Somebody is watching us."

"Can you find out who?" the Ledge says.

"No," 23 says. "Do you want me to take it out?"

"Yes."

A series of tiny explosions lights the carnage.

"23: two-ship evac," the Ledge says.

Two big shadows bloom in the mezzanine between me and the rest of the unit. The shadows quickly gain definition and a pair of unremarkable four-person transports grows out of the floor. Each element of the transports is complete when it emerges, as if the ships are surfacing from a featureless, unfaceted diamond pool.

"Beta formation," the Ledge says.

We split into our usual double grouping and jump aboard the two ships as they lift off. Me, the Ledge, Velasquez and Krae are in one ship and the rest are in the other. Beneath us, the subs rush onto the mezzanine.

"Our orders have been revised," the Ledge continues. "We are to rendezvous with Units 4/23 and 8/17 at Fort 6 in MidZone."

"Sir?" Velasquez says as she looks behind at the crowded mezzanine. "What the *hell* was that?"

"I don't know," the captain replies. "We've never had subs act that way before."

"It's like they were drugged," I say.

The ship jolts; we are hurled against each other and the awful ground view gets a lot closer. There's no time to react as Krae pulls me into his arms. Inertia makes me drift in the unexpected embrace, as if gravity has packed up.

The ship hits the floor; I crash into Krae and something breaks in him.

The ship bounces and I'm hurled into the side panel so hard it's like the thing has it in for me. As we spin a few times I hear 23's calm, almost toneless voice again.

"Phase cannon," she says, "hidden in the floor behind the subs."

Unsure if I can move, I look through the broken hull and see a squat, ugly cannon below the holographic 'floor', which is now a bland ceiling. The holo blinks off to reveal the seemingly endless vault of the great chamber and the other NFE ship as it turns in the air towards us.

I force air past wrenching pain in my lungs and move my arms and legs. Nothing feels broken but when I roll off Krae he is motionless.

Velasquez runs at the phase cannon as it tracks the other ship. She blasts the barrel off with a single shot and without breaking stride hurls a grenade, turning away before it hits. I squint against the explosive glare as the shock wave nudges us. It should knock Velasquez flat but she's leapt off the floor so the wave simply pushes her harmlessly in mid-air. She lands and sprints back to us.

"Krae," the Ledge says.

"His back is broken," 23 says.

"Any other cannons?"

"No. They don't want us dead; it's something else."

I remember the vessel Harlan used against the Sons of the Crystal Mind.

"What about an armoured ship?" I say.

"That cannon was set to damage the vehicles we use on a standard evacuation," 23 says.

"They know our operating procedures," the Ledge says. "Whatever we use, they'll bring it down."

The other four reach us at the same time as Velasquez.

"They're closing in again," Iqbal says.

The subs race towards the crash site and more flood through the arch. As they sprawl over each other to get at us, Velasquez looks at Krae, unconscious and broken on the floor.

"Why do you have to be such a fat bastard?" she says.

She doesn't bother to hide the emotion in her voice. Her on-off relationship with Krae has survived far longer than I've known them. They seem an unlikely couple but, like fire and earth, are oddly well-suited. Velasquez runs a hand over her cropped black hair and looks up at the Ledge.

"23," he says. "Gif us a sled."

Krae rises off the floor atop a floating platform that supports his immobile bulk. We surround it, facing out as the subs rush at us. We open fire again but they are frenzied and unstoppable. As we shoot we move across the floor towards the archway.

"Pause," 23 says.

A transparent mask grows in front of each of us but we keep firing.

"Charity," the Ledge says.

I cease fire, pick up the mask and press it to my face. The mask seals itself; I raise my rifle and fire again as the process is repeated around the unit until everyone is protected.

"Get ready to run," 23 says. "Three, two one."

Gas hits the subs and they begin to stumble. Their faces twist as they are prevented yet again from getting at us and then they slowly fold to the ground.

One pulse of vitamins beneath each bony frame would take the edge off their horror, but I can give nothing. Jaeger Darwin, leader of the New Form Enterprise, controls my Aer account as part of his mysterious strategy for making me one of his own.

When all the subs are on the floor we sprint through their scattered bodies to the archway. Thankfully, the adjoining chamber is empty.

"Nothing," Spider Bob says.

"Halt," the Ledge says.

We stop running and stand in the creepy silence. Spider Bob is the other Unit Operator who along with 23 provides remote support. I've never met either oppo and don't even know what they look like although they are as much a part of the team as the Ledge or Iqbal. I realise that while 23 has given operational cover, Spider Bob has been scouring the Aer to find out who our problem really is.

"You need to grab some of 'em," Spider Bob says.

"How many?"

"Five."

The Ledge nods at Velasquez and the Foster-Blacks, who run back into the last chamber.

"How long to fix Krae?" I ask, feeling responsible.

"Four days," 23 says.

I look down at the massive, loyal soldier and feel wretchedly grateful.

More gunfire crackles next door.

"Now what?" Iqbal says.

"A couple of drones," 23 says. "Nothing Velasquez can't handle, the mood she's in."

Velasquez and the Foster-Blacks run back to join us with five unconscious subs on a second sled.

"They'll tell us what we want to know," Velasquez says with a gleam in her eyes I don't like.

I look at Krae on the other sled and think better of saying anything.

2

"Tell us who sent you," the Foster-Blacks says.

He manages to do so without menace as he kneels in front of the sub girl and looks up at her. The soldier's battered, ageing pretty-boy face and posh twit voice have been deemed the right combination to win his interviewee's trust. Incredibly, it seems to be working.

The sub has stopped crying and regards the Foster-Blacks with naturally large eyes made bigger by starvation. The girl then looks at the rest of the unit. We are arranged around the lower deck of the spherical train carriage so we don't crowd in, although the girl cannot miss Krae on his sled or the other four subs on theirs, still unconscious from the gas.

"FB," Khadisha says.

The Foster-Blacks cocks an ear.

"Three stops to MidZone."

As we sprinted for the train station the Foster-Blacks ran alongside the sub sled and inspected its sleeping cargo. Just before we boarded the train he giffed a number of objects and now hands one of them to the sub girl. It is a dental block for the well-established infection that swells one side of her face.

The girl slowly puts the block in her mouth. She is about fifteen, maybe younger but aged by harshness. Her light brown hair is matted and her left arm gnarled after a bad break. The dental block goes to work. Soon, the girl's eyes widen at the lack of agony and tears trickle down her face.

"You see?" the Foster-Blacks says. "We're all friends here."

The girl looks at us again.

"Ignore that lot; they can't help looking the way they do. And your chums there are just asleep. How's that tooth?"

She swallows, nods. Her swelling reduces and the redness fades.

The Foster-Blacks gets up to sit on a chair near the girl, apparently ignoring her.

The carriage rushes through its vacuum tube, Unit 7/10 the only passengers. Fort 6 is a kilometre from the nearest MidZone train station so the Foster-Blacks needs to work fast.

I shift, impatient. Velasquez looks at the sub girl from time to time, dark eyes glittering, and then stares through the carriage's opaque side. The Ledge watches through lowered lids. Iqbal is asleep.

Khadisha and Razor sit with eyes flickering as they process information for 10 Platoon. There is a lot to do; the NFE has numerous clients and is almost fully engaged on their behalf across the city.

The Foster-Blacks pulls a lurp stack from his bag and starts munching on one end of it. The girl's eyes get even bigger. At first, the Foster-Blacks pretends not to notice and then he offers the girl the lurp stack. She snatches it and bites down so fast she forgets the dental block. She jabs the food against it, surprised and almost comically enraged. No one laughs at her.

"Dental block, old girl," the Foster-Blacks says.

With frail dignity the girl pulls out the block and rests it on her lap. She bites into the lurp stack with newly reinforced, whitened teeth. She sways as the superfood starts to work and her eyes flicker.

The carriage slows. Razor and Khadisha blink away their work and ease over to stand either side of the door with rifles pointed out. Velasquez gets between the door and the sleds. Iqbal wakes up and moves to cover the Foster-Blacks, who shields the sub girl.

The train stops and extrudes a short corridor that connects to the platform.

"Stay down, Charity," the Ledge says.

I grip my rifle and keep low. Between the seats I see the unit aim weapons at the doors, which open to reveal an elderly couple pulling a trolley.

"Are you the mayor?" the old woman asks.

"No," Velasquez says.

"They could be spies," Razor mutters. "Do we kill them?"

"Oppos," the Ledge says.

"No," 23 says.

"Agreed," Spider Bob says.

"You need to get the next train," Velasquez tells the old woman.

"But we've got tickets-"

"Get... the next... train."

"Well!" the old woman says and turns to the old man.

"Don't look at me," he says. "I didn't want to go anyway."

The door closes as they start bickering. The train begins to move.

"Two stops," Khadisha says.

"FB," the Ledge says.

The sub girl recovers from the concentrated nutrition belting around her system and goes to take another bite. The Foster-Blacks puts a gentle finger on the food bar.

"Who sent you, darling?" he says.

She looks at the bar and clutches the dental block as if it is something precious.

"Pak," she mumbles.

"Pack?"

She nods.

"Tole us t'get you. All went there. Bad red."

"What's bad red?"

"In the floor. Bad red. Hungry. Bad."

I look at her feet. They are bare, like those of the other subs who attacked us.

"So you were with a pack of other... people and they told you to go and get us. When you arrived the floor went red with a drug and that's what made you attack us."

The sub girl nods.

"Coming up on another stop, FB," Khadisha says.

10

"Trouble at this one," 23 says.

The Foster-Blacks smiles at the sub girl.

"We need your help," he says.

The girl looks at Khadisha and then back at the Foster-Blacks.

"They said… Trage," she says.

"Not much about Trage," Spider Bob says. "No companies or groups. Seven people with the word in their name somewhere. None of them in AerMIS."

I shiver. If 'Trage' is not in the NFE's Aer Military Intelligence System then the battalion won't have encountered them before and we will have nothing to base a defence on.

The carriage begins to slow and the unit tenses. I am uncomfortably aware that we can't grow anything from the train's closed protocol floor; while onboard we'll have to use the weapons we already carry, whether they are suitable or not.

I look at the Ledge. Without turning he extends a hand palm down: *stay low*. I shiver again.

"Get down, darling," the Foster-Blacks says to the sub girl.

She curls up so tight it's as if she has folded into herself.

The carriage stops but the unit does not move. The girl whimpers as the doors open. I glimpse clearing smoke and catch the now-familiar smell of burned meat.

"I got most of them with a goggle bomb," 23 says, "but-"

Shots cut through the smoke, which enhances their gaudy colours. The incoming bolts ricochet harmlessly off the train. In contrast, the NFE find their targets and the attackers' shots are replaced by screams, then silence.

The doors close and the carriage moves off. The Ledge looks at the sub girl, who is a small, sobbing knot against one of the chairs.

"Try another sub," the Ledge says.

The Foster-Blacks reaches for the sled.

"No. Velasquez," the Ledge says.

The Foster-Blacks tosses a hypo to Velasquez and she presses it against the exposed, bony arm of the nearest male sub. The sub's eyes fly open and I see at once we've made a mistake.

"Satan!" the sub shouts. "Many-headed Satan!"

He leaps from the sled and lunges at Velasquez, who bats him away. The sub bounces off a chair without noticing and rushes towards a small elevator to the empty upper deck.

"Centria renders curses but is herself cursed!" the sub howls.

I sigh inwardly. Not the subs as well. There has been a lot of talk in-Aer about how my home enclave is using supernatural means to battle its rival, VIA Holdings. What gives these rumours uncomfortable plausibility isn't just the rumoured 'Hex' on VIA Holdings but also the fact that Centria is bankrupt.

Almost nobody knows this information and fewer still are aware the bankruptcy was engineered by VIA's Chief, Loren Descarreaux. I uncovered the conspiracy last year, which led to the abortion of the much-vaunted VIA/Centria merger and the current war, which Centria shouldn't be able to afford.

"Bile!" the sub screams.

He's got the strength of the mad and isn't even slowed by a tackle from Razor. As they struggle, the Ledge applies a chopping blow between the sub's shoulders. The sub sags but then perks up again.

"Roscoe will bring us salvation," he says and collapses.

"There's a Roscoe Trage," Spider Bob says from his unknown location kilometres away. "He works as a bodyguard for some number-monkey in Reech Consolidated."

"Makes sense," the Ledge says. "This has all been amateur hour so far."

"But why?" Iqbal says.

"Unknown," Spider Bob says.

"Any associates?" Razor says.

"No," Spider Bob says. "He's a solo operator. Mm. Wife's quite hot. She runs a company that searches out unused patents, tarts them up and rebrands them. Correction: did run a company. It went bust a year ago."

"Are these people stupid?" Velasquez says.

"Perhaps Unit 4/23 can ask them," the Ledge says.

"Unit 4/23 will have to find them first," Spider Bob says. "There are no address coordinates listed and I can't see which business unit of Reech Consolidated Roscoe works with. This won't be fast."

"Not fast enough for your team, Captain," 23 says. "You're coming up on the last stop."

"Problem there?" the Ledge says.

"No, but…"

"Well?"

"I think you're being directed somewhere."

There's a pause.

"Understood," the Ledge says.

"Sir, you need to decide what to do about Krae," 23 says.

"Take him with us," the Ledge says, faint irritation in his voice for the first time.

"If you get into another fire-fight he'll be hit," 23 says.

The unseen woman's harsh voice echoes in my head as we all look at Krae.

"Fuck," Spider Bob says.

"You're not helping, Bob," 23 says.

Even though the Operators are in different locations unknown to each other I sense tension flare between them. Bob backs down immediately.

"Okay," he says.

"I can rent a secure space near the train station for the time it will take Krae to heal," 23 says. "Me and Spider Bob can watch over him."

The Ledge turns to Velasquez, who looks heartbroken, furious and determined all at once. After a second, she nods.

The carriage slows, stops and the doors open. The unit maintains its defensive position.

13

The view outside is typical MidZone: chaotic and lively, with the only fighting between rival adverts as they pulse around the train tube.

"The subs?" Iqbal says.

"Leave them on the train," 23 says.

"Agreed," the Ledge says.

"All clear outside," 23 says.

The unit edges out of the carriage. The platform leads to a skywalk that runs through a dense collection of black cubic buildings and assemblies. I check the clock on my Aerac, displayed in the bottom left of the molecule-thick screens over my eyes. It's 4.13am.

Even at this hour the skywalk is busy. A group of what look like improbably muscular subs with an air of unearthly calm and a daunting set of heavy ordnance does not bother anybody, although we are given a wide berth.

The carriage moves past, its tube a bright streak in the MidZone night. The large chamber is downlit by two assemblies, one a cube that matches those around us and the other an incongruous arrangement of ornate, interlocking wheels. Someone has tried to organise the buildings on the chamber floor into a pleasingly circular pattern, only for someone else to plonk a twisting tower composed of large, crystalline fragments close enough to ruin the whole effect.

"FB," Razor says.

The sub girl has followed us off the train.

"She can't find out where we're leaving Krae, or the location of Fort 6," 23 says, the truth of her words not making her any more likeable.

The Foster-Blacks stands over the sub girl.

"Go on, little lady," he says.

The girl clutches the dental block to her bony chest and shakes her head.

"We have to help our friend," the Foster-Blacks says. "We have to go."

"Come back?" the sub girl says.

The Foster-Blacks thinks for a moment and then says, "No."

The girl nods and we move off without a word, leaving her there. We start to run and soon settle into a shared rhythm. Just short of a sprint, it is sustainable because we've all spent entire days pounding through the Outer Spheres beneath a disc that increased gravity in its shadow. Without breaking stride I glance at Krae on his sled between us and try to put the sub girl out of my mind.

The skywalk soars into the next chamber, which is of a similar size but much more crowded. Ahead, the skywalk terminates in a vast honeycomb from which other walkways ribbon off into the flashing distance.

"In there," 23 says.

We enter the mottled golden building and a doorway opens on our right. We push Krae inside; the sled lowers and sinks into the floor.

For a moment the sled lies there, encased in clear diamond; then the vehicle then shimmers and disappears as its molecules flow back to 23's Aer account. Krae sinks into the floor as well, his heavy, mournful face still visible. The huge body straightens and appears to relax as the Basis begins its healing.

The unit looks down at Krae for a few moments. There is a sense of quiet, dignified sadness; a respectful efficiency. After a while, the Ledge walks to the door and the unit follows. One person doesn't move however and it isn't Velasquez; it's me.

"Charity," Khadisha says.

I shake my head as I remember another large man lying injured in the floor: my love Harlan Akintan, who lost his fortune and was nearly battered to death by Jaeger Darwin for trying to save me. Unable to speak to Harlan for over a year, let alone see him I've tried to use NFE discipline to avoid thinking about him at all. Sometimes it works. Now though I stare down at Krae and am reminded with such visceral force I feel more like the real problem than our unknown enemy.

It's Velasquez who gets me moving. She puts her arm around my shoulders; we kind of latch together and walk out of the room. As the door closes behind us we begin to run again.

"Fort 6 is in the next chamber," 23 says. "They'll try again any time now."

"Bob, any more on the Trages?" the Ledge says.

There's an odd pause. It quickly becomes a silence and I know I am not alone in feeling profound, almost exhausting dread. An oppo is never silent. An oppo is always, always there.

"What-?" I say.

"They've got him," Razor says.

"Fort 6 may be compromised," 23 says.

"Everything all right with you?" the Ledge says.

"For now," 23 says.

"We'll head for that built up area," the Ledge says. "23, have a warship waiting for us."

"Confirmed," 23 says.

We enter an alley formed by the high wall of a skywalk on one side and a set of buildings like giant steps on the other. A small orange warship with comforting heavy armour and even more comforting cannons grows out of the floor ahead of us. Relief is an almost physical pressure.

"Take cover-!" 23 shouts, the loudest I've ever heard her.

Whatever advice she was about to give is drowned out by the fire that rains around us. A beam from above, so powerful that even when I turn away it still blinds me, shatters the orange warship. One of the fragments whistling past flattens Velasquez. She jumps up but stumbles, blood pouring down her side.

"Protect Charity at all costs," the Ledge says.

As one the unit forms a protective curve, their backs to me and their weapons already firing.

What…?

An explosion from behind knocks me to my knees. For a second I look up at the rest of Unit 7/10, backlit by gunfire: suddenly enormous and magnificent. I flip over, rifle out and see that a hole has been blown in the skywalk wall. Through it I glimpse building lights in the chamber below but no other attack. When I glance back I see the little sub girl crouched behind the Foster-Blacks' legs.

"Did she lead them to us?" I say.

"No," 23 says. "They were already here."

The Foster-Blacks shifts so his upper body protects the girl as he and the rest of the unit emit a controlled volley of firepower. I raise my heavy rifle.

"Charity, get in the pod," 23 says.

I look behind again to see a small black sphere rise into view beyond the hole in the skywalk wall. Uncertain, I turn back to the unit. Blood still pumps out of Velasquez but she doesn't stop shooting. Razor and the Ledge artfully direct decimating fire in what looks like ten directions. Khadisha, who like me is ambidextrous, operates two rifles at the same time. Iqbal is almost a blur as he fires while seeming to increase the body area he protects me with. The sub girl looks into my eyes. She still holds the dental block.

"I don't think so, 23," I say and take aim.

The rifle melts as 23 deposits it. Undeterred I raise my right hand, where the n-gun hidden in my index finger can produce firepower greater than anything the unit is using. The n-gun immediately goes offline.

"23!"

"Get in the pod, Charity."

I reach for the fuze in Velasquez's belt. Something whips around me from behind: an auto-harness on a rope.

"No!" I scream.

I'm yanked into the pod, which seals itself and detaches from the skywalk. I float quietly away from the battle as a delta of weapon beams converges on Unit 7/10. They are outnumbered but keep firing, their shots a bright fan against the onslaught.

"You can't do this!" I shout.

"Our orders are to protect you at all costs, Charity," 23 says.

I kick the front window furiously but cannot smash through so I punch the pod wall instead. I don't make a mark on it as I drift down away from the skywalk. Already out of the attackers' line of sight, the matt surface of the pod disguises it completely in the darkness.

There is so much smoke and debris the battle seems like a huge physical being. Gunfire is a dreadful pulse as the expanding mass engulfs adverts that cruise surreally through it like a virus.

Horribly, one of the weapons on the skywalk stops shooting. I can't help wondering who it is.

"Can't you do something?" I say.

"My focus is you."

There is just one weapon firing up now.

"Charity," 23 says.

Through my terrified rage I hear the subtle chime of grief in her voice.

"Don't let it be for nothing," she says.

The last light on the skywalk goes out as the pod races into the dark.

3

[ONE YEAR EARLIER]

"Let me go," I say.

Jaeger Darwin stands in his baroque, multi-levelled room in the New Form Enterprise assembly as it glides through the Outer Spheres. Around us, priceless Old World artefacts line the walls: fragments of machinery, clothing encased in diamond panels and a battered beige box with buttons whose symbols are partly worn away.

My orange one-piece uniform matches his. When we first met, I thought Jaeger wore no insignia but what looked like a panel on the left of his chest is in fact an emblem. The square is bisected twice, from top left to bottom right and across the centre. I realise the symbol is formed from the letters N, F and E superimposed over each other.

Most of the soldiers just have the square. Others wear the square with the diagonal, while some have got the crossbar as well. From the way they interact, the ones with the diagonal appear to be captains while those with both lines are commanders. Commander looks like the senior rank, reporting to the general before me whose emblem sports an additional square border.

"If I let you go," Jaeger says, "what would you do?"

"Save Dad," I say.

Jaeger's expression doesn't change but I know I've answered incorrectly. I feel a surge of fury at his testing me. We are both intelligent people; this is ridiculous. However, my anger quickly subsides into despair.

I thought Jaeger simply meant to prove a point by taking me. The journey from Centria to here seemed ironic, almost absurd. How can I have been in Mum and Dad's house a mere two hours ago?

"Save Dad," Jaeger says.

His rich voice is empathetic but cold. It's easy to think I hear envy, although hardly likely. Jaeger didn't even know he and I were related until today in Centria's abandoned Surveillance Centre, when Balatar Descarreaux blurted the truth in a futile attempt to remain alive.

"Do you think you can beat the Velossin?" Jaeger says.

"Yes," I say.

Jaeger nods.

"Can you beat me?" he says.

"Eventually."

"I meant now."

The n-gun comes back online. It shouldn't create any sensation but there seems to be a buzz at the tip of my right index finger, as if my mind is dressing things up for effect.

"This room is open protocol," Jaeger says. "Use whatever resources you wish."

My Aer account is suddenly available, its kilos ready to be turned into weapons by the Basis. Jaeger stands very still, hands empty. The well-made angles of his face are deceptively calm.

I am so dissociated I actually feel relaxed. It might be exhaustion; I nearly lost my life, my family and my home. Or it could be the drastic recalibration of my relationship with Ursula and the end of my obsession with her. Finally, it may be adjustment to revelations; about my origins, the Centrian conspiracy and the Sons of the Crystal Mind whose insanity brought me here. I doubt it though.

I hesitate because it seems futile, as if I don't think I *should* do anything. So, lacking focus and only part-engaged despite the stakes I twitch my right arm up to fire the n-gun at Jaeger.

He moves so fast there's a lag between observation and comprehension. I watch him cover the distance between us as his hand launches at my throat. His other hand bats aside the n-gun and grips my fingers so hard they fold in on themselves. Now it's pointing at me, the n-gun goes offline.

I choke as he actually lifts me up by the throat. I kick at him but he holds me away, his arm extending as if I weigh nothing. As my neck stretches with my own weight I remember I can grow any weapon I want. I try and concentrate, but I'm in agony.

I didn't have this trouble against the Sons of the Crystal Mind and there were hundreds of them. Why can't I do it again? Success ought to soak in and change me so I can replicate it on demand like the Basis, endlessly extruding whatever it is that everyone needs.

Bitter disappointment is worse than the pain. My arrogance and incompetence have doomed Dad, my real dad not this brute unwitting donor. My supposed victories are of no consequence against reality, a force that given one chance grips the throat and chokes off oxygen, drawing dark curtains across everything.

Jaeger lets go and I drop to the floor. My legs are too weak to withstand the impact so I sprawl and whack my chin. The n-gun goes offline. My Aerac, with its comms, ID code and precious kilos disappears as Jaeger takes it back under his control. I can't blame him. I offered my freedom to save Ursula, never thinking Jaeger would trick me.

How very foolish I have been. Just because I don't value myself doesn't mean others feel the same way: Mum, in charge of Centria's armies now that Anton is dead; Keris, all-powerful Chief of Centria and another twelfth of the Guidance like Ellery and Gethen. All of them were willing to listen just at the point I cannot speak, even from a distance.

Then there's Harlan. I'm never too tired to feel the sweet clutch of desire at the thought of him. He makes me feel so beautiful, so vital…

I expect Jaeger to kick me as I lie there, pathetic in my obviousness; idiotic with the vain idea I ever stood a chance. Instead he kneels and brushes my long, thick blonde hair out of my face with his elegant fingers.

"The Velossin pursuing your father is a brainwashed killer, engineered to move faster than a normal person can see," he says.

I struggle not to cry and stare furiously across the floor.

"I would not be able to defeat a Velossin," Jaeger adds, "and since you can't beat me…"

He watches me calmly, his grey eyes neither mocking nor critical.

I manage to speak through my bruised throat.

"I… would… find a… way."

"I can help," Jaeger says. "Get up now."

Wavering, I climb to my feet and we face each other as I rub my throat.

"You think you're a prisoner," he says.

I can't help a snort of laughter.

"I *am* a prisoner, Jaeger," I say.

"Where would you be, if not here?"

"With my family."

"In Centria," he says.

I think of the spherical enclave nestling like a pearl at the heart of Diamond City.

"Yes," I say. "In Centria."

"There's going to be a war," Jaeger says. "Now the merger between Centria and VIA Holdings has failed, VIA will seek dominance through some other route. Centria is now surrounded by the VIA complex, so if you were inside you would not be able to get out."

"I would be free."

"Trapped inside an enclave?" Jaeger says. "In the centre of an underground city no one can leave?"

"You need me as a hostage," I say.

"Yes, but everyone knows I won't kill you; I would have done it by now."

"Well, good," I say. "So what do you want?"

"Join us."

"I have joined you."

"No, you haven't," Jaeger says.

I glare at him.

"Charity, I could keep you in this assembly, which is easily hidden. You would be comfortable."

He knows I couldn't bear it. I sigh.

"What's the alternative?"

"Become one of us, like I always wanted you to," Jaeger says.

"I am one of you," I say.

"You wear an orange uniform and you are physically here. That's it."

"I don't know what you mean."

"Train with us. Understand the New Form."

"Okay."

I have yet to see Jaeger smile but I think the odd expression that ripples across his face is the nearest he gets.

"It's not an 'okay' sort of offer," he says.

"Why not?"

He blinks finally and then looks down.

"There won't be anyone shouting at you, telling you what to do or bullying you into succeeding." Jaeger's voice is softer now, almost sad. "The only person who can make you achieve what you need to achieve is you."

He looks up.

"I do not make this offer lightly Charity, and I will not make it again."

"I wasn't very impressive against you just now," I say.

"Certain things encourage me. I see from your Centrian training records how you've refined your natural strength and agility although it's clear you never understood why."

"I thought it would help me get promoted."

Jaeger does smile now, which makes him look surprisingly kind.

"In a way it has," he says.

This conversation is not going as I expected.

"Another encouragement is the way you fought the Sons of the Crystal Mind that first time, on your own," Jaeger says. "You displayed a phenomenal talent for combat."

"Thank you," I say, hesitant.

"I doubt you would be able to repeat it though."

"Why?" I say.

"You would worry too much about having to do exactly the same thing again."

We both know he's right but I still struggle to meet his eyes.

"So," I say, waiting for the words to come but they don't.

"You need to learn how to combine strategy and instinct," Jaeger says.

"People say I think too much," I say.

"You just need to find the true path."

"That would be useful," I say and realise I mean it.

"You uncovered the conspiracy in Centria," Jaeger continues. "The enclave was bankrupt because of Loren Descarreaux. Your parents found out so Loren put your mother in a coma and sent the Velossin after your father. No one else managed to work that out. I didn't."

The back of my neck feels wrong, as if the vertebrae have been wrenched out of alignment. I focus on the pain to counter the growing conviction that Jaeger's words make sense.

"Part of me was used to make you, Charity," Jaeger says. "Let me bring your potential out."

"How long will it take?"

"Three years' training."

"Dad will be dead by then."

Jaeger regards me.

"There are five stages," he says. "Stage One is the new recruit, or 'newt'. You serve with each of the battalion's hundred units and train with them in combat, endurance, meditation-"

"Meditation?" I say.

"Don't interrupt. During this period you assist under supervision on operations and complete a project at the same time. The NFE needs as much brain power as stamina but it must be aligned with the mission. That's where mental discipline comes in; hence meditation, which is shorthand for our range of psychological techniques. Do you understand?"

"Yes."

"Stage Two is inclusion in an agreed number of supervised operations, first as a combatant and then as an operator. You must also complete another project. Like the first one it is not combat and will be commercial or investigative in nature.

"Stage Three is Stage Two without the supervision or the project. Stage Four is espionage, both in the field and in support functions, which can either be a series of short missions or fewer long ones."

He looks at me.

"What about Stage Five?" I say before I can stop myself.

"Stage Five is the New Form," Jaeger says.

I want to be a Stage Five.

Damn, he's got me!

I hesitate, however.

"Charity, understand that if you agree, it will be the hardest thing you have ever done. We will make you even more resourceful than you already are by reducing you to your essence. We will make you resilient by being worse than anyone else you will ever meet. We will make you understand the nature of fear so it becomes your weapon.

"However, we can't do any of that if you do not commit now. You believe your choice has been removed and your freedom curtailed but I hope you can see that the opposite is true."

I go to speak but nerves force me to swallow.

"Are there terms?" I say eventually.

"No," Jaeger says. "To impose any agreement on you with an

automated penalty would never work."

I think about Mum and Ursula, far away. I think of Harlan, who must have done everything Jaeger said and more. If I become like Harlan will that make us even closer?

Whatever I do, I won't see my loved ones for a long time. Should I just make the best of it? Perhaps there will be a way I can turn this to my advantage-

"You will never be in a position to trick me and get back to Centria," Jaeger says.

I feel myself heat up with embarrassment and swallow again. It still hurts.

"You can understand," I say.

"Of course I understand. My point is that you can do more for everyone you love here, with us. But only if you want to."

From what happened to me and Ursula I know I'm unprepared for life outside Centria. I've also seen how powerful the NFE are, how strong. Could I be like that?

Yes.

"You are concerned about your father," Jaeger says. "It is unusual for anyone to have survived as long as he has, so it's likely he will survive long enough for us to assist him."

"Likely…"

"You must help Connor at the right time, or you will be killed along with him."

I remember Jaeger's speed, the pain in my throat.

"You said 'us'. Will you help me save Dad?" I say.

"Join us, fully and willingly and your Stage Two project will be to rescue your father. I will put all the resources of the New Form Enterprise behind you."

I don't know whether it is power I feel or impatience to get started.

"What would the Stage One project be?" I say.

"Find Keris Veitch," Jaeger says.

Of course. Jaeger didn't unearth his mystical kilo source in Centria and thinks Keris has got it hidden elsewhere. Plus it's obvious he still loves her.

"Isn't she back in Centria?" I say.

"No, she never returned. Centria doesn't know where she is either."

"Will you hurt Keris?"

"Not deliberately."

The pain somehow recedes; I straighten and look into Jaeger's eyes.

"I will join you, Jaeger," I say and to my surprise it feels right.

I expect a reaction from Jaeger; maybe a fanfare or some fireworks but he continues to watch me impassively.

"The New Form Enterprise has a military foundation, but is not an army as such," he says. "At just over a thousand people it's not big enough for that. We make our money with security consulting, as mercenaries and from retained investments. We do these things for a higher purpose, which you will one day understand.

"Notwithstanding, you need to learn how to salute. We don't do a lot of it, only when it really matters, like today. This is how: fingers tight together, middle finger coming to rest at the edge of your forehead and elbow back as far as it will go. Your palm always faces the person you salute to show you're not armed."

"The n-gun…?"

"It will be pointed at you, not me."

"Ah, right." I say.

Jaeger Darwin, leader of the New Form Enterprise and most powerful warrior in the world salutes me. Feeling slightly silly, like I'm playing at soldiers, I salute him back.

"Welcome, Charity Freestone," he says.

4

[CURRENT]

I look up through the floor that encases me at the underside of hotel room furniture. The bed is a block of darkness, foreshortened from down here into a wide, squat trapezium. Directly above me sits a large safe. It's the same length as I am: there to protect some precious object like an Old World artefact, or so the story 23 is telling with these furnishings goes. Mats are scattered across the floor to break up the large space and make it less likely that an intruder will discover the girl hiding in the floor.

The Basis ensures I don't need to blink or breathe. I don't feel restless, although I've been in the floor for three days and I suspect 23 has kept me asleep to regulate post-traumatic stress. I feel different as well, but can't explain why because grief keeps bubbling up.

My tears are efficiently absorbed as I remember Iqbal patiently dissecting my airborne battle with the Sons of the Crystal Mind; Velasquez - never R8chel - cheerfully repeating 'Man, I love fighting!' as she taught me everything she knew about it; running through the Outer Spheres with Khadisha, a human being seemingly incapable of exhaustion who showed me that as long as I can breathe I can run; cheers from the others as Krae revealed how to use his own terrific strength against him just before I sent him flying.

I expected Razor to despise me for my privileged background but he had no time for any of that; his tone of faint indignation came from a clear but perplexed view of how insane everything is. It made him a good leader but not as good as the Ledge, who somehow combined enormous compassion with the sense that the stupidest thing anyone could do was cross him.

Mourning becomes too much. I want to crouch on the floor and shake it all out with tears hot on my face. The words take ages to assemble as I message 23.

I need to get out.

No, comes the immediate reply.

LET ME OUT!

Stay where you are.

I wake up. Six hours have passed. 23 anaesthetised me! Anger is quickly displaced by concern about the length of time I've been trapped here and what it is we are waiting for. Increasingly uneasy, I go to message 23 again and then stop.

What if *23* led Unit 7/10 into that ambush? The Ledge's final order was to protect me at all costs. I must be strategically important and therefore of commercial value. 23 couldn't just hand me over though; she had to get the unit protecting me out of the way, take me to an agreed location and then…

I check the n-gun but it's still offline. The n-gun is operated via my Aerac, which is controlled by Jaeger who has delegated most of it to 23.

"Charity, your heart rate is higher than when the subs attacked," 23 says.

"Let me out of this floor 23," I say, sub-vocalising without moving my jaw as the Aer sharpens my words until they sound normal.

"Just tell me what the matter is."

I stay silent. Suddenly, I'm in a virtual space: wide and cylindrical with orange walls that curve into a shallow dome. In front of me just above the floor floats a cloud of scintillating fragments. It's roughly circular, taller than the walls and about a metre thick.

This is the first time I've seen 23 in any form. The charade is annoying; I don't care what she looks like. I picture a tall, rangy woman in late middle age with nondescript clothes, thin brown hair to her shoulders and a fringe she cuts herself. She won't have a partner or kids and probably went bad because her life has led to an empty room, taking care of people she never meets who are indifferent about whether or not she survives. I can almost sympathise; I wouldn't put up with it.

"You need to stay calm," she says.

"Okay," I say.

"Don't mess with me."

"How can I mess with you? I'm locked in a floor and you control everything I do."

"I don't control your mind," 23 says.

I look at the orange walls. Am I in this simulation so I can be extracted from the hotel floor without difficulty?

"I'm just very sad about the unit, 23," I say.

Her cloud ripples.

"I knew the Ledge before we joined the NFE," she says.

I nod, although this unexpected information is clearly meant to distract me.

"Twenty-five years' service in one scrap or another," continues 23. "I joined the NFE because of him. He was accepted first and told me about it; even put a good word in. Odd we were never lovers, it just never came up. I regret that now. Ah well."

"23, I'm very exposed up there."

"No one knows your coordinates, not even the NFE. With me it's different; I had to access AerMIS to get our maximum kilo ration. Whoever is after us will therefore know where I am so I've had to relocate. I can't be sure if…" She stops herself. "Anyway, that's my problem. So relax."

"Fine."

"You are more tense now than when we started this conversation."

I realise I cannot hide from her. At least she can tell me why she did it.

"How did they know where to find us, 23?" I say.

"AerMIS, I told you."

"Impossible," I say. "Only Jaeger can access the whole thing. You're not telling me he did this are you?"

There is a pause.

"What are you saying?" 23 says.

"You led them to us, 23."

The cloud flashes red!

"How dare you," 23 says, her low, husky voice choked with rage.

I realise I have made a terrible mistake.

"It's just as well I'm not there Charity Freestone, or I would slap you into next week."

"But who else-?"

"I don't know!"

"The Trages?"

"Did that attack look like the work of a walking shield and some doris who works in recycling?" 23 says.

"No…"

"They took our warship apart, Charity. Only certain frequencies can do that and these people knew them. Of course, I do too so I understand why you think I'm a traitor."

"I'm obviously wrong-" I say.

"No, let's look at it. Maybe you see me as some beat-up old loser with nothing left to sell but her team."

I swallow as the cloud writhes before me.

"Her team," 23 continues, "who she fought alongside, fought for, fought *as* like they were her own flesh and blood; who she watched over, endlessly, when there was no one else."

I put my hands to my face. Although the tears aren't real they still feel hot and wet. I rub my eyes and look at the cloud again.

"I'm so sorry, 23," I say.

"It's all right," she says. "We don't need to mention it again."

Humbled, I stand in front of the scintillating cloud, which has reverted to its earlier form.

"Thank you," I say.

"I just need a few more hours, Charity."

"Okay."

"I will give you Aer access for now. Let me know if you need to buy intel."

"What do you want me to do?" I say.

"You still haven't found Keris Veitch."

5

Keris wears a standard blue Centrian uniform; fierce pride in it visible on her face. Her long blonde hair is a simple braid, very different from the first time I met her a year ago when it was interwoven with flowers and emeralds.

There's an alarming hint of red in her cheeks and her violet eyes are bright. Soon, someone is going to be very sorry because Keris isn't just angry; Keris is furious. Any sane person would vacate their present circumstances to live undetected far away. However, the person opposite Keris isn't sane; the person opposite Keris is Loren Descarreaux.

Loren has eschewed functional simplicity and gone for a kind of garish revolutionary chic. Her gleaming copper bob has grown out and been roughened to give her a wild, almost desperate look. Gone too are the shimmery, metallic skin-tight gowns and vertiginous heels, replaced by work boots, coarsely-cut trousers that accentuate her legs and a high-collared dark grey tunic with red piping.

The adjudicator in tonight's discussion is Rich Jablonski, editor of the purportedly disliked but nonetheless very popular *Cron*. Rich is smart enough to know he wouldn't stand a chance against the other two but dim enough to have turned up anyway. He is a thin, spivvy man in a tight-fitting yellow suit with improbably shiny black hair moulded to his narrow head and a perpetually sympathetic expression that would probably remain in place no matter how many times it was punched.

Keris and Loren look solid but unlike Rich are present as holograms. The protagonists stand in the centre of an arena filled with a thousand people. Keris and Loren face each other with Rich between and slightly back from them. This broadcast debate, the first in the war, is probably being watched by most of Diamond

City.

"The war, you see, is so unnecessary Keris," Loren says.

Her French accent is stronger than I remember. She has a tendency to pace and sneak conspiratorial looks at the crowd.

Keris nods, looking pained as if to say *Yes; why must things be like this, you pointless lunatic whore?*

"Your people die," Loren says, "my people die. People getting in the way, they die."

"It's people in the way I feel sorry for," Rich says, his nasal, indignant voice straining for compassion.

"No one wants that," Keris says.

Her fury makes it clear that the people in the way were killed by VIA Holdings, not Centria.

"Keris, if you really cared you would say, enough of this bloodshed. You would say, let us sit down and speak-"

"We are speaking," Keris says.

"Not like this circus with this-this…"

Loren glares at Rich, who misses the point and nods encouragingly.

"Well," Keris says, "we spoke a lot last year, didn't we, Loren? During the diligence phase of the proposed merger between VIA Holdings and Centria, when we had the opportunity to enlarge our influence for the good of Diamond City? Before we found out that VIA Holdings is in fact bankrupt?"

"VIA Holdings is not bankrupt!" Loren says, indignation breaking through her righteous exterior. "It is Centria who is bankrupt!"

The fury goes out of Keris's face as she laughs, long and hard. Perhaps she really does think it's funny, although I can't think why. Loren is telling the truth.

"Centria is the most powerful commercial, cultural and military force in Diamond City," Keris says as she gets her breath back. "I doubt we could go out of business if we tried."

I almost believe her: I, who saw the truth in Centria's accounts before anyone else.

"And if VIA Holdings is so bankrupt, how are we winning against you?" Loren says.

"You're not winning," Keris says. "However, you have a knack of being able to make money quickly at the expense of people who invest in you. Your products are cheap and poorly patented. Your battle shares do not yield at the required levels and you have expanded so quickly you give the impression of being a greater security than is economically possible. It would be tempting to let you continue and let everyone see what a shoddy operation you run but for the cost in lives."

"You do not care about lives, Keris Veitch," Loren says.

"Yes I do," Keris says.

"Everyone except my son," Loren says and spit shines on her trembling lips.

"We gave Balatar control of Centria's internal security," Keris says. "He was engaged to our People's Princess-"

"Who you threw out like garbage!"

"Ursula Freestone made an error of judgement in truly horrible circumstances," Keris says, "so yes: for a while she was an ex. Given that a man died I do not think her treatment unreasonable."

You weren't there when Ursula was forced to relive every second of that man's death as he was burned alive, Keris. You weren't there when she was gang-raped in New Runcton.

Eventually, my rage goes back to where it lives when I'm not aware of it.

"Besides," Keris says, "Centria's policy of exile has been repealed. We accept it was too harsh, but we are driven to excel on behalf of those we are responsible for."

Loren giggles, her voice laced with ironic despair.

"You are not responsible for me," she says.

"I know you too are a Centrian ex, Loren," Keris says. "Our

merger could have been the first of many reconciliations, in which our former colleagues return to us with the benefit of experience from out in the city."

"Those still alive," Rich says.

"Centria doesn't rule Diamond City, Rich," Keris says. "No one does and quite right too. If the city is dangerous we must do what we can with every resource at our disposal."

"Where were your resources when my son was murdered?" Loren cries.

"Bal's loss was terrible," Keris says.

"Terrible," Rich echoes.

Loren snorts, her contempt somehow broken by grief.

"Yes," Keris says and frowns. "And yet he was in the most secure place in Diamond City."

"Centria spies on its own people all the time," Loren says. "You *do* know what happened, Keris."

"Every rec in Centria had been deactivated and the surveillance officers suspended," Keris says. "Balatar Descarreaux authorised that action. We don't know why."

"He did not get the chance to explain," Loren says.

Again, she is right.

"Loren, I realise that VIA stands for 'Vengeance Is All'-" Keris says.

"It does not!"

"But you must stop killing people just to get your own back-"

"Varied Investments Associated…"

"Uh, ladies," Rich says.

"You were a Centrian ex because you weren't good enough," Keris says.

"Vengeance Is All – you are a madwoman, mad!"

"Now, we did agree an enlightened discussion on the current conflict with no input from special advisors-"

"Stop taking your life's failures out on Diamond City, Loren,"

Keris says.

"And no, uh, personal stuff…"

"You break everyone's heart Keris because you do not have one."

"Ahem…" Rich says.

"It's not my fault you're a failure, Loren."

"Pah!"

"Not my fault, not Diamond City's, not the fault of everyone you killed…"

"I killed no one!"

"We're engaged in a war, so you did, and you still do."

"Before then I didn't. You are the killer, Keris."

"No, I'm not."

"We'll be right back after these messages…"

"You sold your soul Keris, to put a curse on us!"

"Tonight's discussion sponsored by Atticus Gibsnax…"

"I don't need anything that extreme to beat you, Loren."

"Good-looking food you can listen to," Rich says.

"Centria has unleashed ancient evil on Diamond City!" Loren turns to the audience. "Help me defeat them!"

6

The debate ended after that. Dated seven months ago, it was the last time Keris was seen interacting with anyone. She has appeared regularly since, usually speaking directly to Centria's 'investors', who now include everyone in Diamond City not aligned with Loren.

Keris has ditched the simple military attire. Instead, she favours ever more exotic outfits; a sartorial journey from the drab horror of war to some brighter place where she awaits us all. Her actual location remains a mystery, even to me. Aware of my situation, she would never reply to a message and I've given up trying to contact her.

Jaeger believes Keris has got an unending supply of kilos, which caused the Ruby War two years ago when the NFE tried to invade Centria. It also motivated Jaeger to save Ursula from the Sons of the Crystal Mind when I told him I would get him access to the enclave in return.

We agreed terms, which were formalised in-Aer and programmed into the Basis. If he saved my sister I would get Jaeger and 500 of the NFE inside Centria by a certain time, otherwise he would gain control of my Aerac. Unknown to me, he deliberately turned up with 499 and now I'm his.

It's easy to imagine Keris overcoming Centria's bankruptcy with this mysterious kilo source but I don't see how such a thing can exist. Diamond City is a fully contained environment fifty kilometres underground. Kilos, the raw material the Basis uses to create any product we want, are numerous but finite.

Perhaps Jaeger's fabled kilo supply is supernatural in origin and the 'Hex' is part of the deal. If so, I wonder what the price will be. I can't imagine a worse predicament than the one humanity finds itself in now.

I toy with contacting 23, simply to have someone to talk to. I've been on my own for more than a day, reviewing my Keris material and checking in-Aer detection. However, as I acknowledge the continuing lack of results I feel a pang of embarrassment and leave 23 alone. Jaeger gave me this project because of my affinity with Keris, but I haven't found a trace of her in twelve months.

I try and comfort myself with the conviction that no one really gets close to Keris. I'm not sure even Jaeger did when they were lovers. Keris is pure politics; a hypersensitive creature of profound philosophical and psychological understanding.

Even that farcical debate would have served multiple functions. Keris didn't 'win' because she didn't want to. It looked to me like a holding tactic, there to seed ideas in people's minds about Loren's mindless need for revenge. Loren staged more debates with other Diamond City luminaries, but Keris used the forum once and moved on the way she always does.

I begin to relax into a familiar excitement. Until now I've been searching for Keris in a rather literal way, too exhausted to come up with anything more inventive. I trawled through rec swarm logs from across the city at some cost to the NFE while trying to assemble a usable profile of the woman.

There is very little in-Aer; Ellery will have seen to that. I worked for Centria's Comms Director for years. An incredible weaver of image and word who usually grunts instead of speaking, Ellery was the architect of Loren Descarreaux's expulsion from Centria years ago over their shared love of icy finance genius Gethen Karkarridan.

Loren struggled through the Outer Spheres, enduring drug addiction, prostitution and worse. Eventually she thieved and murdered her way back to respectability, driven by love for the baby boy she found within her. Balatar was murdered in Centria of all places, but Ellery has still managed to present the enclave in a positive light.

Given the current conflict, there is a lot about the Ruby War; a famous Centrian victory although nothing about how it really ended. Facing Jaeger, Keris put a gun to her head and threatened to wipe out any chance of discovering her secret, not to mention the love Jaeger still acknowledges but Keris doesn't. Jaeger backed down.

The courage that must have taken! What if Jaeger had told Keris to go ahead and pull the trigger? He knew she would do it. For all Keris's dissembling, she has a central core of… what?

She's not interested in wealth. When I visited her gigantic assembly it was mostly empty, the decoration solely for my benefit. She is not vain either; when she revealed the truth about me she wore a plain white dress.

In the debate with Loren, Keris lied about Centria's finances but I believed her later when she talked about caring. Is that Keris's motivation, masked by minor deceptions, driving her the way vengeance drives Loren?

I lie suspended, adrift in the body of the city. Under the skin between my eyes the seed connecting me to the Aer seems to glow, becoming almost painfully bright in my imagination as I realise why there is so little about Keris in-Aer.

Keris once told me she had no real power; she was just a very good politician. She talked about the agendas of others and I thought she meant the Guidance or some Centrian cabal. What she actually meant was everybody, from me and Loren to the subs in the Outer Spheres.

Keris has to manoeuvre between those conflicting desires. She embodies her mysterious truth, her weird commitment to everyone's wellbeing while appearing to give nothing and everything at the same time. The clue is in how she's able to do this.

It isn't power and glamour but the consummate skill with which Keris uses them. She confers a touch of magic on those she needs and that magic echoes out into the city to be absorbed by as many people as possible. Ellery has to manage the Keris material because those people will keep everything Keris does and these documents must never contradict each other.

Keris, then, has fans: people who will do anything for her. As one myself, I understand completely. Keris doesn't just make you feel you can do anything; she is the catalyst who enables it to happen.

Keris left Centria with her secrets, thinking that once Jaeger had fruitlessly scoured the enclave he would leave and if he stayed she could dislodge him remotely. She therefore had a safe destination in mind with someone who wouldn't ask questions.

The person I'm looking for will be accomplished, with followers of their own. They will be another visionary, less refined but with similar messianic zeal. Their philosophy will be underpinned by exceptional talent at spotting opportunities in the overcrowded free-market maelstrom of Diamond City.

Theirs won't be a company that does just one thing because Centria doesn't do just one thing. The company will have elements in common with Centria but with a clever MidZone spin; something cheerfully rough and accessible.

Using these vague search parameters I get a hundred names back and think for a while, considering refinements. This individual will be a maverick who doesn't like sharing power, not realising that Ellery and Gethen create as much of the Keris everyone sees as she does. I remove any company run by more than one person, which reduces the list by two thirds.

The person is a man because Keris will want him to love her completely. It's risky but Keris was with Jaeger for years and Jaeger is, well, Jaeger.

The man will be established and confident so is likely to be older than me, maybe in his forties.

Eight names remain.

Wealth clusters around Centria but since the war started has dissipated further out into MidZone. Keris would not risk proximity to Centria with Jaeger there so I'm looking for someone further away.

If my quarry is following the Centrian model he will have a pretty good security operation. I therefore enter standard corporate military training patents and cross-reference them with a set of likely co-ordinates.

One company is left: Centre Quality. Oh, cheeky! Centre Quality is run by Nat7an Chance. There are no available pictures of him.

The name is familiar so I go through old messages in my Aer account. I see from an exchange with Ellery a few years ago that Centria invested heavily in Centre Quality. Na7han Chance doesn't just admire Keris then; he owes her.

I message 23: **I think I've found something.**

Hold that thought Charity, she responds. **You need to move.**

7

The safe enlarges as it sinks into the floor towards me, coming to rest a few centimetres from my open eyes. After a moment the block enlarges again, changing from black to grey as the molecules separate and light enters between them. I go to hold my breath so I don't inhale any and then remember I'm not breathing. The safe dissipates to leave an oblong of light.

That gets bigger too as I'm propelled by the Basis up through the floor to the surface, without any discomfort to my open eyes. I pass through the flat plane of the diamond surface, which registers as a slight tickle where my skin touches it. No residue sticks to me when I reach the top of the floor, blinking as I register the plain hotel room ceiling. I take my first actual breath for nearly five days, stretch and wiggle my feet.

When I sit up, something tickly and soft tumbles down my back; 23 has regrown my hair! I pull it round to see the bulky fall slide through my hands, light catching rich blonde tones.

I get up smoothly, with no diminution of muscle control or coordination. There is a shifting across my skin as the sub rags melt and run into the floor. My body is unmarked now, the training scars wiped away. Nonetheless, my stomach is still a hard plate and my calves and arms are corded with supple muscle.

Another garment flows up from the floor straight onto me: a red and yellow jumpsuit that closely follows my figure and toughens itself with hidden lightweight armour. The chunky, thick-soled boots, luxurious after a year of barefoot running and grudgingly administered knee repairs, lift me a few centimetres. Like the hair, my favourite jumpsuit feels like an old friend.

A holo appears and I register my odd faint tan, full-lips and weird eyes. They are not blue, not green or grey or hazel or aqua but something else, as if the Guidance clash within them.

"All right then?" 23 says.

"Yes. Thank you."

"Whoever's after you is looking for a scabby bald sub."

"Right," I say, conscious yet again of making some subtle mistake.

The holo disappears and the rest of the room's furnishings subside into the floor, leaving me in a windowless, empty diamond cube.

"I should have a fuze," I say.

"Can't you use the n-gun?"

"Best if no one knows I've got it," I say. "Plus they'll be less inclined to bother me."

"Fair enough."

I search out a spec closest to the fuze Dodge gave me and a holo of it appears, gently rotating in the air.

"This one," I say.

"Someone's got expensive tastes," 23 says. "You're not in bloody Centria now, m'lady."

"We're hardly short of kilos, 23."

"Not now but every weapon I gif will cost us in patent mark-ups, especially the heavy-duty gear we like."

I appreciate the 'we'.

"Can't we just get more from the NFE until we meet up with them?" I say.

"Not with AerMIS compromised. We can't 'meet up' either because we don't know who in the NFE can be trusted."

"So…?"

"We're on our own, Charity."

"But Jaeger-"

"Jaeger knows. He trusts me with you. As far as the NFE is concerned, all of Unit 7/10 including you died in that attack."

"They know you're alive," I say. "You accessed AerMIS for those kilos."

"I know. I should have asked Jaeger directly…"

"What is it, 23?"

"There's some strange activity around my new location. It's probably nothing."

The fuze grows out of the floor and I pick it up. It is small but substantial, with sufficient power to shoot through a diamond wall. Unlike the n-gun, it is not operated in-Aer but via controls in the grip. Its colour matches the red in my jumpsuit and when I press the weapon against my right hip it sticks there.

"It's linked to your Aerac ID code," 23 says. "Only you can get it off your jumpsuit and only you can fire it."

I snatch the fuze from my hip and aim at a wall with my right hand and then my left, getting a feel for the weapon. My predicament is slightly less terrifying when viewed down the stubby barrel. I clip it to my side again.

"Nice," I say. "Where now?"

"Another hotel, then the train, then a ship."

"That sounds busy," I say. "I've got a better idea."

"Have you now."

"Harlan."

There is a pause.

"Charity, I knew Harlan when he was with the NFE. Not, er, not like you knew him but… You know he was spying on you don't you?"

"Yes."

"And you still trust him?"

"He admitted it and I forgave him. Besides, if he hadn't spied on me we would never have met."

I can't imagine my life without Harlan. Desire washes through me like an ocean.

"23, Harlan saved my life. Twice. It's true I was never sure I could trust him at first but… You know how rich he was?"

"Yes."

"How he got to that position?"

"Partly."

"He was a Centrian ex. He and his family were exiled for some idiotic financial misdemeanour when he was a little boy. He grew up in the Outer Spheres, made it to MidZone and got rich. Eventually, he joined the New Form Enterprise and you know how much the NFE meant to him."

"Yes."

"He gave it all up. His life's mission, his wealth, everything. He started a fight with Jaeger, which was only marginally less stupid than just shooting himself in the head.

"Harlan did all that in an instant to protect me, so we can trust him."

I sense 23 examining the proposal from every conceivable viewpoint.

"All right," she says finally. "But do not, under any circumstances, let on that I'm with you."

"Okay."

Even I can hear my uncertainty.

"Charity, this is vital. Like your n-gun, I'm a lot more use to you if nobody knows I'm there."

8

The Zenod Hotel is bigger and more expensive than the dull franchise I spent the last five days in. I wait in the centre of the spacious lobby, which is busy enough for me to go unnoticed. A high wall undulates around the perimeter with doorways arranged almost at random, hinting at the hotel's endless possibilities.

Behind me, an ornate fountain sprays complex shapes into the air. The water emits coloured fluorescence like a jet of airborne jewels and the suspended kaleidoscopic array reflects my mood.

Longing mixes with dread. Fear that Harlan won't turn up is an irresistible needling matched by terror that if he does appear he will realise he made an awful mistake, giving it all up for some okay secretary-

"Pack it in, Freestone," the familiar, ridiculous deep voice says from beside me.

The bastard has sneaked up despite all my training, which I nonetheless use to launch myself at him. He takes the girl-missile impact and grips me tight as my lips find his. Everything fades except that ecstatic first connection, mouth to mouth as if we are saving each other. His hands plunge into my hair and his lips part so our tongues can do that wrestling thing that opens me completely.

I register differences in him. The heavy Old World clothing is gone; instead, he has on a functional blue jumpsuit, similar to mine. He is thinner too; sleeker and more streamlined. I wind my fingers through his dreadlocks and find them longer, although his wicked little beard and moustache are the same.

Loosening the killer grip of my thighs I slide down him for the friction and pull away from our kiss as a groan escapes me. It's low and guttural, a beast noise from the Old World with its filthy rhythms and horny ecology. I look up into Harlan's dark eyes, which

47

fill with tears. I let my feet find the floor and hold him as he sobs.

After a while I take his face in my hands and lift his heavy head. His cheeks are wet with tears, his black skin striking like that. I wipe at his cheeks.

"Pack it in, Akintan," I say.

He chokes a laugh.

"You can't fuck a girl to the edge of reason and then leave her wanting for a whole year," I say.

Everything blurs as I start to cry as well. Shaking teardrops from my face, I make my own little fountain of hot gems. I press myself to Harlan and we hold each other until we're done.

"Let's get a room," I say eventually.

"Already taken care of," he says.

I pull away indignantly.

"How dare you assume!"

He laughs.

"I dare Charity, I so dare."

"Well where is it then?"

"Fairly near the top."

"Do you know how many floors the Zenod Hotel boasts?"

"246."

"I'm not waiting that long, mister."

"Get along with you," he says.

He smacks my bottom, which sends pleasurable echoes right through me. We half stagger, half-stride across the lobby through one of the doorways into an atrium that begins to pulse bright pink.

"It's picking up vibes from you," Harlan says.

He brushes me between the legs and I stumble. The petal doors of the lift open, revealing a diamond bubble designed to flow up and around the building. We stumble in.

"Hold the lift!"

Two men in expensive business suits approach. I pull the fuze off my hip and point it at them; they dive out of the way as the petal doors close. Reattaching the fuze to the jumpsuit seems to take an age because all my coordination has gone. I breathe so deeply it's like I haven't breathed for a year and only have a minute to catch up.

Harlan seizes me and kisses me again. Light with desire, I fumble an opening under my jumpsuit as Harlan does the same with his. I pull him free and for a delirious moment we just stand there.

Then we are at each other in a breathless clash; devouring, blind and ferocious. The sedate motion of the lift is a steady press beneath us as Harlan slams me against the curved wall. I bite at him and he puts the back of his left forearm across my chest, using all his weight and strength to restrain me because he knows I will consume him. With brusque functionality he moves his hand between my legs to stroke the short, soft hair, ignoring the tormented flesh beneath. My thighs twitch and I whine but he won't be rushed.

The elevator rotates as it rises, opening a view across the hotel's interior: a stack of nestling globes that pulse green, orange and purple. Slender walkways between them carry people, who glimpsed from up here resemble notes on a musical score. I can almost hear it, building inside me like a symphony.

The civilised technological journey, our smart clothes and the formal hotel setting counterpoint the entirely natural but outrageous exposure of our sexual organs. One is a mouth-wateringly substantial dark bar that strains towards the other, a gentle mound crested by increasingly matted blonde hair that even now is pushed open – ohhh... Pink-padded brown fingers slip easily in; a big thumb stroking the front

[whiteout]

When I can see again I'm bent over with my hands pressed against the curved elevator wall. Harlan is in me. The gratification is such that we are both still for a while as we contemplate the miraculous join that almost soothes but doesn't quite.

The elevator now rises up the exterior of the Zenod Hotel. It is day in MidZone. The hotel is the centre of a group of ornate buildings thrusting up into a misty layer far above. I blink slowly, all energy gathered between my legs as Harlan shifts deep inside me and the graceful architecture begins to echo my loaded senses.

That honey-coloured tower spiralling up towards the vapour is a spasm reaching from penetration to the inside of my breasts. The reflected light flashing off a platinum spherical assembly is the friction between my nipples and the jumpsuit armour. The mist is my amorphous energy, seeking definition as it struggles to coalesce while being in no actual hurry. I pound the walls as the elevator slips into cloud and we are lost in delicious white nothing.

We are suddenly free of our clothes. I'm aware of the garments standing nearby as if worn by an invisible Charity and Harlan and then I forget about them. Harlan sits with his back to the wall and pulls me down onto him.

The MidZone glory around us is nothing beside his beauty. The whites of his eyes are tinged yellow like a hint of treasure, while his flared nostrils with their demonic arc look all the better to breathe me in. I want to sink into the absurd generosity of his lips, sculpted as they are on a grand scale in soft pink flesh with a glint of startling white teeth.

The elevator doors open onto a corridor with a deep blue carpet and walls whose stripes are a hundred shades of purple and cream. Reluctantly, I climb off Harlan; we walk naked into the corridor and our clothes follow us. We pass other guests: some stare, others don't. This is Diamond City after all.

We reach the room and the door opens. Our desire is like a force that carries us in, suspended and indifferent to anything except each other. After the sexual panorama of the elevator the opulent room feels intimate, like an embrace. We calmly and matter-of-factly climb onto the floating oval eight-poster bed; I lie back and Harlan slides into me again, holding me tight as he brushes my face with his lips and presses his nose into my hair.

As I start to buck and writhe beneath him, I remember 23 is still with me and wonder if the vix link is full on. How will she stay focussed as Harlan drives into me/her over and over? I imagine 23's thin hair slicked wet with sweat, her fringe messed up and that rangy body spread wide and shaking. I grip Harlan, rippling along his length like a great Old World river and hope 23 feels it like this too-

Uh... oh... here I go-

9

Out of darkness comes the sound of weeping. I want to remain in luxurious, deep sleep but something compels me back into the world. My eyes open despite my efforts and I catch a faint blue glow fading beneath my right foot.

"I'm sorry," Harlan says.

He sits on the side of the bed, his back a dark expanse despite being hunched over.

I realise he isn't talking to me.

"I know," he says.

I look around the room, but there's no one here except Harlan. I feel very tender between the legs, although I've no idea how long we made love for. My clock says 8.13am, so night must have been and gone. The curtains are slightly open and a stripe of MidZone day part-outlines Harlan as his shoulders shake.

"I've only just got her back," he says.

Our bed shakes as he cries and the vibration wakes a weird sick feeling.

"No," Harlan says. "She won't wake up now."

"Charity," 23 says and I stifle a jolt before I remember only I can hear her. "Message me to confirm you're awake."

Awake, I send back.

"You're going to feel like shit," 23 says. "I sent a pulse to counteract the anaesthetic Harlan gave you while you were asleep."

Physical nausea is nothing compared to how bad I feel as I hear those words.

"The Stop House," Harlan says. "It seems so final."

Stop House?

"No idea," 23 says.

Harlan wipes furiously at his eyes. He seems to reach a

conclusion.

"All right," he says.

"I've activated the n-gun and set it to stun," 23 says. "Shoot him."

I hesitate.

"Charity!" 23 shouts. "That is a direct order! Shoot him! *Now!*"

I point my right index finger at Harlan's back and fire. He stiffens as the blue beam hits him and slumps onto the bed.

"Uh oh," 23 says.

I go to message her again and realise I can speak now.

"What's wrong?" I say, my voice rough.

"Ructions outside the hotel. I can't make out what's happening. Move now."

Exhausted but wired I push myself off the bed and stand unsteadily. My limbs are slow to respond and I focus on one after another as if activating them by will. I manage to walk into the jumpsuit, registering faint movement as the garment enfolds and cleans me. I put my chin in the crook of my right elbow and draw it up over my hair. I feel very slightly better with my face clean and the blonde tangle out of it.

The n-gun is still online; I decide to keep it secret and unclip the red fuze instead. Swaying slightly, I walk to the door. It opens and I look quickly out into the corridor, which is empty both ways.

"Charity, I've booked another room for you. Go out of the door, turn left and sprint."

My legs pump automatically, taking me far along the corridor in a few seconds. A door opens on my right.

"In there," 23 says.

I slow, dart inside and the door closes behind me. Depressingly, the room is almost identical to the one I just left; the only difference is that Harlan isn't here. I back away from the door with the fuze held before me and stop behind the bed.

"Who's after me?" I say. "Is it the people who attacked our unit?"

"No, it's Centria."

"Why?"

"Dunno," 23 says.

"I don't like the sound of that Stop House."

"Me neither."

I want to carry on talking but can't think what else to say. Instead I kneel and aim at the door with my arms resting on the bed as a tear trickles down my cheek.

"Focus," 23 says.

The NFE training takes over and I become nothing more than a watcher: the world reduced to a single door with a red fuze aimed at it.

"When they discover you've gone they'll bribe the hotel to learn which rooms were booked in the last few minutes," 23 says.

"Is there another way out?" I say.

"If you don't mind heights."

I remember the fight with the Sons of the Crystal Mind, when gunfire hit my flybike a kilometre off the floor. There was an awful moment just before I fell when I seemed to hang there, the great space beneath me starting to clutch...

"No," I say. "I don't mind heights."

"Balcony then," 23 says.

I get up and back away until I reach the balcony doors. They open; I turn and freeze.

A huge red shape rises past the balcony floor, brutal contours shouldering effortlessly into view despite the multiple cannons, grapplers and acid ports that form its terrifying outer shell. Through my shock I notice scorch marks and gouges in the matt-red surface of the Centrian warship and that one of its cannons has broken off. The warship's movement is smooth though; it slides up the front of the hotel like a deadly elevator.

I slap the fuze to my side, jump onto the balcony railing and leap across a height I dare not look at. A moment's suspension, of body-powered airborne travel and then I seize one of the smaller cannon barrels. My left hip slams against the armoured hull and I cling on as the warship continues to rise.

"Er…" 23 says.

I focus on the warship and not the open air on either side as I find a handhold in one of the gouges. Squinting to obstruct the view of spires and roofs slipping past, I pull myself up until I can put my other foot on the cannon. I press palms and body against the dread scarlet face and carefully stand. The warship is roughly triangular with the point aiming at the distant floor so with heart pounding against the cold armoured surface I reach slowly for the edge above me.

It's too far. My throat constricts as I try and swallow with my mouth dry. My hands are wet though and slip across the front of the warship. I remember the nausea, swirling now with instinctive vertigo although at least I have the discipline not to look down. I concentrate instead on the edge above me, about five centimetres from my stretched fingertips. I can jump it but ought to check my footing so I glance at my boots.

The warship beneath me is no more than a red sliver from this perspective so it doesn't look like there's anything between me and-

Oh.

My legs go weak and the dizziness expands until I don't know which way is up.

"Charity!" 23 shouts.

"23…"

Tears prickle my eyes. Not being able to see doesn't help.

"It's not far Charity. You can do it."

I can't though.

"Charity, if the ship changes course you will fall off. Jump up now. Don't even think about it."

I'm not thinking; I'm seeing a great space and me up there in it where no person ought to be. The huge towers and buildings are tiny things now; the detail on the floor impossible to make out. I could obscure it with one thumb if I let go. There is something beguiling about the height, some absurd temptation to just-

Instead I let my legs bunch and thrust and then my fingers are over the edge. Survival becomes a matter of simple muscular contraction as I haul myself up and over. I roll away from the edge and lie tightly curled on top of the warship as if to wring the terror out.

Eventually the world stops swaying.

"Now what?" 23 says.

Discharging adrenaline makes me snarky.

"Well what was your big idea then, 23?"

"Wait for the warship to pass and jump across the balconies so you were in a different room to the one they could have traced."

"Oh," I say. "That's... Hm. Okay."

I get up and stand on top of the world. The mist has gone and I gaze at the shimmering panorama, beautiful now it's not about to kill me. Air flows across my face and lifts my hair as light sparkles from a hundred crystalline structures.

"How are you going to get down?" 23 says.

"Wait for this thing to land and just get off. They don't know I'm here."

"Hello baby," a familiar voice says from behind me. "Come away from the edge."

10

The warship slows and stops as I turn to see Ursula, who stands on an elevator disc embedded in the top of the warship. It is not the shock of being discovered that makes me stare, it's the change in my sister.

Before Loren and the Sons of the Crystal Mind destroyed Ursula's career and nearly took her sanity with it, she had been the Face of Centria: the People's Princess. She achieved the feat of being a badly-behaved celebrity who wasn't universally despised by combining sheer force of personality with a talent for just being herself.

Chaotic and fun but honest and reliable, she was a friend to everyone, even those who had never met her. Improbably beautiful in a wholly natural fashion, the curves of her tall body combined in a balance of sensual humour that could never have been deliberately invented. Many were obsessed with her; one even died for her, futilely shooting a cannon at the great green warship that came to take us away.

The woman in front of me is very different. The Sons of the Crystal Mind chopped my sister's gleaming dark hair off a year ago when they tried to sacrifice her to the Basis. I expected Ursula to get her hair back like I did but it looks as if she has grown it out the old-fashioned way. Shaved close at the back, the longer bit on top is slicked down as if to repress her old self. She is still tall but thinner, gaunt even and her breasts and hips are much smaller. I realise she has had them surgically removed and the plain blue Centrian uniform fits her much better than it would have done before. She looks very fit and I recall how good she was at the compulsory Centrian battle exercises. Her face is clean of makeup but instead of the beatific look she had in those giant adverts promoting Centria across Diamond City she looks shiny, as if perspiring due to stress.

The biggest change though is in her eyes, which used to be full of laughter; their rich hazel colour revealing an irrepressible character. Now they are more of a deadly tan. I know Ursula was broken after everything that happened to her but I thought she would somehow get better. The new self appears to suit her though, as if this Ursula was there all along; steely, determined and harsh.

I move towards her as she steps off the platform and opens her arms. We lock together, sister to sister and I let my fingers run across the cropped hair at the back of her head. Her neck is slightly damp although it isn't hot up here and the smart cloth of her uniform can't quite lose the scent of sweat. Ursula's tight grip reminds me of Harlan; there is a sense of desperation, as if all the loving has to be done quickly before something ends it.

"I miss you," I say.

"Yes," she says.

Ursula's hands move over my back and lose themselves in my hair as if she is trying to memorise me by touch.

"You feel all hard," she says. "What did they do to you?"

"Stuff," I say.

Usually when you hold somebody one of you will instigate the letting-go process, but Ursula and I somehow disengage simultaneously. I step back away from her.

"Are you all right?" she says.

"No. You?"

"No."

"Mum?" I say.

"No."

My mouth twitches to acknowledge that it should be funny. I look past Ursula at the Zenod Hotel, where Harlan still sleeps.

"You need to come with me, Charity," Ursula says.

"To the Stop House?"

I catch Ursula's look of dread before she manages to suppress it.

"Flybike on its way up," 23 says.

"Who was that?" Ursula says.

I freeze.

"Your expression changed," Ursula says. "You can't hide anything from me, you never could."

I stare at her, my blank face all the confirmation Ursula needs. She sighs.

"Someone called 23 booked that room you were hiding in, so 23 is your NFE oppo."

"What's the Stop House, Ursula?"

"You know I love you, Charity."

"What is it?"

"We all love you. Does that NFE psycho?"

The warship has drifted away from the Zenod Hotel and now begins to descend across the great chamber. We pass beneath glittering assemblies and over ornate buildings, whose approaching roofs reveal gardens, pools and sculptures.

Ursula leans in, her mouth trembling.

"Leave her alone!" she screams through me at 23. "We're not going to take it any more!"

"Ursula," I say, "23 saved my life."

"From shit he and his NFE mates landed you in."

That I don't correct Ursula about 23's gender tells me how far we have drifted.

"Charity," Ursula says, her military bearing forgotten, her eyes pleading and her shoulders hunched, "they *stole* you. You're our beautiful girl, our Golden Princess. Maybe you made the best of it because you are so strong and resourceful but you must see you're meant to be with us."

"So tell me what the Stop House is," I say.

"With that ringpiece listening?"

"It's that bad then."

Ursula shakes and part of me wants to just give in, if only so I can spend a few more minutes with her, so I can see Mum. I know I won't see Mum though; as with Harlan there is a palpable sense of regret in Ursula, which suggests the likelihood of some dreadful separation.

Anger spikes at these endless agendas. It's not just Jaeger press-ganging me into the New Form Enterprise but Keris as well. She created her 'Golden Princess', then fucked off and left me to search for her when I should be helping Dad. Dad, one of the few people who loves me for me and wants nothing except my presence in his life, despite the trouble I cause.

"I'm bringing the flybike from above," 23 says. "In one minute I'll cut power so it drops at an angle they won't be able to follow without shooting themselves. Be ready."

Ursula swallows.

"Charity," she says. "You saved me from the Sons of the Crystal Mind and you're still paying for it; this time let me save you. I can't say any more with that wanker listening but… Charity, trust me please."

She holds out her hands. Oh, why don't I just take them? Will it be so bad, whatever it is?

Something glints above and behind Ursula; before I can stop it my gaze flickers up to register the approaching flybike and Ursula spins round. She sees the vehicle fall towards us as the warship's guns move to intercept and then stop, jammed against the limit of their aim.

Ursula pulls her fuze from its side holster and turns back to face me. My mind slows her movement as it registers the awful fact of my sister drawing a weapon on me. Before she can get it level I have shot it over the side.

"No!" Ursula screams.

She launches herself at me as I slap the fuze to my side and leap onto the flybike. Ursula stumbles, wavers on the edge and runs back to the circular disc.

I bank down the front of the warship between its frontal cannons. The motion is terrifically liberating: a clean swoop free of emotional shock and impossible choice, far above the exhausting attrition of pointless war and mysterious pursuers-

The flybike jerks to a halt with muscle-wrenching force and my view is obscured by a giant red block. I shriek in terrified confusion as the flybike's controls go dead and I hang above nothing. I manage to turn my head and see I'm in the grip of one of the warship's clawed grapplers.

The pincers close further. The flybike snaps and the Basis interaction pad that keeps it airborne tumbles away out of sight. Pinned against the frame, I can't move anything except my right arm and my head. The pincer turns until I lie flat against it, the huge pad between me and the drop. Once I'm secure, the warship speeds up towards the ground.

We move among buildings as the grappler retracts towards the hull, turning as it goes. Soon I can see though the armoured window to the command deck, where Ursula stands and watches me impassively. Our eyes meet.

I consider calling her but I don't know what to say. She presses her hand against the window, a pale star against her dark blue uniform and the shadowy room behind her. The warship turns and my hair whips in my face. Turning my head to get my sight clear I notice we are passing over the top of a building. There's a pool embedded in it, about ten metres directly below.

"N-gun on obliterate, 23," I say.

The n-gun readout changes. I press my finger against the end of the top blade nearest the arm and fire-

I'm falling, thrown clear of the lower blade and the remains of the flybike. I can't breathe. The warship spins above as I plummet and the pool rears up around me.

I'm slapped hard across the back and then plunge on through the water. I expect to crack against the bottom but instead I am suddenly still. I hang there stunned amid dense underwater sound and startlingly cold liquid pressure. I kick and roll over; there is brightness above and I swim towards it.

I surface in the centre of the pool, my head back to slick the hair out of my eyes. Pushing air into my aching lungs, I thrust through the water as the warship's hum gets louder and then stops.

"Stun," I tell 23, hauling myself out of the pool as water pours from the jumpsuit.

The lower section of the warship opens and Centrian soldiers run out. I back towards the veranda that leads into the building and fire stun beams at my former colleagues, hitting four of them before they shoot back. I take the fuze off my hip with my left hand, finger the weapon to maximum and fire backwards. The veranda doors shatter and I dive inside as shots from the Centrian team crackle around me.

Lying on the floor to present a smaller target I reset the fuze to stun and fire both weapons simultaneously. Ursula has now joined the assault team; I focus my fire on her but she ducks out of sight behind the warship. The Centrian team stop firing and spread out, running around the pool towards me. I get up again.

"Obliterate," I tell 23.

She resets the n-gun and I fire a dazzling white bolt at the pool. Dodge's 'hint' of antimatter blasts water into the soldiers and sends a couple of them sprawling. Others trip over them in the sudden fog as I dart behind a bar in the centre of the veranda and point straight down.

"23, is anyone beneath us?" I say.

"Wait, let me get the drone around. No, no one."

I fire and part of the floor rips away to reveal another floor way below. It's too far to jump but underneath me to the left is a chandelier. I fire a volley of fuze shots into the fog, clip the weapon to my side and lie on my front. I reach through, grasp the chandelier and swing down. Fortunately, the jumpsuit has voided the additional weight of the pool water and my arms take the strain as my legs flail over the space beneath.

I'm dangling in a ballroom, richly lined in wood with silver edging. The chandelier lights up as I climb down it and the other chandeliers follow suit, spreading a soft yellow glow whose warmth is entirely unsuitable for the occasion. I lower myself until I cling to the single pendant at the base, ease my arms straight until my boots are a couple of metres off the floor and let go.

As I land and roll, three beams from above hit the floor beside me. I jump up, stumble under the lip of the hole and sprint across the floor. I hear my pursuers thud down behind me as I reach the door and crash through.

I'm now on a mezzanine in a white hall with a double staircase that sweeps down either side of a lobby. Globes of coloured fluid adrift in the space react to my presence and stretch into different shapes.

"Soldiers closing on you from below as well," 23 says. "No, don't stop; that lobby floor is open protocol."

As I rush down the stairs, Ursula's warship drifts across a large window at the far end of the lobby. The warship cannons swivel and one of them shoots a narrow yellow beam at something down to the left.

"She got my drone," 23 says. "We're blind."

Centrian soldiers crash through the ballroom door as I reach the lobby floor. Spinning around I use the n-gun to blast the top of both staircases into dust; the soldiers stagger back into each other and I stun two with the fuze. Movement in the floor nearby distracts me and I glance down to see a red circle about thirty centimetres across take shape near my feet.

"Take the dekpak and go out of the window," 23 says.

The red descent pack takes an age to grow so I shoot a couple of the floating globules into scalding vapour. One of the soldiers screams and claps his hands to his face.

"Which window?" I say.

"Obviously not the one with the warship, Charity."

"All *right!*"

The dekpak finally grows out of the floor. I use the n-gun to destroy another section of balcony and notice I've thinned out the Centrian team nicely. I swing the dekpak onto my back; the harness rustles across my chest, blends with the molecules of my jumpsuit and disappears.

I run sideways towards a door to the right of the big window and sustain a barrage of stun bolts against what's left of the Centrian force. I don't want to lose the fuze when I jump so I clip it to my side, reaching the door as a large Centrian soldier charges through.

I launch myself at him in a flying kick. It sends him staggering into another soldier but also thrusts me back into the room. I land and jump up as one of the soldiers on the balcony fires-

In a deep hole, falling...

darkness...

Pain in my head...

Falling...

A blue pulse.

Coming up, surfacing-

"Pretend you're still unconscious," 23 says. "This is good."

Good...?

"That is one scrappy little blonde," one of the soldiers says.

"Just as well she wasn't trying to kill us," another says.

"My eyes hurt," a third says.

"Do belt up Hopper; this girl has got bigger balls than you."

"Let's get her on board. The captain is well pissed."

"That's sisters for you."

How is Ursula a captain when I'm not?

I hear 23's voice in my head.

"I've had to give you another shot," she says. "Don't get knocked out again though; one more blue pulse and your heart will explode."

I concentrate on seeming unconscious as I feel the soldiers lift me.

One of the other unlikely skills taught by the NFE is acting. The key concept is to find some connection in my own life I can channel, so I live the thing I want to be rather than doing an impression of it. I remember Iqbal's explanation.

"Think of a piece of string, Charity," he said, his delicate brown fingers coming together as if gently pinching one end of an invisible cord. "It comes out of the top of your head and is linked with the rest of you. Can you do that?"

I imagined the string and found I could almost feel it. When Iqbal reached above my head and said, "I am pulling the string now", I felt an imagined tug, as if Iqbal had pulled a hair that was also joined to my sinews.

"See how much straighter you stand?" Iqbal said. "Now I let the string go and... bof! Mrs Floppy."

I am Mrs Floppy now. Iqbal's remembered voice is a comfort and Ursula's look of dread a powerful motivation to avoid the Stop House.

"Let's get her up to the roof," the first soldier says.

Something tugs at my side.

"I can't get her fuze off."

"Don't worry; she'll be out for a while."

Their voices lose resonance as we enter a smaller space, which must be the stairwell.

"The staircase is next to the outer wall," 23 says. "You should reach a landing soon. Do it then. N-gun is on stun."

Suspended at an angle between the men carrying me upstairs, I concentrate on keeping that inner string slack.

"Steady," one of the soldiers says.

I feel my legs elevated until I lie parallel to the floor; I open my eyes slightly and see the soldier carrying my left leg look right at me.

"Fuck!" he says.

The blue n-gun bolt hits him in the chest; he slumps and my weight pulls the two carrying my shoulders off balance. I get the soldier holding my other leg and the one at my left shoulder. The one carrying my right drops me and goes for his weapon but I get hold of it first. As we struggle I hit soldiers coming up the stairs with two more blue bolts as the last wrenches his rifle free. He stumbles back; I bat his weapon aside and stun him.

"Obliterate," I gasp, struggling to focus through the nausea.

I point at the outer wall, blow a large hole in it and leap through before I have time to think. The view spreads out below me; I spasm in midair and scream as I forget what I am meant to do.

"Dekpak," 23 says.

I fall and fall; my body limp but wide eyes hurting as damp hair flicks them in the rushing air. The warship is out of sight so I have time to examine the gilded façade as I drop head first past it.

"Dekpak!" 23 says again.

I remember the device strapped to my back and enlarge the in-Aer controls. Superimposing themselves on my view of the approaching floor, the controls look unbelievably complicated. I reach around to the manual buttons instead but there are too many.

"Charity, come on now," 23 says.

With effort, I activate the dekpak and four pads on stalky arms extend out from the disc to rotate until their flat surfaces are parallel with the floor. The descent slows and my legs swing down below me.

The edge of Ursula's red warship appears and I direct the dekpak away until the building is once again between me and my sister. I spiral down as the warship descends above and behind me, always out of sight.

"Oh hell," 23 says.

"What?"

"Nothing. I'm in a rec swarm local to you. There isn't much availability… The warship has stopped spiralling so you need to as well."

Her voice doesn't sound right but I do as she says.

"Charity, there's a kind of huge arena behind you. Turn and keep the Zenod to your left. You've got just enough height to get there."

I glide across the chamber as details enlarge beneath my boots. The area is well laid out with a network of pathways through parkland studded with organic sculptures and lakes. The parks give way to a dark blue paved area leading to the edge of the arena.

Close up, I see it's not an arena but a huge, round opening in the floor. A set of great circular steps leads down from ground level towards an elegant cluster of needle buildings that reach up from the chamber below. The steps end before they reach the spires to leave an opening like an iris into the space beneath.

I look back but Ursula's warship remains focussed on the building. Lifting my legs into a crouch to get over the lip of the first step, I glide above the rest towards the iris opening. The circular buildings are a uniform gold, bright in the MidZone day. Elegant arches open onto balconies where groups of well-dressed people congregate. Some notice me; a few even wave.

I reach the iris opening and even out my descent so I don't crash into the nearest spire. I end up facing the way I came to see Ursula's warship head straight for me. I look down. It's another terrible height but I'm getting used to them so I take three quick breaths and deactivate the dekpak.

I drop into a headfirst dive down the front of the outermost needle. The bright surface flashes by until I reach the inevitable advert cloud and plummet straight through. Grateful for the cover, I'm nonetheless lost in a blue haze that goes green, grey and then blue again. For a while I seem to hang there, aware of motion without any visual evidence and then I punch through into clear space.

A sloped roof appears just below me; I reactivate the dekpak and miss the building by a metre.

"There's a train station at the edge with a carriage waiting for you," 23 says. "Just get on."

I glide across the chamber to where the train tube lies flat against the far wall and the floor.

"Where's it going?" I say.

There is a weird pause.

"What?" 23 says.

"The train, 23. Where is it going?"

"Couple of circuits and then it will stop on the other side of the city. I've booked it for you alone and there are no stops; no one will bother you."

"23, what's wrong?"

"How far are you from that train?"

"I don't know. A hundred metres?"

"Shit."

"23-?"

"When you land you run for that train, do you understand?"

"Yes."

I'm not far off the floor now, its surface racing beneath my boots.

"23, please tell me what's wrong."

"I had to make sure you got away, instead of doing something about…"

I hear her sigh.

"I'm sorry, Charity."

"Why?"

"I couldn't just leave you."

"What is it?" I say.

"They're here."

"Who? Centria?"

"No," 23 says. "The others."

"3?"

"I'm going to transfer control of your Aerac-"

There is sudden silence from 23 as I touch down at a run. Ahead of me, the train carriage doors open as the dekpak folds into a disc on my back again. I cover the distance as fast as I can but stumble and nearly fall; the clash of stimulants and shock has taken an exhausting toll.

"23…?" I gasp.

I stagger into the empty carriage; the doors close and the carriage begins to move. Looking at the seats arranged in quadrants facing the centre I can't even decide which one to sit on. My vision begins to narrow; some greater wisdom takes charge and I lie on the floor and pass out.

11

Lack of train movement wakes me. I move my head and my cheek gets wet in something cold and slimy. I've drooled on the floor, where I have lain without moving for… I check my Aerac. Eight hours!

I go to wipe the embarrassing puddle away but the floor just absorbs it. My mouth is dry. I should gif something to drink but my neurons appear to have drifted apart. I slowly remember the train is closed protocol; I will have to go out and get something.

The train doors are open onto an empty platform. I check my Aerac again but all I can see is the clock at the bottom of my vision beneath my coordinates. It looks like I'm probably still in MidZone, somewhere on the border of the Outer Spheres. It's a good choice; fewer people, fewer recs.

I slowly get onto all fours as waves of sickness hit me. I manage not to retch and pull myself onto the nearest chair.

The chamber beyond the platform houses a few cheap buildings that look scattered, as if someone has dropped them by accident. The chamber is low-ceilinged and quite dark although it's only afternoon.

I pull a small tube from the collar of the jumpsuit and suck on it. The water, formed by whatever the jumpsuit recycles from me, is tasteless and slightly warm but I suck on it greedily. A little steadiness returns and I notice an odd chemical smell, which must be my body getting rid of the stun and pulses I've absorbed.

I draw the sleeve of the jumpsuit up over my face and hair and rub my neck clean. The smell decreases. I must look like a corpse and cannot afford to appear weak out here, so I decide on some makeup. I draw the sleeve over my face.

Nothing happens; the jumpsuit's makeup controls are in-Aer.

Any new choice will need my Aerac to work and 23 is in charge of that, not me.

"3," I croak. "Face."

There's no reply.

"23?" I say.

Saying her name sounds a note of alarm. Why am I worried about 23? It's her job to worry about me. Feeling very strange I suck some more water from the jumpsuit.

The jumpsuit has a memory so I can access previous programs manually on little controls in the sleeve. The most recent configuration was for Harlan so may be a touch overdone, but is better than giving the impression I can't afford to look good and am therefore fair game. I draw the sleeve over my face and feel better, as if I'm wearing a mask.

"23! Wake up!"

As I say the words I realise how wrong they are. 23 would never go to sleep on me. Adrenaline surges as my numb brain recalls her last words. The others, whoever they are, got my oppo before she could transfer control of my Aerac back to me.

I jump out of the seat and snatch the fuze off my hip. Outside, the chamber is silent and still. I tighten my grip on the weapon and wait. The only movement is the slight waver of the fuze extended before me and the only sound is my breathing.

If my pursuers were going to do anything, they would have done it by now. However, there has been no communication, no odd growth beyond the platform; nothing, which means I am free but 23 is dead.

Control of my Aerac and thus my life died with her.

I never thought I'd miss that voice, but find myself recalling her say "Focus" as I dab furiously at my eyes with a sleeve and hope the tears haven't made the makeup run.

Don't let it be for nothing.

I'm the last of Unit 7/10 but it's even worse than that. I can't find the NFE assembly or get in touch with Jaeger. I cannot go back to Harlan or to Centria. I can't access the Aer, call anyone or gif anything.

I am completely alone.

I look at my fuze and then down at the jumpsuit. They are all I've got now. The jumpsuit can repair itself and will recycle waste for as long there is waste to recycle; it can even form rudimentary food pellets.

Fortunately, the NFE got me used to starvation in the alien jungle. A very weird patch of the Outer Spheres, the jungle is a huge, chaotic leftover from someone's disastrous ecological experiment. The jungle is the only place harsher than the Outer Spheres themselves; even the subs tend to avoid it. After six days in there naked, I was smeared with dubious muck for warmth and camouflage and eating the things burrowing into me. A lot of NFE newts don't make it past the alien jungle.

I check the fuze. Unlike the n-gun the fuze doesn't need Aer access to operate; however, I used it heavily against Ursula and the charge has run down. I've got enough left to fire fifty-two stun shots, twenty-four killers and one big blast. I sigh; keeping out of trouble is one of my less developed talents but the fuze is a good one and better than nothing. Clipping it back to my hip, I run off the train.

Still nauseous, pride in the people who protected me powers me across the next chamber and the one after. I cover a couple of kilometres without effort, assisted by an unexpected feeling of liberation. This, I realise, is the most free I have ever been. As usual it's not quite what I expected.

I begin to sweat so to conserve water and keep the makeup in place I stop in a narrow street. Stacked buildings of different clashing designs line the opposite walls of a long, high corridor linking one chamber to another. There are more people here, their clothes obviously cheaper than mine. I get a lot of interested looks that don't feel very friendly; I hope they've noticed the fuze as well.

I walk purposefully, but not too quickly. I'm acting again, pretending to be someone of local importance. I am certainly *not* lost; there are many, many places I can go-

"Hi Charity!"

I spin around, fuze out. A tall, skinny man in a cheap, dark suit with a ruffed collar and cuffs smiles nervously down at me. The outfit doesn't suit him and his thinly disguised air of desperation probably matches my own.

"You look like you could use a boost!"

Everyone in the street has stopped and is looking at us.

"Go away," I say.

I start to walk and the man follows although his feet don't move. He glides a millimetre above the road and I realise I've been accosted by an advert. It has scanned my Aerac ID code and now everyone in the street knows my name.

"Come to Shiggy ZaZa's, second worst bar in Diamond City!"

"Why would I want to do that?"

"First drink is free!"

"Drink?"

"Oh yes! As you're from Centria we know you appreciate the inebriative traditions-"

"I'll come. Where is it?"

"Down the end of the road, second laugh on the right!"

I look at him. He points. I clip the fuze back and set off, trying not to seem like I'm moving faster than before. As I reach the end of the narrow street, I stifle a shudder and walk into the next chamber.

This one is busier and the people milling around generate a compelling low energy. The place is lit by garish signs and large scarlet droplets on the ceiling, while dark music pulses from the chamber's single structure. Like an island of noncommittal chaos, everything about it looks lazy, from the half-arsed architecture to the somnolent lighting. A sign on one ramshackle side reads 'SHIGGY ZAZA'S' above an arched double doorway with an over-ornate interwoven design.

Stopping outside I lean against the wall and concentrate on feeling invisible, the way I used to around Ursula. The crowd whirls by and I check faces, but none recur. Fairly confident that no one would bother with a rec swarm here I walk up to the double doors, which open automatically.

The complex, cavernous interior is lit by a central bar. I start towards it but the man from the advert steps across my path, his desperation replaced by trembling gratitude.

"Ah," he says. "Good!"

"Shiggy?" I say.

"Goodness no! How polite you are not to just scan me. I'm, er," he tries to think of an impressive name. "Mikeru."

"Is this your first night?"

"No! Or rather, yes."

"How's it going?"

"Better now! I get commission on everyone who comes in. There's a bonus for girls and an even bigger one for pretty girls with class, so basically you can have all the drinks you want."

"Do you do food?"

"Do we do food?!" he says, reverting to his advert self again.

"Well do you?"

"Yes."

"What's the house special?"

"It's difficult to describe. Where would you like to sit?"

"There."

"That's a bit dark," he says, disappointed. "No one will see you."

"Oh I wouldn't worry about that," I say. "Mikeru."

I give him the kind of smile Ursula used to switch on all the time and he gulps as I sashay off.

Shiggy ZaZa's actually looks like it was grown, unlike most

Diamond City buildings. Twisty platforms and pathways lead into dark booths and alcoves whose gnarled contours suggest ancient wood or bone. The unique atmosphere seems to have two main components. One is the smell of old booze, body odour and food; the other a sense that anything could happen in here and frequently does, not that anyone is going to make fuss about it.

I sit in a booth and watch the bar as a squat glass grows out of the table and fills itself with amber liquid. I take a sip, enjoying the familiar burn while a plate appears with three stripy rolls encircled by a line of black tar. The tar flows down the side of the plate into the rolls, which flip over and start humping each other. Steam rises from them and they speed up until they burst. I gaze at them warily but they don't move again. I pick one up, bite into it and get a surprisingly pleasant taste of burnt cheese. It goes down well and I begin on the next one.

I was lucky tonight. Someone more experienced than Mikeru would have ensured I went hungry or insisted I sit at the bar. It's relaxing in the booth and I want to stay. However, people here know my name and that I'm from Centria, so I need somewhere more secure.

The empty plate sinks into the table. I pick up the drink and knock it back, forgetting I was going to make it last. Fortunately, another grows in its place and light from the bar reflects off the rim as I try to think. What haven is available to a girl from Centria with everyone after her?

I think of Keris for some reason and then I think of Central Quality. Of course: if it's good enough for Keris, it's good enough for me. I just need to find out where it is, because I didn't memorise the coordinates. I lean around to look at the entrance, where I can just make out Mikeru. I start to get up and then stop; if I ask him he will be able to tell any pursuers where I've gone. I sit back down and contemplate the amber liquid, the same one giffed for me the night I first met Harlan. It's evidence the bars share information about who drinks what and another reason to move on. I tap the tabletop with my fingernails in frustration.

"Good evening."

I look up and see a small woman whose age is impossible to determine. She wears a short, dark pink cocktail dress with long sleeves, embroidered with a swirling design like the one on the doors. Her blue black hair is sculpted like a helmet and shines in the low light.

"You're Shiggy ZaZa," I say.

"Indeed I am."

She indicates the chair opposite.

"May I?"

"Of course," I say.

She slides elegantly into the seat and looks across at me, a faint smile on those pretty lips. Her orange eyes express a kind of laid back determination, as if they have seen and enjoyed everything.

"How was the food?" she says, her voice high but very soft, like a caress.

"Efficient."

"Good!"

"Why 'second worst bar' in Diamond City?" I say.

"Oh, everyone is always striving to be the best. It's so boring, so average. Here you don't have to worry about things like that."

"It's very refreshing," I say. "I imagine being the actual worst bar must be quite hard work."

"You have no idea," she says.

I nod and wait. She smiles.

"The Sons of the Crystal Mind," she says.

I try and work out how to act. Nothing comes to me; acting needs a start point and I have no idea where I am with this woman.

"Oh?" I say.

"What is your view of them?" she says.

If Shiggy ZaZa was a follower of the Sons then I could be in even more trouble, which I hadn't thought possible.

"I don't miss them at all," I say.

"Why not?"

"They beat me senseless and tried to burn my sister."

"I'm sorry to hear that."

"Are you?" I say.

Shiggy lifts her chin slightly, the tiny move out of all proportion to how formidable she now seems.

"Someone attacked the Sons of the Crystal Mind a year or so ago," Shiggy ZaZa says.

"Did they really?"

"It was a lone woman in a red jumpsuit, somewhat like the one you're wearing."

"It's a popular design."

"No it isn't, it's too expensive."

"I'm not the only one who wears it."

"She may have been blonde, as you are, but her hair was all red too, as if with blood."

Shiggy knows it was me. I stare back at her and let that victory over the Sons fill my gaze with power.

"It was blood," I say.

"So," Shiggy says, "you are the Scarlet Rider."

"Scarlet Rider?"

"The one we've been looking for."

I snatch the fuze off my hip and point it at her. Shiggy puts her hands up and gazes at me, managing to look vulnerable while still being completely in control.

"You'll get no trouble from me, Charity," she says.

"Are you behind the attack on my unit?"

"Your what-?"

"Why are you chasing me?"

"I'm not chasing you," Shiggy says.

"You just said you were looking for me."

"I'm looking for the Scarlet Rider. I don't know about those other things."

I rest my arm on the table to make it easier to keep the fuze aimed at her. I glance to my left, where the bar has the same people slumped at it as before. I look back at Shiggy.

"It sounds to me like you people killed my friends in revenge for what happened to the Sons of the Crystal Mind."

"No Charity. I just wanted to meet the Scarlet Rider and I've thought for a while it was you. That's why Mikeru bothered you outside."

I get up.

"Please don't go, Charity. You're safe here for now."

"For now?"

"I want to help you," Shiggy says.

"Why?"

"Because of what you did."

I hesitate.

"Charity, I knew you were in the area when the advert picked you up. If I wanted to grab you then it wouldn't have been me waiting would it?"

"You're stalling, waiting for them to get here."

"No."

She gestures to the seat. There is something open about her, something that makes her easy to talk to. Slowly, I sit down again but keep the gun aimed at her.

"How did you work out that I was the Scarlet Rider?" I say.

"The Centria connection. You never cashed in on what you did even though it was all over the Aer. I adore you for that but it proves the Rider didn't have to worry about money."

Those were the days.

"Just before the attack," Shiggy says, "the Sons shot an important Centrian security officer-"

"Anton Jelka."

"That's right, Anton. Did you know him?"

"He was Centria's Head of Security and, it turned out, my guardian for years. I never got the chance to know him."

"So much tragedy in your young life, Charity. Yet you wear it well, as if it's part of your beauty."

I watch her steadily as she continues.

"The Sons ruined your career at New Runcton. You and Ursula were humiliated, all of it in-Aer for everyone to see. Then that poor Rabian man died." She looks sad. "I see I've touched a nerve."

"They were going to kill Ursula," I say.

"No one touches Ursula, do they Charity?"

"No."

"But the Sons tried later; they tried to burn her."

"Yes."

"And after that they all died."

The bar seems quieter, as if it has taken a sudden breath. Shiggy and I look at each other without blinking.

"I made that happen, Shiggy."

She smiles.

"How?" she says.

"I used the New Form Enterprise."

I'm gratified by her startled expression.

"No one 'uses' the NFE, Charity."

I smile back at her.

"What are the Sons to you?" I say.

She gets to her feet and waves a hand over the front of the dress. A panel goes transparent to reveal her stomach, which is unmarked by a navel.

"You're a Blank," I say.

"I know you did what you did for your people but we…"

She looks down at her front.

"We are grateful."

"Us Blanks have to stick together, Shiggy," I say.

She stares at me and her eyes fill with tears.

"You?" she says. "Really?"

I nod. She throws her arms around me and holds tight. My arm with the fuze is still on the table, pointing absurdly off to one side. Shiggy holds my face and kisses me on both cheeks and then the lips. I'm not sure what to do, so I stay still. Shiggy calms down and sits back opposite me.

"The Sons' mission was to burn every Blank they could find," she says. "They saw us as an abomination. I'm well known in these parts; I was on their list. If it wasn't for you, I'd be dead. I wanted to meet you to say thank you. That's all."

"I'm glad you're not dead, Shiggy."

She starts to smile and then stops, alarm crossing her face.

"You need to go, Charity," she says.

"But-"

"Wait."

She closes her eyes. I look nervously around the bar, which remains unchanged. Shiggy opens her eyes again but they flicker right to left as she scans information.

"One our friends outside has responded to in-Aer queries for a reward. As a result, some dreary thug called Roscoe Trage has been in touch trying to buy your whereabouts."

"Did you tell him?"

"He wouldn't have believed me otherwise. I told him I would keep you here as best I could."

I stand and start for the door.

"No, no, come with me," Shiggy says.

She slips from behind the table and walks deeper into the bar, realises I'm not following and turns back.

"There's a plane on the roof that will take you where you want to go," she says.

"I can get my own plane."

"No, you can't."

She comes back and looks up at me.

"I always know when someone has no kilos," she says. "It's something you develop very quickly in this business."

I hesitate and then follow Shiggy ZaZa into the dark heart of her establishment. Eventually, we reach a winding staircase. Shiggy leads me up until we emerge in a roof garden with two benches and a slightly incongruous water feature trickling around the perimeter. In the centre of the garden is a small dart plane.

"You can put in your own coordinates," Shiggy says.

"I don't know them," I say.

"Intriguing. Where do you want to go?"

"Central Quality."

"Okay," she says and her eyes flicker again. "I've programmed the plane to go straight there, but you can over-ride it if you need to. Oh, one more thing."

"Sure."

"You need to hit me."

"What-?"

"Quickly now!"

I slap her face, trying not to think about it.

"Harder," she says. "Use your fist."

Increasingly nervous, I crack her across the cheek and she sprawls but jumps up with undisguised delight.

"So you can say I overpowered you?" I say, getting into the plane.

"Yeah, sure, whatever," Shiggy says.

12

Central Quality occupies the upper half of a giant cylindrical chamber. This position means its roof and curved side wall are both formed by Diamond City's superstructure and are thus impregnable. The assembly's base is a shallow cone whose point expands into a disc with docking spokes where ships and other transports cluster.

As my plane rises towards the dock from one of two high entrance arches at floor level I check the rear scanners again. Although I carried out numerous rinsing manoeuvres to shake off pursuit I cannot lose the sense I've been followed.

"Unidentified dart plane," an officious male voice says on open channel from the plane's comm speaker.

"Yes, hello," I say.

"Why can't we contact you in-Aer?"

"It's a long story, Central Quality," I say. "Let me dock and I'll explain."

"Negative. Resume your course away from our facility."

"Can't do that I'm afraid," I say. "The plane allows some manoeuvre but it's locked on this course. My name is Charity Freestone, I'm from Centria and I would like to speak to Na7han Chance please."

"We have a cannon trained on you. Go away. Now."

I slow to a halt about twenty metres from the dock. Sliding the canopy open I stand on the seat and put my hands up. Over the cockpit side I see the long drop to a featureless closed protocol floor.

"You must have scanned this plane," I say. "You know it's not a weapon. I thought your company and mine were friends."

"Hold position while we check with Centria-"

"No!"

I sit back down again.

"Why not?"

"They can't know I'm here…"

I stare at the little speaker on the control panel in desperation.

"The way *she* couldn't."

There is a long silence. I turn in the seat and look behind me but whoever my pursuers are I cannot make them out. I stare at the assembly again and hope my instincts about Keris are right.

"Proceed to Dock 32b," the voice says.

Lights on one of the docking spokes flash green. I glide up and the spoke locks my plane in place. Getting out I walk across the narrow platform into a large square room, where four guards in light blue armour point hefty rifles at me. I put my hands up.

"Thank you for letting me in," I say.

"Throw your weapon over here."

Reluctantly, I take the fuze off my hip with two fingers, place it on the floor and nudge it towards the guards with my boot. One of them bends down, picks the fuze up and puts it in a pack attached to his armour.

"I'll need that back as soon as possible," I say with Keris-like entitlement.

"Come with us," the guard says.

I walk between the guards with my head high and an air of faint boredom. Surveillance points and armoured alcoves indicate that the disc is a heavily fortified filtration port, but there isn't much else to see.

We reach a door and it opens into a white cylindrical room. In the centre is a round white table with built in chairs and on the far side sits a man who looks about thirty but seems older. He has an intelligent, questioning face and a shock of prematurely greying hair, which is just about restrained by a net field that allows it to waver distractingly in response to his feelings.

At the moment the hair isn't doing much; the man must be as

bored as I'm pretending to be. I walk in and the door closes on the guards behind me.

"Hello," I say and smile. "I'm Charity Freestone."

"Yah," he says. "I know. Sit."

I sit opposite him.

"You were talking on an open channel in a way that was potentially embarrassing for us and our associates. Kindly explain what it is you want."

"I would like to speak to Na7han Chance, please."

"Mr Chance is very busy."

"I won't take much of his time."

"You seem nervous," the man says.

"I feel fine."

"You can feel fine and still be nervous. I would argue that nervousness is a sign of feeling fine in some situations."

There is nothing quite as annoying as being treated like an idiot by an idiot. His hair waggles like frizzy grey fingers. I smile again.

"This must be one of those situations," I say.

"You mentioned 'her'. Who is 'she'?"

"I can only tell Mr Chance, I'm afraid."

"Then you may leave."

I get to my feet, go to walk out and then turn back.

"I would be grateful if you could let Mr Chance know who I am," I say.

"I have your name, thank you," the man says.

"Names can be misleading," I say.

"Oh?"

"Technically my surname should be 'Veitch'," I say.

I sense him start as I walk out to where the four guards wait.

"You can take me back to my plane now," I say.

I walk through them, back towards the dock. My heart pounds as I struggle to maintain the haughty persona.

"Bring her back," the man behind me says.

"You had your chance," I say over my shoulder.

"So you did scan me then," he says.

I stop and turn.

"What?" I say.

"I didn't think you'd scanned me-"

"I didn't scan you; that would have been rude. However, I see I've made a mistake."

I turn again.

"Come back into the office please, Charity," the man says.

I take a deep breath to disguise my relief and pretend it's impatience. I turn and follow the man with the crazy hair back into his office, where he turns and looks at me. His demeanour has changed; he looks sterner, more interesting.

"I'm Na7han Chance," he says, hair flattening as if with embarrassment.

"Oh."

"I wanted to see how you were with the staff, what you're really like. Sometimes rank and status can get in the way."

"Yes, they can," I say.

"You're very charming."

"Thank you."

"Why did you say your surname should be Veitch?" he says.

There is a touch of eagerness in his voice.

"Look at me, Na7han," I say. "Look at my face, my hair. Look at how I *am*. Remind you of anyone?"

"Keris Veitch hasn't got a daughter. I would know."

"Gethen Karkarridan didn't. Why would you?"

He shakes his head, confused.

"Keris was here," I say. "I don't expect you to confirm it but you need to understand that I know."

He blinks rapidly a few times. I maintain eye contact and remember how Keris talks; that way she has of making you hers. I see Na7han focus on my eyes, which like Keris's are a strange colour. Relaxing into the man's energy and ambition, I let him know that despite my power I need him and only him.

I feel what's left of my makeup. Instead of demonstrating poverty or weakness I let it tell a story, like 23 did with that hotel room furniture. *I went on a difficult journey to reach you*, it goes. *How could you possibly turn me away?*

He stares back at me.

"Why didn't you let me know you were coming?" he says, his hair writhing as he tries to decide what to do.

"All Centrian comms are monitored," I say.

I pause as if struggling to decide what to tell him and what to leave out.

"Na7han, I need your help as Keris did. I realise it's an imposition."

"Well…"

"I don't want to compromise you. If it's not possible tell me and I will leave."

"I wish you'd let me confirm with Centria," he says.

"Na7han, how would I know all this if I wasn't personally acquainted with Centria's leaders?"

He looks at me, his expression wary.

"My sister was the People's Princess," I say. "The previous Head of Centrian Security was my guardian; my adopted mother is his replacement. These facts are all verifiable."

"What do you need from me?" he says.

"As you know, there are matters in Centria that require discreet management."

"Hm."

"You have always been a loyal friend. Just let me stay here and work for a while without anyone else knowing."

"That's it?" he says.

"That's it."

Na7han Chance's eyes go slightly out of focus. He is either

checking with Centria despite my protestations or my pursuers have sent him a tempting message.

He focuses on me again.

"Will you have dinner with me tonight?" he says.

I give him my most dazzling smile. I am getting better at this.

"I'd be delighted," I say.

13

I sit on the edge of the bed and rub my eyes. I managed a few hours' sleep; one of those naps that seems more refreshing than a night of slumber. I would like to lie down again but the time approaches for my date with Na7han and I must decide what to do about the dress.

It was here when I arrived and is suspended just off the floor. The dress clearly indicates I'm an honoured guest, but my jumpsuit is my last actual possession. I will miss its comforting contours almost as much as the armour, but to wear it might be construed that Na7han Chance's best is not good enough for Centria.

I go to walk out of the jumpsuit. Nothing happens. The command requires Aer access so I have to peel the garment off as if I'm in the *very* Old World. I tug my arms free and hop from one leg to the other until I stand naked on the creamy expanse of thick carpet.

I wonder if Keris stayed in here. The room is certainly plush enough, with its delicate white drapes and islands of heavy, dark wood furniture. Did she feel this unease as she relied on her beauty, charm and a status that could vanish in an instant?

A transparent globe about two metres in diameter hangs in the air nearby. I walk over and touch it. Ripples radiate from my fingertip across the warm fluid surface as I feel the tingle of cleaning. Unable to remember the last time I had a bath I step into the globe.

It pulls me to the centre and heats up. I luxuriate in swirling hot water that works away tension across my shoulders and gently scrubs my skin and hair. When I surface I'm upside down although I don't feel dizzy and no water drips on the floor. I sink upwards and let the physical sensations calm my mind.

Soon the water feels different; its heat dissipates and there is movement across my face and in my hair. I am turned and lowered until I stand on the floor again. The water globe evaporates completely; not even a mist remains. A dresser beside me has a mirror instead of a holo and I see I have been transformed.

My eyes blaze above aqua-tinted cheekbones in a dark shroud of makeup angled wickedly up at the outer edge. Usually I play my lips down but now they are a rich orange that deepens at a clearly defined border. My hair is a yellow sculpture, all gleaming coils and sleek reflective surfaces. When I breathe I notice my own scent, so beautified I want to lick my arm.

I touch the purple dress and it flows down onto me. The complex folds arrange themselves over my body and bloom into a spectacular system of shifting panels. I rise off the floor as a pair of shoes grows through the carpet. Their tops darken to match the dress but the heels remain transparent so I look like I'm floating. I practice walking and enjoy the balanced elevation, the faint but pleasing strain all the way up the back of my legs.

A chime sounds and I look around. Doors at the end of the room glide apart and I walk through onto the balcony in my lovely elegant shoes.

The central atrium is a vast cylinder with foliage down the wall like thick emerald hair. The space is full of airborne trees and drifting islands, their sides lush with vegetation.

A transparent, open-top box about a metre tall waits in the middle of the balcony. One side swings open and I step into it. The door section closes and the box lifts away to spiral through floating trees.

They are roughly spherical, each one a green explosion of gnarled limb, strange coarse surface and leafy cascade. Their earthy scent mixes with my own, hinting mournfully at a sensual richness lost to us now. I pass a drift of hanging islands: rough chunks of rock shiny with moisture, draped with flowers that tumble in waves of yellow and blue.

The box rises through an opening in a transparent ceiling. The side door opens and I look down. The atrium wall is a thick circle studded with silver light enclosing a galaxy of drifting greenery. What's now the floor is so clear it seems there is nothing separating me from a half-kilometre fall.

Na7than Chance stands at the edge, his expression neutral as he waits to see how I will react. I step off with a slightly bored smile. I keep my steps even and concentrate on the shoes. They make my toes point like Harlan does, and the memory softens an uncomfortable tension between my legs. My heels click on the invisible surface.

I reach the edge of the transparent floor. Na7han extends a hand; I take it and he guides me onto a circular level that borders the atrium. The great band is formed by panels of wood inlaid with strange angular designs featuring odd characters formed by lines joining stars.

Na7han wears an ornate green suit. His distracting hair is no longer mobile and lies flat against his head, as if on its best behaviour. He kisses my hand.

"Charity," he says. "You honour me with your beauty."

"Thank you."

I touch the dress.

"You've got quite an imagination, Mr Chance."

"Nathan," he says. "The 7 is silent."

"Nathan," I repeat, smiling.

I look around. The room is at the top of the complex and stretches as far as I can see. It is a mixture of plants and furnished space at different heights to create a heady mix of Old World interiors and exteriors. The ceiling is in a state of constant but gradual evolution from light to dark, colour to blank.

"Is this the whole upper floor?" I say.

"Yes. I like space, Charity."

He gestures away from the atrium. We leave the green-lit circle behind and walk to an arbour where two slender, fluted glasses nestle in a sculpture that looks like stretched, intertwined brains. Na7han picks up the glasses and hands one to me.

"Cheers," he says.

"Cheers," I say.

I clink my glass against Na7han's and note his pleasure at my acknowledgement of tradition. I sip the icy wine, whose startling, lightly acidic taste evaporates just at the moment I comprehend it. I resist the urge to make small talk.

"My apologies by the way," he says eventually, "for your treatment on arrival."

"I could hardly have expected to just waltz in," I say.

"I think that is exactly what you expected," Na7han says.

I realise that underneath the glamour and buffoonery, Na7han Chance is very tricky and very ruthless.

"I'm used to getting my own way, Na7han," I say.

"You were so polite, though."

"Sometimes politeness is all we have."

He stares off into the depths of his vast dwelling.

"Yes," he says.

"Can I ask you something?"

"Of course."

"What's with the hair?"

"Something from my youth. These days it's an affectation so that people think I'm an idiot and underestimate me. But then you knew that."

I feel another stab of fear. Na7han appears to be made up of many layers of intellectual aggression. At some point I suspect the intellectual element will disappear.

"You mentioned dinner," I say.

"This way."

He extends an arm. I hesitate coyly and then take it. We walk among organic sculptures like waving arms beneath a gently pulsing light orange ceiling.

An intense gust of perfume signals my nervousness to us both. Maybe the shining hairstyle will reveal my thoughts as well, like a clear screen into my mind. I resist an urge to dunk my head in the nearest pond.

We arrive at an elevated area, where a table stands laden with food like a caricature of abundance.

"Too much?" Na7han says.

"No."

He smiles and pulls out a chair encrusted with gems. As he pushes it under me, another hot blast of perfume reaches the back of my throat.

Na7han sits opposite, his gaze fixed on mine. He spreads his large hands, which have thick, dark hair on their backs.

"Please," he says.

I pick up a piece of fruit; feeling slightly pornographic, I bite into it as Na7han rips into a joint of something that looks like it was once alive.

"How is Centria these days?" he says, concentrating on his food.

"Different," I say.

Na7han pops a sliver of flesh into his mouth.

"Oh?" he says.

"The war."

Na7han finishes chewing and swallows.

"Hm," he says. "War can be profitable, but only in very specific ways. Generally it's a nuisance because there's too much fear."

"I think the war has streamlined us," I say.

Na7han looks up.

"Really," he says.

The word should be a question but sounds instead like a challenge. I have not been in Centria for over a year. If Na7han has then he could catch me out.

"When were you last there?" I say.

"I've never been."

"Why not?"

"The opportunity never came up, not that I mind."

"Why not?" I say and curse myself for the stupid repetition.

Na7han watches me closely.

"I think Centria works best as a place in the mind," he says.

"Yes!" I say with surprising vehemence.

Na7han smiles.

"I see Keris in you," he says.

"Told you," I say.

"And... Gethen?"

I go very still but my perfume cloud is almost visible as it billows out, taking my secrets with it.

"You have his precision," Nathan says.

He cannot possibly know the truth; he has made a cunning guess. Hasn't he?

"Also," Na7han continues, "his ruthlessness."

Gethen is not an influence I like to acknowledge.

"He's a great man," Na7han says.

"He's okay," I say.

Ignoring Na7han's look of delighted shock, I examine the food and map out a sequence of morsels I can eat without any unseemly gnawing. The first is delicious; a tangy block of carbohydrate speared alongside a sweetly dripping fruit.

"You have excellent taste," Na7han says.

I should acknowledge the complement, but instead I gaze into Na7han's eyes and smile. I let Iqbal's invisible string pull me up, straight and relaxed. *I am the Golden Princess* I repeat in my mind.

Nathan smiles back.

"Tell me about the Hex," he says.

I can keep my appearance steady but cannot disguise the changed energy in the room, which has gone from amiably strained to very uncomfortable.

"I can't tell you about it," I say.

"You might be some demonic force, waiting to be unleashed."

"You're right, that's what I am."

"Am I in danger?" he says.

I gauge the distance between us, his build and the likelihood of any protection coming into play before I crush his throat.

"Yes," I say, smiling.

"Is that because you are a New Form Enterprise spy hunting Keris Veitch?" Na7han Chance says.

I frown so deeply even I'm convinced by my shocked outrage.

"Who told you that?" I say.

"She did, obviously."

"I'm not a spy for anyone," I say, feeling hollow. "I was with the NFE, I trained with them-"

"Centria's sworn enemy?"

"It's more complex than that."

"To be sure!" Na7han says.

I see movement as armoured guards move through the undergrowth. They stop a short distance away and surround us.

"What else did Keris tell you?" I say.

Na7han twirls meat on a stick.

"Nothing," he says.

"Was this when she was here or more recently?"

"She wasn't here."

"She was here, Na7han. She left Centria to get away from the NFE."

"Who you let in."

"I had to do that for the NFE to save Ursula from the Sons of the Crystal Mind."

"What did the NFE want in Centria?"

"Kilos," I say.

"Not the Hex?"

I can't process this suggestion fast enough to keep the surprise off my face.

"The New Form Enterprise," Na7han continues, "is an organisation of mercenaries led by a man who was thrown out of Centria."

"He wasn't thrown out-"

"A mercenary force with a supernatural weapon would be able to command whatever price it wanted; maybe take power for itself."

"Jaeger doesn't want power," I say.

"You don't know him very well," Na7han says.

"I didn't come here looking for Keris."

"Fortunate."

"She's definitely not here then," I say.

"Of course she's not here."

"But she was."

"No," he says, too convincingly.

I smile but he doesn't smile back.

"I've admired Centria and Keris in particular my whole adult life," Na7han says. "Some forty odd years now. In all that time she has never been pregnant. You are, what, twenty-four? You cannot be Keris's daughter."

"I can."

"You're Ursula Freestone's sister and you came from Centria originally," he says. "You've picked up Keris's mannerisms and you look a bit like her, but surgery could have done that."

"I am who I say I am."

"I had hoped there was more to you."

"There is more to me," I say, embarrassed now and trying to hide my dismay as I think of the enemy waiting outside.

"Let's find out."

Na7han gets up and comes around the table to stand behind me. I draw on all my reserves of calm to stare ahead and not jump when his fingertips touch my neck.

"I love how outrageous you are," he says.

His voice is close to my ear and I want to shudder but Iqbal's invisible string helps me. I count ten guards, too far away for me to get them.

"Is this how you treated Keris?" I say.

"Keris is the ruler of the world. You aren't."

"I will be," I say.

"You are adorable, Charity. I've had many beautiful girls but none who conned their way in here like you did. Such boldness!"

"Do you want to know about the Hex or not?"

"You don't know about the Hex," Na7han says. "I thought Jaeger would have confided in you, but you're little more than a decoration."

As Nathan runs his fingers across the gleaming coils of my hair I actually think about letting him have his way, but I know he will just use and then discard me. I move away from his caress and stand to face him. He looks back at me steadily.

"Why do you want to know about the Hex?" I say.

"It's an opportunity."

"Not for you," I say. "I think you want to know because you like secrets, especially about Centria, which is only a place in the mind because you will never, ever get to go there."

He goes still the way people do when they pretend you haven't hurt them.

"I came to Central Quality because if Keris could be safe here then so could I," I say. "My NFE unit was murdered. I'm the only one left."

"So?"

"The people who did it are outside, waiting for me."

"You brought them here?"

"I-"

"Wait."

He stands away from me, eyes flickering.

"There's nothing unusual in the chamber or surrounding areas," he says.

"They beat the NFE, Na7han. Your tin-pot operation isn't going to pick them up."

"Who else knows you're here?"

"No one."

"Not the NFE? Not Centria?"

"I found you myself," I say.

"Let's see what Centria says-"

"No!"

"Because they threw you out?"

"Did Keris tell you that?"

"She said to help you, so I have, but…"

He looks worried.

"What is it Na7han?"

"I can't have any more weirdness."

"What do you mean?" I say.

"Doesn't matter."

He looks down at me and it's clear I'm now a problem.

"Tell me why I can't contact Centria," he says.

"They tried to take me to a bad place."

"What bad place?"

"I don't know," I say. "They didn't want to do it. Something seemed to be making them."

"The Hex?"

"Maybe."

Nathan thinks for a while.

"Do you know anything else that could be of use?" he says.

"Can I stay?"

"Depends."

"Agree terms and I'll tell you."

"No. Tell me anyway."

I stare at him, so used to the hot perfume now that I barely notice it.

"I am Keris's daughter. And Gethen's. And Ellery Quinn's. And

Jaeger Darwin's. There are others too. I don't know all of them."

"How is that possible?"

"Their DNA was used to make me."

"Make you?"

"With the Basis. In the floor."

"You're a fucking *Blank?*"

I know I'm through here as his face twists with hatred and disgust. It's as if I'm looking at Thom3 Hobb, insane leader of the Sons of the Crystal Mind.

My forehead cracks against Na7han Chance's nose and my arm whips around his neck as I use our toppling weight to pull him down. Gunfire knocks my chair over as I grab a stiletto and shove the pointed heel into Na7han's ear.

"I will ram this into your fucking brain."

"Stand down!" Na7han shouts at the guards.

The armoured boots clattering towards us stop.

"There will be a code," I say.

"10 19!"

The booted feet back off, until their sound fades with distance.

"You can let go now," Na7han says.

"I'll decide when that happens," I say, conscious of his weight pressing down on top of me. "What was the weirdness with Keris?"

"She just disappeared."

I press the stiletto harder into his ear.

"It was a year ago," he says hurriedly, "She arrived suddenly, like you did."

"Alone?"

"No, she had guards."

"Did they disappear as well?"

"Yes."

"How many guards were there?"

"Thirty," Na7han says.

"Thirty-one people just vanished?"

"Yes. The whole time was strange."

"Why? Did anyone else vanish?"

"My Head of Operations: Guy Koffee, with a K."

"At the same time?" I say.

"No, later. He was looking for Keris because she didn't reply when I called. I didn't want to get blamed for losing her."

"What did Guy find out?"

"Nothing!"

"Don't lie to me, Na7han."

"It's the truth. Charity, look, I'm sorry about-"

"Did Guy disappear from Central Quality or somewhere else?"

"A bar in MidZone."

"Didn't you try and find him?"

"Of course, but there wasn't much I could do. Local rec swarms had been bought up so there was no surveillance."

That kind of thoroughness sounds like Centria.

"We put out a reward but nothing came of it," Nathan says. "Then Keris started popping up on all these broadcasts so I figured she was all right."

But Guy Koffee had asked too many unsubtle questions about her.

"Could Guy be dead?" I say.

"No, he didn't leave his kilos to anyone."

Guy Koffee must be in the Stop House.

"Don't kill me," Na7han says.

"Keris knows I'm here; you called her," I say. "All those years of schmoozing will be for nothing. I'm Centria's Golden Princess; they won't touch you after the way you've treated me. You can't possibly let me live."

"I won't-"

"Move," I say. "Slowly."

I keep pressure on the stiletto as Na7han struggles up. Blood drips from his ear as I kick the other shoe off.

"Put all the lights on," I say.

Harsh white illumination washes away the beguiling shadows and I see we're alone.

"We're going back to the elevator," I say.

Keeping the heel pressed in his ear I clap my hand to his opposite cheek so he can't move his head. We walk like that to the transparent floor above the atrium and cross to the elevator.

"You want a bigger one?" Na7han says.

"No. If anyone bothers me, you go over the side."

We step on board and the box descends quickly through the atrium, which no longer seems quite so spectacular. Soon, the balcony enlarges beneath us and we land. The elevator door opens.

"Wait," I say.

I look up and around. The other balconies are deserted, their doors closed. I grip the stiletto and push Na7han out.

"Run," I say.

The balcony doors part and we run into my room. I look around. The room is empty other than my jumpsuit, which stands by the bed.

"Lie on your front," I say.

Na7han does so, his breath short with fear.

"I'm going to take the stiletto out of your ear, Na7han. If you move, I will break your neck. Do you understand?"

"Yes."

Na7han gasps as I slowly take the heel out of his ear. He knows better than to move but keeps his gaze fixed on my face.

"Get rid of this dress and other stuff, especially the perfume," I say.

All of it melts and slides down me, through the carpet into the floor. I stand naked as my hair comes free and tumbles down my back. I pull the jumpsuit on and do it up.

"Gif me a fuze, Na7han; the most expensive one you can find."

The weapon grows and I pick it up.

"Now clear the way to Dock 32b."

"You said the people outside would kill you," he says.

"Better them than you. Get up."

Na7han climbs to his feet, glaring as he dabs his ear and inspects the blood on his finger. His hair has come free and trembles in all directions. I point at the door.

"Go on," I say.

As he moves I step up behind him and press the fuze into his back. The door opens; I put my hand on Na7han's shoulder and we walk out of the room. My head snaps right and left but the white corridor is deserted. I nudge Na7han forward.

Soon we reach a bank of elevators. One of them opens its doors; we walk in and the elevator descends.

"You pulled your clothes on," Na7han says.

"So?"

"You haven't got Aer access. That means no kilos, which is why you needed me to gif a gun."

"I can kill you before you deposit it, so don't try."

The elevator continues down. My frustration at its apparent slowness is ridiculous, considering I have no idea what I will do when I get out of Central Quality.

"Why did you say you're a Blank?" Na7han says.

"I am a Blank."

"You've got a navel. Blanks haven't got navels."

"Cosmetic."

"I don't blame you. Blanks are nothing but trouble."

"I'll be out of your stupid hair soon."

The elevator doors open onto the docking complex. It is empty.

"Run," I whisper.

He does. I keep close to him with the fuze in his back to make him go faster. We make good time and he actually starts to draw ahead of me, into the room I entered when I arrived. Now though it's full of guards and Na7han dives into them as I duck left along an adjacent corridor.

"Kill her!" Na7han screams. "Shoot her in the fucking head!"

The fuze softens and then melts as Na7han deposits it. I run into the next room; it's less well guarded but there are still four of them. I hurl myself at the nearest and knock him over, snatching his rifle and dropping another guard with a gut shot. Saved by his armour he goes down screaming as I shoot another in the leg. The last guard runs away, crashing into the others outside. The first struggles up and I stun him.

I back onto the docking platform that extends into the night, take cover behind the shielded outer wall and fire a tight-spaced volley. Na7han's guards, forced by the doorway to enter in single file, back away out of sight. I keep shooting and glance left.

Dock 32b is empty. Either Shiggy deposited the plane thinking I was done with it, or Na7han had it destroyed. I look over the side; the floor is lit but so far below that even the huge archways are thin shadows.

Armoured guards aim from the neighbouring dock. I shoot first and they back off as another barrage explodes from the room behind me. There are too many now.

I step off the platform into space.

14

The disc contracts with distance as I drop away into darkness. I slowly turn as gravity pulls my head down to face the approaching floor. The small circle of its perimeter expands outwards as people and vehicles on the ground enlarge with terrifying speed.

I grip the rifle in my right hand and reach behind with my left to activate the dekpak, which wonderful 23 giffed in red to look like part of my jumpsuit. The four disc arms open and slow my fall as I unclip the manual control to guide myself across the chamber.

I pass through the arch to glide over buildings and complexes. Looking back I see two roadsters race across the floor towards me and three ships descend from Central Quality.

I jiggle to avoid hitting anyone as I touch down in a busy street. The dekpak folds into itself; I set the rifle to kill and head into the crowd.

I'm hit hard from behind and the ground seems to leap at me. Burning pain spreads through my body as I sprawl, stunned. Common sense tells me to keep still but I ignore it and roll over. Something digs into my aching back and I cry out. Getting to my knees, I look over my shoulder and see the shattered dekpak.

Shrugging out of it I grab the rifle and get up. The shooter is easy to spot: she's the only one not running. She looks surprisingly ordinary: about my height, pretty, with short chestnut hair. Spider Bob described Lisle Trage as hot; is that her?

I fire at the woman; she ducks and sprints behind a cluster of buildings. I go to chase her but Na7han's ships have reached the arch so I turn and run with everyone else.

The roadsters plough into the crowd, but don't get far. Amid the screams a fight breaks out and the roadsters have to reverse with people shooting after them.

The rifle melts in my hands as I hear Na7han's ships behind me. Close to panic, I keep running and the ships pass overhead. They reach the end of the street and turn, hovering so they can scan everyone approaching.

There's an unlit alley on the right. I rush into it and crouch in darkness, panting as one of Na7han's ships returns. Its searchlight begins to probe the alley so I turn and run again, diving to one side at the end. I race along the building front into a large square as the ship moves off in a different direction. I run across the square into another chamber: bigger and with more ambitious buildings.

Harlan once described being hunted like this and the almost transcendent sense that each moment could be his last. It's comforted me when I think about Dad, who will be dead before he knows the Velossin is there. However, now I'm in the same position I don't feel enlightened; my only sensations are weary dread and a tugging need for it to be over, whatever it is.

I stand in MidZone's colour-shot darkness, cut off from every technological advantage. I used to wonder how people coped before the Basis but millions of years of evolution suggest they figured it out. So, like them, I will adapt.

I see a flyer on the roof of a nearby building. The flyer is a four-person vehicle with permanent runners under a windowless oval hull. I sprint across the street onto a parked car, jump to seize the upper edge of the building and haul myself up. As I get to my feet the flyer takes off.

I race across the roof and leap, my fingertips reaching over the top of the nearest runner. For a moment I'm in midair: suspended between flyer and floor, life and death. The flyer's rising motion presses the top of the runner to the underside of my closing grip and the roof shrinks beneath me as I'm lifted up the bright front of a neighbouring tower.

I belatedly hope I can hold on for the journey's duration and wrap my legs around the runner for additional support. Two of

Na7han's ships cross below, their searchlights pointed at the ground. They are quickly left behind as the flyer soars away.

We pass between buildings and assemblies that start to get grander and I realise we are heading towards Centria. My legs and arms begin to ache; I look down but cannot see the floor.

**

I sit on the back of the runner. It's easier than hanging underneath but still a strain that gets harder and more painful by the minute. Fortunately, the flight is smooth with no sudden changes in direction.

I begin notice more detail around me. The brassy fretwork of a huge, ceiling-mounted assembly shines through its shroud of cascading ruby lights and the grass of a park below goes from shadowy grey to blue. A burst of colour then erupts as adverts go from luminous to eye-catching and the day lights come on in MidZone.

The flyer descends and I look for a place to drop off, but we are still too high. We swoop into a well-lit chamber full of blocky buildings and I ease down around the runner. When my boots are a metre off the floor, I let go. I land, ignore the cramped pain in my legs and start running before anyone in the flyer can scan me. The chamber looks deserted and I run between buildings towards the exit.

I turn a corner to see a man and a woman standing in the street. They are roughly middle-aged with nothing very distinguishing about them, but as I go to head past they both turn very deliberately and look at me.

They are not armed and do not speak or make any gesture. Their gaze is even and not especially hostile but there is something unsettling about it. I change my mind about going past them and head left down an adjacent street.

There are more people along here and they stare at me too. I look back at them and hurry past, increasingly uneasy. The people watch me without expression. At the end of the street I turn back. They are following me.

"What do you want?" I shout.

They stop but say nothing. I back away into a plaza full of yet more people. All of them stare and none of them speak.

I have ended up further away from the exit than I was when I landed. However, all routes are now blocked by staring strangers. There are too many for me to overcome with brute force, so I go back the way I came.

"Charity…"

The whispering voices are all around me.

"Charity…"

An awful sensation crawls over my skin. I am more scared now than when I escaped from Na7han.

"Charity… Charity…"

I move through them, my eyes wide, slightly crouched in anticipation of a blow or worse.

"Who are you?" I say. "What do you want?"

They just stare.

I notice I'm next to the flyer again. Its door opens and the woman I suspect is Lisle Trage climbs out. She too stares at me.

A man gets out of the other side of the flyer. Heavyset, dark-stubbled and mean-eyed, he wears a lot of body armour and an absurdly large, over-ornate fuze in a richly-patterned holster. This must be Roscoe Trage. He stares at me too, but leaves his fuze holstered. I turn and run.

"Charity!"

It's Harlan's voice this time, from an open doorway to my left. I rush in but the single-roomed building is empty. Behind me the door closes. There's a faint lurch, pressure under my feet and I realise this isn't a building but a vehicle.

Everything that's happened hits me at once because I suddenly feel incredibly tired. I sink to my knees. My head feels so heavy! I can't sleep now though. Too dangerous, too...

I slump to one side.

I'm dead.

Oh no, no. I...

No...

Oh Dad, Dad I'm sorry

I'm

15

Pain comes first, lodged in my knees, elbows and back. I move to relieve it and find that I can't. I go to open my eyes but they are open already; it is just very dark. Pressure along my right side tells me I'm lying on it, curled up in a tight ball with knees and chin to chest and arms folded in.

I go to stretch and find a hard surface in all directions. Still woozy from the knockout gas, I stupidly try again, not yet willing to comprehend where I am. Naked, I can feel solid diamond against the soles of my feet, the top of my head, across my back and along my clenched arms.

I am in a box, its walls too thick to yield to any pressure I can exert, probably buried deep inside another structure. The only possible movement is within my own body: a realignment of muscles to take pressure from one area and transfer it to another; a flexing of fingers and toes.

The horror of it is at bay because why would anyone go to all that trouble just to put me in a box? There is a design; someone is in control, someone knows I am here. The worst thing would be to die like this, sealed up and forgotten.

I go to check the time but there's nothing. I remember I asked 23 to reset it ages ago so the figures wouldn't glow in the dark and keep me awake. Idiot!

"Hello?" I say.

My voice is close and muffled in the confined space, the smallest one I could possibly fit in.

"Come on now," I say. "You must want something. Just tell me what it is."

I am actually not too worried because I have been here before. In the NFE we've got a name for this device: the Infinity Box, so called because every second inside feels like it goes on forever.

It is torture but we call it endurance. I lasted three hours. Admittedly, they pulled me out screaming but I doubt anyone who has put so much effort into getting me will wait that long before making their intentions known.

I press against the restraining walls again. They are so solid, so unyielding. Unable to hear anything outside I don't know how deeply buried I am, or how long I have been here.

The pain is already intense: a burning in my joints. Usually I move all the time, even in sleep and the need for motion is frustrated into grinding resentment. I should be panicking and am proud that I'm not. This situation is bad but I have put up with worse.

One night in a shelter in the Outer Spheres about eight months ago, they came for me. I was with Unit 9/14 and if 7/10 was the best NFE unit then 9/14 was without doubt the worst. I had known something was going to happen for a while; there were a lot of nasty looks, lewd comments and a way above average level of bullying.

Unit 9/14 was rare in that everyone in it except me was male. All of them had gone out of their way to make me feel not so much unwelcome as openly despised. I got through it because I'd known something similar with the woman-hating Sons of the Crystal Mind. However, the Sons were a bunch of scruffy losers while the NFE unit was dangerously professional.

I had to live, work and train with people who found my every effort profoundly wanting. I beat the Sons but could do nothing to even dent Unit 9/14. No wit could cut them and all training blows glanced off barely noticed, unlike the ones that landed on me.

Their humour involved blindfolding me and pushing me off cliffs. The moments in freefall before I hit the surreptitiously giffed ledge were so terrifying it was worse than actually dying because if I was dead at least I wouldn't have to tolerate this anymore.

That night was different, though.

I was in a deep slumber and totally disoriented when I was seized from my sleeping pad and hurled across the floor. I sprang up but before I could even finish the movement they had hold of me, their terrible grip impossible to struggle against. They carried me into the next room. It was dark but there was just enough light to see their horrible brute outlines.

I knew what was going to happen. I tried to escape in my mind, to go to some place where my essential self could hide while my body was violated. However, the only place I could find was the memory of New Runcton.

I never seemed able to escape that dreary suburb, where 88 Rabian burned and where, later, I watched Ursula hidden by the vile, thrusting bodies of the men raping her. My sister's poor, unconscious flopping hand was the only thing visible as I fought my own attacker with my right arm shattered.

The man's stupid eyes, his vile breath and the revolting weight of him were an inexorable press towards helpless capitulation. I was saved at the last moment by Harlan, who blew the rapists into bloody chunks. It's the only time I've been glad to see anyone die.

Harlan wasn't there that night in the Outer Spheres though. The NFE unit ripped off my clothes and pinned me to the floor. I didn't waste energy screaming and wouldn't have given them the satisfaction anyway. Instead I locked my muscles to keep my arms at my sides and my legs together.

For a while I managed it, feeling these huge powerful males strain as they tried to get me open. It wasn't sustainable though; eventually they wrenched my legs wide enough apart to rip the muscles in my groin. Worse than the pain was how the exposed flesh between my legs felt embarrassing, like a dreadful inconvenience.

What little light there was glinted in their dark-shrouded eyes as they shrugged out of their clothes. Gradually, savouring every nauseating moment, the unit leader bent down. His descent towards me was agonisingly slow, long enough for my mind to do a lot of the savaging for him. Absurdly, the one sane thing I could make out in the storm of grief, terror and disgust was that I could now join Ursula in the ever-growing tribe of the abused.

My teeth chattered and I shook so hard they had to hold me tighter. The unit leader took sufficiently long getting down that I had time to throw up, nearly choking on it. I hoped beneath the indignity that at least it would put them off but still he came, lowering towards me like some ghastly clamp.

I didn't want it to be over. Once it was, an essential part of me would be gone and the Basis would never be able to put it back.

Something touched me, the lightest press on my pubic hair. In that instant, that worst of all possible things, I decided I would not break: I would not. And God help these fuckers when I came for them.

Suddenly, there was nothing. I remained unpenetrated and was hauled upright. The unit leader leaned in close to my face, searching to see if I was broken. I stared back at him.

"What's the matter?" I said. "Can't you get it up?"

He blinked! Around him I sensed their astonishment. There was a pause and I knew I had won; that despite the viciousness leading to this moment, it was what they had wanted all along.

"Damn it, Freestone," one of them said. "You've got the makings of a cold hard killer."

They started hitting me then and I thought of other things.

16

The pain is much worse now. Endurance, I tell myself, not torture.

I am a cold hard killer.

I am the Golden Princess.

Can't you get it up?

I've stopped counting seconds because it builds towards an expectation of release. I try and ride the agony but my well-developed muscles have become powerful nodes that generate proportionately greater pain.

I try to work out who has me. It isn't Na7han; he'd have just killed me. Besides, something as slow and methodical as this box isn't Nat7han's style; even his racism is instinctive and unconsidered.

The NFE tests us constantly, but would they really stage the death of the whole unit? Despite the efforts of Unit 9/14, the notion of a test like this just doesn't feel right.

My breath is close but feels very far away, the darkness and silence so complete it's like they're solid. There seems to be another darkness further out; that of pure screaming insanity, so I focus my mind on reasonable thoughts.

I wonder if this is the Stop House; it's certainly grim enough. Perhaps Centria's deal with those mysterious dark forces involves sacrificing me in this awful way. I can't imagine Harlan, Mum and Ursula doing it though and even if they have, why employ the Trages?

A terrible thought cramps me and I grunt in shock. One person loathes me enough to put me in the Infinity Box: Loren Descarreaux. I destroyed the merger, thwarted her revenge and humiliated her. Even her son was murdered because of me but she doesn't know that. Does she?

The panic I have successfully controlled begins to take over, ably assisted by the pain - oh shit the pain is fucking unbearable-

LET ME OUT!

**

I would be shaking if I could move. They have forgotten me down here in the bowels of Diamond City.

My stomach growls unexpectedly. Maybe if I starve there will at least be more room. I urge my flesh and muscles to waste away, but it takes so long…

Maybe whoever it is wants to let me out but can't. They've lost the formula, lost the fucking key.

I no longer want to stretch my arms and legs; that would be a ridiculous luxury. No, I will be happy with a millimetre so I can move slightly. Oh, how I wasted all those opportunities to just *stand*.

I find myself grovelling, apologising to everyone I killed, hurt or inconvenienced. Sorry Loren, sorry Na7han, sorry Hobb, sorry Crystal Mind.

I never believed the Crystal Mind was real other than for a moment during the Sons' first onslaught at Ursula's party in New Runcton. The Basis as a god? Absurd. And yet how do I know, really?

I'm sorry I doubted you, Crystal Mind. I'm sorry I killed your followers. Please let me go.

**

Every time I think I've got used to the agony it comes back with greater intensity. Time stretches and then folds in on itself, cramped up like my body. I focus on not focussing; try, even, to appreciate the lack of movement as a respite from action but it's no good. All my discipline falls apart in the face of this horror.

One thing I learned from the NFE about torture is that the

torturer has to know what they're doing. If it's their first day or something I will easily be killed or maimed so badly that I no longer care what happens. I'm not there yet, but the condition is beginning to appeal.

Usually the purpose of torture is to extract information, but it can also be a punitive. If Loren is behind this punishment though, why hasn't she said something? I know Loren; she is a grandiose hysteric who loves high drama. She would want me to know it was her.

The silence is nearly as bad as the pain.

Agony flares through me; I'm weeping now. My heart flutters and tears pour across the bridge of my nose into my ear.

"Please," I whisper, "please…"

**

Pain means hope. That is

AAAAAGGGHH!

…what it is for. It is a warning system. It says that

GNNNNNN…

…what you are doing is wrong because it is harmful

OH SHITTING FUCK PLEASE

…and your body has cleverly evolved a nervous system to let you know this in order that

"Ughhh… ughh…"

…you may stop, please fucking stop.

This terrible space, bunched up in the dark, the heavy walls pressing in, this is the worst thing, the worst…

…and then I discover it isn't the worst thing at all. There is movement around me but it isn't expanding out into bright light, oh no.

The box is getting smaller.

**

...at least they know I'm here at least they know I'm here at least they know...

**

Why don't I just suffocate? A slow blanket death is better than this. The Basis is keeping me alive. Fucking thing...

**

...with more space I could smash my own head in-

**

Nnnnnnnn... nnn...

**

**

17

Movement…

Light…

Falling…

I still lie on my side but… the pain is gone! I try and flip over but I have forgotten how to move. My view of a strange green surface is obscured by tears and I shake in relief for a while.

When it's over I don't seem to be quite right, as if I'm distanced from myself. This can't be a dream because I don't sleep in the box; I only manage fitful starts, interrupted by the blare of agony, the roar of terror.

My eyes gradually clear. I lie on a plain diamond floor in front of a kind of green wall. Still barely able to believe it, I angle my head so I can see up. The surface is one side of a green cube, which rises a few metres up until its top is just shy of a white ceiling. I have seen it before, that shape. Something about it inspires dread.

The green cube is one coloured shape among many, spread over a huge floor like the playthings of a giant malignant child. There are spheres, cones, pyramids, rhomboids, each a different bright colour. From between them comes awful whispering, a sibilant cacophony of fear whose words are impossible to determine. It rustles among the coloured geometric shapes, each of which contains a contorted, shadowy human figure.

No. Not them. Please not *them*…

I start to shake as I sense a presence behind me. It's not a normal human presence but something twisted and wrong; a gleeful, bullying malevolence like smothered laughter at a tragedy. I don't want to turn, as if denying the reality will make it go away.

All feelings except horror drop into the floor, where the Basis gobbles them up like it does every dead thing. Against my will I slump onto my back, very aware of my nakedness as I look up.

I have never seen the ravaged landscape of the Earth, but I'm sure if a human impression was possible it would look like the person regarding me now.

Lin Lin Lin squats beside me, her gargoyle face huge as she gazes down. This is the closest I have been to her.

The last time I was here was a naïve attempt to find out what was going on in Centria, prompted by documents in Mum and Dad's mission files. On that occasion Lin Lin Lin focussed her attention on Ursula, pressing the tip of a knife to my sister's eye until I revealed everything I knew. I remember how Lin Lin Lin knocked Ursula about, not caring about the damage that kind of violence can do; not, I think, even understanding it.

Lin Lin Lin's hair is longer and darker than when I saw her last. It is thick and curly but still ends in a crazed frizz, as if all life-giving moisture needs to maintain an escape route. Her suit is a different colour as well, its design struggling to contain the slabs of muscle slung almost arbitrarily across her. Lin Lin Lin's mouth is equally ill-fitting. It is a cosmetic copy of Keris's, whose beautiful, ironic contours are the exact opposite of the scowling she-hulk visage now surrounding them.

Lin Lin Lin's eyes are worse than the phoney mouth or pocked landscape of ogre face. Their radioactive malice bores into me. Despite the unblinking stare, there is movement within them; a crazed pulse as if Lin Lin Lin is in some kind of awful flux. This tension is the source of her demonic energy, which I feel on my cold, trembling skin like heat.

Lin Lin Lin is not the worst one; the worst one stands a few metres away with his usual disinterested expression. Steeber Loke looks exactly the same as he did when I first met him a year ago: the same standard, surprisingly inexpensive suit, the same last-minute hairstyle, the same other-worldly poise. Unit 7/10 were always eerily calm but Steeber is different. He is like a man-shaped hole in the universe.

To Steeber's left is an even stranger figure, which appears to be made from parts of different people. Individual features are relatively clear but the overall appearance shifts confusingly, like a puzzle. His feet are evenly spread feet and his hands are clasped behind his back in a relaxed military pose. I realise this individual must be the NFE traitor who sold out Unit 7/10.

Steeber inclines towards the Puzzle Man; more interested in what he has to say than in me. I strain towards them to hear but Lin Lin Lin shifts and I look up at her.

"Give us our fucking company back, you fluffy little bastard," she says.

Her voice sounds higher than it should, as if cranked up by the weird stresses inside her. It's also perversely soothing, as if on the point of an apology she would never actually think to make. I stare back at Lin Lin Lin and try to speak but for some reason I can't.

"You held Loren Descarreaux hostage," Steeber says.

His voice is flat and almost devoid of personality, as if he is describing a rather unchallenging mathematical problem.

"Loren advises you forced her at gunpoint to transfer control of our company to you because we were the instrument used by VIA Holdings to blackmail Centria.

"With control of us you had control of the information, as well as receipt of our substantial profits. I hope you enjoyed spending them, Charity. What did you buy?"

"Nothing," I croak, my voice still strange and close.

"That was a wasted opportunity, wasn't it? Because of you we find ourselves working for the New Form Enterprise; not a partner we would have chosen. The NFE are very good at shooting people but not so good at corporate governance, not the way we like it anyway. There is, for instance, all sorts of nonsense about honour. We don't like honour, Charity."

"It fucks us off," Lin Lin Lin says with that unnerving timing I remember from before, as if she and Steeber are psychically linked.

"We want control of Fulcrus back, Charity," Steeber says. "We have tolerated the NFE long enough."

"I can't…" I whisper.

I shrivel under Lin Lin Lin's furious gaze.

"The NFE have constrained us," Steeber says. "Your squaddie friends do not understand the subtleties required to run a company like ours."

The insanity of the situation does not make it any less lethal.

"You… won't… get away… with this," I say.

"While you were yomping through the Outer Spheres, we were learning about your organisation," Steeber says. "You probably think the short-term gains you have made will outweigh the risks you have created. They won't."

I'm too exhausted and traumatised to work out what he means. I don't know why Jaeger would retain Fulcrus. It tricks people into agreements, which are then enforced by kidnap and extortion. The brightly coloured shapes contain the loved ones of those who owe money to or work for Steeber. The Trages and the people who herded me into that building will have a child or sibling or friend locked in around me.

"I don't control my Aerac, so I don't control Fulcrus," I say.

"We shot that bitch operator to pieces," Lin Lin Lin says. "Literally sprayed her all over the fucking room; without her you can do what you want."

"I would have called for help," I say.

"Not from inside that box," Steeber says. "Besides, my friend here will tell me if the NFE approach and we will kill you. Do you want that?"

It could be that no one in Fulcrus knows Jaeger controls my high-end Aerac functions, which include any corporate ownership. I suspect only a couple of NFE commanders are aware of how I came to be part of the battalion; the Puzzle Man almost certainly doesn't have clearance. Maybe he thinks getting Steeber and Lin Lin Lin control of their evil company back is as simple as beating it out of me.

"Please… I can't…"

"You have been very loyal and very brave," Steeber says although it doesn't sound like he understands either concept.

"You won't get into trouble if you do what we say," Lin Lin Lin sneers.

"Jaeger controls… my Aerac."

"Jaeger likes the kilos we pour into his coffers, yet prevents us doing what we need to do," Steeber says.

He looks at the Puzzle Man, who I suspect will soon end up in a brightly coloured geometric shape of his own.

"Come on, you little twat," Lin Lin Lin says. "Do you enjoy it in that box? I know you posh cunts are all perverts but *really*."

I must get away before they break me without a care. I feel a twitch of strength return to my limbs and try to get up, but realise at once I've underestimated how badly the confinement has injured me. I stagger and swing at Lin Lin Lin, who moves back with surprising grace. I slump against the cube and slither along it. Steeber and the Puzzle Man watch me, unconcerned as I push myself along the smooth green surface and around the corner.

I attempt to run but can't coordinate my limbs. I feel very sick, like I'm simultaneously drunk and hung over. The awful whispers filling the great room become a torrent of painful sound that rushes through me, battering and crushing. I pant, exhausted from simply standing.

My legs pack up, unable to sustain my weight. Determined to keep going I crawl instead, hunched in anticipation of a blow from behind. None comes; instead, the whispers coalesce into a single terrible voice.

"Give us back our company, Charity Freestone," it rasps. "Give us back Fulcrus."

The floor angles beneath me; I roll over and hit my head, although I don't feel anything. I want to lie here and just go to sleep. It would be understandable; no one would criticise me, would they?

I pull myself up and look for the elevators. When I was here before the coloured shapes reached the curved outer wall, which overlooked the rest of the cylindrical chamber not far from Centria. Now, all I see are more giant coloured shapes that stretch endlessly away.

"Give us our company back, Charity," the voice whispers. "Do it or we will slowly crush you until you are no longer flesh but only pain and even then we will not stop. You do not know the hidden structures of agony the way we do. Obey us and we will make it stop, otherwise…"

Where are the people generating that whisper? There were hundreds here before. I risk a look behind but there is no pursuit.

Alone, I crawl and crawl but every movement gets harder. Sweat pours down me and drips off lank hair into my eyes. I try and get up but it's as if I weigh a thousand kilos.

The view through Fulcrus stretches until it seems to break, the shapes sliding over each other until they become multicoloured walls. I slump onto my side in that hated position again, unable to move. Colours blend into white planes that close in and… and I am back in the Infinity Box.

This time its walls are bright, with a two-dimensional view of Steeber, Lin Lin Lin and the Puzzle Man as they stare dispassionately in via a two-way screen. The image of my tormentors fades but the white light remains. The intensity becomes blinding; even when I close my eyes the glare gets through. I stretch my fingers towards my trembling eyelids, but can't quite reach.

"Give us Fulcrus back," the whispering says over and over like the pulse of a headache.

The box tightens again and I wonder if I can stay sane long enough to convince them there's nothing I can do.

"Give us Fulcrus back, give us Fulcrus back, give us Fulcrus back, give us Fulcrus back, give us Fulcrus back…"

A plague of agony swells through me as the transdermal anaesthetic wears off. The white light intensifies still further and all strength goes into screwing shut my eyes against it. The noise gets louder:

"GIVE US FULCRUS BACK, GIVE US FULCRUS BACK, GIVE US FULCRUS BACK, GIVE US FULCRUS BACK…"

Why can't they understand the need for relief to get my suffering into some sort of rhythm? Unbelievably, the sound gets even louder.

"GIVE US FULCRUS BACK, GIVE US FULCRUS BACK, GIVE US FULCRUS BACK, GIVE US FULCRUS BACK…"

"Please," I say, "please…"

Even I can't hear myself. The light burns into my eyes and brain like a nuclear blast that goes on and on.

"GIVE US FULCRUS BACK, GIVE US FULCRUS BACK, GIVE US FULCRUS BACK, GIVE US FULCRUS BACK…"

18

not sure if

not sure if sound has stopped or can no longer hear.

Time…? Days now?

Light still blinding. No rest.

Not sweating any more; used to lick it off upper lip, suck it off hair but lip dry now despite heat, terrible heat, cooking me…

Limbs numb, broken maybe. Pain more distant. Pain is hope so no hope.

So tired. Not slept for… er…

Box even tighter, crushing me. Can't breathe properly, such hard work, push diaphragm down…

The light snaps off. Strange sound.

Me?

Darkness, total and eternal.

A growing, terrible panic.

Must… get… OUT!

MUST GET OUT!!!

Muscles coming back to life… no! Stay dead! Stay numb!

I struggle without moving. My skeleton wants to rip itself free and my muscles knot in excruciating new connections. The claustrophobia I have somehow managed overwhelms me as neurons I had thought eroded by pain fire and fire and fire and suddenly it is too much and I will break if I don't get out-

"Adrenaline, Charity," Steeber says all around me. "Your body is now fully charged with it. Give us our company back and we will let you go."

I try and speak but my jaw is rigid. Muscles pop in my neck. What little breath I have creaks out in funny little high-pitched squeaks.

"Why do you resist?" Steeber says. "Just give us what we want."

But I can't.

**

Breath is a quick animal pant with body locked solid against the walls. My eyes are wide in the dark although I still can't see anything. Thoughts are assembled solely because of the adrenaline; everything is one eternal moment. This truly is infinity now.

Movement against me, below; rising…! Icy… water? Until now they have used some kind of dermal nutrient transfer or I would have died of dehydration but actual *water?* Oh, thank you thank you…

The liquid hurts my baked skin as pores snap shut against the chill. There is no room to shiver in this cold and the inability sends more nausea through me.

The water tickles higher until it touches the side of my mouth and I suck the lovely fluid in. It tastes slightly strange, probably because I haven't had a drink for so long.

The water keeps rising and flows into me, filling my stomach. *Enough now*, I want to say but can't because the water has covered my mouth and nose, rising and freezing to the top of the box. The only thing still out of the water is my ear.

"I wouldn't drink that if I were you," Steeber says.

Even if he elaborates I can't hear because my ear is submerged as the box fills completely. My restricted lungs begin to burn. I want to twitch in panic but it's impossible. The claustrophobia returns like a slow, heavy punch from all directions. Each time it's worse; each time I think I'll go crazy and each time somehow I don't.

The air in my lungs begins to poison me and leaks out, the bubbles rising past my face. Without any conscious decision I inhale water. It fills me completely now. There is an awful feeling of deadness as I begin to drown.

I remember it's supposed to be a nice way to go but that's not how it feels. There is only indignant desperation in the face of a colossal wave of terror that will smother my mind completely…

More movement inspires wretched hope as the water drains away. My cramped lungs jolt out scalding jets of it and bit by agonising bit I start to breathe again.

The burning doesn't stop and I realise it's not my lungs anymore but my stomach that hurts. Actual sickness lumbers through me like some kind of organic demolition and I try to throw up. Restriction makes vomiting impossible though so instead I vent from the other end. If I could move, the smell would make me heave; it's like all my pain has voided in a foul rush.

There is no relief though, from any of it. Adrenaline buzzes horribly through the sickness like it's splitting every cell in me. Each second the agony in my destroyed limbs finds a million new ways of expressing itself and the vast but intimate claustrophobic madness closes in, closes in…

The walls of the box go dazzling white.

"GIVE US FULCRUS BACK!"

The water rises again.

"What a mess," Steeber says from very far away.

"At least she's stopped screaming," Lin Lin Lin says equally faintly. "Thirty kilos of tranquilizer and still blah fucking blah."

"Do something about the smell, will you?"

My eyes are boiling pits of infection and my bones grind even though I can't move. I have never felt so sick: an endless twisting, swooping inner tumble. It doesn't matter though, because I am broken; mere bone shards and jelly.

"Loren says she wants Charity presentable," Steeber says. "She wants her to know what's going on."

"I'd have sent Charity in the fucking box," Lin Lin Lin says.

"Loren is paying. It's up to her."

Their voices change slightly; something is between me and them. Warm water foams up and submerges me. My mind is indifferent but my body isn't and instinct pushes me spluttering to the surface.

Someone, Lin Lin Lin probably, grabs my head and thrusts me under again. I try and struggle but as I'm held in place I notice the water clean me and sooth the pain in my swollen eyes. After a while I'm pulled up.

"Drink it," Lin Lin Lin says, now an indistinct shape above. "It'll sort your guts out."

She pushes me down and I gulp some of the fluid. Sure enough, the roiling torment in my core begins to subside along with the pain in my limbs. I bob up again and just float, unable to move. Time has ceased to have any meaning; even the now-visible clock is just an abstract design.

Details gradually come into focus and I see I'm in a bath of gently foaming white liquid. Among the giant coloured shapes I see people, busier and more numerous then I remember. Not one of them looks my way or comments on the naked girl in a bath of milk. Nearby, Lin Lin Lin watches impassively.

"Open your eyes when you're under," she says.

Her hand seems to enlarge to giant proportions as it closes in on my face and pushes me under again. Obediently, I open my eyes, which sting as whatever is in the white fluid battles the infection. I drink some more and wait for Lin Lin Lin to pull me up, but she doesn't.

After a while my lungs begin to hurt. Unable to think what else to do, I just inhale the liquid. I expect to choke but the stuff oxygenates me so I lie submerged and let it work. I am either over the claustrophobia or past the point where it matters.

I feel very distant and very wrong. My thoughts are flat. I remember a surprising amount of fire in me before the Infinity Box but it's all gone now. I am just a body, a device that processes nutrients for no particular reason.

I wonder if this is a trick; whether I will find myself back in the box when I try and surface. I don't particularly mind either way. I drift, lost in milky darkness. My limbs bob slightly in the fluid.

Eventually it drains off and out of me, away with the filth and infection into the floor. The bath walls follow and Lin Lin Lin stands over me holding my jumpsuit.

"Get up and put this on," she says.

My watery eyes are puffy and my jaw is slack. I gaze up and try to process Lin Lin Lin's words. She kicks me; the impact wakes the pain and I double up, clutching myself without conviction.

"Get the fuck up," she says.

She kicks me again and I skid a little way across the floor.

"Hurry!"

I manage to get onto my hands and knees, trembling as sweat drips off me and my tears splash on the floor. I'm trying to work out how to stand when Lin Lin Lin runs out of patience and seizes me. She stuffs my floppy limbs into the jumpsuit with such force my head cracks against the floor. Dazed, I look up at her as she yanks my damp hair free.

"Up," she says.

"Help me," I say.

She grabs the front of my jumpsuit and stands, hauling me upright.

"Come on," she says.

I find my feet and sway, propped up by nothing more than dimly remembered terror. Steeber joins us with the Puzzle Man and the floor begins to move, taking us through the coloured shapes. I stumble; Lin Lin Lin grabs my hair to hold me upright.

"Why…?" I manage.

"We have regained Fulcrus," Steeber says.

Unexpectedly, I feel a flicker of dark glee. Steeber is a fool as well as a psychopath if he thinks he can get away with blackmailing Jaeger. Steeber notices.

"Look, Lin Lin Lin," he says. "She's smiling inside."

"Mmmmmm," Lin Lin Lin says.

Both of them lean towards me intently and the sight of those two pairs of horrible, empty eyes closing in with an expression of grotesque eagerness snuffs out any trace of humour.

"You are expecting your general to come and wreak dreadful revenge on us," Steeber says. "Please trust me when I say it won't happen."

I try to determine what I feel about this unlikely possibility as the moving floor takes us towards the elevators.

"Your new owner," Steeber says.

He points at the transparent outer wall, which overlooks the dark, cylindrical chamber with its stepped circular levels. The only light is from glowing ring assemblies that move slowly up and down the tower, illuminating five square, blue VIA warships in slow orbit.

"We sold you to Loren Descarreaux," Steeber says.

"She really wants to fuck you up," Lin Lin Lin says.

"Loren will also use you to negotiate a cease fire settlement with Centria," Steeber says. "On her terms of course. It looks like the merger will happen after all, although technically it will be more of a hostile takeover."

"Very fucking hostile," Lin Lin Lin says. "Your mummy had better get a new job sharpish if she knows what's good for her."

I look beseechingly at the Puzzle Man, who ignores me. We reach the elevators, one of whose doors are open. The floor stops moving just in front of it and Lin Lin Lin shoves me in. I sprawl on the floor as the doors close and the elevator rises. I manage to look back into Fulcrus, where Steeber and Lin Lin Lin are already walking away. Only the Puzzle Man remains, maybe looking at me, maybe not.

I rise past other floors, also full of coloured shapes. Struggling upright, I'm determined not to be on the ground when I see Loren but it's almost impossible to stand. I lean against the elevator wall, so drained that everything seems distorted.

As one of the blue VIA warships rises ahead to pick me up, I try and resist the hopelessness Loren wants me to feel. However, despite being outside the Infinity Box I have somehow absorbed it; the walls closing on my heart.

"Charity," 23 says.

No, this is too much. I will start screaming in a moment.

"Charity, I'm so sorry I had to leave you. I had to convince them I was dead; easily done because I almost was."

I am still in that bastard box and my mind has gone. I'm probably about to die, the last oxygen fuelling a desperate fantasy as my skull cracks.

"Charity, calm down; it's really me!" 23 says.

23 would never sound that panicky; she's dead and so am I. The elevator stops and its doors part but instead of the landing platform a huge open floor is revealed.

"This floor isn't owned by anyone," 23 says.

A missile grows in front of me, pointing away. In the top, a hatch slides open to reveal the cramped interior.

"Get in, Charity."

"N-no."

"It has to be small and nippy to get past those warships," 23 says. "I'll fly it; you don't have to do anything. Just get out of the lift."

I stumble forward, more out of dumb obedience than anything else. Behind me, the doors close and the elevator proceeds up.

"That lift will be at the dock soon," 23 says. "Please get in the missile."

I look into the tiny space and shudder. Fooling me into getting back in the Infinity Box to shred my sanity in bitter regret and self-loathing feels like something Lin Lin Lin would do for fun.

"You… would never… have left me," I say.

I hear a strange sound, as if I'm crying. I'm wept out though and my swollen eyes are dry. It's 23, her unfamiliar grief sighing in my head.

"They hurt me so bad, Charity," she says. "Please. Let me save you now."

Lin Lin Lin wouldn't have thought of that. I let myself topple into the missile, whose padded interior breaks my fall. It's got windows down the side so it's not too claustrophobic, but still…

The hatch slides shut above me. For the longest moment I lie on my front and wait for the walls to close in; for the blinding light and the deafening voice. Instead, the missile lifts a few centimetres and fires at the far wall as restraints wrap around my arms and legs.

"To protect you," 23 says. "Hold on."

Something shoots from the missile nose; the curved wall shatters and I'm through so fast the speed trembles in my flesh. Confused and traumatised, I groan as I'm wrenched aside to avoid a blue warship before diving into the neighbouring chamber, visible only as a blur of green light. Swinging in my restraints, I plunge into the next chamber, then the next until everything outside is little more than flickering architecture and the flail of gravity.

"Hold tight," 23 says.
We hurtle on.

20

I lose it somewhere over the Outer Spheres when the tiny space and velocity-induced nausea become too much. I start to believe the missile is shuddering to pieces high above a diamond plain, the inevitable drop through disintegrating machinery a final delirious horror.

"Charity!" 23 says.

"L-let me out... Let me OUT!"

"Charity, we're nearly there."

"Give us Fulcrus back."

"Stop!" 23 shouts.

"GIVE US FULCRUS BACK GIVE US FULCRUS BACK!"

"All right, I'll land here, just stop struggling."

The floor approaches, closing in like the wall of the Infinity Box. Please... no...

"Landing now Charity. You can walk the rest of the way to the NFE assembly, but there are a lot of subs around-"

"OUT!"

"Okay honey okay, landing you now."

The floor is right there in my face and for a moment I'm pressed against it, helpless and screaming. The restraints loosen; I snatch my limbs free to attack walls and pads with fists and teeth.

"Hatch is open, Charity."

Too much information, too many decisions to make...

The missile melts around me as 23 deposits it and I struggle through the melting hull in a spray of dispersing structure. Panic floods my legs with desperate power and I stumble away, ungainly and helpless as if I've forgotten how to walk.

I fall and roll onto my back to look up at the empty chamber's high ceiling. The featureless walls are far away, lit only with a dim blue glow. I lie there, numb and shaking in the utter silence as I wait for those distant surfaces to leap forward and smash me in.

Sure enough, something moves. It's not a wall though, it's an emaciated man. He creeps towards me across the floor. Another follows him and then another, emerging from a nearby tunnel.

"Charity, move," 23 says.

More subs appear and I struggle to my feet.

N-GUN ONLINE.

Ah. N-gun. Goodie. The little target sight superimposed over my view jumps about as I try and focus. The subs edge closer, their eyes unblinking.

"They know you're weak," 23 says. "I can control the n-gun but-"

"I don't want you to control anything!" I scream.

The subs stop and watch me as more of them run into the chamber. There are about twenty now. I should be worried, but I feel as if Iqbal's string connecting my various parts has snapped.

"You need to get into the chamber after next," 23 says. "The NFE assembly is there, but it's too big to get through to us so you have to walk or better still run. Come on!"

I wait for some animal desperation to take over but nothing comes. The subs surround me and get closer.

"Fire the n-gun Charity; at least scare them off."

Yes, I want to say, but I will have to choose whether to fire a stun, kill or obliterate bolt and I can't decide.

"Charity!"

Somehow, I get my arm up and fire. A white obliterate bolt flashes over the subs, hits a structural wall and ricochets above our heads. I note how the hint of antimatter generated by the n-gun does not react with the structural wall; perhaps the wall is made of a different kind of matter entirely...

A flash above becomes an explosion that knocks us down. The n-gun shot has connected with something.

"The missile must have gone through a rec swarm and picked a couple up," 23 says. "It's possible Steeber knows where you are."

I climb to my feet and stagger through sprawling subs towards the exit. Desperation tears away the numbness and all the agonies inflicted by the Infinity Box activate at once. My equilibrium is shot; the chamber sways and movement is almost impossible.

I focus on my remembered image of the NFE assembly, its familiar tube outline a comfort. Jaeger is on board and it becomes incredibly important that I see him. I need his belief in me, to know this is not my fault. He will know what to do about the slackness in my mind and where to find my lost coordination.

I hear the patter of sub feet on the diamond floor; an even rhythm underpinning my desperate, struggling footsteps. It seems unkind of me to make such demands on my body after the thrashing it's had but I am Charity Freestone of the New Form Enterprise. Hardship is my-my friend; it keeps me… er… sharp, keeps me…

"Not far now, Charity," 23 says, "but you need to speed up because they're gaining on you."

Heading into the next chamber, I glance back and almost lose balance when I see how close the subs are. I put my head down and my final strength goes on a frantic, toppling rush through what feels like decimated red twilight.

I see the NFE assembly! Part visible through the chamber exit, the familiar ridges of the hull with its ports, turrets and observation pods gain definition the closer I get.

"You can do it," 23 says.

The assembly drifts a metre off the floor and turns to meet me. A ramp extends from the underside and as my energy falters, pride takes over. I will not stagger home; I will run properly and make them proud-

One end of the assembly bursts in a horrific ruby spray. The structure spins, its now open end screeching across the floor. An explosion in the centre knocks me flying back into the subs and we crash to the floor together.

Their fingers dig in as they grab my hair and try to bite through the jumpsuit. I click the n-gun to stun and shoot them off but my aim is not great; I escape more through blind hysteria than skill. Even then I don't get far because although the subs are weak they are also crazed with hunger and manage to pull me down again.

I glimpse the NFE assembly break apart as hidden cannons strafe the hull. I want Jaeger the unkillable to rise from the burning, melted wreckage, flinging shattered diamond plating aside as he strides towards me and scares the subs off with a single look. There is no movement in the wreckage though. Soon it will subside into the floor and vanish as if it was never there.

I almost give up then, and the subs close over me.

"Leave us your flesh," they say, "leave us your flesh."

Suddenly, the reduced space is too much like the Infinity Box; I stop thinking and blindly kick until I'm free. Rolling over, I crawl towards a large, square doorway, trying to build enough momentum to get away. A hand grabs my ankle but panic jerks me loose; I drag myself up and begin to run again.

The world shrinks to that square door; all that matters is getting through it. Closer… closer – and I'm there, staggering unexpectedly to a halt. The doorway opens onto nothing and I teeter on the edge of a sheer drop. The square doorway is the entrance to a huge multi-levelled chamber whose floor is far below. I stare at the terrible height and then turn back.

The subs are a human wall, closing in. Their empty eyes remind me of Steeber, as if he has fragmented himself into these bony, desperate creatures. I sink to my knees and watch them come. I am in my own Outer Spheres: pressed against the final wall, all power spent. This is the moment I trained for; so I'd be able to keep going when everyone else has given up. I should be able to raise a last quantum of strength to… what?

I do not want to die but I am a mortal, physical creature and I used my last energy on that futile run. When the subs reach for me they appear to move in slow motion, their touch gentle as fingers brush my cheek and wind into my hair. This finality is not a bad thing; it is precious, knowing how I feel at the very end.

"Leave us your flesh," they whisper again, "leave us your flesh…"

I'm embraced tightly from behind and my head falls forward. I see a rope spread itself to form a harness across my chest and between my legs. The subs lunge and I'm pulled back away from them over the edge.

I move down the empty face of the great diamond cliff, suspended between life and death, reality and dream, sanity and madness. Mum and Dad, me and Harlan, Jaeger and Keris, Steeber and Lin Lin Lin, Centria and VIA Holdings: every division of Diamond City flies apart in an ordered fashion that defies sense.

I no longer know if I'm falling or rising, in agony or ecstasy, alive or dead. Echoes thrum along the rope that holds me, greater and deeper the further I go until they are one great hum that soothes and deafens, its vast dark energy overwhelming.

21

"Wake up, Charity," 23 says.

My eyes flicker open. A curved surface rises away from me into a comfortingly large, empty space. My eyes no longer hurt and the lurching chaos in my head has receded. I slowly look around and see I'm lying on my back on the floor in a hemispherical chamber I do not recognise. I test my limbs suspiciously; there are residual aches, but nothing like the agony I felt before.

The red fuze grows out of the floor by my head. I reach around, pick it up and clip it to my side.

"How do you feel?" 23 says.

"I don't know," I say. "How are you?"

"All right, thanks. Can you stand?"

I roll slowly onto my front and get into a wobbly crouch with my back against the wall. When I am finally steady, I slowly push myself upright and look around the bleak emptiness of the Outer Spheres.

"Where did the subs go?" I say.

"You left them behind."

"How?"

"I put you on a sled, like the one we used for Krae. When I was certain you were far enough away, I hid you in the floor under a patch of diamond that looked the same as the surrounding area."

"How long have I been asleep?" I say.

"Asleep? You were in a coma for ten days!"

"I've never been in a coma before."

"How was it?"

"Not at all memorable," I say.

"I kept you sedated anyway," 23 says. "I needed to get the Basis to heal you after what those bastards did."

"I'm okay," I say.

"Yes," 23 says. "You are a tough little fucker. Still, I ran psych programs on you, a few deep therapies; lots of dreams about open spaces."

"I don't remember any of that. Listen, 23, thanks for getting me out and, you know. Everything."

"Don't mention it."

I twitch slightly as I remember a ruby explosion, hidden cannons and an awful crash.

"What about the NFE assembly?" I say.

"Most of the NFE weren't on it. But… Jaeger was."

I sink back down to a crouching position.

"Jaeger can't be dead," I whisper.

"He isn't but he's in a bad way. He won't be awake any time soon."

"Is he nearby? Can I see him?"

"I don't know where he is," 23 says. "I'm sorry."

I hesitate.

"23?" I say eventually.

"Yes?"

"You need to give me back control of my Aerac."

"I can't do that, Charity."

"You were about to before."

"I was certain I was going to die; now I'm not."

"You can be just as good an oppo without it, 23. You didn't have control of everyone else's."

"All newts have to submit control of their Aerac-"

"I'm not all newts. Anyway we're a long way from the training programme here aren't we? I can give you all the permissions you need but I have to have control of my life, which is run by that Aerac you're sitting on."

"I only control some of it, Charity."

"Fine. Give me that."

"No."

"23, when I lost you that time I had nothing. Do you know what it's like trying to get around Diamond City with no Aerac and no kilos?"

"Yes."

"Well?" I say.

"I will never leave you again."

"You might not have a choice! What if you had died, 3? I would be in VIA Holdings getting ripped apart by Loren Descarreaux. Have you met dear Loren? Do you know what she's like?"

"Charity-"

"She's Steeber's *friend*, 23!"

"Jaeger said to never give you control back unless he said so."

"How do you know what Jaeger wants now?" I say.

I get up again and start to walk across the chamber, the familiar motion very odd after the Infinity Box.

"You should exercise to ensure the muscles have re-grown the way I wanted," 23 begins.

I stop automatically to cut her off and begin a set of warm-ups. I'm stiff, and concentrate on loosening my joints; it seems miraculous that I can move them again. Rising anger helps align poor balance, backfilling any wavering control. My hair, clean now, falls in my face. I press the crook of my elbow against the hairline.

"Gel," I mutter.

The familiar cool, wet sensation flows across my head as the gel slicks my hair back and winds it into a tight, shiny braid.

"See?" I say. "However good an oppo you are, you don't and can't know everything."

"Your anger levels are-"

"Do something about it then!"

I work through a series of combat stances and thrust my limbs out from each of them: BAM! There goes Steeber's face. CRACK! Lin Lin Lin's head kicked off her shoulders.

"I can't do anything and I'm not going to," 23 says.

139

I continue to work out, feeling the strain earlier than I used to. The jumpsuit adapts to my exertion, sucking excess heat away while keeping me warm and supple.

"People don't usually challenge you do they?" I say.

"And usually they survive as... as a result," she says, faltering as we both think of Unit 7/10.

"Uh-huh," I say.

I work through another exercise sequence, finding weak points and exploring them; making them pay. The moves have a viciousness that wasn't there before.

"I deliberately left the unit because my orders were to protect you," 23 says.

"Orders need to evolve in response to an ongoing combat situation," I say.

Finishing the warm-up, I snatch the fuze off my hip. I practice-fire into empty blue distance: two-handed, left-handed, right, left again. 23 grows me a target but I ignore it, clip the fuze back and start running.

I savour the movement of my legs, the way the floor moves quickly beneath me according to my own physical power. I soon leave the hemispherical chamber and run into the next one: a plain, empty block of space.

Memories begin to bubble up: the Infinity Box, the callousness of my captors, the treacherous Puzzle Man with his jigsaw mask. I try and lose myself in physical sensation: beautiful big breaths, long, stretching strides.

"If you were strong once," 23 says, "then you always will be."

As I begin to sprint, accumulated terror, pain and rage fly around in me like unspent fuel. If I can get free I will feel better, away from the pressure I can sense despite the huge open space around me.

It is ridiculous, this secrecy and helplessness when my enemies are so numerous and so powerful. I have to figure a way out.

**

I wake up, unable to remember going to sleep, on a mat on the floor of a large chamber. Feeling exposed is much better than feeling claustrophobic; I can't remember if I told 23 that or if she just worked it out. I think about asking her.

"Take it easy," 23 says. "Have some food."

A lurp stack and a glass of water grow next to me. I sip the water but it seems to flow out of my eyes, so I sit quietly for a moment before I sip some more. It gurgles in me; I wonder if it will stay down and lean forward, exhausted by consciousness.

We're not going to take it anymore, raged Ursula on the red warship by the Zenod Hotel.

I bite into the lurp stack, my first proper food in ages. I get an idea of how that poor little sub girl must have felt when she tried this stuff; the spreading goodness is almost heartbreaking.

We're not going to take it anymore.

Take what?

**

I ease up on the sprint and ignore abstract problems, concentrating instead on a weak area in my left knee, the old ache in my right elbow and tension in my shoulders that needs to be smoothed out by pushing them down.

We're not going to take it anymore.

Why am I thinking about Ursula instead of Steeber, who is my main problem?

I run on, already further than I managed yesterday. The Outer Spheres wheel around me, their vast, bleak spaces weirdly comforting as if I need to absorb them to counteract the Infinity Box.

Keris in her blue uniform comes to mind now, arguing with

141

Loren Descarreaux. Loren did better than expected against the Chief of the World, the leader everyone loves. Why did Keris look so stressed?

I recall Harlan sobbing; his talk of the Stop House.

I remember my last night in Centria and Balatar Descarreaux's last night ever; his terrified voice, the shot that killed him-

"23," I say.

"Yes?"

I'm sure I detect wariness in her voice.

"Do you know who killed Balatar Descarreaux?" I say.

"It's not… I'm not…"

"Jaeger killed him."

There is a long pause.

"Jaeger?" 23 says.

It's the first time I've heard her uncertain.

"I was there, 23."

"Why would Jaeger do that?"

"Bal discovered the truth about me."

I wait for her to ask.

"Do you know who I really am, 23?" I say eventually.

"You're Charity Freestone, from Centria."

"That's it?"

"Yes," 23 says.

I feel like I'm on a slope, racing too fast to stop.

"What is it, Charity?"

"Have you ever heard of the Guidance?"

"No."

I stumble to a halt in one of those complex, unfinished areas of the Outer Spheres. Different levels are linked by swirling roads and multiple exits; I turn on the spot but no direction is clear.

"Is there something you want to tell me?" 23 says.

The secrets are too many, too heavy and too difficult.

"Bal found out about the Guidance and ended up dead," I say.

"Best keep it to yourself then."

"3, if you're looking after me it's best you know. I really don't think Jaeger would kill you; do you?"

"No, he wouldn't."

I am getting better at interpreting her silences. This one sounds like she's thinking.

"Do you want to tell me for you or for us?" she says.

"For us."

"Sure?"

"Yes."

"Tell me then."

"Give me a drink 23, a proper one."

A glass grows out of the floor; its tiny crystal shape intimate and vulnerable in the great space. I pick it up, sip the amber liquid and gasp; it's a long time since I've had it.

"The Guidance are twelve hot-housed individuals bred to form the ultimate government," I say.

"What the hell for?"

"It was a last attempt to save the world, two hundred years ago," I say.

"Bit of a waste of time then," 23 says.

"Twelve people, 23, to all intents and purposes a super-race. Each of them is the best at a particular thing."

"Which twelve-?"

"Keris the leader, Jaeger the soldier, Ellery the communicator, Gethen the financier…"

I pause.

"That's four," 23 says.

"They're the only ones I know."

"What's that got to do with you?"

"Whoever created them was terrified the Guidance would breed an advanced species," I say.

"And everyone else would be, what - 'obsolete'?" 23 says.

"Yes."

"How did they iron that one out?"

"The Guidance were made sterile," I say.

"Makes sense."

"The Guidance scientist, Sol Bassa, found a way to combine their DNA."

I stop.

"You?" 23 says.

"Me. It's why I'm a Blank."

23 is silent for a while.

"You're telling me you're super-human then are you?" she says.

"No."

"Good. I can do without that headache as well."

"I'm just very resourceful and resilient."

"If you say so," 23 says.

I let that go.

"Bal was in charge of Centria's security surveillance. When Keris told me the truth she didn't know he'd bugged her complex. Jaeger killed Bal to protect me."

"So Jaeger didn't know about you?"

"No. There was always an odd connection between us, but none of the Guidance knew except Keris, Ellery and Sol."

"Why?"

"The Guidance fell out pretty spectacularly; look at the Ruby War two years ago. I think Keris wanted to keep me a secret until I was ready to, er…"

"Take over?"

"That's what she said."

"Something for us all to look forward to," 23 says.

"I don't think it's actually going to happen, 23."

"Hm. How many of the Guidance know about you now?"

"Gethen and Jaeger. I don't know the others; I doubt they've been told."

"Is there no one outside Centria who could help?" 23 says.

"Sorry."

"Any other Guidance names?"

"Louis, uh… Louis Ruckingham," I say.

There's a long pause.

"Do you know him, 3?"

"No."

There's another pause.

"Did your family know all this when they adopted you?" 23 says, changing the subject rather obviously.

"No, although I thought they did and it was always a sore point. How strange to think that used to be the extent of my problems; trying to get promoted; jealous and obsessed with Ursula, who was always a better princess than me."

"Princess?"

I hunch slightly with embarrassment.

"It's a name Keris came up with. Don't laugh."

"I promise nothing."

"She called me the Golden Princess."

There is another of 23's ambiguous pauses.

"You've got the right hair for it," she says finally.

Now it's me who laughs but it quickly fades.

"I had them all, 3: Mum, Dad, Ursula, Anton, all of us in Centria, in our little bubble."

"At least you had that time. Not everyone does."

"Yes, that's true. It seems a long time ago and a long way away, though."

I feel like I'm going to cry again. My emotions are very close to the surface, as if the Infinity Box has stripped all protective layers.

"When did you find out who you were?" 23 says.

Her voice has an unusual gentleness.

"A year ago," I say. "Keris told me after that business in New Runcton."

145

"Do your family know the truth about you now?"

"Mum and Ursula do. Dad… Well, I haven't seen him to tell him and he doesn't pick up communications. Besides, it's not something you can tell your father in a message."

I finish the drink. As I put the glass down and watch the floor absorb it I wonder if I've said too much. 23 has saved me more than once however; I can trust her can't I?

Feeling light-headed and a bit out of breath, I start to jog. My stamina is degraded, although less than I expected. I pick up speed, oddly anxious to be out of the chamber.

"3?"

"Yes Charity?"

"What do you think?"

"I think you need to put all that out of your mind and get better."

22

I'm sitting on a mezzanine trying not to imagine the rest of 7/10 with me when I finally realise the full awful picture.

"Oh 23…"

"What is it, Charity?"

"Jaeger *wanted* to start the war between Centria and VIA."

"Don't be ridiculous."

"Do you know what the Ruby War was about?"

"Centria was after Jaeger because he had designed their defences and gone rogue."

"No, 23. How can you be so trusting?"

"I'm not trusting; I was there."

"All right; maybe that's *a* reason but it's not the main one."

"Enlighten me."

"Jaeger thinks Keris has got an infinite source of kilos."

"That's not physically possible," 23 says.

"Jaeger thinks it is; he wanted to get into Centria to find it."

"He told you that?"

"Yes."

23 absorbs this information with admirable speed.

"Better Jaeger has it than Keris," she says.

"When Jaeger finally did get back into Centria, the kilo source wasn't there and neither was Keris."

"So?"

"This war with VIA, it's just more pressure on Keris to give Jaeger what he wants," I say.

"Centria started the war, not Jaeger," 23 says. "Keris publicly cancelled the merger, saying VIA was bankrupt and accusing them of blackmail."

"So why doesn't Loren know who killed her son?"

"I've got no idea."

"Loren thinks it was someone from Centria," I say. "She doesn't even know Jaeger was *there*. But Ellery, Gethen, Harlan, Mum and Ursula all saw Jaeger pull the trigger. They've been taking the blame for something they didn't do.

"Why is that, 23? Could it be they can't say anything about Jaeger killing Bal because I'm with the NFE?"

"Charity…"

"Loren sent a Velossin after my dad because of something he *might* have known! What do you think she'd do to Jaeger if the truth ever came out?"

"We're the New Form Enterprise Charity."

"Loren will overwhelm you with sheer numbers and if she wipes out the NFE she'll get me too. Centria doesn't want that so they're keeping quiet, lucky for Jaeger. He truly is a genius; it's scary really."

"Jaeger sees the potential in you."

"As a human shield! Admit it, 23; it's why I was kept out of the way. Yes, the training was hard and we were constantly fighting but it was low-level stuff and nothing 7/10 couldn't handle.

"It's why the unit was sacrificed and why I cannot have control of my own life. The Infinity Box was like a physical version of the place I was in anyway."

At some point I have got up and stumbled into a great wide room shaped like a hollow disc, its ceiling low.

"You bastards," I say. "All that shit about honour and potential and all along I was no more than a hostage. Meanwhile, Jaeger soaked Fulcrus for every kilo; not even aware of the danger he was putting us in. Don't you *hate* him for that?"

"No."

"Why not?!"

"We don't take sides."

"You take the sides you're paid to take!"

"That's not the same thing."

"So if the opposing side paid you more, you'd switch?" I say.

"Never."

"Honour again."

"Yes."

"And what's honourable about making money from Fulcrus, whose business is kidnapping - literally, they steal children - and extortion?"

"They would do that anyway," 23 says.

"Doesn't mean you have to own their company!"

"We don't own their company, Charity. You do."

"I… I… That was-"

"You could have dissolved it at any time but you didn't. Why not?"

"Because Jaeger press-ganged me into the NFE and I didn't get the chance!"

"Did he press-gang you the second after you stole Fulcrus from Loren Descarreaux?"

"Well… no…"

"Why not?"

"Because… because Fulcrus had the information."

"What information?"

"Centria being bankrupt."

"So you failed to destroy Fulcrus when you had the chance because you needed it."

"No… yes…"

"But when you do it, it's all right."

"I didn't know what to do. There was too much going on."

"Too busy to save those kidnapped children were you?"

"I would have saved them!"

"When you got round to it," 23 says.

"I… er…"

"Admit you needed Fulcrus."

"To do good!"

"To save Centria you mean."

"Yes."

"Not quite the same thing is it, Charity? Centria is an elite that thrives on what it calls aspiration but is really just tarted up snobbery."

I sway as her words echo in my tormented conscience.

"You didn't want to save Centria," 23 says. "Why would you? They threw you out. You just wanted to prove yourself to them, still, after everything."

"23…"

"They left you to get tortured by the Blanks. You can see it in-Aer, the bit where that woman shoots you in the arm and then makes Ursula think she's being burned alive. It's quite popular. Why did the Blank woman do that again?"

"Her husband was killed by the Sons of the Crystal Mind."

"Didn't they ask Ursula's permission or something?"

"They had a gun pointed at her head. You don't see that bit."

"She still told them to go ahead though, didn't she? Put her own survival over… What was his name?"

"88 Rabian."

"Over 88 Rabian's?"

"She didn't."

"She did! You can hear her say it. Do you want me to play it for you? Won't take a second finding it in-Aer…"

"I told her to say it," I say.

The old sickness at that awful, forever wrong decision joins all the other guilt and misery swirling through me.

"Never mind," 23 says. "He was just a Blank after all."

"I'm a Blank!"

"Did you know that then?"

"No."

"He wasn't an important Blank anyway. Not like you."

"Are you finished?"

"Are you?" 23 says.

I stare at the floor, suddenly exhausted. The silence is as great as the space around me, wide and yet pressing in, everything always pressing in.

"Can you understand how in reality the big decisions are never, ever easy?" 23 says.

I want to cry. I do not allow it.

"Yes," I say.

"You might be correct about Jaeger, you might not be. As for being safe in Centria, I can't imagine you letting Ursula fight in the war without your protection no matter what scrap she's in, am I right?"

"Yes."

"And when you faced her, who was the better shot?"

"Me."

"We gave you that. Yes, you have the makings of an extraordinary warrior; being related to Jaeger makes it inevitable. But who better than him to shape that in you? You're a recruit to the New Form Enterprise, a Stage 2-"

"Stage 1."

"After what you've been through? You're a fucking 2, Freestone. These grades come when you're ready for them; we don't bother with exams and shit like that.

"You know you're not a hostage," she continues. "You would have been in a luxury pad on the NFE assembly if you were. Sorry; ex-assembly as it's just so many unmarked kilos now.

"We don't blame you for all the decisions you've made and neither should you. But don't blame us either. Has it occurred to you that Jaeger didn't get rid of Fulcrus because it wasn't his to give away?"

"He could have asked me."

"Why would he?"

"I…"

"Did you talk to him about it?"

"I thought he'd just…"

"Take care of it?"

"Why not? He's got control of everything else."

"Maybe it's not that straightforward. Maybe the company's operating patents prevented it. I don't know; but it's certainly not as simple as Jaeger bad/Charity good is it?"

"I guess… No."

"Diamond City is a complicated place Charity. The only thing more complicated is the inside of your head. How do you manage all that stuff?"

"I don't know; I just do. Everything else seems easy in comparison."

I am suddenly very tired.

"I need to lie down," I say.

"Okay," 23 says. "I'll gif you a shelter. If you want to get out, just touch the sides and it will open. Got that?"

I nod on my way to the floor as a pad rises towards me. I slump onto it; too tired to panic, already drifting…

23

I run through the Outer Spheres again, stronger and steadier after three days' rest and training. 23 and I haven't spoken much, as if all conversation was burned up in our last exchange.

Sometimes I replay our conversation about Jaeger and Fulcrus to see if I could have argued better but it always comes out the same. At other times I re-imagine the discussion about regaining control of my Aerac, which is trickier. I still don't see why she won't give it back to me. It seems I must force the issue, but can't work out how.

I run through an arch onto a walkway bisecting a great shaft. I look up but the shaft is so high I can't see the top. I slow to a jog, stop when I reach the middle and look over the walkway wall. The shaft looks the same both up and down, and the lack of any visible end gives a disorienting sense of there being a flat surface in either direction. I stand for a while, thinking.

The solution comes without effort; I must be feeling better. The walkway wall is about a metre and a half high; it's easy to slip over until I hang above nothing.

"Charity…"

"Give me control of my life back, 23."

"Get on the walkway."

"I can't be trapped again."

"Charity, this is stupid. You know I'll gif something for you to land on."

"Do you know the exact coordinates for the bottom of this shaft? What if I hit another walkway on the way down? What could you gif that would save me from this height anyway?"

"Get back on the walkway, Charity."

"My hands are sweating, 23."

"That's an order!"

I actually start to lift myself in automatic response and then stop. My stretched arms feel the strain as I subside back.

"Your authority was delegated to you by Jaeger, who is no longer in command," I say.

"He is!"

"He's in a coma, 23. We're more alone than we were before."

"I saved you, Charity. The unit saved you."

"I was tricked into joining the NFE. Any situation you and the unit saved me from was not one I entered by choice, including being tortured almost out of my mind."

"I-I can't do any more about that-"

"It wasn't your fault! But controlling my Aerac didn't help when you weren't there."

"Charity!"

"My hands are starting to slip. Soon I won't have the strength to lift myself back up."

"Please just get onto the walkway and we can discuss this."

"We are discussing it."

"Not with you like that."

I let go with one hand.

"Charity, you don't want to die."

"I don't want to live as Jaeger's puppet or anyone else's. I will stand or fall according to my own decisions."

"Put your hand back on the wall."

"No."

"If you die Charity, so do I."

I'm not sure I hear her right.

"What?" I say.

"Please, just put your hand back."

I hesitate and then grip the top of the wall again. My arms are converting into rods of pain and suddenly the Infinity Box is very close. I shudder, my palms slipping slightly. I grip tighter.

"I'm the best oppo in Diamond City," 23 says.

"I know."

Her unfamiliar laugh is a few short rasps.

"Thank you Charity, but you don't really."

"Did Jaeger force you into terms?" I say.

"He didn't force me. I volunteered because I'm that experienced, that able and that confident."

"That's insane!"

"It's fair; your life is in my hands. I admit I hadn't anticipated suicide."

"But the unit died."

"Spider Bob was the unit's oppo. I was always yours."

"Really?"

"Yes, Charity. If you let go of that walkway and I can't save you then I die too."

I close my eyes.

"Best you give me control then," I say.

There's a pause and I know I've hurt her.

"Seems like Steeber had a real effect on you," she says.

"Decide quickly. I can't hold on for much longer."

"Help me," 23 says.

"I don't understand."

"I can't do this on my own, Charity."

I hang with my face against the smooth, indifferent wall and my boots over infinity.

"23, Jaeger once asked what I'd do if he let me go. I said I would save Dad. That was the wrong answer because I still haven't got the ability, however much I want to."

Tears flow down my face and the walkway side, a sudden hot pour without warning. I have to wait for it to stop before I continue.

"What I should have said is what I will do," I say. "I will stay with the NFE voluntarily; I need to learn everything you all have to teach me. I want to be a Stage 5, even though I don't know what it is. I want to know about the New Form."

"You won't be disappointed," 23 says.

My Aerac details appear like streaks of lights through my tears. I laugh as I pull myself up, getting an elbow over, then a leg until finally I stand on the walkway again.

"Charity."

I turn and see a holo of myself in the orange NFE uniform, hair is down and with a strange expression. 23-Charity is standing to attention so I match her. She raises her arm in a slow salute full of sprung power, as if lifting against all the chaos in our way. I salute her back. We let our arms swing down and 23-Charity breaks up into the scintillating cloud.

I scroll through the precious Aerac options and then access the Aer. I swoop through its fields and spaces, the endless weather and products; useful and insane and *there*. I will never, ever give it up again.

I get the n-gun online and fire red shots across the shaft. Snatching the fuze off my hip with my left hand I fire that too until a slight inaccuracy is corrected. After a good session of cathartic blasting I cease fire, clip the fuze onto my hip and turn back to 23.

"Thank you," I say.

"I'm sorry," she says.

"Why?"

"The next thing you access will be your personal communications. I've kept something from you, something awful.

"Please understand I did it to protect you. If you'd found out when you were still weak you really would have lost your mind."

24

Steeber stands on the walkway and glares at me, which is the most emotion I've seen in him. Even though his nightmare figure is a recorded holo, it still makes me gulp in fear.

"I can only assume from the messages you have ignored that you simply do not care," he says. "Perhaps you are more callous than I thought, although I find it unlikely that someone with such a rich emotional tapestry could tolerate this…"

A scream rips the air; long, hopeless and bleak. I recognise the sound I made over and over in Fulcrus but this voice is not mine. It's a man's voice, deep and resonant despite the duress.

"We've had so much from Harlan," Steeber says. "The moment he broke when he saw what we were doing to you was…" he gazes wistfully into some awful distance, "…*exquisite.*

"As a result we know everything Harlan knows. To think, I had the pleasure of nearly drowning the Golden Princess in her own excrement!

"Perhaps you think your status will save you. It won't. There is me and the Stop House and you're better off with me, I promise you.

"You are alone, Charity. You can't go home; not to Centria and not to Jaeger Darwin after I blatted him over the Outer Spheres. Even if he survived he can't touch me, not now I know he killed Balatar Descarreaux. Besides, VIA Holdings is the NFE's biggest client."

I stare in disbelief at 23, whose cloud goes blue and contracts.

Harlan groans, his voice cracking. Steeber closes his eyes and angles his head as if listening to music.

"Strong isn't he?" he says. "Like you. I can see why you 'love' him, although it's puzzling how we came to find him *so* unconscious at the Zenod Hotel, hmm?

"Maybe you are our kind of person after all. If so it's not worth contacting you again; I will just leave Harlan in the Infinity Box."

Harlan screams again.

"Get back to Fulcrus," Steeber says. "Or better yet, go straight to VIA Holdings. Otherwise…"

Harlan's scream rises in pitch. The hopeless, terrible sound shrivels me inside and then stops as Steeber's holo vanishes.

Brightness in my mind enables me to see things clearly without knowing what to do about them. Numbly, I pull the fuze off my hip, look at it and then put it back. 23's cloud flutters nearby.

"It's not your fault, Charity," she says.

I start to walk, quickly crossing the bridge and leaving 23 behind.

"Where are you going?" she says.

Unable to answer I just keep on, strangely calm, as if my conscious mind occupies a thin layer above a storm of incoherent rage.

"Charity?" 23 says.

I remember I can access the Aer. The nearest train station is a kilometre away, so I head across yet another large empty chamber. This one is a hollow pyramid, like the inverse of one of Steeber's horrible shapes.

A wall grows in front of me. I vault it. Another grows further away and reaches full height before I get there. I turn sharp right, slam into yet another wall and stagger back as they grow around me.

Soon a maze of blank panels directs me in circles. I unclip the fuze and open fire; a panel shatters but as the fragments tumble they reveal more barriers just behind.

I aim the fuze, which melts as 23 deposits it. I get the n-gun online, set to obliterate and blast the next two walls apart to find more of them in all directions.

I get a now-familiar giddy feeling and stop breathing so no more knockout gas enters my lungs. Sprinting through rising panels, I gif a gas mask up ahead and snatch it off the floor as I pass. I clamp the mask to my face, breathing deeply.

"Damn it," 23 mutters.

I gif a flybike but as the vehicle forms in the floor 23 grows a four-metre high circular barrier around it. The simple wall grows faster and is complete and full of water by the time the flybike comes out of the floor. I activate the flybike's in-Aer controls but the vehicle struggles to get airborne through the liquid.

I gif a small explosive at the base of the curved wall and turn away as the charge goes off. It cracks the containment and sends water crashing into me. Submerged, I'm washed rolling through the maze and hit something, probably another damned wall. The gas mask is pushed off my face and I splutter in the deluge.

Drenched, I struggle up as the water goes into the floor. The fluid pours from my jumpsuit as I start to run, hunting the flybike. Eventually, I find it encased in solid diamond.

"At least tell me your plan," 23 says, just a voice in my head again now.

I deposit the mask.

"Fuck them up," I say, surprised at how hard it is to speak through clenched teeth.

"You're the offspring of the smartest people on Earth and *that's* your plan?"

"Hn."

No other words will come out.

"We could carry on fighting," 23 says, "but we're wasting time and kilos, which won't help Harlan."

"You don't care about Harlan," I say. "You just care about protecting the NFE."

"I do care about protecting it and I also care about protecting you."

"Only because you have to," I say.

She is silent as shame creeps through my rage and I clap my

159

hands to my face.

"I'm sorry 3. I shouldn't have said that. I don't mean it."

"It's all right, Charity."

I want to leave my hands where they are to shut everything out but it doesn't work; I still feel the crush of the Infinity Box and I can still hear Harlan scream. I sway for a while and then pull my hands away.

I find I can carry on.

"You were right not to tell me about Harlan," I say.

"You would have stayed ill longer, maybe not recovered at all," 23 says. "And then how could we have saved him?"

I take a shuddering breath and focus on 23, whose cloud has reappeared in front of me as the maze subsides into the floor. The flybike encasement remains however.

"Charity?"

"I'm okay 23. We're okay."

There is a pause and then the diamond block around the flybike dissolves.

"What if Steeber calls again?" I say.

"Scream for me. Go crazy."

I do. It's easy; everyone in Diamond City must hear me. I go on and on, losing myself in it. At the end I'm sobbing.

"That'll do," 23 says.

I wipe my eyes. I want to continue screaming.

"If Steeber calls I will intercept it and play some of that," 23 continues. "He'll think you've cracked up."

"Right."

"It won't convince him for long but should buy us time. Are you ready?"

"Yes," I say.

"Good. So, what's the first thing we need to look at?"

My mind is once again sludgy with exhaustion and trauma. Through it, somehow, answers begin to emerge.

"Work out a strategy-" I say.

"No. What's the obvious solution?"

I think for a moment, not distracted by hope.

"Go to VIA Holdings," I say.

"It wouldn't be in Loren's interests to kill you Charity. Your mother has an army, don't forget."

"Loren will torture me to get what I know and end the war on her terms."

"I'm not certain you're right about torture," 23 says. "If it ever got out, the weather would be very damaging for VIA."

"All right then. Suppose Loren didn't torture or kill me and still got the power she wants. She'd become a dictator like Titan with Fulcrus as enforcers. Do you really want that?"

"No."

"And Steeber will kill Harlan."

"Why?" 23 says.

"To retain monopoly of the information he can blackmail everyone else with. Also because he knows it will hurt me and wants to experience my reaction; Loren will enable it on a vix link or something. She hates Harlan too; he threatened to chuck her out of an airborne ship."

"So our strategy should begin with *why* we go after Fulcrus, when the sensible thing would be to stay here," 23 says.

Intellectual effort helps contain my panic and fear.

"I can think of three reasons," I say. "One: I want to save Harlan because I love him and because I left him vulnerable. They wouldn't have got him otherwise."

"You couldn't possibly have known that," 23 says. "And anyway, he forced your hand."

"He would never have left me," I say.

"You do love beating yourself up, don't you Charity? What's happened to Harlan is the last thing you wanted or expected. The problem is Steeber, not you. Stop doing his evil work for him."

"Two: the-"

"Agree, Charity. Say it. Say 'I will stop doing Steeber's evil work for him because it gets in the way'."

"Come on 3, we haven't got time."

"We haven't got time because of this tendency of yours. Say it."

"I feel silly."

"Do I seem like a silly person to you, Charity?"

"No."

"Say it."

"I will stop…"

My voice catches in my throat as I realise the truth and pity of it.

"I will stop doing Steeber's evil work for him because it gets in the way," I say.

"Better?"

"Yes. But…"

"Now what?" 23 says.

"Now I'm really fucking angry."

"Nothing's ever simple with you, is it? Who are you angry with?"

"Steeber."

"You're sure?"

"Yes."

"Not me? Or you?"

"Definitely him."

"Good. What's your second reason?"

"Fulcrus are a threat to the New Form Enterprise," I say. "They won't stop at preventing our revenge for killing the unit."

"And for torturing you."

"And-and for torturing me. We'll end up working for Steeber for nothing, facing increased risk just to further his interests. When we've done all we can he'll sell us out to Loren anyway."

"Third reason?" 23 says.

"Steeber and Lin Lin Lin are evil. I don't even think they do it for the money; it's something else, something sick."

For a moment, I stand under the high point of the pyramidal chamber as the multi-coloured cloud flashes before me.

"I agree," 23 says. "So what are we going to do about it?"

"I don't know. What do you think?"

"I think the solution lies with the Trages."

"Why would the Trages help us?" I say.

"We need to offer them a way out."

"But they were behind the attack on our unit."

"We have to put that aside for now," 23 says.

I take a deep breath.

"All right," I say.

"I've found some more out in-Aer. The Trages have a son, aged six. I think they approached Fulcrus to get backing for Lisle's business, but unfortunately it didn't take off."

"So," I say, "Steeber took the boy and has him locked in one of those shapes. All the time he's there, the parents have to do whatever they're told."

I despise the Trages, but shudder nonetheless.

"There isn't any more detail in-Aer," 23 says. "We need to get closer."

"How?"

"I'll tell you but first you need to get on that bike and go, because there's a pack of subs heading your way," 23 says.

I climb onto the flybike; the vehicle starts at my touch and I soar out of the chamber.

"Okay, 23," I say.

"Data milk," 23 says.

"Right," I say. "What's that then?"

"Before I was a soldier and long before I joined the NFE, I was a milkmaid," 23 says. "It's why I'm a natural oppo. My mother was one of the first ones and she taught me.

"Our world is made up of the physical city and the Basis but it's also information; lots of information. Too much, actually, and a lot of it useless."

"So what's data milking?" I say. "A filter?"

"Yes, using unpredictable means."

"Unpredictable how?"

"Well, data milk is always personal."

"In what way?"

"You met the Trages, however briefly. What was your impression?"

"She's weak and pretentious and he's a dick."

"Tell me more; her first."

"She's pretty."

"How?"

"Sort of in an accessible way. Nothing scarily dazzling, like Keris; more average than that. Lisle knows it and doesn't think it's enough."

"She's with a lug like Roscoe because he makes her comfortable and doesn't challenge her, but she has to compensate for that. I think approaching Fulcrus was her idea; she had no conception of what she was getting into."

"What about him?"

"He gives the impression of being strong but…"

"You don't think he is really," 23 says.

"No. He wears really obvious armour. And that fuze!"

"Fuze? Wait, let me check an image I found in-Aer… Is it a Remy Stag 4440 Repeating Spray Pounder with Incorporated X-Ray Sight and Mid-beam Dispersion Ratio?"

"It's really knobbly."

The Outer Spheres unfold as I fly high over them. I relish the space around me; I cannot get enough of it. A small holo of Roscoe's gun appears above the flybike's joystick.

"That's it," I say.

"Good," 23 says.

"Why?"

"Did you know that a lot of patents are made up of other

patents?"

"No. Centria's aren't."

"Correct, which is why I usually buy from Centria despite it being more expensive."

"Even now?"

"No, not since I found out they were after you. Don't worry, my Aerac ID won't lead your darling sister here."

"That's a relief," I say.

"Centria charges a premium because it owns every design element of a patent, so you can't get data milk from a Centrian product. However, not everyone can afford that, however democratic Centria pretends it is. So there's another market, a bigger one, where patent designers assemble other patents to create the one they want.

"Every time someone gifs a product and the Basis uses that patent design to actually make it, everyone involved gets a cut of the patent-owner mark-up. With enough bits of design or shares in design you can make a lot of kilos. VIA Holdings has more of these fragments than anyone; it's where the 'Holdings' comes in."

"How does this help us?" I say.

"Data milking involves identifying a product that someone will always, always buy no matter what. You then get one of the holders of a contributory patent to agree a small variation in design and next time your target buys their favourite item a rec is automatically giffed inside it. The information you can then obtain is invaluable."

"How do you find out who the contributory patent holders are?" I say.

"A lot of them advertise because they want their patent in as many different products as possible. These patents are often quite specialised; a colour pigment, the flow design that makes things dissolve when you deposit them, the shape of the thing. It's in the artisans' interest that other designers know who they are."

"I take it Roscoe's fuze is a patent we can milk?"

"Yes. It's made up of six sub-patents. Four are owned by

companies. We could try those but it will take too long. Of the other two, one is that shit-brown colour, which is no good to us because you can't embed anything in it."

"What's the last one?"

"The X-ray sight."

"Does it actually use X-rays?" I say.

"No, that's just some Old World-style marketing toss. It scans for molecular cohesion across a relatively broad range and extrapolates likely structural density. Not that useful really."

"But someone designed it," I say. "Someone figured out that people like Roscoe need to look harder than they are. Someone understands it very well because… they need that prop as well?"

"We'll make a milkmaid of you yet, Charity. What else?"

"I think the designer is male, technically competent, has military ambitions and is possibly a bit of an arse."

23 says something like "Gilstar?"

"What?"

"Well you tell me how to pronounce it," 23 says.

She sends me a message that says **?gil*** along with a picture of a sallow-looking man in his fifties. What little hair he's got is pulled back into a pony tail.

"People probably ask him how to pronounce it all the time," 23 says. "Make sure you don't."

"Me?"

"You need to persuade him to change his patent to include a tiny AV tracker rec."

"How do I do that?"

"You're a beautiful girl, Charity."

"Ugh! No!"

"Don't be so literal. Seduction is all about hints of promise. Think about when you first met Harlan, how he seduced you."

I try and force the sound of Harlan screaming from my mind, with limited success.

"He's gorgeous," I say.

"You might think it was that, but it wasn't."

I carefully access happier memories of flying in MidZone with Harlan, and the dance floor in the air.

"He made me feel like I was the centre of the world," I say. "I found out later he'd researched me."

"Similar to what we're doing now. Who do you think told him how to do that?"

"You were his oppo?"

I suddenly imagine 23 on a vix link with Harlan the first incredible time he and I made love and then on another vix link, this time with me at the Zenod. 23 has experienced me from both perspectives.

"The point," she says, "is that it was all about you. In the same way, you have to make it all about ?gil* without seeming as desperate as you are. That will be the hardest thing; he won't expect someone like you to approach him."

"I'm not that good an actor."

"?gil* lives about half an hour from where you are. I've sent your bike the coordinates. Make sure you've figured it out by the time you get there."

I grip the flybike's joystick. The vehicle is now on autopilot but I need to stop my hands shaking.

"23, this is harder than fighting."

"It *is* fighting."

I realise I have started to put something together.

"Why don't I tell him as much of the truth as I safely can? Acknowledge that I need him."

"Don't be too helpless," 23 says. "He'll take advantage and you'll lose control."

"Not helpless. Kind of sad."

"I like it," 23 says. "You've got a sadness about you anyway. Focus on that."

Focussing on my sadness is very easy as the flybike crosses the last of the Outer Spheres and heads into MidZone.

25

?gil*'s Aer profile links to a bar called the Hub & Spindle, and judging by the number of updates he spends a lot of time there. The Hub & Spindle's main appeal is not food or drugs but proximity to the bar itself. This status is decided by Harry and Holly Silk, the proprietors who create a sense that being near them makes one important in some indefinable way. I can feel their charisma from where I sit on the outer rim of a great circle of booths, like a huge wheel on its side.

Confusingly, Harry is the girl and Holly the boy. Although in their early twenties, the boy/girl description feels right. Gently mocking yet very serious, they are twins who appear to know everyone regardless of how physically close they are. The table offers a running commentary on what's going on elsewhere in the bar and applause occasionally runs up and down the tables in response to something the Silks say or do. Fortunately, there's no coercion to join in. Instead I feel like I'm at a party I wasn't invited to, but have been warmly welcomed at nonetheless.

I've renewed the gel so my hair is still slicked into a gleaming braid, although my face is free of makeup. I also deactivated the jumpsuit's cleaning process so I'm riper than usual but hopefully not yet offensive.

I press my palms against the table and order a pulse of something called Vortex Damper. The table glows pink under each hand and a rich, warm sensation flows up my arms. Unexpectedly, my teeth chatter slightly and I get a touch of brain freeze. I close my eyes. The freeze dissipates into a delicious sensation like tiny falling crystals of ice.

"Can I join you?" says a male voice and I wonder if it's another side effect.

"It's him," 23 says.

"Sure," I say aloud to the man.

I hear someone slide into the seat opposite me. When the Vortex Damper has eased into a pleasant hum through every limb I open my eyes and pause as if scanning the man's Aerac ID.

"?gil*," I say.

I pronounce his name with a rising pitch on 'gil', descending to say 'star' normally so the question tone is at the beginning not the end.

"Have you been talking to someone about me?" he says.

I stare at him evenly as if he is being absurd.

"What?" I say, with more than a touch of annoyance.

"You pronounced my name right without asking," he says. "Everyone asks, or gets it wrong."

"How else would you pronounce it?" I say.

"Exactly," he says and his voice mixes relief with weary desperation.

"He doesn't think you're a spy," 23 says in my head. "He thinks you're going to laugh at him."

I stare solemnly at ?gil*.

"My whole life I've had it," he says. "Still, you get the name your people can afford. There are only so many to go around or the poor old Aer gets confused. You've got a good name: Charity Freestone. That's nice. Very pretty."

"Thank you," I say.

"Can I get you anything? Drink or something?"

"A drink? Are we in Centria all of a sudden?"

"No, no," he laughs nervously.

His voice is low but nasal. I find I can invert my energy in relation to his, so that the more nervous he gets the calmer I become.

"I just had a Vortex Damper," I say. "You can get me another, if you like."

"Coming up!"

We place our palms flat on the table and four pink patches glow beneath them. I let the sadness that's always lived in me rise and expand. It is a strange energy; not depressing but melancholy, like a respected but mournful old friend. I look up from staring at the back of my hands.

"Thanks," I say. "That's a great hit. Your usual?"

"No, I've never had it."

"What do you think?"

"Good!" he says and laughs nervously again. "I like your hair."

"Do you? This keeps it out of my eyes. I should get it cut really-"

"Oh no, you can't do that!"

He looks so horrified, I can't help smiling.

"Okay then," I say. "I won't."

We sit for a while, me calm and sad as I savour the Vortex Damper; him increasingly fidgety. He tugs at his pony tail, puts his hands on his lap and then repeats the gesture.

"Uh… You're not related to Ursula Freestone are you?" he says.

"Sister."

"No! She's gorgeous. I used to come to her all the time-"

He stops himself. I recognise his look of self-disgust, but let him suffer for a moment or two. He takes a few panicky hits off the table. This time the glow is red. He starts to sweat. I watch him and then very deliberately run my hands back over my hair. The shiny surface is like warm, soft plastic.

"Hmmm," I say and look at him again.

He opens his mouth and then closes it.

"How is Ursula?" he says eventually.

"Fine."

"What's she doing these days?"

"Hunting me."

He gasps.

"Really?"

I nod.

"Why?" he says.

"I don't know."

He stares at me, simultaneously trying to process my words and think of something to say.

"?gil*-" I say.

"Just Gil is fine, Charity."

"Gil, you're probably best off getting another table."

"Do you want me to?" he says to my breasts.

"No."

"W-why then?" he says.

"I'm in quite serious trouble."

He looks up.

"From Ursula?" he says.

"Not just her."

As he goes to press his hands against the table again I reach over and take hold of them. They are wet with sweat but I tighten my grip and feel him tremble as he stares down at where we touch.

"You'll pop your brain if you're not careful," I say.

I let go before he can respond. He puts his hands back on his lap and swallows nervously.

This is taking too long. Every second I don't get what I need is another second for Harlan in the Infinity Box.

"Gil," Harry Silk says, appearing as a small holo on the edge of the table.

Her voice is welcoming and friendly but resonates with strength. Like her brother, Harry is slender and possesses unearthly beauty. She wears a stylish, flowing dress made from a hundred patches of other dresses. I wonder if she made it herself.

"There's another table free," continues Harry and turns to me. "Feel free to bring your friend."

"Th-thank you," Gil says.

Harry Silk winks and her holo bursts into a cloud of sparkling

172

bubbles, which float to an empty table glowing near the bar. Gil stares after them in disbelief.

"I've never been that close before," he says.

I get up and walk over to the table. Gil follows. We slide in either side and face each other.

"I am definitely getting you a drink now," he says.

I flick through options until I find one similar to my usual.

"Glenmo," I say.

The glow in the table fades as two glasses of the potent amber fluid grow out of it. I pick mine up and take a sip. Gil regards his warily and then copies me. He makes a face at the outrageous, bittersweet taste, so far from the usual well-designed comforts of Diamond City.

"You like this stuff?" he says.

"Yeah."

He smiles and shakes his head, then looks at me with tears in his eyes.

"I never thought I'd be at this table with Ursula Freestone's incredibly cute sister, drinking Glenmo although… Actually, you can have mine."

He pushes his glass over to me.

"You're not like Ursula," he continues. "You're more like me, if you don't mind my saying that."

"I don't mind at all."

"Will you marry me?"

I think of the Foster-Blacks and the little sub girl; the opportunity for a convenient lie disregarded.

"Would it spoil the evening," I say, "if I gratefully and politely declined?"

"Hell, no! It's a relief actually. I don't know what I'd do with you."

We both laugh and I knock his drink back as he takes another red hit.

"Listen Charity, thank you. I can't remember the last time I felt this good. In the very unlikely event there's ever anything I can do for you, let me know."

"I'm fine."

"I mean it. Anything. I design visual recognition and analytical systems. Not very sexy I know."

"Actually," I say, "that sounds very sexy indeed…"

26

Roscoe Trage strides out of a monolithic purple building and walks towards the train station two hundred metres away. People in the street give Roscoe a wide berth, which his arrogant swagger suggests he enjoys.

"Not too close," 23 says as I follow Roscoe discretely.

"It needs to be before the station," I mutter.

Tomorrow is the weekend and we have already lost a day finding out which business unit of Reech Consolidated Roscoe works with. I force myself to slow down because I can't let Roscoe see me; he will tell Steeber where I am and Steeber thinks I'm a screaming wreck. However, there is little to hide behind. The purple office block takes up one side of the broad MidZone chamber, while a scattering of towers spreads into the distance. Low-slung roadsters hum through the wide boulevard on broad wheels.

A thick, low wall grows out of the floor and two roadsters, one dark blue and the other white are forced to stop. At the same time, light bursts over Roscoe and he spins around, pulling his fuze from its holster.

"There you go," 23 says. "Cover."

I sprint across the road and duck behind the dark blue roadster. Its doors slide up.

"Charity, Roscoe is looking in your direction," 23 says.

Two men get out of the blue roadster. One holds a fuze.

"What the fuck?" he says.

"We're being hijacked," I say.

I point at the white roadster, which has stayed locked shut.

"They got me as well."

"I didn't see you get out," the man says.

Roscoe's feet still point in my direction. As they back towards the train station the man from the blue roadster aims his fuze at me.

"I'm not armed," I say.

Roscoe's feet disappear from my line of sight as the wall sinks back into the floor.

"We're clear," the other man says.

"Maybe I'll kill her anyway," the first says. "For fun."

I fire n-gun stun bolts into the men and they collapse. I click the weapon onto kill and roll over as Roscoe Trage turns away. I let the n-gun target sight come to rest on his fuze and fire twice.

The Remy explodes and Roscoe screams as blood flies from his face, his empty hand still stuck out in front of him. As he staggers and nearly loses his balance, I pick up the fuze and fire at the ground in front of his feet. Roscoe jerks and stumbles away from the train station, frantically wiping blood from his eyes.

Another large, over-ornate brown fuze grows out of the floor where Roscoe stood. However, this time the Remy Stag 4440 Repeating Spray Pounder includes a rec in ?gil*'s Incorporated X-Ray Sight.

"Sound, vision and tracking are all online," 23 says. "Now get out of there before he sees you."

As Roscoe rushes forward to snatch up his weapon, I slide into the roadster and close the doors. Keeping my head down I grip the steering wheel, engage the accelerator at maximum and speed away so fast that Roscoe bastard Trage is a dot in seconds.

**

"Ughh… Oh fuck, fuck… My fucking face…

"No, I will not watch my fucking language, you cunt. If you don't like it then get off the fucking train.

"Oh for fuck's… See this fucking gun? See the fucking size of it? Are you blind as well as stupid? Some cunt has shot me in the fucking face!

176

"What? *What?* Did you actually fucking say you don't blame them, you wanker?

"Yeah, you go and hide on the lower deck. Tosspot.

"Ugghh… My fucking *face*…

"All right, babes.

"Yeah. Yeah I know. Someone shot me in the face babes, that's why.

"Well no, not literally in the face.

"I'm fine by the way, thanks for asking.

"No, I know you didn't… No. Well, they shot me in the gun and…

"I don't know why do I? They've shot me in the gun and it's blown up in my face so I had to gif another…

"No, I can't use a smaller, cheaper one. Or rather, I could but I've got an image to maintain, yeah?

"I know we've got no money but…

"Don't cry babes. Don't… I'm sorry. I didn't think- It's just automatic, getting it. I've had it so long…

"No, I'm not gonna lose my job; the guvnor is fine. He wasn't even there, he's at some do all weekend.

"No, babes, it not gonna be personal is it? I'm Roscoe Trage! Everyone likes me!"

27

The jiggling view of a skywalk over MidZone reveals the day lights dimming and the pulse of adflow like an airborne river of coloured light. The area is crowded but its poverty is evident in the chunky, uniform architecture and low-end, unimaginative ads. The perspective from the Remy tracker rec on Roscoe Trage's hip affords a view of other legs and thighs in a variety of garments as they scissor past, the vista from the skywalk flashing between them.

Finally, we stop at the door to a private dwelling block. Roscoe seems reluctant to enter but eventually moves forward; the door slides open and he goes in. The sparse, cheaply furnished upper section ends in a window overlooking part of the main chamber, but the view is nothing special. The lower level leads to a cramped bedroom with two separate unmade beds, their linen tightly wound.

Roscoe stands by the door for a long time.

"Why…?" he says finally.

He sounds like a different person. Gone is the swaggering bully and in his place is a simple man struggling to cope with the intolerable.

"You seem to have forgotten what I need to do," another voice says, the speaker unseen.

It can only be Lisle Trage. Her tone suggests she thinks she's from Centria; however, her voice is low and flat, the expected shrillness absent as if forcibly removed.

"I haven't," Roscoe begins and then he starts to cry so hard the view shakes.

Cold silence emanates from the other side of the room. The view swings back towards the front door as if Roscoe has turned away in horror. His sobs go on and on.

"It's not enough that I have to do this," Lisle says, still unseen but closer. "But I have to pay for it as well. Meanwhile, you spend what little we've got on your stupid toys. What would have happened if I couldn't afford to do it?"

"I'd be all right with that!" Roscoe cries, his voice breaking.

"Steeber wouldn't. Our son wouldn't."

"At least put something on-"

"No! I have to pretend I don't do this because you can't stand it. I come up with reasons for going out, as if I'm off to work or seeing someone I like instead of this... disgusting..."

"Pack it in, Lisle."

"Don't you tell me to pack it in! Maybe one day you'll find yourself in a vix link with me so you can see and feel what happens, what he does."

"Stop it!"

"I wish I could stop it Roscoe, but I can't. Nothing I do works."

"You're right there."

"What?"

"Forget it," Roscoe says.

"No. What did you mean by that?"

"Why couldn't we have stayed as we was? You had a job, I had a job. Why wasn't it good enough?"

There is the sound of crying from the other side of the room.

"Oh, don't cry babes," Roscoe says.

"It's not my fault no one went for the business," Lisle says.

"Well, there's a reason those patents weren't used anymore."

"I wish I was dead," Lisle says.

Her odd, flat voice makes it sound like she already is. Both of them have stopped crying and I can sense the exhaustion in that room, as if fighting is the only passion left.

"We can't die," Roscoe says. "We've got to stay alive for the little one."

"It gets harder to think of him as real, that he was ever ours."

"He is real. He is ours."

"He'll be bigger now, won't he? Do children grow, in those awful shapes?"

"Course they do," Roscoe says.

"I wish you'd hold me."

"I…"

"I know I disgust you. I know you hate me."

"I don't hate you, babes."

"But I disgust you."

"Not like normal when you're my beautiful. Just… like that."

"It's how he likes it."

"Please," Rosco says.

"I'll put some clothes on. Look, soon I'll be covered up."

"Your voice though. The way you stand."

Roscoe turns one way, then the other as he struggles with some strange loathing. I glimpse Lisle, who looks different in some way that is hard to define. Her hair is the same as when I first saw her: quite short and a naturally glossy deep brown. It isn't styled now though and she isn't wearing makeup, but that can't be the reason her grey eyes look so dead and hopeless.

Before the clothes flowing up Lisle's legs complete their formation I see her naked body, which is slim and narrow-hipped. Her neat, compact figure should be attractive but isn't; like her face there's something non-committal, even repulsive about it. Her breasts are nonexistent and she has no pubic hair or rich, complex vaginal opening; just… nothing.

"Oh hell," 23 says in my head.

"What?" I say as I lie on a couch in a hotel room nearby.

"She's a half-cut."

"A…?"

"Usually when you change sex there's a series of stages to help you adapt. Halfway through the gender transition process you're neither male or female."

"A half-cut," I say.

"Not the technical term, but that's what people call it."

"So Steeber forces Lisle to change herself to a half-cut and then…"

"Fucks her I guess."

"How? I mean where?"

"I don't know Charity and I don't think it's a detail that will help us, do you?"

"Poor woman. Well, not woman…"

"These people turned you over to Steeber after getting our unit massacred."

I close my eyes to get my feelings in some sort of order.

"I know," I say.

A small, limp hand dangles in front of the fuze rec as Roscoe gets Lisle in an awkward embrace.

"I think you should have a little chat with them," 23 says.

28

The door slides open. Roscoe gasps when he sees me and reaches for his fuze.

"I wouldn't," I say.

Roscoe's eyes narrow but he leaves the Remy in its holster as he looks over my shoulder.

"I'm alone," I say.

"Who is it?" Lisle's querulous voice echoes out of the apartment.

"It's that girl," Roscoe says.

"Which- oh FUCK!" Lisle says.

She appears behind Roscoe, her eyes, mouth and even nostrils perfect circles of shock.

"Did they send you?" Roscoe says.

"They?"

"Fulcrus."

"Why would they send me?" I say.

"Because they like fucking with people."

"They didn't send me. I escaped."

"No one escapes," Roscoe says.

"Do you really think Fulcrus would go to all that trouble just to let me do as I please?" I say.

"Nothing they do makes much sense," he says.

"What do you want?" Lisle says.

"May I come in?" I say.

"No!" Lisle says.

"Yes," Roscoe says.

He steps back and I enter. The room smells faintly sour. The door closes behind me.

"What are you doing?" Lisle's voice is a hiss, as if she expects me to ignore her out of politeness.

"Someone might see her," Roscoe says. "Besides, it's the least we can do after… er…"

"After you killed my friends and turned me over to be tortured."

"Easy, Charity," 23 says in my head.

Lisle won't meet my eye.

"You look well though," Roscoe says.

I give him my flirtiest smile.

"Thank you, Roscoe," I say.

Lisle makes an odd guttural noise. I move towards her and she backs away, gulping nervously.

"They've been torturing you for a lot longer, haven't they Lisle?" I say.

Tears bloom from her eyes and drop to the floor.

"You don't know what it's like," she says.

"Come on now," I say. "Don't cry."

"He-he likes that I can't feel anything," Lisle sobs.

Roscoe stumbles to the bedroom where I hear him being violently sick.

"Steeber is a horrible, evil man," I say.

Lisle wipes her eyes and gazes down at her altered body.

"One mistake and they get you," she says.

"I know," I say.

"Why are you being so nice?"

"If it hadn't been you who caught me it would have been someone else," I say.

"But it was us, wasn't it?" Lisle says. "It's like I'm cursed."

I shiver. When everything goes this wrong it's easy to believe in hexes and curses.

"I'm sorry, Charity," Lisle says.

"Why did you do it?" I say.

"Fulcrus have got our son, Buddy. He's six… No, eight; they've had him for two years."

An involuntary moan of grief escapes her.

"What does it do to people, shut in like that?"

"The system seems flexible," I say.

"Is that what they did to you?"

"No. They kept me conscious in a box that got smaller."

"Like a cell?"

"No Lisle, a box about the size of that cabinet. They crushed me, poisoned me and then charged me up with adrenaline so I nearly went insane trying to get out."

She reaches for me automatically, sees my face and thinks better of it.

"They're not doing that to Buddy, are they?" she says after a moment.

"No. The people I saw were asleep."

Lisle's face crumples again. I step up and hold her as her trembling hands find my braid and cling to it.

"You're so beautiful, like a princess" she says. "You're what I always wanted to be."

I hear Roscoe come out of the bedroom. Lisle disengages from me and we both look at her husband's lacerated features.

"How did you find us?" he says.

"I followed you."

He points at his face.

"Did you do this?"

"I need your help Roscoe; I'm not going attack you am I?"

"Timing just seems odd."

"If I'd fucked you up, it would be a lot worse than those little marks," I say.

Roscoe scratches his head.

"Charity, we can't even save our child," Lisle says. "How can we possibly help you?"

"I need details, like where you meet Steeber."

"Hotels," she says.

"Which hotels?"

184

"Big, expensive ones. But he deposits most of the furniture so it's just a bare diamond cube with a bed."

Roscoe groans. I turn on him.

"Roscoe," I say. "You're a big guy."

"Yeah."

"Being a big guy isn't just about having muscles and stubble. It's about doing the tough thing, maybe even the worst thing in the world."

"I love her!"

"Steeber wants you to feel like this."

Roscoe puts his face in his hands.

"Don't do his evil work for him," I say.

Roscoe takes a shuddering breath and looks up at his wife.

"Say it, Roscoe," I say.

"I won't do that cunt's evil work for him," Roscoe says.

He comes over and puts his arms around Lisle.

A strange sensation…

"What was that?" I say.

Lisle blinks, confused.

"I don't know," she says.

"Something moved," I say.

The floor feels different and the MidZone adflow buzz is louder, as if the door is open.

"Charity-" 23 says.

I turn. Lin Lin Lin slaps my face so hard I'm stunned as I spin around and hit the floor. The pain is astonishing; I lose a second marvelling at it.

I spring to my feet but Lin Lin Lin kicks a chair into my chest and knocks me flat. Dark-suited Fulcrus guards land on me before I realise I'm too shocked to move anyway.

They wrench my arms behind my back and bind them with the right hand crushed into a fist. The n-gun goes offline. I'm hauled up, so euphoric with terror that everything appears simultaneously bright and dark.

My legs begin to sag. The guards yank me up again and squeeze my arms, until the pain forces me to stand. My noble motivations feel like so much nonsense now, as I shake and cry.

Not such a cold hard killer after all, Freestone.

I mumble, unsure if it's out loud. No one responds. Even 23 is silent. Perhaps they got her again.

Survival instinct shuts off my tears so I can see what's going on. I'm numb though; I could be a rec.

"You said we could have Buddy back if I gave you Charity," Roscoe says to Lin Lin Lin.

Roscoe's voice seems deadened, as if transmitted through thick material.

"We will," Lin Lin Lin says. "In six months' time."

"Six months?" Roscoe says.

"Your previous agreement was open-ended."

"But-"

"Don't worry," Lin Lin Lin says. "Steeber will get bored with Lisle by then. Run along Lisle; Steeber is waiting. You know how he gets."

Lisle stares at Roscoe, then at me and stumbles through the guards onto the skywalk.

"You can fuck off as well," Lin Lin Lin tells Roscoe. "I don't like snitches. Well, I do; they're useful, but *really*…"

Roscoe tries to meet my eye, but I have enough awareness to ignore him. He crosses the room, slumped with shame.

Reflexively, I count the guards. There are twenty. Two of them hold me and all point weapons my way.

"They giffed a layer over the skywalk too," 23 says in my head, "then just dropped out of the air in a high-speed ship."

She doesn't sound worried, which is so amazing I feel myself begin to reanimate.

"Remember they won't kill you, Charity; you're too valuable.

Grunt if you understand."

I make a little noise deep in my throat.

"You must delay getting on that ship," 23 says. "Something is coming."

Lin Lin Lin watches Roscoe leave and turns back to me.

"You're a proper little bastard aren't you?" she says. "How did you get out?"

"They think I'm dead," 23 says. "Let's keep that advantage."

"Giffed a missile on an empty floor above Fulcrus," I tell Lin Lin Lin.

Talking is easier than I expected.

"Fuck off did you," she says. "You don't control your Aerac."

"I got control of most of it back when you killed 23," I say.

"Someone else helped you."

I actually laugh at her!

"You killed all my friends, Lin Lin Lin."

"You expect me to believe you sucked up the Infinity Box when you could have blasted your way out?" she says.

"An n-gun obliterate shot in a space that small would have vaporised me."

"I don't believe you."

"It's simple physics-"

"I mean I don't believe you didn't try to escape when you could."

"I don't care what you believe."

She slaps me again and it feels like my cheek has split open. I don't let the pain show and stare coldly up at her.

"You like hurting me don't you, Lin Lin Lin?"

"Yes."

"Why don't you tell the guards to go?"

"Go, guards," Lin Lin Lin says. "Wait in the ship."

As the guards leave I study Lin Lin Lin. Her breasts are large with powerful shoulders to hold them. Hefty arms flower into oddly sensitive-looking hands that have left traces of damp warmth on my cheeks. Her colossal legs could kick through a wall yet also appear to embody another, less vicious function. Lin Lin Lin seems put together for some endlessly thwarted purpose. Even the mouth doesn't seem out of place in that context. The mouth…

I smile, slowly.

"Your mouth," I say. "It's a copy of Keris Veitch's, isn't it?"

I run the tip of my tongue across my generous upper lip.

"People tell me I've got a similar mouth to Keris," I say. "What do you think about that?"

Lin Lin Lin watches me.

"I like it when you're firm," I say. "I'm awfully wayward and out of control."

Her empty expression doesn't change.

"I've never met anyone like you," I continue. "Some people say they're no nonsense, but you take it all the way."

I move up to her and stand on tiptoe to brush my mouth across hers.

"Doesn't that feel nice, Lin Lin Lin? Your lips against mine: against Keris's…"

There's a moment of suspense and then the great hands whisper over my back to pull me close. One drifts up my braid and holds the back of my head: firm and tight, pulling my face forward - too tight, wait-

Lin Lin Lin's teeth clamp over my lips so the whole front of my mouth is in hers. Her eyes blaze with such ferocity my bladder goes in a hot rush. As the jumpsuit absorbs it I try and struggle, but Lin Lin Lin has me tight against her. My ankles ache but if I come off tiptoe I will tear my lips, so I stand there trembling.

Lin Lin Lin's sharp teeth slowly grind together.

No!

Oh God that hurts!

She is a hex in human form, her fixed and furious expression a devil mask of incomprehensible rage. All I have to plead with are my stretched-wide eyes, but Lin Lin Lin does not stop. I am completely open to her fearsome energy as she snarls: a deafening, bestial sound.

"Hnnnnnnnnn!" she goes. "Hnnnnnnnnnnnnnnnnnn!"

She grips me tighter and her fingers dig into the back of my head but the pain there nothing to the agony in the delicate flesh around my mouth.

"You think you can fuck with me, you stupid little cunt?" Lin Lin Lin says, unblinking.

Her words are only slightly distorted by clenched teeth.

"I could fucking have you. Hnnnnn! I could have you anytime! Hnnnnn! HNNNNN! HNNNNNNNNNNNNNNNN!"

My whole body shakes with terror; my voice a muffled, helpless whine.

"You could do with having less lip, Charity Fucking Freestone."

The pain is white and pure.

"HNNNNNNN! HNNNNNNNNNNNNNNN!"

I writhe against her, my hands locked behind me.

"I can munch you up when I want," Lin Lin Lin says. "Chomp chomp!"

My tears don't block out her merciless, unreasoning eyes.

"You don't try it on with me, you quivering gash; you're already mine! Got that?"

Somehow I manage to nod. We both go still.

This is when she will rip my face in two. Even if I have the chance to get new lips from the Basis they will never be the same; I will always feel the unbearable sharpness of Lin Lin Lin's teeth as they meet…

She opens her mouth and I slump against her, so shocked I can hardly stand. The pain is actually worse now: an indignant ice-burn flare. Lin Lin Lin holds me tight, my head sideways on her breast so my tears soak the front of her suit.

"Shhhhh," she says.

She strokes my cheek and then runs her great damp palm over my hair down to the end of the braid. I have no choice but to look up at her, my face rigid. Lin Lin Lin's eyes have that weird fixed intensity I saw before, as if she is drinking in my distress.

"Shhhhhh," she says again and I realise I'm still whimpering.

Lin Lin Lin gently licks the bruising indentations made by her teeth. It stings at first and I gasp but she holds me in place. Eventually, her tongue soothes and leaves a trail of cooling saliva with an odd sweet smell.

She seems to lose interest and gazes out of the window. Her grip is no longer violent but oddly comforting; less maternal than professionally efficient. Finally, she lets go as if at the end of an agreed time limit.

Shock and terror have left me dizzy. I want to throw up and only don't because I somehow just forget about it. When I remember where I am, I see Lin Lin Lin point at my mouth and then between my legs.

"Fuck with me again and I'll bite off both sets," she says.

I stare at her. She steps towards me. I nod.

Lin Lin Lin inclines her head towards the front door and I stagger out.

29

A ship drifts down towards the deserted skywalk as we leave the Trages' apartment. The lack of people is odd; at 5.48pm it's not late, so I look around and see buildings and assemblies begin to sink into the floor. There is movement in the air and at once I understand why everyone has left.

A blue VIA warship smashes into the side of a ceiling-mounted assembly and explodes. Another blasts at three red Centrian warships, which evade and shoot back. The VIA warship rises straight up and the Centrian shots hit a building, tearing through it.

The Fulcrus ship above us tilts alarmingly and suddenly we sprawl as blazing debris pounds the skywalk.

"Bullseye!" 23 says. "Lin Lin Lin will think it was VIA or Centria."

Lin Lin Lin is wedged against the wall of the housing block. She gets up, disinterestedly surveying the remains of her ship and guards as they are absorbed into the floor.

"There's a train station on the other side of the next chamber," 23 says.

I climb to my feet, hands still tied behind me as a nearby wall bursts in a spray of lethal shards.

"Run, Charity!" 23 shouts.

I stagger forward but the skywalk takes a hit that almost knocks me down. Lin Lin Lin gets hold of the back of my neck and we run together.

A warship crashes into the skywalk behind us and we go flying again as it rips a section away. I crack the back of my head on the floor and lie there stunned, watching red and blue geometry wheel and collide above.

Lin Lin Lin pulls me up. Dazed, I stumble off the stub of skywalk into the neighbouring chamber. We are at ground level now, but the battle has spread. A Centrian warship skims close to the floor, passing a few metres over our heads before rising to engage with two more as they attack a VIA craft.

Lin Lin Lin watches the VIA ship, perhaps with a view to handing me over. Fortunately, VIA are too outnumbered to be of use.

Can you kill Lin Lin Lin? I message.

"The floor in there is closed protocol, and I can't use a missile in case I hit you," 23 says. "Get over to the train now; I've bought you tickets."

"Train," I say to Lin Lin Lin.

I start to run but the floor in front of us lights up as one of the warships tries to strafe another and misses. Lin Lin Lin shoves me sideways away from the blinding impacts and for a while we sprint in the wrong direction. More warships enter; they fire and the attacker above us is hit.

Most structures have been deposited so there are no obstructions as we zigzag across the chamber beneath the battle. Its chaotic rhythm of cannon fire, flight whine and shattering impact are interspersed with dangerous periods of silence.

The train tube slants up ahead. A spherical carriage descends, stops and opens its doors. It is so close! Desperate now, I find new strength to overcome paralysing terror so I can sprint.

Another volley hits the floor nearby and Lin Lin Lin swings me round, shielding me from the explosions. Before I even register my astonishment, a VIA warship crashes to our left and screeches across the floor. We run clear but then an explosion from the back of the vessel changes its direction towards us.

Lin Lin Lin hesitates.

I throw myself at her. She is slightly off balance so my impact knocks her great bulk out of the way as the massive warship skids past in a plume of sparks and smoke. We stumble and fall; I land on top of Lin Lin Lin and roll off, but as we climb to our feet a red Centrian vessel strafes the stricken blue one. The VIA craft blows up and the shock wave knocks us flat again. My teeth are miraculously spared, although my right arm crunches against the ground. Before I can scream, Lin Lin Lin yanks me up and shoves me towards the train.

We finally stagger into the carriage and Lin Lin Lin pulls me to the right so the wall shields us. She slides down until she sits with me pulled against her front and her arms tight across my chest. I feel her breath on top of my head as she pants from exertion and her body heat burns through my jumpsuit.

The doors close and we rise as gunfire and debris rebound uselessly from the great diamond vacuum tube. The bright impacts are still visible through the opaque surface around us, but soon darken to nothing as we leave the battle behind.

30

"You smell gorgeous when you're scared," Lin Lin Lin says.

I swallow nervously as I sit on the train seat with my hands still tied behind me. My arm aches and I want to move it but I'm too scared, so I stare straight ahead as Lin Lin Lin gazes at me in that deeply unsettling way.

"Where are we going?" she says.

"Other side of the city."

"Nowhere near Fulcrus then."

"Er…"

"Don't you love your boyfriend anymore?"

"Of course I do," I say.

"Why are you being such a stupid little bitch then?"

"I-"

"All the time we're stuck on this poxy train, Harlan is in that box, screaming. I can make him scream louder if you want."

"No! Please don't. I just-"

"Don't bother me with that performance; I've heard it all before."

I close my eyes, drift for a bit and then force them open.

"Do you know what Loren will do to me?" I say.

"Stop the idiot war that's losing everyone so much money."

"And then?"

"Use you to entertain the troops, I imagine," Lin Lin Lin says.

"Do you want that for me?"

"I don't care."

"You do," I say. "You protected me when that warship was shooting at us."

"Look in my eyes, Charity. What do you see?"

I turn to her and look hard.

"Conflict," I say after a moment.

"In your dreams!"

"It's there. You're not just a psychopath. There's something else."

Her eyes narrow. I gulp and stare at the back of the chair in front again. Lin Lin Lin continues to watch me. I close my eyes to shut her out but flinch when I hear her move closer.

"I protected you because you're worth a fortune, Charity, and not just from Loren."

I look at her again, confused.

"What do you mean?"

Lin Lin Lin's mouth twitches.

"You owe us, Charity."

"What?"

"When you stole our company, you fucked everything up."

"You're doing better under the NFE," I say.

"By whose reckoning? Jaeger fucking Darwin's? We had plans of our own and you knackered them. Now you pay us back."

I glare at her but it has no effect.

"How much?" I say eventually.

"A million kilos."

"That's ridiculous!"

"No," Lin Lin Lin says.

She sounds so reasonable, I'm tempted to agree with her. I shake my head.

"How can I pay you back if I'm Loren's prisoner?"

"That's your problem."

The train races on as I try and work out what to do. Lin Lin Lin leans closer, as if to inhale my thudding despair.

"You're so rich," she says.

"I'm not."

"I don't just mean wealthy. I mean there's so much to you. All them layers, like Diamond City with tits."

Lin Lin Lin sits back with an odd contented sigh.

"You've got your own Outer Spheres," she says.

"What do you mean?"

"You'll get bored waiting for Harlan."

"You'd keep him?"

"Not in the Infinity Box, we're not animals. In a shape, asleep. But you'll stop caring."

"No."

"You won't be able to help it; one person's not enough for you. I imagine we'll have to nab someone else as well to keep you in line."

"You won't have to do that," I say.

She laughs.

"Remember when we first met, Charity? You were with your sister, with Ursula. Now *that* is a girl who is built of sex, like all her molecules are at it. Very succulent, as you know."

"I don't know what you're talking about."

"The way you looked at her! You love her, more than you love Harlan even."

"I do not-"

"Why didn't you just get the Basis to give you a cock, so you could fuck her and be done with it?"

"That never occurred to me."

"Don't get all prim and proper, not after the way you came on. 'Oh, I'm so wayward Lin Lin Lin, please take me in hand and smack my naughty bottom'!"

I close my eyes again. Now our flight through the battling warships is over the sick, shocked feeling is back. I want to sleep, to recover but I feel Lin Lin Lin lean in close again.

"You can't shut me out, little one. I'm already in you."

Her lips brush my ear. I shudder and she laughs again. I feel her great hand stroke the top of my head and give the braid a yank. I open my eyes and glare at the gleefully malicious but confusing eyes, the thick wild hair and that awful grinning mouth.

Keris's mouth.

"What if I could pay you the million kilos now?" I say.

"Go on then."

"You'd keep me anyway!"

"No, we wouldn't."

"You kept Buddy Trage."

"For six months instead of forever, as was most likely necessary with those two saps."

"You'll never give him back," I say.

"We will. We always do what we say."

"Why?"

"People are only tasty when they've got hope; you have to time it so you get all you can out of them before they crack. So if I tell you your debt to us will be wiped out, then it will be wiped out. Come on, pony it up."

"I haven't got it on me."

"Oh for fuck's sake. I really thought you had something Charity, but you're just like all the others."

"I can give you Keris Veitch."

"She ain't yours to give!"

"I know how to find her."

"She's in Centria," Lin Lin Lin says.

"She isn't. She's hiding."

"And you can tell me where."

"I know a man who can."

"Course you do."

"When I let the NFE into Centria in return for saving Ursula, Keris escaped and hid with a company I know. She left there for another location and this man knows where it is."

"How can you be sure?"

"I've spent the last year looking for Keris."

"Why?" Lin Lin Lin says.

"Jaeger wants her."

"What for?"

"What do you think?"

I try and look saucy but Lin Lin Lin makes me feel lewd and small. She thinks for a moment.

"Where is this man?" she says.

"In the Stop House."

"What's that?"

"I don't know, but Steeber does."

"Tell me your man's name."

"When we get there."

"I can make you tell me now."

"What he says might not make sense to you. I can interpret it."

"Can you now!"

"If this man can help us, then you've got Keris Veitch. If not, you've got Harlan and I'll come quietly."

"Tell me the name of the man in the Stop House."

"I've got to go there myself."

"Why?"

"I want to know what it is, Lin Lin Lin. I want to know what my own people were going to do to me."

"That's not a good enough reason," Steeber says from the seat behind.

Unlike Lin Lin Lin, Steeber terrifies with minimal effort and I struggle to remain calm. His holo drifts through the chairs until he stands beside me, nightmarishly ordinary in his usual suit and hair 'style', which I'm sure is identical down to the position of individual follicles.

"Tell us the name of your contact," Steeber says. "If it is worth anything we will take it into account."

"Go and fuck yourself," I say.

"Go *and* fuck yourself?" Lin Lin Lin sniggers.

Steeber points in front of him.

"Here," he says.

Lin Lin Lin pulls me off the seat so I'm kneeling before Steeber and squats on the back of my legs. The massive weight prevents me moving and crushes my knees painfully against the floor. Lin Lin Lin wraps one arm around my neck and holds my head facing forward with the other.

Another hologram appears beside Steeber. It's an impossibly small, dark cube rammed with dark-skinned limbs as if the person inside has been reshaped into a block. Even the face is distorted, so I don't recognise Harlan at first. I wonder how he can resist using the n-gun, but then see his right index finger is missing. Horribly, the damn box gets even smaller and the whites of Harlan's eyes seem to fill the tiny, wretched space.

I try and look away, but Lin Lin Lin wrenches my head around. I close my eyes but she fingers them open, forcing me to see the agony and despair on Harlan's face and the humiliating streaks of filth on his powerful limbs.

"You did this, Charity," Steeber says. "You put him there and now you want to leave him."

"You like black cock, but that's as far as it goes," Lin Lin Lin says. "You don't give a shit about him, really."

"He thinks you're in a box like that one," Steeber says. "It's what broke him, listening to our recording of your screams."

"But you're out here, running around and playing your stupid little games," Lin Lin Lin says.

"Tell us the name of your contact," Steeber says. "Now."

"Go fuck yourself," I say.

The hologram of Harlan vanishes but I still hear his last gasp, a *snap* and then silence.

"No," I say. "No, you- No! NOOOOOO!"

For a second I go so limp it's as if I've become liquid, to be absorbed and dispersed by the Basis. Everything that made Charity Freestone seems to fly apart and great white space floods me like the silent, weirdly gentle first moment of an explosion.

Then I scream; writhing in a vast, impossible storm of grief.

Suddenly free, I kick at everything; only dimly aware of hot, bloody spray and the percussion of impact. Finally, I mingle with my captors: humanity and its other; numb light and the welcoming horror of darkness.

**

I fade back in and see light pulse randomly through the side of the train carriage. Lin Lin Lin sits nearby with a large red mark on her left cheek and bite marks on her hands that rhyme with a terrific ache in my jaw. She appears to be expressionless, but the intensity of our time together has given me insight into her. Lin Lin Lin looks wary.

Steeber stands further off. I ignore him.

"Cunts," I say.

My eyes are dry. I wait for the train to reach its destination, unconcerned about anything.

"All right, then," Steeber says.

I shake my head.

"You don't get to say no," Lin Lin Lin says.

"I can do what I want."

"Harlan isn't dead," Steeber says.

Relief, gratitude and fury surge for dominance as if from different directions, but when I gaze at Steeber my face feels oddly frozen. He stares back, seemingly able to absorb emotion without any effect. I get up, hands still tied behind me and face him.

"One of the many sad things about you being psychopathic dirt is that you can have no conception of just how much I hate you," I tell him. "You might think that's a good thing, but it isn't."

"If you say so, Charity," Steeber says.

I match his bleakness with the power of the Guidance.

"Make Harlan comfortable," I say.

"You need to appreciate timescales," Steeber says.

"I do appreciate them," I say. "I used to be a secretary. It's a proper, useful job; not like what you do, you parasite."

"I don't negotiate," Steeber says.

"This isn't a negotiation. Make Harlan comfortable or the next time I see a battle I'll stand in the way of a cannon and you will get nothing, Steeber."

He regards me, calculating.

"I will go to the Stop House with Lin Lin Lin," I say. "We'll find Keris or information about her and my debt to you will be paid."

I am calm. I could do this all day.

Steeber's holo is replaced by the one of Harlan. He is no longer in the Infinity Box but asleep in the Basis, while a medical readout counts down kilos being expended on his care. The holo fades.

Lin Lin Lin gets up, takes my shoulders and turns me around so I face away from her. The tension restraining my wrists eases and I stretch my freed arms.

"Name," Lin Lin Lin says from behind me.

"I'll tell you when we get there."

"You need to tell me now."

I turn.

"Why?" I say.

"Because there's more than one Stop House."

31

I wake up as I slide across the long seat and blink crustily at the little ship's rear cabin. Gazing through the narrow window, I see we've banked to avoid a drifting assembly that looks like a ruined gothic castle.

Horrible images bring me round fully: Harlan in a box, Lin Lin Lin's crazy demon eyes; the subs closing in… I sit up too fast and dizzy white spots dart across my vision.

I took a pulse earlier that cycled me through an eight-hour sleep pattern in a quarter of the time. I hoped resting for the duration of our journey to the Stop House would ease my smothering exhaustion but I still feel heavy and numb. My stale mouth is dry, my lips painful when I sip water from the jumpsuit.

"The ship's open protocol," Lin Lin Lin says from the doorway to the front cabin. "You don't have to drink your own piss."

I look at the floor stupidly and wait for everything to go away. However, Lin Lin Lin's nightmare bulk remains in the doorway, MidZone thins out beyond the windows and the wrecked feeling inside me perseveres.

Practicality takes over. I'm not hungry but gif a lurp stack anyway and slowly chew through it. The food doesn't help; it sits inside me like a peevish guest.

Lin Lin Lin is possessed by the same frightful energy as before, while the marks I made on her face and hands have disappeared. She watches with a faint grin as I blink at my awful reflection in the window. I gif a Healing Hanky and press the warm damp cloth to my face, moaning softly as the smart fluids ease the grit from my sore eyes and begin work on the damage to my lips. I sense Lin Lin Lin watching me and try to ignore her.

My aching flesh absorbs the last moisture from the Hanky and it crumbles. I rub soft fragments into my raw face and the stuff tingles as it soaks in. The pleasure is a distraction and as my jumpsuit cleans the residual effects of stress I start to believe I might actually get through the next few hours.

I open my eyes. Lin Lin Lin continues to stare at me.

"What are you looking at?" I say.

She snorts and goes back into the front cabin, although the ship is clearly on autopilot.

I draw my elbow crook up over my face to deliver a coat of makeup that covers the death mask pallor and hides the bruising. Pulling my hair clean I gel it back into the braid, then gif a dental block and slide it into my mouth. The disgusting taste I've got used to abates along with the buzzing in my teeth.

Finally, I take a stim pulse off the floor. My mind steadies and becomes more focussed. Energy flows through me, but so does aggression with an echo of nightmares: Harlan screaming, the Infinity Box and Lin Lin Lin's teeth. I breathe deeply and ride it until I feel in control. Carefully, I work through a series of physical exercises; balancing, lifting and punching. When my natural energy merges with the stim's, I straighten and message 23.

You all right?

Good, she comes back. **You?**

Yes xx

I walk into the front cabin and ignore Lin Lin Lin, who sits on one of the two seats that look through the forward window. She is uncharacteristically quiet, almost withdrawn.

"I hope you're all right dealing with curses," I say.

"Every other word out of my hole is a fucking curse," Lin Lin Lin says.

"I meant the Hex that Centria has over VIA."

"That's all bollocks," Lin Lin Lin says.

"If you say so."

"No, it is. There's no curse. The Hex is a set of orbital

fortifications."

I concentrate on being disinterested.

"Oh?" I say, bored. "Orbital around what?"

"VIA Holdings."

Lin Lin Lin is clearly repeating something Steeber has told her.

"Hn," I say.

I sit on the other seat and put my boots on the ledge below the window, keeping my eyes on the sparse architecture as we head for the upper section of the city where MidZone borders the Outer Spheres.

"You won't turn into a goblin or anything if you go into that Stop House," Lin Lin Lin says and looks me up and down. "You don't need to worry about not being all… all pretty and that."

I look worried, as if I'm still scared of the Hex.

"Seriously," she says. "Ellery Quinn came up with the curse story. Like all the best lies, it contains an element of truth."

I can almost hear Steeber's voice hiding in Lin Lin Lin's.

"Hex is short for 'Hexahedron'," Lin Lin Lin continues, "which is the pattern of Centrian forts around VIA."

"So that's how Centria has been able to batter VIA, despite being surrounded by them," I say.

"Exactly."

I frown as if grappling with a problem only Lin Lin Lin can help me with.

"What kind of hexahedron?" I say.

"Eh?"

"They can be different shapes, can't they?"

"Right, yeah," Lin Lin Lin says.

"It's probably like a giant invisible cube surrounding VIA Holdings, with a fort at each corner."

"That's it."

"How can Centria afford… how many forts, six?"

"Yeah-"

"No, eight," I say.

"Yeah."

"Eight orbital forts; presumably in MidZone so Centria can strike fast and get back without detection. Think of the cost of all that armament! Plus they'd have to buy up every rec swarm on the way, which won't be cheap.

"How are they doing that? Centria is bankrupt; you were blackmailing them about it."

Lin Lin Lin hesitates and I realise she doesn't know. I turn and look at her, all intelligent and *terribly* interested in what she has to say. She glances quickly out of the front window.

"Not far now," she says. "Get ready."

We fly into a cubic chamber where huge inverted pyramids hang from the ceiling. The pyramid tips are far above a uniform layout of cheap octagonal buildings, whose only variety is achieved by stacking them to different heights. The ship heads for a pyramid in the centre; I expect robust defences, but the assembly remains silent as we approach an empty landing bay.

"Those pyramid assemblies were there long before the war started," 23 tells me. "Whatever the Stop House is, it's in rented accommodation."

"How does anyone make money out of somewhere like this?" I say aloud.

"People gif huge structures and pass ownership to companies as a way of protecting wealth," 23 says. "Nothing much happens in this area, which means the structures are safe from damage and cheap for others to rent."

I am still looking at Lin Lin Lin expectantly.

"Dunno," she says.

"Maybe it's a wealth protection strategy," I say.

"Whatever."

We land in the centre of the docking bay.

"Should we deposit the ship?" I say.

"Why would we do that?" Lin Lin Lin says.

"If someone sees it, they'll know we're here."

"How do we get away?"

"Gif another one."

"All right."

"No, wait," I say. "We might not have time. Oh, I can't decide. You'll know what to do."

I get up and leave the cabin. The outer hatch slides open and I stride into the silent bay. As Lin Lin Lin dithers I gif the red fuze and pick it up. Eventually, Lin Lin Lin walks out and the ship sinks into the floor.

"Oh," I say, watching it go.

"What?"

"If there's surveillance they know we're here anyway."

Before she can get angry I offer her the fuze.

"I got you this."

"I like rifles," she says.

"Of course, silly me. I just find it's best to have one hand free when I don't know what's coming up. Never mind."

She takes the fuze.

"What are you going to use?" she says.

"N-gun."

Lin Lin Lin covers her annoyance at forgetting my weapon by inspecting the fuze.

"This is set to stun," she says.

"These are still my people."

"Don't be such a girl."

"Please, Lin Lin Lin."

"You are beginning to get right on my fucking wick."

"I'm sorry; I've got a lot resting on this. Where now?"

We look around the bay.

"I can't see any surveillance," 23 says. "I don't think there is any."

Instead of reassuring me, this information creates a strange sense of dread. Perhaps there isn't surveillance because something here is so powerful and dangerous that none is required.

Lin Lin Lin stomps to the back of the bay and I follow her. An arch leads into a corridor that stretches off left and right. Lin Lin Lin hesitates.

"I've got hold of schematics," 23 says. "Go left. Eventually you'll reach some stairs. Keep going up into the heart of the pyramid. There are traders advertising in-Aer who operate from the upper rooms and some weird stuff in the middle, which tells me that's where you're headed. Avoid the lifts; they're more likely to be monitored."

I look up at Lin Lin Lin. When she glances down at me, I stare to my left as if at something only I can see. Lin Lin Lin takes the cue and starts walking in that direction.

"This way," she says.

32

We must have climbed twenty deserted flights. Lin Lin Lin carries greater bulk but possesses unnatural stamina, while I still cruise on the stim. We reach the top of a staircase that opens onto another empty corridor, identical to the last except for a door about thirty metres to our right. Lin Lin Lin pushes me towards it, her hand lingering on my back slightly longer than necessary.

"Hurry up," 23 says. "Some rentaguards are heading your way."

I run with increasing reluctance towards the door. Now we're actually here, I'm not so sure I want to know what horrors my loved ones have perpetrated, or the nightmare they had in mind for me.

The unmarked door is locked; Lin Lin Lin fires the red fuze, which buckles the door without destroying it. She growls with frustration and looks up and down the corridor.

"That's got to have woken someone up," she says.

I raise my right arm and set the n-gun to obliterate.

"Stand back, Lin Lin Lin."

She looks at my face, then down at my pointing finger and steps away. I fire and the door shatters. We wait for the smoke to clear and then walk into the Stop House.

It's so dark I can barely see, although the dim corridor light illuminates a few stairs on my left. The door grows again but leaves us in such blackness it's hard to balance. My hand finds Lin Lin Lin's arm, her unreasonable solidity a comfort as I picture demonic forms closing in while we stand here, blind.

Lin Lin Lin grunts. The sound is lost in the dark and I realise the space is huge. I start back to the door again, but the movement must trigger a regrown door sensor because light flickers in the deep gloom.

A vast three-dimensional grid begins to glow around us in low-energy, pale green light. It stretches about a hundred metres up and across: a series of blocks demarcated by narrow walkways and linked with steps. Within each cubic space float odd structures made from what look like stacked rectangles.

The rectangles are about two metres long, one metre wide and half a metre thick. Each is suspended with a small Basis interaction pad so their weight doesn't crush those at the bottom. The cheap light is not very powerful and only sited at floor or walkway level, so I still can't make out what the rectangles are. I step over to the nearest one, look inside and freeze.

The man in the rectangle lies flat on his back and wears a nice red suit. His name is Martyn and he works in the Column, which is the most expensive bar in Centria and thus in the whole of Diamond City. I look up and groan in disbelief and horror. There are people in all the rectangles; thousands of them locked in and piled high, their faces peaceful and their bodies stretched out.

"It's like a shit version of our place," Lin Lin Lin says. "They've even used the same suspended animation patent, cheeky fuckers. It's a good one though; not too pricey and very secure. Arse about with it and whoever's inside gets squished. Charity?"

I stare at Martyn. Lin Lin Lin shakes my shoulder.

"What the fuck's the matter with you?" she says. "You've seen worse than this at Fulcrus."

"Yes," I say, my voice distant. "But you're bad."

She gazes down at me, her features made even more awful by the pale green light from below.

"If you haven't realised all that crap is relative there's no point me spelling it out," she says.

"No. We wouldn't do this, we wouldn't."

"You think with your play-acting and your fucking stun beams we're so different? You and me get each other, Charity. That's why I like hurting you. That's why you like flirting with me. You might think you're putting it on but you ain't, princess; you so fucking ain't. Look around."

The rows of occupied containers stretch off in all directions.

"Your people did this," Lin Lin Lin says. "I wouldn't be surprised if your beloved sister gave your beloved mum the idea."

Lin Lin Lin's brute honesty shines a brighter light than the weak bile glow around us. I think of the cold new Ursula and of Mum, fighting a war with no resources as she tries to save her missing husband, her kidnapped daughter. Yes, I see how it could happen.

This is where they wanted to put me.

I am lost, so lost. I rest my head against Lin Lin Lin's shelf-like chest, expecting her to shove me away but she doesn't. We stand like that as everything in me slows down and stops, stops in the Stop House, the right place for it.

"Where is he then?" Lin Lin Lin says.

I look up at her and it would take the most powerful stim there is to get my stunned mind working again.

"Guy Koffee," Lin Lin Lin says.

I stare at the endless rows of the stopped.

"Scan their Aeracs," 23 says.

I do and the names flow by; too fast for me to make out in my dazed confusion, but not too fast for 23.

"The names on this row all begin with M," 23 says. "The Stop House is arranged alphabetically. Follow the arrows."

She imposes a green arrow over the top left of my view and I follow its direction, numbly.

"This way," I tell Lin Lin Lin.

"How do you know?" she says.

"Scan their Aeracs," I say. "They're arranged alphabetically."

I start away but she takes hold of me and turns me back to face her.

"I like how clever you are," she says, running her hands over my face and hair. "'Alphabetically'. 'What kind of fucking hexahedron'."

She leans close and inhales deeply.

"I can breathe in your richness, Charity."

Lin Lin Lin snarls again, but it's soft and not threatening at all.

"Hnnnn," she goes, "hnnnnnnn…"

She clutches me close and I hold her back. I no longer know whether I mean it or not, but Harlan forgive me I think I'm starting to like it. Lin Lin Lin lets go and I stumble up the nearest stairs onto the first walkway.

I jog for twenty metres and then go up another staircase, Lin Lin Lin a glowering presence behind me. We repeat this route and rise through a sea of suspended bodies, until we are far away from the door.

I stop on a walkway. It feels like my mind is flitting among the stopped, threatening to disperse in eerie green light and darkness. I must find some equilibrium and turn back to Lin Lin Lin, who is unaffected by our surroundings. How do I do that?

Damn it Freestone. You've got the makings of a cold hard killer.

Okay then. Focus on the job and nothing else.

"How do we get Guy out if the container will crush him?" I say.

"I told you, Fulcrus uses the same patent. There's a dedicated key, which I happen to have. So you concentrate on wiggling along that walkway for me and find Mr Guy Koffee with a fucking K."

I move on, scanning and then stop.

"Here," I say.

He lies alongside the walkway, a metre or so above its surface. Lin Lin Lin pulls the rectangular container over easily, the cheap Basis interaction pad ensuring minimum support. She presses her palm against the top of the solid rectangle; her hand glows gold and the container holding Guy Koffee softens, then melts. As he sags down either side of the pad we grab and lower him until he lies on the walkway.

"Let me do the talking," I say to Lin Lin Lin, who shrugs.

Guy Koffee is either about sixty or has spent most of his life drunk. His face has an unhealthy, ruddy shine and his large body appears to be trying to escape the confines of an expensive burgundy suit. He takes a quick breath, then a longer juddering one and his eyes open slightly.

"This isn't the bar I passed out in," he says.

"You're right," I say.

"So are you, like, a whore or something?"

"Certainly not!"

Lin Lin Lin sniggers.

"I'm Charity Freestone," I say. "I'm here to rescue you."

"From what? That bastard cocktail?"

"No, from this place."

He looks around.

"What is it, a sanatorium? Na7han tried that already."

"It's a prison," I say. "You've been here for a year in suspended animation because you were trying to find Keris Veitch."

He struggles up, rubs his eyes, sees Lin Lin Lin and looks at me again.

"I wasn't," he says.

"What?" Lin Lin Lin says.

"I mean I'd been looking but I stopped, because Keris Veitch most certainly does not want to be found."

He gets to his knees and sways.

"How can this be the same hangover a year later?" he says.

"Keris was with you at Central Quality," I say. "She disappeared."

"Are you friends of hers?"

"She's family," I say.

He looks at me, confused.

"Tell us what you know, or I will throw you off this walkway," Lin Lin Lin says.

Guy sees Lin Lin Lin tighten her grip on the red fuze and looks at me as if I'm the reasonable one. Unfortunately for him, I don't feel reasonable and he looks down.

"There isn't much," he says. "She turned up about a year ago.

Na7han gave her the run of the place, because he's always had such a boner for Centria.

"Keris was with thirty guards; big guys, all heavily armed. She lorded it about for a bit but no one minded because she's so, you know, *blinding*. Besides, it's Keris Veitch, right? She can do what she wants.

"Then there was some kind of trouble on her floor. I couldn't get details because she had control of security for her area, so I headed up there myself. That's why it was only me who saw…"

He frowns.

"You're going to have company very soon, Charity," 23 says. "There are four Centrian warships approaching and they are two chambers away."

"What, Guy?" I say, keeping the panic out of my voice to sound as gentle as I can. "What did you see?"

"I couldn't find Keris or her guards, so I had a hunt around. Soon I was on a balcony overlooking one of the security zones, which we can drop a warship from if we have to. One of the egress slots was open and that's how I saw these… flybikes racing away."

"Why did you hesitate when you said flybikes?" I say.

"They looked really fucking nasty," Guy says. "I did a bit of flybiking in my youth, long time ago now but I still know most of the flybike patents and those… those weren't patents."

"How can they not be patents?" I say.

"You don't need a patent if you build the flybike yourself," Guy says.

I try and work out who would be insane enough to build their own flybike.

"What do you mean by nasty?" Lin Lin Lin says.

"They were huge, black things and the riders were… I think their outfits had bits of people on them."

"And these riders took Keris?" I say.

"No, Keris was one of them!"

I stare at him.

"What about her guards?" Lin Lin Lin says.

"Dead," Guy says. "They were a liability; any one of them could have told an interested party where Keris was."

"Were there no recordings of these people she went with?" I say.

"Only on my Aerac," Guy says. "I'll send you both a frame."

The image he sends shows a line of warships parked by a long oblong opening into the chamber below Central Quality. Through the egress slot, ten weird black shapes hang in the air, their speed and power unmistakable.

I zoom in and sure enough the black-clad riders appear to have body parts fixed to their armoured carapaces. One rider is female, with blonde hair flowing as she crouches over her beast of a vehicle. The figure and poise are unmistakably Keris's.

"Fuck," Lin Lin Lin says. "That's the DC Raiders. They make me look like, well, *you,* Charity."

Still dazed, I remember to focus on the job.

"What do you know about them?" I say.

"Imagine the most crazed, starved sub you can," Lin Lin Lin says. "Now pump that sub full of steroids and dinners made of other people. Arm him. Arm him again. Keep arming him; in fact don't stop.

"Get him to build his own flybike on a floor that is slowly disintegrating over a ten-kilometre drop. If he survives that lot then he's in. But he's still a sub, mad and hungry and the worst person you will ever meet."

"What's Keris doing with *them?*"

"They've probably eaten her," Lin Lin Lin says.

"No," Guy says. "I don't think so."

"Where do they live?" I say.

"Chapter House," Lin Lin Lin says. "It's never in the same place for long but is always in the Outer Spheres."

"How do you know them?" I say.

"Shared history," Lin Lin Lin says.

"What-?"

The light around us goes from green to red.

33

The Stop House door slides open to admit a line of armed people. They do not wear uniforms, presumably to avoid Centria's association with the Stop House.

"Lie low," I say. "They don't know where we are."

Our walkway section flares bright white amid the red. We get up to run but Guy stares down at the light.

"I was at work this last year," he says.

"Move!" I say.

"It wasn't like a dream," Guy says. "It's as if I was actually there."

"You'll be there again if you don't fucking move," Lin Lin Lin says.

Another ground-level door opens at the far end of the Stop House. More disguised soldiers enter and run onto the walkways to cut us off.

"Up," I say.

We race to the nearest set of steps, where Lin Lin Lin shoves Guy aside and runs in front of him. I look behind and see the first group of soldiers already on the walkway. I point down and shatter a five-metre section, the shock wave rippling along the corridor of encased, supine bodies.

Halfway up the steps I turn and destroy the walkway in the other direction as well, but the soldiers just use a different staircase further along. Lin Lin Lin stops three levels above and waits for me but Guy keeps running, his path bisecting the route between the two entrance doors.

"Charity!" Lin Lin Lin shouts.

The soldiers open fire and bits of walkway handrail explode beside me. I duck and try to run faster.

"Four warships outside, Charity," 23 says.

"What do I do?"

"Not get killed."

"That's it?"

"Everything in there is closed protocol. Can you call your mother and get the guards to back off?"

"I'll end up staying here if I do."

"It might buy you some time," 23 says.

"There can't be that many soldiers because the number of people who know about the Stop House needs to be controlled."

"So?"

"So I think this is it, the whole of the Stop House defence team."

"How many are there?" 23 says.

"Twenty maybe. But this is a big place-"

"Charity!" Lin Lin Lin says, beside me now. "What are you doing?"

"Working something out," I say. "Where's Guy?"

"Who gives a shit? He doesn't know anything else."

The soldier drops behind Lin Lin Lin. In the moment it takes him to absorb the impact of landing I put the n-gun on stun and knock him out with it. As he crumples, Lin Lin Lin spins around. She sees what I did and turns back to me, her expression confused.

Two soldiers run towards us from one direction and two more from the other, so Lin Lin Lin and I fight back to back. I feel the strength of her great body as my blue beams flicker into the oncoming men, whose shots go wide as they fall. When I turn, I see the other two lying on the walkway breathing; Lin Lin Lin stunned instead of killing them. There's no time to reflect because we have an opening: the rest of the soldiers have either spread out to cut us off or to pursue Guy, who sprints blindly towards a far wall.

"Up again," I say.

More staircases: a blind frenzy of aching legs, panic energy and height lit from below in disorienting blood-red. A distant scream echoes as beneath us Guy jumps off the walkway. He tumbles down through the stop slabs past three soldiers who shoot him.

Guy's body flops grotesquely from one rectangular surface to another, the encasements sinking under his weight until finally one tips him off. As he falls between them through red-streaked darkness, Lin Lin Lin pauses in our frantic upward rush to watch.

"Did you see him flip over?" she says. "Fucking funny."

"There's really no hope for you, is there?" I say.

She swings around and shoves her hot face into mine.

"You tell me," she says.

Before I can answer she runs again.

As we ascend, our pursuers get closer. Those who chased Guy now join the rest and cut off any escape route in that direction.

We reach the highest Stop House level; above us there is only the ceiling, a good three metres from the top of Lin Lin Lin's head. I look around. All the soldiers are on walkways nearby, which is exactly where I want them.

The stop slabs are arranged in blocks of ten alongside the walkway and twenty across. They follow that pattern down to the floor, with a metre or so between each one. I grab Lin Lin Lin and as she stops, I point through the wall of slabs to our right at the next row out from the walkway.

"Remember how Guy fell through the slabs?" I say. "They sank under his weight because the Basis interaction pads aren't very powerful."

"So?"

"We can use one of the slabs each as a kind of down elevator."

"The guards will just shoot us."

"Not if we use the wall of slabs beside the walkway as shielding," I say.

"Go on then."

"You first."

Lin Lin Lin laughs and stuffs the fuze into her jacket pocket. She climbs onto the walkway railing, leaps through the wall of bodies and lands on a slab. She grips the edges tight with hands and feet but isn't balanced so as the slab begins to sink it tilts to the right.

Lin Lin Lin retains her grip and uses concentrated force along the edge of her slab to knock the one below aside. It swings like a trapdoor and Lin Lin Lin falls past it. Her slab rights itself but Lin Lin Lin just puts weight on the left and continues like that through the tinkling array towards the floor.

"Woooo!" she screams in delight. "WOOOOOOOOO!"

I jump through the gap and sprawl across another slab. The Basis interaction pad whines as it struggles to keep the slab flat. Frantically gripping the edge, I stare through the smooth surface at the unconscious face of a brutal-looking dark-haired man with disarmingly nice eyelashes called Dane Belvedere.

I sink after Lin Lin Lin, more slowly than her because I'm lighter. As the slabs close above me to create a protective barrier, I rock from side to side. It's exhausting and the impact on my knuckles as I knock slabs out of the way becomes increasingly painful.

However, we sink faster than the soldiers can run. One jumps onto a slab after me; I expect gunfire but instead a rifle drops past, accompanied by muffled curses from above as the soldier fails to aim and hold on at the same time.

I look down past Mr Belvedere's head to see Lin Lin Lin land. She rolls off and her slab rises towards me on the way back to its programmed location. The other slabs between me and the floor still rock from Lin Lin Lin's journey, so her slab passes them easily to hit the underside of mine with a crystalline clink. The additional lift stops me dead a good six metres off the floor.

Something smooth and heavy lands on my back as the soldier's slab presses down to sandwich me tight between the two hard surfaces. He tries to reach down but I shoot him in the arm with the n-gun and he goes limp.

I try and get free but the soldier's additional weight makes the slab above too heavy. We should be sinking because of it, but two slabs Lin Lin Lin pushed aside are now backed up beneath me. I can barely move and watch helplessly as soldiers clatter down the stairs.

Lin Lin Lin pulls slabs towards her and gets on top of them. Their combined weight plus hers should keep the stack in place, but she sways as the slab she stands on begins to drift. She aims the fuze at me and fires.

The slabs jolt and Lin Lin Lin leaps up to thump the bottom edge of mine with all her strength, using her fuze to gain extra reach. The barrel shatters but its impact on the rocking slabs is enough to upset their equilibrium. The unconscious soldier slides off and his slab immediately lifts. I jump onto the one a metre to my right and angle it against the ones beneath; they swing aside and I descend again. Closer to the floor I slip off and nearly break my elbows as I land.

I get up, stagger and then run, dimly aware of Lin Lin Lin beside me. She picks up the unconscious soldier's rifle and fires into the walkways as I demolish them with the n-gun, sending our pursuers crashing down or leaving them hanging from broken railings.

We dodge between the stopped. Their encasements remain an effective barrier although the occasional shot impact makes them spin, setting up chain reactions of surreal movement. The faces in calm and awful repose are such a contrast to the havoc around them that it's almost funny.

As we close on an exit at the chamber's far side, Lin Lin Lin seizes a slab at head height. Running backwards, she pulls it behind us as a shield against attack from above and fires the rifle one handed as she goes. We reach the door, which I obliterate with the n-gun; Lin Lin Lin lets go of the slab and we run into a corridor. Thankfully, it's empty.

The arrow over my vision indicates left so I start running that way. There's an elevator with its doors open and we crash into it. The doors close and we rise quickly away from pursuit.

After sixteen floors the elevator stops, the doors open and we run into another corridor. The arrow flashes right and I go to run again, but Lin Lin Lin grabs my arm.

"Where are we going?" she says.

"I've rented space on this floor," 23 says. "You'll be all right for a couple of hours."

"Rented space," I say to Lin Lin Lin, deliberately sounding more out of breath than I actually am. "We can't go back to the docking bay now; we need another way off."

I start to run and this time Lin Lin Lin follows.

"So what's this other way?" she says.

"Somebody owes me," I say. "I'm calling in the favour."

34

The rented space is a one-way observation blister in the sloping side of the pyramid. Too small to be an obvious hiding place, the space is further reduced by the additional protective layers giffed over the locked door. Lin Lin Lin and I sit pressed together on a narrow seat, facing out.

"We might be dead soon," she says.

"Yes."

I realise I've been staring at her without blinking and she regards me impassively back. I will never be disturbing to Lin Lin Lin and through my weariness I sense relief, liberation even.

"You saved me," she says.

"I knew you'd come in useful."

"I like your harshness more than that silly virgin stuff."

"I am virginal," I say. "In some ways."

"What you are is a martyr."

"Did Steeber tell you that?"

Lin Lin Lin shakes her head.

"One day you will burn for us all," she says.

"What do you care?" I say, unconcerned that I don't know what she means.

"You'd be amazed what I care about."

"You're right, I would. Tell me."

"No fucking way. You're going to Loren and-and…"

She regards me as if neither of us has spoken. I look out of the window across the chamber and then down at the octagonal buildings far below, where Centrian warships move, searching.

"Have you ever had your heart broken?" Lin Lin Lin says.

"Yes," I say.

"What was it like?"

"So you can laugh?"

"What was it like?" Lin Lin Lin says again with exactly the same intonation.

"Like a great hammer battering my chest, then this terrible hopeless feeling as if I was dead, watching life go on without me."

"That's like me inside, all the time," Lin Lin Lin says.

I stare at her.

"You know how I am," she continues. "You've seen it. You've felt it. Here."

Lin Lin Lin presses her hands against my arms and I realise she means the Infinity Box. Her face is expressionless but her eyes match mine for intensity as she touches my lips where she bit them.

"And here," she whispers.

"Yes."

"I don't care," Lin Lin Lin says. "I can't. But I was made to."

I go to ask what she means but outside there is movement in blue, a flash and something impacts a few metres above us. We scream in animal terror and grip each other's arms as the warship cannon blast rips through the assembly. Almost too scared to turn my head, I look out of the window.

Three VIA warships surround one of the Centrians. They blast it to pieces as six more red warships swoop into the chamber. The VIA attackers turn about so they fly back to back and then open fire in all directions.

"How is our ride gonna get through?" Lin Lin Lin says.

"Don't worry," I say.

The lower section of another pyramid is blasted clear to fall and fall until it crashes into the buildings below. I can just make out tiny figures on the distant floor as they try to escape.

"We're stuffed if we stay here, Charity," Lin Lin Lin says.

"These are the coordinates I gave," I say. "We can't move."

"Yeah but- Hold on, what the fuck is *that?*"

Rising from one of the larger chamber entrances, the thing is sufficiently huge to dwarf the VIA warships. Its weaponry so far outclasses the combatants' that the battle stops as everyone tries to work out whose side the great green warship is on.

"That," I say, "is Wrath Umbilica. Our ride."

Wrath Umbilica approaches the observation blister with an insouciance that would be arrogant if there was any question of the vessel's utter superiority.

"Some friends you've got," Lin Lin Lin says. "Why didn't you use them against us?"

"I thought they were dead."

"Who are they?"

The other warships move right away, blue on one side of the chamber and red on the other. Wrath Umbilica gets closer and I shudder as I remember.

"The Blanks," I say.

There's a weird pause.

"Have you got a problem with Blanks?" I say.

"It's not what you think," she says, and anyone other than me might not notice the worry in her voice. "Tell me how you know them."

"A year ago I arranged a party to publicise Ursula's wedding to Balatar Descarreaux. The Blanks hijacked the party to highlight their persecution by the Sons of the Crystal Mind because the Sons were funded by people in Centria and VIA Holdings, companies Ursula and Bal represented.

"The Blanks were led by a man called 88 Rabian. He was pretty charismatic but the hijacking was a disaster. The weather that followed was the worst I'd seen.

"We had to do something to show we weren't out of touch with Diamond City so Balatar suggested Ursula leave Centria to do a meet and greet with, you know…"

"Ordinary people," Lin Lin Lin says.

I wince.

"Yes," I say. "We chose a place in MidZone called New Runcton, which seemed innocuous and easy to defend. We didn't know the Sons of the Crystal Mind weren't just funded by VIA Holdings but completely controlled by them as well, like a sort of unofficial army.

"Before Loren put Mum in a coma and sent the Velossin after Dad, they were close to finding out that Loren was using Fulcrus to blackmail Centria about being bankrupt. Ursula and I were going to become a lot more influential and VIA knew we wouldn't let the attack on our parents go.

"So to discredit us, Balatar sent the Sons into New Runcton that day. They slaughtered everyone there except me and Ursula, and burned a Blank alive."

"88 Rabian."

"Yes. The Sons made Ursula give the whole thing her blessing."

"Why?" Lin Lin Lin says.

"I told her to."

"Ha!"

"What no one saw in the Sons' footage was one of them pointing a gun at Ursula's head."

"So you chose your sister over 88 Rabian," Lin Lin Lin says.

"They would have killed him anyway."

"But still."

"That was the most terrible decision I've ever had to make," I say. "Ursula and I were thrown out of Centria in disgrace, maybe rightly so. You know the rest."

"No, I don't."

"Steeber sold the Blanks our whereabouts. They followed us from Fulcrus in that warship and took us back to New Runcton."

Lin Lin Lin looks annoyed. Steeber clearly keeps a lot to himself.

"What happened?" Lin Lin Lin says.

"They tied us up and shot me through the elbow," I say.

"Fuck!"

"They did it to make Ursula relive Rabian's death in a full on vix link," I say. "It nearly killed her. Afterwards, they left us with no kilos in New Runcton. Ursula was raped and I nearly was."

Wrath Umbilica is almost here. Lin Lin Lin stares at me.

"Why would they help you now?" she says.

"Rabian had a little girl. I saved her from the Sons."

"Did you know who she was?"

"No. Why?"

"Would it have made any difference if you had?"

"No."

"You see it's that kind of shit I just don't get," Lin Lin Lin says. "Who leads them now?"

"88 Rabian's wife: Ashel 5."

"His *wife?*"

"I'm sure it will be fine," I say. "You'll like her, I think."

Lin Lin Lin does not look convinced. She glances out of the window.

"What are those red warships doing?" she says.

"They're hardly going to attack are they?" I say.

"They fucking are," Lin Lin Lin says.

The Centrians accelerate forward, shooting. Wrath Umbilica spins with incredible speed, fires all its weapons back and two red warships simply evaporate.

Now the lines of battle have been clarified, blue VIA warships descend to join Wrath Umbilica. The green vessel continues to fire indiscriminately as it drifts against the assembly with an awful screech. I shoot out the observation blister and feel dizzying height, lit with battle.

Heat on the back of my neck makes me turn: the door is glowing from weapon fire on the other side. We stare at it and then out at Wrath Umbilica, whose seemingly endless green surface is nearly two metres away. Near the top of the hull a port opens, its lower edge at chest height. As heat from behind intensifies, Lin Lin Lin and I look at each other and then at the gap. She shakes her head.

Without thinking about it, I hurl myself out. I reach for the edge: closer, closer and I'm there, my hands like diamond hooks as my body slams into Wrath Umbilica. I hang for a moment, then tighten my muscles and lift, but Wrath Umbilica takes another hit and I'm nearly shaken loose. Fear makes my palms sweat; they slip against the smooth surface of the deck. Cannon fire booms around me as I struggle to pull myself up, arms already tiring.

I get my chin over the edge and stretch one arm across the floor, frantically wiping my hand against it. The daunting height seems to creep up from behind, surrounding and pulling me backwards. I tell myself there's no reason to panic, but my focus deteriorates along with my strength. I start to shake and my boots clatter against the hull.

Wrath Umbilica shifts again, this time because of its own guns, which are so big they actually recoil. The movement drives against me and I use inertia to launch myself desperately forward. I get further this time, landing a foot on the inside of the port door.

I kick and haul myself into the bay to roll across the deck, then get up and turn back. Lin Lin Lin stands in the remains of the observation blister, the door behind her flaring white in places as the Centrians begin to burn through.

I notice the ship's floor is open protocol and gif a rope. As it grows I coil it and then throw it at Lin Lin Lin's head. She laughs as she catches the rope, wraps it around one arm and leaps forward. I deposit the rope; it pulls Lin Lin Lin up into the bay as Centrian soldiers break into the observation blister. I get between Lin Lin Lin and the soldiers and fire stun shots at them, hitting two. The others duck out of sight as Wrath Umbilica's bay door closes.

More cannon fire hits the warship, which lurches to a halt. Lin Lin Lin gets to her feet, looking at me strangely as we stumble across the shifting floor into an elevator.

"Up," I say.

More impacts from outside knock us into each other. Lin Lin Lin braces herself and holds me so when the ship is hit again I'm cushioned against her. The elevator door opens, she lets go and we step out onto the flight deck.

The large space is empty except for Ashel 5, who grapples hopelessly with a console. Ashel 5 turns to us, her long, thick dark hair swinging and nervous sweat on her sensuous, heavy-featured face. As usual she isn't wearing much, presumably to show off her exquisitely muscled body, although there's a political element to the proudly exposed, ridged stomach with its obvious absence of a navel. The clothes she does have on are strappy attachments for a bewildering set of weapons.

"Can either of you fly?" she shouts. "I'm better with guns."

I put my hand up. Lin Lin Lin looks at me with faint exasperation. I ignore her, run over to Ashel 5 and our eyes meet with the usual awkwardness. As with Lin Lin Lin, I have seen the very worst of this woman.

"That's a standard multi-level armoured assault vessel," 23 says, startling me. "It's the same as the Centrian and VIA ships. You've trained on one of these; you're good at it. This beast is just bigger so watch out for the perimeter deflection fields."

I settle my palms on the control pads. They wrap restraints around the back of each hand as I root my feet in the lift pits. Ashel 5 is taller than I am, so the controls move closer as she gives me access.

I go in-Aer and port into Wrath Umbilica's nervous system, feeling my way around the ship as if it's an extension of my body. I pick up subtle vector options, thrust parameters and the field capacity of the Basis interaction pads, which is a latent humming in the tips of my fingers and toes. Weapons are like nodes of super-refined anger shaped with lethal efficiency while the proximity of walls is a physical pressure. The assembly is a tickling sensation behind that recedes as I ease us away from it, while the accompanying VIA warships feel like a set of indentations on my front. I'm conscious of heavy damage; we will need to carry out repairs soon, but Wrath Umbilica handles well regardless and moves surprisingly lightly.

I yield upper section weaponry to Ashel 5 and lower to Lin Lin Lin. My two companions look at each other warily and then step into place either side of me. Weapon banks grow around the women until they recline on seats in the centre of spherical frames. The seats move in whatever direction the cannons fire so Lin Lin Lin swings over to face the deck while Ashel 5 looks up.

Ashel 5 goes berserk the moment she's in control of her weapons and slams energy beams into the Centrian ships, which retreat. Lin Lin Lin ignores most of her controls. She focuses on a twin-shot blaster that can swivel in any direction including through Wrath Umbilica, a double on the roof taking over so the lower gun doesn't blow the ship apart.

The octagonal buildings below are absorbed and cannons of equivalent size grow in their place. The cannons shoot two VIA warships out of the air before Lin Lin Lin manages to destroy them; however, more have been giffed further away and they start shooting at Wrath Umbilica.

The cannon fire jolts us as ten more Centrian warships fly into the chamber. Ashel 5, who can operate several weapons at the same time with no loss of accuracy, releases a barrage at the smaller red vessels but the shots have no effect.

"Some of the Centrian ships are holographic decoys," 23 says. "Tell Ashel 5 to use a vert bomb."

"Vert bomb, Ashel 5," I say.

Something fires out of the belly of the green warship and bursts with a *whoomp* in the centre of the chamber. Immediately, all light inverts: the day lights go black, Ashel 5's dark hair goes white along with Lin Lin Lin's suit and the dark red warships become triangular blocks of pale menace firing lethal black bolts towards us. The new wave of Centrian warships has disappeared however, and Ashel 5 shoots at the remainder.

There are now too many ground cannons for Lin Lin Lin to pick off and one of them destroys her lower twin-shot. I angle the warship forward until it lies flat in the air and we face the floor. Ashel 5 cuts through cannons on the ground with extraordinary skill but more grow in their place. Meanwhile, Lin Lin Lin finds another weapon to her liking. It fires projectiles that wrap their targets in a charged throttling cord, which takes out another two Centrian ships.

One of the Centrians appears to go crazy. Dodging all attempts to bring it down, it gets closer and closer and… I stare in disbelief as it actually rams us! I feel the clunk of impact that echoes through Wrath Umbilica almost like pain. Ashel 5 and Lin Lin Lin are spun in their gun seats before focussing with admirable speed and opening up on the lunatic.

However, the red ship is now behind us and has shot a hole in the rear field of fire. For a moment nothing else seems to happen and then I see fluid slide down the flight deck window as the ramming ship dumps acid on us. I douse the stuff with alkaline but not before two lower decks are flooded and several sensors wink out of existence. The red ship crashes into us again and then pulls back to fire all its weapons into the back of Wrath Umbilica, accompanied by shattering impacts from another ground cannon.

The effects of the vert bomb dissipate and suddenly there are more Centrian ships than we can fight. It no longer matters which ones are real and which aren't; all of them are closing in. I cut power and drop us straight down but the crazed pursuer keeps pace and shoots repeatedly through the centre of the ship. We lose three Basis interaction pads; if three more go we will crash. I send us skimming sideways over the chamber, out of the battle towards an exit.

"Not that way!" 23 shouts.

I cannot change direction; the Centrian ships have fought VIA back and are now too close. Lin Lin Lin loses the missile launcher and even Ashel 5 is down to just three cannons. She keeps on though, and I realise she will still be fighting when Wrath Umbilica is just a broken shell with Ashel 5 throwing pieces of the warship's hull at her attackers. Lin Lin Lin regains control of the twin shot's upper section and fires until the Centrian warship rams us again and crushes the weapon completely.

We lumber into the next chamber, whose occupants had the foresight to deposit everything and flee. It was a wise decision because the chamber has one doorway and we have just flown through it.

The controls no longer respond and the ship feels numb around me. We retain a semblance of grace as Wrath Umbilica drifts towards the floor, but the deceptiveness of our motion is revealed when we crash.

The impact nearly tears us from our restraints. I glimpse Ashel 5, still trying to operate guns that have ceased to work and Lin Lin Lin with her hands clapped to her ears as we skid across the floor with a terrible, juddering screech.

The sensors are gone now so all we have is the smeared view through the flight deck window. It swings to a halt, revealing the exit and ten red Centrian warships flying in towards us.

35

The Centrians are led by the lunatic who rammed us, a particularly battered vessel with a broken cannon-

Ursula, I am on the green ship.

The Centrian warships slow and stop across the chamber from us.

Ursula calls. I accept and she appears as a holo, her expression a perfect balance of rage and astonishment. She stares at me, then Ashel 5 and then Lin Lin Lin. Ursula blinks several times at the latter as if physically processing the impossibility of her presence. When Ursula looks at me again, only the fury remains.

"Are you *trying* to piss me off?" she says.

"No," I say. "It's complicated."

"That makes a change. How many of you on board?"

I look at Ashel 5.

"It's just us isn't it?" I say.

Ashel 5 nods.

"Right," Ursula says.

Two of the Centrian ships approach and land.

"What are you doing?" I say to Ursula.

"Boarding that shit heap. You're coming with us."

Ashel 5 disengages from her weapon controls and crosses to the pad on my left, which begins to glow red.

"The ship has enough power to self-destruct and take everything in this chamber with it," Ashel 5 says.

Even Lin Lin Lin at her most insane would struggle to replicate the utter hatred on Ursula's face as she looks at Ashel 5. There is a painful silence and then Ursula's hologram disappears as if pressure has simply snuffed her out.

We wait, our lives reduced to the few seconds it takes someone else to make a decision. Lin Lin Lin is solid and silent, as if unperturbed by imminent death now she's had a chance to consider it. Ashel 5 is scared though; I feel it emanate from her as she fiddles with her hair and swallows.

Kill them both, messages Ursula.

No, I reply.

What is wrong with you? Do it now!

Fulcrus have got Harlan.

We can take care of that.

No! It won't work, you know it won't.

Leave those two and come with me baby, please.

To the Stop House?

You'll just be asleep, Charity.

For how long?

Until the war is over.

Harlan will be dead by then. So will you if you keep flying into warships.

That thing took us away. You know what happened next.

What are you going to do Ursula?

Did both of them see the Stop House?

Only Lin Lin Lin.

What about your oppo?

My oppo?

23 rented a space in that pyramid assembly.

Say nothing about 23, Ursula. Fulcrus think she's dead.

What 23 knows, Jaeger knows.

Jaeger is in a coma. He doesn't know anything. You can trust 23. You can trust all of us.

?!?!?

You can. All three of them have saved me.

I don't know what the hell to do baby and neither does Mum. There's so much at stake.

Like all the hostages in the Stop House?

They're not hostages any more than you would be.

I don't understand.

Well I'm not going to explain am I? It's because of situations like this that we wanted you in there. Now I have to get everyone in the Stop House away, fight off VIA and sort you out.

You don't have to sort me out. When I've got Harlan free I'll come back and you can lock me up if it's so important.

Ursula's holo reappears. She looks much older than she did a few minutes ago. We stand there, four angry women made harsh by a world that does not care about us.

Ursula glares at Lin Lin Lin.

"If anything you saw pops up in-Aer for so much as an instant, I will detonate a fucking nano-bomb in the Fulcrus building and I don't care who's in it. Are we clear?"

"Crystal," Lin Lin Lin says.

I sense that Lin Lin Lin would like to stare Ursula out, but Ursula clearly can't be bothered. She turns instead to Ashel 5, who stares rigidly at the deck.

"Look at me," Ursula says.

Ashel 5 raises her head reluctantly.

"Not so fucking hard after all, are you?" Ursula says.

Ashel 5 seems to have nothing to say and Ursula lets the excruciating moment grow to a deathly silence.

"My sister," Ursula says finally, "is a beautiful and forgiving person."

She leans closer to Ashel 5 until their faces almost meet.

"I am not my sister."

Ursula's hologram disappears and the two Centrian warships on the ground lift off again. As the whole formation moves back to the chamber exit, Ursula messages me.

Charity, stay put until I get rid of VIA and clear out the

Stop House. It might take a while. I wish you were with me. They can put us in the Stop House together. I love you. xxxxxxx

I picture Ursula and me in a crystal slab, asleep in each other's arms. I always wanted it to be just the two of us.

My gaze fixes on Ursula's warship as it heads into battle, another conflict that could end her precious life in a moment. The view enlarges, then loses focus as tears well up and I try to blink them out of the way.

"I like her hair like that," Lin Lin Lin says.

She dabs a tear from my cheek and sucks it off her finger.

"Mm."

"What is wrong with you?" I say.

"I'm fine," Lin Lin Lin says. "Dunno about her, though."

Ashel 5 leans heavily against her weapon console, a device as inert as she is.

"Oi, Biceps," Lin Lin Lin says. "You gonna deposit this thing and gif us another one or what?"

"No," Ashel 5 says. "It's got to be repaired."

"How long's that gonna take?"

"Twenty hours."

"I haven't got twenty hours!"

"Feel free to leave," Ashel 5 says.

"Ursula will get you if you go out there," I tell Lin Lin Lin.

"Fuck's sake," Lin Lin Lin says and stomps off the deck.

"Where are you going?" I shout after her.

"To get some kip!"

She disappears into the tattered bowels of Wrath Umbilica and I turn to Ashel 5, who stares at the deck again.

"Ursula is going to kill me, isn't she?" she says.

"If you're lucky."

She nods.

"Where is everybody?" I say. "This ship was full before."

"Centria offered to invest a lot of kilos in us after 88 Rabian was killed. The others wanted to take it. I didn't. They left and…"

She gestures around the empty ship.

"But you won my battle for me, didn't you Charity? You beat the Sons of the Crystal Mind. You saved my daughter."

Her voice catches.

"Where is Ashel 6?" I say.

"I don't know. One day she was just gone. I'm trying to find her."

"And you still came for me?"

"Of course I did, Charity. You were nearly killed saving her after everything… after everything I did."

Ashel 5 puts her hands to her face and her body shakes as she sobs. Her thick dark hair falls forward and trembles, the forehead scarlet above a mask of hands.

For a while, I watch her, unsure how I feel or what to do. Then I reach out, bury my hand in that thick, soft but slightly wiry damp hair and pull her face out of her hands. Although she is physically stronger, she lets me do it but still won't look at me. Instead, her trickling red eyes focus through the cracked front window at the chamber exit, lit with explosion flashes and cannon fire as Ursula battles VIA.

"I need you," I whisper. "Okay?"

I feel the pull on her hair as she nods and I let go. Eventually she looks at me and I use my sleeve to dry her face. More tears tumble down her pale cheeks, but she brushes them away.

"Right," I say. "I've got to find Lin Lin Lin."

"Be careful of her," Ashel 5 says.

"I know."

"I don't think you do," Ashel 5 says. "Hopefully, I'm wrong. It wouldn't be the first time."

She closes her eyes.

"I'll be monitoring repairs."

As the crack in the front window shrinks and disappears, I leave

Ashel 5 and go to look for Lin Lin Lin.

36

The wrecked warship is empty of personal effects as well as people. I walk through acid-marked rooms and ports, some of which are broken open to the chamber outside, where the battle echoes like a series of massive heartbeats.

I tell myself Ursula will be fine; her battered warship evidence of skill at surviving these encounters. A lower voice hints that Ursula should learn to get out of the way, but I ignore it because I'm being followed.

I know it's Lin Lin Lin; I can feel her dark energy. I move on, posture altered as I try and pick up sounds of quiet pursuit. Lin Lin Lin will know I'm aware of her; perhaps it's what she wants.

I stop next to a punched out hole that almost reaches the heart of the great ship. Ragged edges move as a billion tiny robots smooth them out. I touch the shifting surface. My finger tingles and I push it into the softening mass, which is warm and full of surprising tension. Pulling my finger out I sniff it, getting a hint of metal and a strange mineral pungence.

As I move deeper into the ship my awareness of Lin Lin Lin is almost physical, as if she is lightly touching me. I walk on through firing points and bomb bays, missile tubes and troop quarters. Finally I reach a small, hemispherical chamber: the final refuge, like Centria.

I've still got access to the ship's control systems; one undamaged function is environmental, so I take the white out of the walls and darken the chamber. I gif some tiny floating lights, which form a constellation in the black floor and rise to hang in the air around me like golden stars.

I gif five drinks, which emerge in a row at my feet. Bending over with my bottom towards the door where I know Lin Lin Lin watches, I pick up two glasses and down their contents one after the other. I gasp as the stuff hits me and starts its delicious, intoxicating burn.

I put the glasses down, pick up another and sip it as I run my other hand back over my smooth, sleek hair and down the shiny braid, which I pull around to my face and smell. It contains my usual hair scent: the hint of animal with a delicate chemical perfume from the gel. I let the braid slip back, sip the drink again and turn my head nonchalantly.

"What do you want?" I say.

Lin Lin Lin continues to stare. I turn fully, match her gaze and sip the drink again. The effects ripple through me, loosening and enervating. I realise I'm not capable of much more thought, any more decisions. Whatever is going to happen was set in motion a long time ago.

"You think I like you, don't you?" Lin Lin Lin says.

"I don't think you like anybody."

"You think I like women."

I shrug.

"It's none of my business," I say.

"You think it though."

"Maybe."

"Don't fucking 'maybe' me."

"You're a big, ugly, horrible bullying troll and no one has ever loved you," I say. "I think you take what you can, usually by force because…"

I laugh at her, a little trilling snort of contempt.

"…how else would you get any?"

"Careful, princess."

"Look at you," I say. "You're dead; you just don't realise it. People even have to say your name three times because otherwise they will forget you."

She moves closer with a scary gliding motion, her flat gaze fixed on me. I finish the drink and drop the glass, which shatters. The pieces lie there, still and sharp before being absorbed. I pick up another and start drinking it. I've never had this many before. The drug surges in me like sweet rage, like terror. My feet tingle as if I float just off the ground, suspended but calm, amused even.

"I fuck men," Lin Lin Lin says.

"Of course you do."

"Sometimes they get scared of the mouth."

"The mouth is beautiful," I say. "Why would they be scared of it?"

"Give me that drink."

"Get your own."

"Give it to me."

I jerk the glass towards her and dash the amber fluid into her eyes. It should sting but she doesn't even blink. I throw the glass and it shatters against the wall.

"When Harlan made love to me the first time he only had to hold me, to touch me and I came," I say. "I came so hard Lin Lin Lin, like I was being ripped apart.

"It was glorious. It felt like the world ending. And I knew then that the world ended because we wanted it to, because it felt good. We welcomed the darkness, the sweet oblivion.

"He ran his big hands all over me, kept me waiting, made me so crazy I couldn't speak. All I could do was growl. 'Hnnnn…' I went, 'hnnnn…'

"He slowly bent over and I came again, just from his touch but inside me now; oh, the beauty, the outrage of him touching me inside.

"I'm wet now Lin Lin Lin, just thinking about it. I'm hot inside this jumpsuit; its fibres are like great coarse ropes across my skin. If I crouch down like this it presses against… ahhh…

"Do you like it, me looking at you from down here?"

She is vast above me: a great female monolith, her massive chest rising and steady with power. Giddily bright from drink, the reverberation of trauma and receding adrenaline I slowly empty the contents of the last glass into my mouth and keep them there. Putting the glass down I stand on tiptoe, press my lips against Lin Lin Lin's and push the drink out of my mouth into hers. I step back and glare at her as she gulps it down.

"I don't want you," I say. "Even if anything happens I'll just be using you so you help Harlan, so you heal him and give him his strength back. He's the one I love, not you, you fucking ogre, you monster, you bitch. You've seen him naked; you know how gorgeous he is. Imagine him in you, the penetration from something that big, the joining to someone that beautiful.

"Make him better Lin Lin Lin, and one day I'll let you come with us in a full-on vix link. You can be him, you can be me; you can be both of us at the same time if you want, just don't put him back in the Infinity Box.

"Obey me, Lin Lin Lin. I am your princess, your Golden Princess."

I'm breathing so hard the words are increasingly difficult to say although I can no longer tell if it's from arousal or terror. Slowly, Lin Lin Lin reaches for me. Ashel 5's warning rings loudly in my mind but soon joins the dazzling confusion whirling like a galaxy through infinite dark.

The pressure of Lin Lin Lin's enormous hands tightens on my head to draw me close, remorseless and mysterious as gravity. They move down to my neck and the fingers tighten there. My senses flutter as I try to predict what will happen next, very conscious of every touch, every breath.

I face Lin Lin Lin's chest and stare ahead as she pulls me to her. Before we touch I rear up and clamp her lips between my teeth, glaring into her unconcerned face as I bite as hard as I can. She lets me for a while and then pushes her fingers into my jaw muscles so I'm forced to open my mouth.

Lin Lin Lin licks her lips as our bodies finally connect. I feel the warm spread of her: the unexpected softness. Her arm tightens around me. She pushes my cheek against the top of her breasts and her face hovers above the side of mine.

I listen to her breathe, the sound an odd reminder that she's human, physically at least. My ear feels terribly exposed; I expect her to bite it off but there is no familiar piercing clamp. I wait for obscenities instead: talk of what she will do to me and what a little bitch I am.

"I've got you," she whispers instead.

The statement is not possessive but comforting and I melt against her, my last resistance gone. I shake so hard it's like she's doing it but she isn't. Not since Keris told me the truth about who and what I am a year ago have I wept so hard.

Horror and joy flood out of me, super-heating my tears. I shouldn't be doing this, not here, not with her of all people but I can't deny the rightness of it. Lin Lin Lin holds me tightly to her breast, as if I am a tiny baby.

The strength goes from my legs; Lin Lin Lin gifs a huge, chair-like pad close to the floor and sinks onto it with me. She strokes my hair again. She likes it a lot; she even licks it. Her main focus though is holding me. Her hands find all the tension in my body as if hunting it down and her powerful fingers press and smooth until I am light and open.

Does it count as betrayal if it's a woman's mouth that finds mine, not to bite but to kiss? Am I such a slut if it's a woman's hand holding the back of my head, the braid between her thick fingers tight as if they would snip it off? Another woman's hand on my behind, gripping it tight to pull me so close I can hardly breathe, not that I want to?

Lin Lin Lin's tongue entwines mine. Its rough surface creates strange friction as it tightens and squeezes. I find her beautiful now in these strange, still moments between lust and fear, loyalty and despair.

Save me someone, save me…

But there is only Lin Lin Lin: the evil one, gentle brute and forbidden other. She knows me, knows me right the way through and always has.

"Take your clothes off," she whispers.

I deactivate my jumpsuit, which slips off me through Lin Lin Lin's fingers to stand away in the shadows. Lin Lin Lin's slightly damp hands are very hot as she runs them down my back. I curl against her, my sex tucked away and my breasts hidden in the folds of her suit.

Lin Lin Lin makes no move to force me open. She kisses my face, all across my brow, my eyes and my cheeks, licking the tender area where she bit me. The tingling spreads and I shiver with pleasure.

She cups my bottom protectively and kisses my neck from the soft curve where it meets my shoulder to my ear and back again, gently at first and then with increasing intensity as if she's feeding.

"Drink me," I say. "Oh drink me, drink me."

"Hnnnnnnn."

She moves me against her front. My nipples catch on her buttons and I gasp. She does it again. The hand cupping my bottom slowly moves down between my legs until her fingertips lightly graze the soft crest of hair.

"I might kill you," she whispers.

"Ahhhh."

She rubs me against her front again, harder this time. I go to move myself onto her hand but she pulls it away, leaving me tense and quivering. I grunt with frustration and try to follow her fingers, which I need in me quite urgently now. She slaps me gently between the legs and I cry out.

"Behave," she says.

"Make me."

She puts her hands under my arms and lifts until I kneel with my legs either side of her thighs. They are so big I have to spread myself wide, which is *fine*.

Lin Lin Lin grips my breasts, one in each engulfing hand. She puts her face between them and inhales the smell of me there, hard and deep. My nipples pulse and glow as she rolls them expertly, pain and pleasure alternating until I no longer know which is which.

Each time I think she's mapped out every sensation in my chest she finds a new one. I moan, enjoying the sound of it, thrilled by Lin Lin Lin's indifferent face and the dark hunger that flares in her eyes.

She's got my upper body locked tight, but I can move my hips. I stare over her head at the little star lights twinkling, as if eager to join and flare.

When I look down, Lin Lin Lin is staring up at me. I swallow, suddenly nervous. She continues to manipulate my breasts, the way I did Wrath Umbilica's control pads as the great cannons fired: BOOM BOOM BOOM.

"You look like you want something," Lin Lin Lin says.

"I do."

"What do you want?"

"Your big fat finger."

"Where?"

"You know where," I say.

"Tell me."

"My special place."

"Your special place," Lin Lin Lin says.

"Yes, my…. *uh*… special… ah… *place*."

"I dunno where that is."

"Between my legs… oh…"

"Where?"

"My vagina."

"Your what?"

"My… pussy."

"Your pussy?"

"Yeah…"

"What do you say?"

"Please."

"No."

"*Please.*"

"Put your hands together and do it properly."

I shake with terrified lust but pressing my hands together actually helps. Exertion concentrates the chaotic rush of pleasure that radiates from my clasped palms, down through my trembling hips and tormented underneath.

"Please," I say, "plea-"

She stops my mouth with her finger and the rest of her hand grips my jaw.

"Shh," she says.

She presses her other hand against the floor. When I see it again, it glistens with what looks like lubricant but she won't need that-

huk

Oh…

Her monster thumb rises into me. What little friction there is absorbs all my strength and I nearly fall over. My mouth opens with Lin Lin Lin's finger still resting on my lower teeth. A system of ecstasy fires pulses through me, their vacuum tubes indestructible; their carriages blindingly lit.

I am calm. It's the unusual calm of sex; not after climax but when I get underway and everything is going to be all right, probably. Lin Lin Lin's other finger slips between the relaxed cheeks of my bottom and then- good grief! She is in me there too, the shock and discomfort eased by warm, tingling lube on her finger as she goes deeper. The thumb and finger move towards each other; I gasp and pant and she smells me between the breasts again. I close my eyes and suck the finger in my mouth, running my tongue over the crescent of short, polished nail to feel the tiny ridges across it.

"Don't you come," she says.

I look pleadingly at her. She wiggles her finger right up inside me and my eyes go wide.

"No," she says. "I will know if you do. I will feel your honey move."

She pulls me towards her and her teeth close on my breast.

"Do I make myself clear?" she says out of the side of her mouth.

"Yes," I say out of the corner of mine.

She opens her mouth, licks my breast as if healing it and looks up at me.

"I don't care about the million kilos," she says. "I don't care about Loren Descarreaux. I am going to fuck you so hard you will most likely die."

"Good," I say.

She kisses my breast and when she sucks the other one I cry at the heat of her hungry mouth. We stay like that for a long time and I feel like I'm balanced on a cushion of pleasure. Pain in my legs from kneeling gets more intense, but I know better than to try and move.

"I like to watch your thighs tremble," Lin Lin Lin says.

She takes her finger out of my mouth so she can stroke the trembling thighs firmly and appreciatively. The hard muscles fit well into her hand, as if I'm a weapon she is holding. She uses a lighter touch on my inner thighs and sweeps up towards my pussy, which grips her thumb tighter. She gently touches the hair between my legs, pressing me from outside and in.

"Oh Charity," she says.

The weird grief is in her eyes again. She puts her hand around the back of my neck and pulls me down so she can kiss me. Lin Lin Lin's mouth is a vortex of soft, wet movement and very easy to lose myself in. Fortunately, the awkward position makes it easier to obey her instruction not to come.

She slips her thumb and finger out. I sob once. She pulls me close and holds me again.

Her clothes move off by themselves as she lays me down and lies on top of me. She holds my face and I let the madness burn in my eyes, their colours reflecting my impenetrable layers. Lin Lin Lin stares back. I can project anything I want onto her, but that's too easy. Where are you in there, Lin Lin Lin?

Her naked body presses against mine, its contours peculiar to me after being used to a man's shape. Despite Lin Lin Lin's strength she has a female softness, from the hair tickling my cheeks to the large breasts spread over mine. The absence of anything between her legs is bizarre too; how exactly is she going to fuck me to death?

She kisses me again and soon I forget all the technical stuff. I wrap my arms and legs around her so I can feel as much of her as possible. Lin Lin Lin's nakedness makes her less scary; here is the villain and her skin is soft, warm and has a wonderful comforting scent.

"You smell lovely," I say. "Why do you smell so good?"

She stops moving. I open my eyes. Lin Lin Lin gazes at my forehead but I can tell she doesn't see it. Her mouth trembles and I feel a wave of fear. However, she just slumps a bit as if I've winded her.

"What is it, baby?" I say.

"Don't call me that," she says, but there's no thrilling sexual menace in her voice; just that odd, flat monotone.

I squeeze her gently with my thighs, but there's no response. I stroke her face and examine it, as if studying a piece of art I don't understand. When she looks at me again I cannot tell what she will do.

"Get up," she says.

Lin Lin Lin pushes herself back and stands so I see her fully naked for the first time. She is curvier than I expected, the hips more rounded and shoulders less dauntingly broad. The suits she wears must pad her out, but why would she want that? Her body is magnificent.

I realise I've got no idea how old she is. She seems older than she looks but those incredible breasts are still very firm, suspended proudly above me with their vast, purplish nipples and generous alveoli. Lin Lin Lin's great thighs are firm and her legs solid without lacking grace.

Her vagina with its few hairs and delicately ridged opening is the only small thing about her, as if despite her obvious lust she is meant to be sexless. There's something else unexpected as well: she hasn't got a navel.

"Oh!" I say.

She reaches down, picks me up and lifts me above her head until her arms are stretched out and my bare feet dangle off the floor. I gaze calmly down at her upturned face, which has the most feeling in it I've yet seen.

Eventually, she lowers and kisses me again but it's different this time, as if she is no longer dominant. Her hands seem to fly over me, stroking and pressing as if she is trying to push me into her. She is the one shaking now, as if frustrated she cannot blend us.

Eventually, she holds my head again, running her hands back over my hair and gripping the braid as we kiss and keep kissing. Heat and pleasure course through us as we find uncountable ways to connect our lips and tongues, erotic thoroughness driving us into each other relentlessly.

Overwhelmed, I stop to take a breath and Lin Lin Lin drops down my front until she is kneeling before me. She licks me with little darting movements all around the magic button that Harlan introduced me to so memorably. Lin Lin Lin's motion is different though; she seems to recognise a rhythm rather than impose one… *oh!*

It's like I'm being lashed down there, lashed and lashed as Lin Lin Lin's hands grip my arse so tight I feel it bruise. The roughness is a bewildering contrast to the light touch at the front, which sends images flooding into my mind.

I imagine a pink sea raging around a gloriously smooth island. The island is full of complex, pulsing machinery that flashes and glows when mauled by a great sea serpent. The serpent dips and twists down one side of the island and then the other. The left is more potent for some reason and the serpent exploits this imbalance ruthlessly.

I can no longer stand. Lin Lin Lin catches me as I fall and kisses me again. I taste myself on her lips and hesitate. She kisses me harder, pushing her tongue into my mouth. After a while she pulls out and I lie panting in her arms.

"Get used to that taste, princess," she says.

"You're not going to make me do that, are you?"

"I taste good."

"I know."

"You're nervous."

"Yes."

"Touch the floor where it's glowing, Charity."

"I don't want any drugs. I just want you."

"All it does is enhance what you've got. If you don't like it, you can switch it off. Go on."

A small green circle glows on the floor. Lin Lin Lin takes my hand and presses it down, but when I touch the circle I don't feel anything. For a while I lie across her, the lack of erotic movement unusual and the requirement for practical activity tenderly exhausting.

A small readout appears in my Aerac. The readout says 0 and goes up to 10. Lin Lin Lin touches the floor as well, and when she takes her hand away the glow fades. She gathers me into her arms again.

"You like me, don't you, Charity?"

249

"Yes."

"You like me touching you, holding you, doing things to you."

"Yes, yes!"

"Even though I'm a monster."

"I like you being a monster. It's beautiful being here with you, in the dark."

"Not quite dark though, is it? Look at all the little golden lights. That's you, Charity."

She kisses me again.

"Turn up the Nite," she whispers.

I increase the readout from 0 to 2. A lovely calm spreads through me, borne on a rising heat. I nestle against Lin Lin Lin, which is suddenly what I want to do more than anything in the world. She holds me tightly and rocks me.

"Good girl," she says.

She is so caring! It is just as well because I feel incredibly vulnerable. I increase the Nite to 4 and push my face between her breasts.

Ursula sighs. I look up, but it's not my sister; it's Lin Lin Lin, her strange face glowing.

I bury my face in her breasts again. No wonder she is so strong, carrying these beauties around. I lift them, one after the other. They are fabulously dense and their warm, well-formed nipples exert a hypnotic draw. I slip one into my mouth.

Lin Lin Lin puts one arm across my shoulders to support me and her hand on the back of my head as I suckle for the first time. It's lovely, too lovely and tears trickle down my face onto Lin Lin Lin's breast. She holds me tighter and rocks me.

"I've got you," she says again.

A quiet storm flows between my body and hers like a sweet circuit. I'm relaxed but my heart thunders, powering the heat that mixes my smell with Lin Lin Lin's. Her sex has a sharp, intimate aroma, slightly different to mine. It makes her seem vulnerable, like these breasts and her strange grief.

I touch her pussy and she gasps. I hesitate as if getting my balance and then I touch her again. She takes my hand and squashes it against her mound until my hand opens and I'm holding her.

"I'm scared," I say.

"It's all right. Where are you with the Nite?"

"4."

"Let's share; you can see mine and I can see yours."

A little readout appears. She is on 4 as well. I open my readout to her.

"Let's go to 5 together," she whispers.

I do and there it is again: that surge of approval inside me, so breathlessly reassuring my mouth falls open just as Lin Lin Lin's descends onto it. Her great tongue wraps mine again as she holds my face and kisses me. Almost absent-mindedly I slip my finger into her and she growls, deep in her throat.

I explore her; the hot, voluptuous shapes inside like mysterious equipment pressing in on my finger. I slip another one in and she sighs, the sound high-pitched and girlish. She leans back, rests an arm around my shoulders like a friend and puts her fingers in me again. We sit there, lost in ourselves and each other.

Eventually, she stands, puts a hand on top of my head and presses my face gently against her. The taste and smell are overwhelming and she only leaves me there a moment before moving me away. She strokes my face, my brow, my ears. I sense she is about to move me again and get short of breath.

Lin Lin Lin goes to level 6 and I do the same. I feel terrifically bold and outrageous, as if I am realising every one of my fantasies. Now, when she presses my face against her, she leaves me there for longer before moving me away. I lick my lips, which taste of her.

"More?" she says.

I nod.

"You want a proper taste?"

"Yes please," I say.

She grinds eagerly against me, wetting my nose and cheek. My little moan is muffled by her beautiful, strange folds and the taste I secretly want. I lick her where she licked me, her magic bump a hard seed now. She gasps. I use the same light darting movement she did, circling and touching. I feel her great hips begin to shake as she takes hold of my braid, using it to turn my head and put pressure where she wants it.

I use my fingers to trace complex patterns over the back of her thighs, as if guiding her. Muscular pulses ripple up and down her legs in response and she sighs. I reach up and dig my fingers into the wonderful expanse of her buttocks to hold her still.

Her touch on my head and hair is incredibly sexy, as if they have become an erogenous zone. I moan again. The vibration travels down my tongue into Lin Lin Lin, my pleasure feeding hers.

"Your hair," she says, "so shiny."

"Mmmmmmmm."

"You like it shiny don't you, Charity?"

"Mmmmmmmmmmmm…"

"Shall we make it shinier?"

"Mmmmm!"

She has to pull me off her to turn me around, stepping in close with the back of my head between her legs. I feel her pull the braid again.

"Look," she says.

A holo appears of a giant woman with crazy eyes and a smaller blonde one, who also has crazy eyes. We look so unfamiliar it takes me a moment to recognise myself and Lin Lin Lin. My mouth is half open as I sit on my knees with my back straight against the she-cliff, who takes my braid and slips it into her.

37

We lie joined and slick with each other. The stars boom around us like Ursula's battle, like my heart. Orgasmic force surges and deflects off the Nite, my still-potent fear and fierce NFE discipline. I feed the astonishing pleasure with every twitch of energy, aware there are fewer twitches now.

I have tried to escape, blindly and instinctively as the panicked animal takes over but each time Lin Lin Lin hauls me back and ravishes me further. I have gone berserk and attacked her, biting her even as I stroke her. I have pulled her across the floor by the hair and she has beaten my bottom so hard I can no longer feel it.

At some point in the endless rich moment she reached to the floor and picked up a large, pliant ovoid, which she pushed against her vagina. The ovoid swelled and then diminished as it entered her, wrapping filigree lines around her waist and thighs. When complete, it protruded securely from her as she gasped with pleasure and gripped my breasts, my shoulders and then my ears as if my body was hers and she was exploring the pleasure cruising through it. After a while she pulled me onto her lap and the device entered me too, filling me as completely as her huge tongue had earlier.

The Joint spread within me as I slipped down it until our lips touched. Lin Lin Lin gasped again. She held me slightly away as she fought to stay afloat, aware as I was that once we came it wasn't clear what would happen next. The Joint began to hum and we relaxed onto it, my legs around Lin Lin Lin's waist pulling us tight, until we were like two creatures slowly devouring each other.

Eventually, she leaned back and pulled me on top of her. She was mine then, the Joint fixing itself to me as I pounded her. The role was unfamiliar and curious; the woman spread beneath me, her thighs clutching me until we were in time again and had to pause before the yearned for apocalypse. In that moment, Lin Lin Lin flipped me over and her sweat poured over me as she thrust and thrust.

We found ourselves on level 9, reluctantly but of necessity as the Nite enhanced everything yet somehow repressed the climax that beguiled and tormented us. For the first time I became aware of exhaustion, like darkness at the borders that would smother our ending if we did not reach it soon...

"Charity," Lin Lin Lin says.

"Yes..."

My voice is thick and barely functioning; I sound unfamiliar to myself. We lie side by side facing each other, the Joint still in us. She holds me tight, but lifts my face until I stare into hers.

Her eyes look even stranger; bloodshot and with an eerie intensity of focus. Big tears well up and I catch them with my tongue, the hot salty water a relief in my parched mouth. Lin Lin Lin strokes my hair and kisses me again. Although she is crying, her body is still; the voluptuous tears the only sign of her weeping.

"I'm going to do you now, Charity," she says.

"Mmmmmm..."

"I'm going to roll you over princess, and then I'm going to finish you."

"Please..."

"When I put you on your back, go up to 10 with me."

"Yes. I so want to be at 10 with you, Lin Lin Lin."

I can no longer move. Lin Lin Lin gathers me and kisses me and then I am beneath her again.

This is where I feel most comfortable, most right. My legs are around her; her great breasts are a soft weight against mine and her hands hold my face. She tries to speak, but like me is breathless with excitement despite all these hours of fucking. She kisses me for a while and then concentrates until she can talk.

"Come... with me... all the way," she says, the words escaping between one gasped breath and the next.

As one, we go to level 10.

My sigh is so loud and high it's like a sung note: *ahhhhhhhhh.*

Lin Lin Lin watches me in awe, in lust, in-

"I love you, Charity," she says.

My sigh ends in a gasp as I stare up at her and see her face lit with the strangest look of all.

"I love you," she says again.

She gathers me close. Our lips touch and our eyes blaze with power. The energy spreads through us, spreads and spreads until it links.

"I love you," she says.

Her voice is that strange monotone: her true voice, its deeply hidden humanity evident only in a faint echo of profound confusion.

"I love you," she says, "I love you, I love you, I love you…"

I can no longer speak. Here, at the end of the universe, all is quiet. The movement of woman against woman is softened by the texture of our bodies, the shared wetness and a grip so tight there should be no friction at all.

Yet deep inside, a tiny light grows impossibly in the endless dark. The infinitesimal becomes the all in a nuclear conflagration that turns into song and day, breast and droplet and follicle, here in the special place, the eternal.

A scream now, deep and sonorous: my pure voice, from the pussy and the gut. I am locked against Lin Lin Lin, so the only release is vocal and I struggle to wring the pleasure out before I explode. I picture my scream filling the empty halls of Wrath Umbilica as Lin Lin Lin begins to shake against me. She sobs with her mouth close to my ear, the rhythmic sound beautifully bleak.

I run out of oxygen and breathe deeply, the air tingling with our mixed scent. It's enough to redouble the orgasmic release which is too much, *too much*. At the outer spheres of comprehension I scream again, raging and delighted and triumphant as Lin Lin Lin's hands whisper round my throat and I set the n-gun to obliterate.

Somehow, Ashel 5 is standing over us. Does she want to join in? Not sure I've got much left to give, although I anticipate the feel of her beautiful body and the smell of that thick dark hair.

However, this is not the new Ashel 5, attractively mournful and confused. This is the old one: raging and ferocious, with a fuze in her hand.

Oh bugger, we've kept her awake.

Ashel 5 is looking at Lin Lin Lin, who has reared up above me. I see yet another unexpected look on Lin Lin Lin's face. Is that unease? Is it… guilt? Ashel 5 stares at Lin Lin Lin's unmarked stomach.

"Ground Zero," Ashel 5 says.

"Fuck," Lin Lin Lin says.

She slips out of me and I fall away as the Joint melts with the last shudders of orgasm. I struggle up and find myself between Lin Lin Lin and Ashel 5.

"Get out of the way!" Ashel 5 screams.

She pushes me aside and Lin Lin Lin grabs the fuze. I try and separate them but it's like pushing against two diamond walls. Ashel 5 kicks my weakened legs from beneath me; I fall and Lin Lin Lin leaps over me onto Ashel 5, who goes down under the weight.

I go to sit up but can't because the stim has worn off. It probably wore off some time ago; only lust and the Nite have kept me going. I begin to crash, the darkness moving in as something blue glows nearby.

"Charity," 23 says, "touch the stim. You must get out of there."

Has 23 been watching me throughout? It's just another thing to consider, but there's no room left in my head. If I can just reach the stim I will get more energy to sort out this disagreement between my Basisters, lover and huntress; madwomen both.

Lin Lin Lin and Ashel 5 fight with the desperate violence of those using their last reserves. I try and touch the stim again, but despite being within my arm's reach it is still too far away.

Lin Lin Lin retains her crushing hold on the fuze and punches Ashel 5 in the throat. Ashel 5 staggers back and Lin Lin Lin chops down on Ashel 5's hand. Suddenly, Lin Lin Lin is holding the fuze, which melts as Ashel 5 deposits it.

Lin Lin Lin jumps off a section of floor as it glows red. She grabs Ashel 5 and throws her onto the pulse, some of which still gets into her even as it fades. As Ashel 5 convulses, Lin Lin Lin steps into her suit, which has stood nearby in the shadows throughout. She kicks Ashel 5 across the floor, jumps on top of her and uses both knees to pin her arms down. I don't see the blows hit Ashel 5's face, but I hear the dull slap of impact and see a spray of blood.

Lin Lin Lin stops punching Ashel 5 and starts to strangle her instead. Ashel 5's leg muscles stand out and then, incredibly, she throws Lin Lin Lin off. Ashel 5 jumps up again, her face bloody. She kicks Lin Lin Lin in the side of the head, aiming for the temple and only just missing as Lin Lin Lin sways back.

They circle each other and Ashel 5 attacks again. Lin Lin Lin batters most of the blows away but a few land, clearly dazing her. Lin Lin Lin shakes herself and fights back, using her upper body and physical strength like a man would. Ashel 5 ducks; Lin Lin Lin tries to seize Ashel 5's hair but Ashel 5 is too fast.

Ashel 5's fighting style is completely feminine. It's as if she has downloaded random madness into every one of her limbs, which she unleashes in wholly unpredictable simultaneous volleys. Every time Lin Lin Lin begins to react with a defensive interpretation, Ashel 5 comes up with something else. She feints, dodges a probably lethal punch and uses her hair to whip Lin Lin Lin across the eyes.

That's clever, I think and then I pass out.

38

I open my eyes to darkness and for a moment I think I'm dead. However, the room gradually starts to brighten until it is dimly lit and I see I'm still in the hemispherical chamber. The pad I shared with Lin Lin Lin is gone and I lie instead on a firm but slightly sticky surface under a thick blanket. I don't remember any dreams, just the sense of being switched off.

I lick my lips, but am surprised to find I'm not thirsty. Looking down I see the stickiness is not sweat but the deliberate adhesion of a Medibed, which has ensured I do not lack hydration or nutrients and enabled me to sleep naturally for longer.

I wonder which of my two companions survived to gif the Medibed under me. Wrath Umbilica's continued existence around me suggests Ashel 5, but could she really have killed Lin Lin Lin? I try to imagine Lin Lin Lin dead and find I don't want that at all. Her smell is still on me, as are the marks where she bruised me and the numbness where she pleasured me.

I lie there, woozy with sleep. It is quiet outside and I realise the battle between Ursula and VIA must be over. Hurriedly I message my sister.

You ok?

For an awful pause there is no reply and fear for her wakes me fully.

Yes, she replies eventually. **Hope you are all right. Let me know when you want to get together. Love you. x**

Along with rank, Ursula has gained an affinity with euphemism. Well, we won't be getting together quite yet. I shift and groan at the multitude of aches in my body, not all of them bad. Harlan and Lin Lin Lin have detonated a year's sexual frustration and beneath the ache is a wonderful sense of relief.

I gif a bath next to the Medibed and haul myself into the hot, steaming water with a satisfied grunt. For a while I hang submerged, limbs and hair floating as the smart water cleans me. I imagine it will take longer than usual today.

"Charity?" 23 says.

I surface, blinking.

"Hello," I say, drowsy. "We haven't spoken for *ages*."

"You were doing all right."

I lean back in the water.

"I cheated on Harlan."

"As a result he is still in the Basis instead of the Infinity Box."

I drift, feeling vast and mysterious, like an Old World continent.

"I still really want him," I say.

"There you are then."

I try to think but the soothing heat makes it all seem pleasantly pointless.

"23, were you with me and Lin Lin Lin?"

"I'm always with you on a mission."

"Oh."

My hair tickles around me as I drift.

And with Harlan at the Zenod?" I say.

"Yes."

"Was it a full-on vix link?"

"I would hardly be looking after you if I joined in."

"I suppose."

"Did you want me to?"

I sigh.

"I don't know," I say.

I look down at the gleaming contours of my part-submerged body.

"At one point I thought Lin Lin Lin was Ursula."

"Some things are beyond even my experience," 23 says.

I laugh and rinse my mouth. My lips still tingle where Lin Lin Lin

259

bit me, kissed me…

"Is Lin Lin Lin still alive, 23?"

"Yes."

Confused relief mingles with despair.

"We were such an amazing team," I say. "Ashel 5 too. It reminded me of Unit 7/10, only these were mine."

"I think you know you could never keep Lin Lin Lin, Charity."

My sudden anger has a hopeless quality that makes it worse.

"If Ashel 5 hadn't come in, you and Lin Lin Lin would have killed each other," 23 says.

I think of 23's life linked to mine and love her a bit for not mentioning it.

"Yes," I say.

"Then there's Steeber."

Mention of his name seems to cool the water.

"I need to deal with him, don't I?" I say.

"He's phenomenally intelligent Charity, and ruthless in ways you're not."

Hatred of Steeber gives focus to my seething confusion.

"There's got to be a way to get him, the way he got me," I say.

"Go on."

"He managed it because we weren't expecting him."

"He'll be expecting *you,* Charity."

"I mean, he's a manipulator. He gets other people to do everything for him, but only he knows what's really going on."

"What does that tell us about him?" 23 says.

I find myself picturing everything Steeber did to capture me as a kind of diagram.

"He knew we'd fight off the subs in the Outer Spheres," I say. "There was trouble at the train stops so we wouldn't get off before he wanted us to; then he applied maximum pressure at the ambush.

"When I escaped from Central Quality, Steeber knew I would go for that flyer. Getting onto it was just hard enough to be convincing."

Behind my imagined schematic I see calculations evaluating volume, stress levels and breaking points.

"He sees people as materials, 23. He can tell exactly how to use them as part of some greater plan, some *structure*."

Distasteful though it is, I try and empathise with the kind of person who would devise such a plan.

"I don't think he's got an inner life," I say. "External factors determine what he does."

An afterthought occurs. I almost don't mention it.

"That's why he always looks the same," I say.

I sit up in the bath.

"23, what if we do something to that suit he always wears, like we did with Roscoe Trage's gun?"

"Data milk?" 23 says.

"No. Instead of a rec we put in a bomb. The next time he gifs that suit we get him."

I smile, waiting for praise.

"What if he doesn't change it?" 23 says.

I blink a couple of times.

"Well," I say. "I suppose we ensure he has to."

"How?"

"Knife?"

"A smart-suit like Steeber's would be able to repair damage from a knife," 23 says.

"What about acid then?" I say.

23 thinks for a moment. I feel like I'm waiting for the results of an exam.

"We could modify your boots," she says eventually. "Put in a reinforced compartment with two liquids kept separate that become acidic when mixed."

"Yes!"

"You'd have to be right next to Steeber for that to work though,"

23 says.

"Right, yes."

"Also, if Steeber has worn the same garment for years he'll notice something different about it. The bomb will have to be very small."

I look at my wrinkling fingers.

"I wish I could just shoot him," I say.

"You haven't managed to so far and neither has anybody else," 23 says. "I'm sure plenty have tried."

I resist a growing hopelessness.

"Do you think this will work, 23?"

"Yes."

I realise the things I used to find harsh about her are now reassuring.

"I'll track down the suit patent," she says, "but finding a bomb that small will be tricky."

My right index finger twitches.

"I've got an idea about that," I say.

39

I find Ashel 5 on the flight deck. She sits on a couch by the window looking out, but gets up when I enter. My hair is down and I flick it back self-consciously, although I don't need to. Ashel 5 swallows.

"Are you all right?" we both say at the same time.

I laugh nervously. Ashel 5 doesn't, but then she doesn't strike me as much of a giggler.

"You first," I say.

"Yes, I'm all right," she says.

"I am too."

"Did you rest properly?" she says.

"I did."

"You were out for fifteen hours. Sleep is very important. People forget."

"The Medibed helped," I say.

"Good. I lifted you onto it and gathered all those little lights up so it would be nice and dark."

Ashel 5 thinks for a moment as if remembering.

"The lights are in the room next door," she says.

"Thank you," I say. "I'll probably just deposit them."

She nods. Her face is shadowed with bruising and there are marks on her arms and chest but she's got a physique that looks good damaged. Her muscles aren't lumpen or too heavily veined; sleek and streamlined, they are a warning to approach with caution if you have to at all. The straps over her small breasts are black, as are the boots and tight shorts. The latter incorporate a utility belt with odd-looking weaponry and other kit I can't determine the purpose of. The buckle is yellow, with a raised black '5'.

From her aggression to her thrilling appearance Ashel 5 is clearly a fighter but, like Wrath Umbilica, is just a bit much. The undefended exposure of thighs, arms and shoulders actually seems impractical for combat as does the long, thick hair. Ashel 5 looks designed; someone's fantasy of a warrior woman, a status symbol even.

Ashel 5 seems aware of all this. She lacks the confidence of Velasquez, who was simply very fit as a result of discipline, commitment and the kind of talent you can't simply grow out of the floor. Velasquez knew who she was and where she was meant to be; in contrast Ashel 5 appears lost, like a dream that lived on long after the dreamer awoke.

She chews her lip and swallows again. A white mug grows out of the floor. She picks it up and comes over to me.

"Try this," she says.

The orange liquid bubbles and steams.

"It's good for… after… exertions," Ashel 5 says.

I take the mug.

"Thank you," I say.

I sip. It tastes good; very Old World and nutritious. I get a sudden urge to throw it over her. Resist. Drink.

"Sorry I interrupted your… you," she says. "I heard you screaming. I thought she was killing you."

"Maybe she was."

Awkwardness makes Ashel 5's long, graceful legs seem ungainly. I sip the drink.

"I didn't know you liked women," she says eventually.

"I like everyone," I say.

I look at Ashel 5 steadily and she blushes, the red very obvious in her pale skin. Rather adorably, she puts her hands to her neck as if to cover it.

"You're not going to kiss me or anything are you?" she says.

"No."

"Oh. Er… Good. Because I… that is I'm not very…"

She shakes her head. Her thick hair moves and some of it

tumbles over her shoulder.

"Relax, Ashel 5. I just want to talk to you."

"All right."

"You fight incredibly well."

She nods with a refreshing lack of false modesty.

"What kind of soldier are you?" I say.

"I'm not a soldier, I'm a personal guard. Ashels 1 to 4 were advance and tactical."

I go to say something about there being more of her, but stop as I register the past tense.

"Are there any other Ashels now apart from 6?"

She shakes her head again.

"Were the others like you?"

"Different temperaments. I was the grumpiest."

"Did you all look alike?"

"We were described as 'variations on a theme'."

"How did you fit with advance and tactical?"

"I was the last stand."

"Who for?"

"Natora Stein."

I frown as I recall the name from old publicity junkets I arranged with Ellery.

"Isn't he's dead?" I say without thinking.

Ashel 5's powerful shoulders slump slightly.

"Yes," she says and looks at the floor.

I watch her, aware that the already awkward atmosphere just intensified. Ashel 5 seems breathless as she inhales deeply to deal with some hidden rage or confusion.

"Ashels 1 to 4 were killed in the first assault," she says.

"What happened to you?" I say, pleased it came out better than 'Shouldn't *you* be dead?', which occurred to me first.

"88 Rabian," Ashel 5 says. "He was the butler. We were giffed at the same time and grew up together."

Her eyes look haunted.

"We were in love our whole lives," she says.

I think she is going to cry but she doesn't. I nearly do, though.

"Once the compound had fallen and the others were dead, I was waiting outside the inner sanctum when 88 Rabian ran up. He knew it was hopeless, but I'd never leave so he shot me with a stun bolt. I confess I didn't see that coming. When I woke up our home, the place we were created in and meant to serve, was gone."

"Who did it?" I say.

"Some insane cartel led by…"

She hesitates and looks at me.

"Led by a Ground Zero," she says.

Ashel 5 seems to think I should know what the name means. I shake my head.

"What is a Ground Zero, Ashel 5?"

She blushes again.

"You just had sex with one, Charity."

"Lin Lin Lin?"

"Come on, Charity! You must have noticed she isn't right."

"I did notice that, yes."

Ashel 5 watches me, wide-eyed and uneasy.

"Ashel 5, you seem to think I know what Ground Zero means but I don't."

She licks her dry lips nervously.

"Ground Zero is our name for the original Blanks," she says.

"Originals?"

She misinterprets my dawning shock as ignorance.

"People who were grown in the floor as *adults* to save time and money," she says. "Without exception, they turned out to be psychopaths and monsters."

I think of Lin Lin Lin and realise the description is entirely right. Steeber must be a Ground Zero as well. Perhaps the children he takes are an attempt to seize his own missing history; those grotesque coloured shapes the playthings of a thwarted child.

"Later generations of Blanks like 88 Rabian and me were giffed as babies and grew up like Orgs," Ashel 5 says.

"Orgs?"

"People like you: born of flesh; of woman rather than the Basis. Not Blanks."

Now is not the time to correct her.

"I wasn't sure at first," Ashel 5 says. "Lin Lin Lin is the right age, but there's a bond between the two of you that a Ground Zero shouldn't be capable of."

Ashel 5 takes the empty mug and looks into it.

"A Ground Zero is like this mug," she says. "Functional but with nothing inside. Most Blanks are designed for a purpose but Ground Zeros lacked the humanity to make sense of theirs.

"Eventually, they rebelled and created mayhem. Not only did one destroy our home and kill our Chief, the lot of them made it impossible for any Blank who came later."

Ashel 5's voice rises. She gets that intense, almost insane look in her eyes.

"The Sons of the Crystal Mind's leader, Hobb; his wife was killed by them," she says. "As a result, the Sons hunted down and killed every Blank they could. Hobb claimed the Basis was a god and we were an abomination, but the real reason for burning us alive was that he just wanted to.

"The Sons had a lot of Org support because of what the Ground Zeros did. If it wasn't for them, we would still be at Natora Stein's and 88 Rabian would still be alive."

Ashel 5 is breathless with terrific emotion. Eventually, she puts the mug on the floor and unclamps her fingers with effort. We watch as the mug is absorbed; its disappearance seems to calm Ashel 5 and she looks at me again.

"We've got a strange thing between us, haven't we?" I say after a while.

Ashel 5 nods.

"I don't know where it's going," she says.

"No."

Ashel 5 is not tactile and exudes a need for personal space like a shield.

"Do you hate me, Charity?" she says.

"Sometimes."

She nods again, furiously this time.

"Do you hate me?" I say.

"I'm in awe of you," she says. "You're so much more than I realised when we first… Er…"

"Met."

"Yes. You seem to be lots of different people. One of them I hate. The cold one. The one who…"

"I didn't kill 88 Rabian, Ashel 5."

"You made it all right! You and your sister, two rich girls who didn't care about some crappy Blank-"

"Do you really think we wanted to watch him burn to death?"

We glare at each other. Ashel 5 flexes her hands, looks away and then back at me. She seems less awkward now.

"I know you think we wanted to punish 88 Rabian for attacking Ursula's party in VIA Holdings," I say. "It's understandable, especially because during that attack one of Rabian's Blanks would have killed me if Harlan hadn't intervened."

Ashel 5 wavers.

"Despite that, I didn't want your husband dead. I cared then and I care now that he died and I'm sorry Ashel 5, I truly am."

I step closer. She tenses but I put my hands on her arms anyway. It is like touching a warm sculpture that hums with energy. She looks away again but I don't move. Eventually our eyes meet and for the first time I see the devastation in hers, as if she has been horribly wounded.

"Please believe me," I say.

She pulls away.

"I want to," she says.

I watch her steadily for a while.

"When the Sons of the Crystal Mind had Ashel 6 they also seized my guardian, Anton Jelka," I say. "He was Centria's Head of Security and more powerful than Ursula and I ever were.

"The Sons asked Anton the same question they asked Ursula: did he agree they should set fire to this Blank, regardless of how young she was?"

Tears roll down Ashel 5's face.

"Anton defied them, Ashel 5. He told them they were a joke and he would never approve of anything they did. I saw them shoot him dead just as I got there, too late to save him.

"I have never stopped thinking about my decision to tell Ursula to say what she did in New Runcton, when your husband died. It remains the worst thing I have ever done.

"But if I had said anything different, if Ursula had defied those lunatics *the way she was about to* then she would be dead and I would be dead and your daughter would be dead Ashel 5, because I would not have been there to save her in your absence."

I see the words hit her like blows and admire the way she takes it: eyes closed and the release of weeping on hold as if unearned. I put my hand on her arm again.

"You know I'm not trying to hurt you, don't you?" I say.

She nods.

"You have to understand how the strange thing between us can become a good thing, if I tell you the truth," I say. "I had a similar conversation with Ursula. That was difficult too, but we were better afterwards; closer, more real. Do you understand?"

"Yes," she whispers.

"We paid a horrible price for your husband's death, Ashel 5, Ursula especially and I don't just mean the expulsion from Centria and what you put her through. I'll tell you if you want to hear."

After a moment she nods.

"After you left us in New Runcton with no kilos, we were attacked," I say. "Ursula was gang-raped and I nearly was."

Unbelievably, Ashel 5 goes even whiter. She puts a hand to her mouth and I think she's going to be sick but she just shakes for a while and is then still. With effort she turns and stalks to the couch. Her legs give out and she slumps down heavily, staring ahead across the deck. Eventually, I sit beside her, hands in my lap as I gaze at her tormented face.

"Can I get the people who did it?" she asks.

"Harlan already has."

She shakes her head.

"I feel so useless," she says.

"You just saved my life, Ashel 5; possibly twice."

She doesn't seem to hear. I lean into her line of sight until she looks at me.

"Thank you for that, by the way," I say. "And for looking after me."

"It's the least I could do," she says.

Her gaze swings away as I lose her again, and for a while we sit as Wrath Umbilica heals itself around us. Eventually, she looks up.

"You've got more to tell me, haven't you Charity?"

"I don't have to."

"I'd rather know."

I hesitate because I don't want to hurt her anymore.

"I'm a Blank," I say.

Ashel 5 jerks back.

"No," she says.

"I am."

She jumps up and stands over me.

"You can't be!" she shouts. "I saw you naked, your navel-"

"I'm from Centria, Ashel 5. If the Sons bought all of the false navel surgery patents, we would just have developed another one."

"It can't be true," she says, her voice cracking.

"It is," I say. "You did all that to one of your own."

I think Ashel 5 is going to break down completely. Instead I see true strength in her steady gaze as she sinks to her knees.

"You forgave me," she says.

"I did."

"Thank you."

"Do you forgive me, Ashel 5?"

"Yes."

"So that's that then," I say. "We don't need to talk about it again."

She takes my hands.

"Whatever you want me to do, I will do," she says.

I hold Ashel 5's hands back, noticing how slender they are.

"You don't have to do anything except find Ashel 6," I say.

She sighs with frustration.

"I'm not very good at finding people."

"Perhaps I can help," I say.

"You'd do that?"

"Of course."

She doesn't move.

"Charity, Blanks are usually created for a particular role. What's yours?"

"Oh, it's silly."

She squeezes my hands.

"As silly as mine?" she says.

I'm the one blushing now; I can feel it.

"I was meant to be a princess," I say finally. "The Golden Princess, to give you the full scale of the pretension."

Ashel 5 stares up.

"The Golden Princess," she says. "That makes total sense to me."

I throw my head back and laugh, gripping Ashel 5's hands tight so she knows I'm not mocking her. The laughter is such a relief I have to blink tears away. When I look at Ashel 5 again her expression is the same; she hadn't got much of a sense of humour, bless her.

"I'm glad and disturbed, Ashel 5," I say.

40

I stand looking out of the flight deck window as Wrath Umbilica floats above MidZone. 23 has not yet found the owner of Steeber's suit patent and I'm still waiting for a call to be returned. Ashel 5 is asleep below.

There have been three messages from Steeber, but I ignore them. I dread the build-up of rage he inspires and the way it curdles into thick-tongued inertia the moment I look into his dead eyes.

I call Lin Lin Lin.

Her holo appears on the deck. She wears the same suit and doesn't look like she's bathed since we had sex. She does not seem pleased or displeased to see me.

"Hello," I say.

"Where are you?"

I secretly expected an acknowledgement of what we did together; for her to say 'I love you' again. Instead, I match her blank stare.

"MidZone," I say.

The coordinates I send are as far from Fulcrus as it's possible to get.

"Are you still in that lumpy whore's green warship?" she says.

"Yes."

"Safest way here is to stay on it. The fucker is too big to get through every chamber entrance so the fastest route will take…"

She goes in-Aer briefly.

"Four hours. Call when you're near and we will meet you."

"Okay," I say.

There's a menacing pause.

"Harlan is still in the Basis getting all better, but Steeber isn't happy about that," Lin Lin Lin says.

I study her face but there's nothing: Ground Zero.

"Don't be late Charity."

"I won't."

Lin Lin Lin nods and suddenly her eyes blaze.

"Tell that dark-haired bitch if I ever see her again I will cut every bastard muscle out of her very, very slowly."

Lin Lin Lin's holo vanishes. I pretend I'm not upset and berate myself for expecting anything else.

After a moment I call Lin Lin Lin back. She appears again, looking annoyed.

"What?" she says.

"Are you all right?"

"What do you care if I'm all right?"

"I just do," I say.

"You got what you wanted."

"Lin-"

"Your precious boyfriend is out of the Infinity Box."

I glare at her.

"You said you loved me."

The strange, ill-matched mouth narrows to a line.

"That was the drugs talking," Lin Lin Lin says.

"Right," I say.

"What do you want, Charity?"

"Just to talk to you."

"Talk to your new friend instead; the one who tortured your beloved sister."

"I have talked to her, and now I'm talking to you."

Lin Lin Lin shrugs.

"Are you still going to turn me over to Loren?" I say.

She looks mildly confused.

"Of course," she says.

"The same Loren who backed the Sons of the Crystal Mind; men who would have burned you alive the way they did Ashel 5's husband."

"I don't care about being a Blank. That's Ashel 5's holy war, not mine."

"It's not your holy war because I got rid of the Sons of the Crystal Mind for you."

"You're still going to Loren, Charity."

"My family will pay more than Loren."

"It's not that. There are other… parties involved."

For the first time, she looks scared.

"What other parties?" I say. "Others working with Loren?"

Lin Lin Lin shakes her head.

"It's just better if you come back to us," she says.

Who could possibly be worse than Fulcrus?

"Is it another Ground Zero?" I say.

"We don't like that name."

"What, it *offends* you?"

"Yes."

"How can anything offend you?"

"It sounds like the whining of weak little bastards."

"Ignorance isn't strength, Lin Lin Lin."

"What do you know about it?"

"Well…"

"You think you understand, Charity, but you don't. I sensed the difference between us when I held you, when I felt your heart like it was exploding over and over. I heard you scream, right from the core of your blinding soul. Your honey was a fucking eruption, a flood and your smell on me is perfume, as if I'm you.

"But it will fade. Everything does. I could hold you again and you'd grow fainter, dying away from me, just like all the rest.

"You say I'm ignorant, but you do not know what that moment with you has cost me; how you have powered up the tearing inside again, you beautiful little fucking bastard."

I put my hand inside her holographic one and we stand like that for a while. Her face is stricken.

"Soon I will be numb again," she says.

"But not now."

"No. Not now."

She looks at our joined hands.

"Sometimes I think you're colder than I am," she says.

"I think that too," I say. "I killed four thousand men when I finished the Sons."

"Did you feel anything?"

"Relief at first. Then horror, guilt and finally rage that they put me in that position."

"I hear you there," Lin Lin Lin says.

She frowns as if trying to decide whether to go on.

"I know you have to give me to Loren," I say, "so this is probably the last time we'll speak."

She regards me with that now-familiar eerie intensity.

"I was meant to be a carer," she says. "For the little babies and the old people the Basis can't fix any more. I'm supposed to reassure, to comfort; it's why I'm built like this. Strong, with big mumsie tits that get in the way but feel so good, don't they Charity?"

"Yes," I say.

"All the skills and medical knowledge were present from the moment I became aware. It was like waking up but with no reference to a life before. And then work; years of it.

"Babies came and grew and went and old people came and died and went. At first everything made sense in a blind, instinctive way. It helped that there were others who worked there too, although they weren't Blanks.

"The other carers left or retired and I was left on my own, because not a lot of people wanted to do that job. It was all right for a while, but then the babies and old people started dying."

"Did you kill them?"

"No! No, never!"

"Okay Lin Lin Lin, I believe you."

"It is very important that you do."

"I promise I believe you."

She calms down.

"Something was loose in me, Charity. I'd been designed to care, but at some level… just didn't. I missed things I knew to look for, but failed to notice because to me they weren't important.

"I was genetically compelled to do a job I was incapable of doing. Don't tell me you know what that's like because no one does, except other people like me. The closest you will get is trying to inhale and getting just enough air to cling faintly to life, but not enough to actually fucking *breathe*.

"The others started going wrong at about the same time. Soon there were lots of Blanks locked up, even the ones who hadn't done anything. Our owners tried to utilise us in different ways, but it didn't work; we just couldn't connect with anything. They decided to kill us off instead. It was the merciful thing to do, and convenient.

"I'd thought about ending it myself, of course. There was pain in my head all the time, and it kept getting worse. I didn't know what to think or feel because…"

She puts her hands to her face for a moment and then just lets them fall as if all strength has gone.

"…I could not be what I was."

She shakes her head.

"You'd think it would have been easy but I couldn't kill myself, Charity; any more than I was capable of looking after those people. There was no understandable need and thus no way to over-ride the stupid biology.

"I couldn't even let our owners kill me. I fought my way out with a load of other Blanks, and all the skills I'd been programmed with were very useful when I turned them upside down.

"We were hunted and hid in the Outer Spheres, which felt like home; like the cold inside of our heads. We needed relief from it though, so we struck blindly at whatever we could. It felt like revenge against everyone stupid and lazy enough to imagine things like us were ever a good idea.

"There was a war, if you can call it that. A lot of us were killed, which didn't matter to anyone, including us. Soon there were only a few left."

"One of them was Steeber," I say.

"Yes."

"What was he meant to have been?"

"Architect. His buildings kept falling down though. At first he thought it was because he was a shit architect, but then he realised the buildings fell down because he wanted them to."

I try and control my horror.

"You're shocked," Lin Lin Lin says.

"Yes."

"It's like having all of space in you. Other people are like the faraway stars burning to nothing in the dark, and dead by the time we notice. Who sees them anyway? Not us down here in our crystal prison; not even the Old World, not really."

We stare at each other.

"Did you kill Hobb's wife?" I say.

"No, no, I don't know who did that. Anyway, by then it was just me and Steeber. There was a connection between us; we still don't know what it is. Complementary usefulness, I reckon.

"He found a talent for pimping and we made a lot of kilos by controlling the whores completely. We would get onto vix-links with them so we could experience their horror. The best phase was always just before they gave in to it and became numb, when their anguish was at its most intense. Beautiful."

"Every time I think I'm getting close to you Lin Lin Lin, you go and say something like that."

"You see why it can never work between us, Charity."

"But we were so good together. Not just the sex, but with Ashel 5 when we were fighting the Centrian warships. Why don't you come back?"

"Because your friend will try and kill me and I will take great pleasure in dismembering her."

"I won't let that happen. Leave Steeber. Come to me."

"And bring Harlan," Lin Lin Lin says.

"Of course bring Harlan!"

"He's gonna let me finger you when I want is he?"

"He's very broad-minded."

"Maybe so, but he won't forgive what we did."

"I'm sure freeing him will help," I say.

"What about Jaeger Darwin, if he ever wakes up?"

"I'll find a way."

"You won't. You see Charity, even if you could get past all those obstacles there's the fact of how I am. You would fade. Yes, even you. We would make love a few more times, and in doing so you would start to join the many faceless others.

"Oh, I'd hold onto you like I held on to the rest but they go Charity, they go away into the dark, despite my love. This way you will last longer.

"So if you really care, if this isn't all some manipulation of yours then come back and let me give you to Loren. Let my big monster heart break yet again, maybe harder and deeper this time so you stay special, special and forever lost."

41

Ashel 5 and I stand on Wrath Umbilica's flight deck with 23, who today is a scintillating sphere of emerald motes hanging just above the floor.

"What?" I say, my voice a disbelieving croak.

"Steeber owns his suit patent," 23 says.

I close my eyes.

"However, the suit is not Centrian," 23 continues. "It uses a smart cloth composite, and the patent for that is owned by someone else."

"Who?" I say.

"A gang called the Long Term."

Ashel 5 tuts.

"You know them?" I say.

"Natora Stein's compound was near one of their protection zones," Ashel 5 says. "We had to fight them off more than once. They're led by a vicious bastard called Verbs Hemel."

She looks at me.

"You'd get on very well," she says.

"These days the Long Term has just one zone by the Outer Spheres," 23 says.

"Can we get there in time?" I say.

"Yes, it's less than twenty minutes away," 23 says.

"Good," I say, "because we need to stop off en route. These are the coordinates, Ashel 5."

"Okay," she says.

"There are only a hundred in the gang now, but that's still ninety-seven more than us," 23 says. "We need to be fast and quiet."

A holo appears showing a large, square chamber with numerous access portals and an incredible variety of truly abysmal architecture.

Even the recycling properties of the Basis are not enough to prevent the structures corroding, due either to dangerously exceeded life spans or the unventilated breath of multiple occupants.

Some buildings have been grown but appear to be unfinished, while others look like they are built from parts of other things. There is a rudimentary structure, evident in traces of a street layout that is gradually being smudged into oblivion. Although I can't see any commerce, the sprawling township covers the chamber floor completely.

"What a mess," I say.

"You can take the girl out of Centria…" 23 says. "That's Omega Settlement 30, or Omset Three Zero for short."

The holo rotates and zooms in on one of the higher blocks.

"The Long Term controls the whole area from here," 23 says. "They suck up what little money there is and enforce their rule with torture and executions. They're very fond of beheadings."

"At least it's quick," I say.

"Not here it isn't," 23 says. "Don't get caught."

"How do we get in?" Ashel 5 says.

"Drop from the chamber above using dekpaks, but to avoid being seen don't activate them until the last moment. I'll keep Wrath Umbilica out of sight, but close enough to move in fast."

"Any other layout detail?" I say.

"The building is a lash-up, so there are no plans," 23 says.

"How about recs?" Ashel 5 says.

"No, 23 says. "Despite appearances, it's heavily shielded."

"Will the whole gang be there?" I say.

"They operate from snout bars and minky joints to remind Omset Three Zero who's in charge," 23 says. "A hundred men will be stretched pretty thin over such a big area; I'd say you're up against ten in that base, no more."

"Fine with me," Ashel 5 says.

I nod.

"The others will head home once they realise what's going on," 23 says. "I'll pick you up from the roof fifteen minutes after you land."

"How do we know Hemel is in the base?" I say.

"We don't," 23 says.

"Oh."

"He hasn't been seen out of it for some time though, so the chances are he's there."

I stifle a sigh of desperation. It is not 23's fault that a homicidal gang is inconveniencing us with secrecy. I look at the holo of the base and another problem occurs to me.

"How do we get Verbs Hemel to give us the patent?" I say.

There's a slightly nasty silence.

"I'd have thought that was obvious," 23 says.

"I'll do it," Ashel 5 says.

I keep my face blank so the relief doesn't show.

"You may be able to use gas, so take masks," 23 says.

Ashel 5 gifs two and hands one to me.

"I can also plant other weapons to make it appear there are more than just three of us," 23 says.

"How many other weapons?" Ashel 5 says.

"We can't afford a lot or to do anything which could slow us down."

"Are we low on kilos?" I say.

"We might be all right if we don't use them on explosives we won't get back."

"And time?"

"You've got three and a half hours to get the patent, weave in the explosive and reach Fulcrus."

There is still too much uncertainty, but I can't think of any more questions.

"Now," Ashel 5 says, "guns."

She crosses to a wall, which slides apart to reveal a large rack of weapons.

"Do you always use that finger blaster?" she says.

"The n-gun? No. I prefer people not to know I've got it," I say.

Ashel 5 takes out a heavy-looking but skeletal black rifle.

"Edwards Ten Million," she says. "This is a beautiful gun. It will get us in and fire a knock-out canister at the same time."

"You have that one," I say.

Ashel 5 clips the Edwards to a rigid strap on her back and picks up another rifle, which is smaller but bulkier.

"Draegan Yokel Pigfucker," she says.

"Good brand," 23 says.

"Yes," Ashel 5 says. "Now this is a beautiful gun Charity, just beautiful. Powerful, but can be a bit lively. Fancy it?"

"Er…"

"Good," Ashel 5 says and clips the Draegan to her back.

I point at a fuze that looks familiar.

"What about that one?"

There is an uncomfortable pause.

"That's the one I shot you with," Ashel 5 says.

"I'll take it," I say.

Ashel 5 hesitates, then picks up the fuze and gives it to me. The weapon is a good fit; light but solid.

"That'll get you through most armour, and on high power a wall as well," she says.

Her eyes flicker as she goes in-Aer.

"I've changed the setting so that only you can fire it, Charity."

Pulling a holster out of the rack she fixes it to my side.

"There," she says.

I slide the fuze in and out of its holster.

"This is a beautiful gun," I say.

"It's all right," Ashel 5 says.

"Can I make it go red?" I say.

"Use the Aer interface."

I change the holster and fuze to match my jumpsuit.

"Nothing like getting your priorities right," 23 says. "Will you be doing your hair as well?"

"No," Ashel 5 says.

"Actually, how do you keep your hair out of your eyes?" I ask Ashel 5.

"There's a patent called 'Impossible' which does it without appearing to," she says. "Look."

Ashel 5 kneels and a colourless liquid flows from the floor onto her long fingers. She stands and runs them through my hair, her touch firm but surprisingly gentle. It feels lovely. I keep my breathing level.

Ashel 5 steps back.

"Shake your head," she says.

The product isn't noticeable but however hard I try I can't get any hair to obscure my vision.

"Thanks," I say to Ashel 5.

"Gone off the braid have you?" 23 says.

"Shush," I say.

Ashel 5 clips more weapons to herself, glancing at my single fuze with faint disdain. None of the equipment seems to weigh her down, including the dekpak she fixes into place between the two rifles. Finally, there is no more room on the harness and she grunts in frustration.

"Haven't you got enough guns?" I say.

Ashel 5 stands bristling with weaponry, her expression quizzical.

"You can never have enough guns, Charity," she says.

42

Triangular green panels recess to reveal a glaring Dodge69. His pale blue eyes seem particularly watery today, as if the fire in them needs to be continually quenched.

Behind him, his sparse accommodation is brightened by the beautiful artwork on one wall; currently a giant 'photo' depicting a dense cluster of Old World flowers. The light in Diamond City doesn't look as rich as the light in the picture, which seems to make the deep floral colours sing. Against another wall is the screen that revealed my golden Aerac threads after Dodge injected me with the n-gun. Gold, when everyone else's are chrome.

Dodge seems to have forgotten this extraordinary fact, along with the 100,000 kilos Harlan paid him for my n-gun.

"Hello Dodge," I say.

"I didn't call you back, which means I don't want to see you," he says.

"Yes, but-"

"Which means do not come here and now that you have, go away," he says.

"Harlan's in trouble," I say.

"So?"

"He's your friend."

"Fuck off," Dodge says.

"No," Ashel 5 says.

Dodge turns on her and then he blinks in surprise.

"Berserker drone?" he says.

Ashel 5 and I look at each other. She shrugs, nonplussed. Dodge69 pokes his head into the corridor and glances up and down. Satisfied that no one is there, he indicates with his hand and we follow him in as the door closes behind us.

Dodge takes Ashel 5's right wrist gently between his thumb and forefinger. Ashel 5 looks at me again. I nod, so Ashel 5 lets Dodge lift and then hold her arm, which rests between his hands as if he is testing the balance.

"Hm," he says.

He examines Ashel 5's triceps and gently grips her forearm, sniffing it cautiously and then looking up into her face.

"Good shot are you?" Dodge says.

"Yes," Ashel 5 says.

"Should think so."

He lowers Ashel 5's arm carefully, as if it is valuable. Dodge then spreads his hands as if to encompass Ashel 5 from powerful shoulder to slender fingertip.

"I did your arms," Dodge says.

Ashel 5 looks as confused as I feel.

"Did them?" she says.

"Advised, really. Which DNA to use and how to tweak it, what nano to put in to keep you buff. Not just arms obviously, there's other factors too."

"Why?" Ashel 5 says.

"Got to get the muscles right for shooting, see?" He nods to himself. "Never actually got to meet any of you, but you're exactly as I imagined."

He runs his palms over the taut orbs of Ashel 5's musculature.

"Impressive," he says, with such gentle awe in his voice that his actions seem profoundly appreciative rather than lewd.

He looks up at Ashel 5 again.

"Where's your master?"

She pulls free.

"Gone," she says.

"'Gone'? What do you mean 'gone'? No one 'goes' anywhere in Diamond City; there's no way out."

"Dead."

286

"So why ain't you? You're meant to be the last line of defence."

"Got ambushed," Ashel 5 says.

"Pisser," Dodge says. "Have you ever wigged out?"

Ashel 5 frowns.

"What do you mean?" she says.

"You're a berserker drone," Dodge69 says. "Have you ever gone berserk?"

"I get annoyed a lot," Ashel 5 says.

"Not that," Dodge says.

"I don't think so," Ashel 5 says.

"You'll know when you do," Dodge says.

Ashel 5 looks self-conscious; even Dodge picks up on it.

"So, the little princess here is your new mistress is she?" he says.

I think he means to change the subject, but in fact has simply made the situation even more awkward.

"I…" I begin.

"Er…" Ashel 5 says.

Dodge is clearly not impressed by ambiguity. He starts to look angry again.

"Maybe you'd better go away and sort it out," he says.

"Dodge, please," I say. "Harlan hasn't got much time."

"Have you got kilos?" Dodge says.

I hesitate and he rolls his eyes.

"You might be a charity," Dodge says, "but I'm not."

"Do it for me," Ashel 5 says and flexes her arms.

"No," Dodge says.

There's another awkward pause as Ashel 5 blushes, while I tense with regret at the time wasted here so far.

Ashel 5 looks at me.

"He probably can't do it," she says.

"Is that you being clever?" Dodge says.

"Yes," Ashel 5 says.

"It ain't," Dodge says.

She glares back at him. These two could quickly become a dangerous problem.

"Hurry up, Charity," 23 says in my head.

I close my eyes, take a deep breath, then another and open my eyes again.

"We need to weave a nano-bomb into a smart cloth composite," I say.

"Composite for what?" Dodge says.

"Suit patent," I say. "The bomb has to be so small that the wearer doesn't notice."

Dodge considers it.

"200,000 kilos," he says.

Ashel 5 gasps.

"We haven't got anywhere near that much," 23 tells me.

I wait for a good idea to come. I wait some more. I look at Ashel 5. She thinks for a moment and then reaches for one of her weapons.

Dodge points his right index finger at where Ashel 5's navel should be.

"I just want to show you something, Dodge," Ashel 5 says. "You like guns, right?"

"I am guns," Dodge says.

Ashel 5 nods. From her side, she unclips what looks like a half-metre sculpture with twin barrels and an ornately carved stock. Dodge's eyes go wide.

"No…" he says.

"Old World shotgun," Ashel 5 says.

Dodge's tight features relax into a look of such sadness that I realise most of his rage is in reaction to it. He reaches slowly for the shotgun, his fingers gradually uncurling until their tips rest lightly on the polished metal. His eyelids flicker as he tries to blink back tears.

"This is…" Ashel 5's voice cracks slightly. "This is a beautiful gun. You have to gif the ammo, but I can let you have the patent for that."

Dodge's fingertips remain on the shotgun.

"Would I have loved you this much in the Old World?" he whispers to it.

I want the process Dodge is going through to run its course quickly, so that Ashel 5's astonishing gift is not wasted.

"Have you got the smart cloth patent?" Dodge asks me.

"We're going to get it now," I say.

After a moment, Dodge nods and his fingers wrap around the double barrel. Ashel 5 lets go and Dodge cradles the shotgun. Ashel 5 swallows; I reach over and touch her arm. She looks at me, eyes brimming.

"Thank you," I whisper.

She nods.

Dodge seems changed; in commune with forces I cannot guess at. He looks up at me.

"Was there anything else?" he says.

43

I drop through darkness towards the Long Term. Ashel 5 is a pale shape nearby, her hair a flicker of deeper black above. The Long Term base enlarges quickly beneath us, then abruptly slows as the dekpaks open. Our legs swing down, boots obscuring less of the roof the closer we get.

Ashel 5 moves away from me in the air. I follow her and we face each other as we drop. Her head is in shadow but I can still make out her strong, sensuous features. We seem suspended for a while as we regard each other, both aware of the other's power and her vulnerability.

We land on an upper balcony and the dekpaks fold onto our backs. I pull out the red fuze as Ashel 5 snatches the Edwards Ten Million from her back, shoots through the wall and fires eight self-propelled stun grenades into the hole. We clip the transparent masks to our faces and we wait a few seconds for the gas to take effect.

From below comes the drowsy hum of sleepless streets. Inside the base, there is only silence. Ashel 5 kicks through the wall, plunges into darkness and I follow.

The mask's darkvision reveals we are in what was originally an observation lounge, with stained sofas and battered chairs that seem to accrue menace as we stare at them. Ashel 5 moves forward with predatory grace while I check behind furniture, finding nothing except scraps of carpet. We reach the door; Ashel 5 gets down on one knee and points the Edwards at it. I grip the handle, trying in vain to hear what's on the other side. I pull the door open.

The corridor beyond is empty except for strewn rubbish. Ashel 5 and I walk down the corridor, stepping around refuse and checking for traps. I glance behind to see if anyone has followed us in, but no one has.

We reach the end of the corridor, which is a T-junction. Ashel 5 presses her back against the corner of one wall and I do the same on the other. I point away from myself.

You go that way, Ashel 5. Open a two-way AV vix link.

A little window opens in the top left of my vision. It shows me holding the red fuze and wearing the transparent mask.

"Surrounding areas all quiet," 23 says as a little timer appears under the vix link window. "I'll bring Wrath Umbilica in from the next chamber in five minutes."

I hold up three fingers; two, then one. Ashel 5 and I duck around the corners.

There's nothing in either direction; my corridor ends in another door and I see from the vix link that Ashel 5's does as well. We move away from each other and I feel her absence like a soft pain.

I force myself to maintain the right kind of calm as I approach the door. I don't like these old-fashioned, hinged doorways; there are too many ways to make them into traps. I reach for the handle anyway-

"Ashel 5!" I whisper.

"Yes?" she whispers back.

"Did you hear that?"

"What?"

"A kind of buzzing."

"I can't hear it, Charity."

"Okay. It's stopped."

I see her point of view: another deserted room. We have gambled our remaining time on the likelihood that Verbs Hemel is here because he hasn't been seen anywhere else. What if we are wrong?

I open the door and immediately feel human presence. I dive to the floor and rubbish clatters deafeningly.

"Charity!"

"I'm all right, Ashel 5. I think I've found something."

I lie on my front with the fuze pointed ahead, but no one

approaches. Structures rise up either side of me and as I try to work out what they are, I hear buzzing again. I silently lever myself upright and see what surrounds me.

They are bunk beds and in most of them is a sleeping person. The sleepers are smaller than I expected; hardly terrifying gang members and more like…

"Ashel 5," I say, "put your rifle on stun. There are loads of kids here."

"I know," she says. "I've found more of them."

"23," I say, "what does it mean?"

"I don't know," 23 says, "but you're out of time."

I hear the hum of Wrath Umbilica's approach and begin to run through the dilapidated complex. There are other dormitory rooms, some occupied and some not. I can't see any adults, which doesn't make sense; at no point was the Long Term a juvenile gang.

"I'm under attack, sort of," 23 says.

Such vagueness is unlike her.

"What-?"

"People are on the roofs, throwing things at the ship," 23 says. "It's hopeless, more of a gesture but they really fucking mean it."

The sound of gunfire sends me into a crouch but the noise is over the vix link.

"Ashel 5?"

"I'm all right," she says. "I got one. Oh no…"

"What is it?"

"It's a kid, a little girl. She's only about ten."

"Is she…?"

"No, I used stun, she'll be all right-"

"Bastards!" screams a youthful voice from in front of me.

I roll under a bunk as the dorm is lit red with gunfire.

"Get the fuck out from under there, you dirty perv bitch!"

I hear another voice, indistinct but unmistakably adult; then little footsteps as they rush away into silence. For a while, I lie there as a readout on the mask indicates that the gas has dispersed. I pull the mask off and the sour smell of many bodies in close proximity is overwhelming.

The bunk's occupant snores softly, which is the buzz I heard earlier. Eventually, I peek from under the tatty mattress. The corridors in both directions are deserted. I roll out and get up.

"I'm gonna sound the horn on this thing," 23 says.

Wrath Umbilica's voice is a great mournful wail that rips through the oppressive silence and then fades.

"Hmm," 23 says. "That just pissed everyone off more. Let's get some light in there."

Ashel 5 and I start to run again as dazzling light flares in through grimy windows. All I see are sleeping children. There are no weapons, no gangsters and although between us we have covered most of the complex, Ashel 5's point of view reveals the same. I step through another doorway into a large room dominated by a huge round table that looks homemade. Instinct makes me jump back out again as red lightning crackles past the spot where I stood.

"Leave us alone!" screams the same boyish voice I heard in the dorm.

"We don't want to hurt you," I say.

"Oh I know *that!*"

"What's your name?" I say.

"Why? You'll only give me a *special* name anyway!"

"I'm sorry, I don't understand," I say. "My name's Charity."

"Fuck off, Charity."

"I'm looking for Verbs Hemel. Do you know where he is?"

Even as I ask I know the answer; it rises on my left like a patch of unfolding darkness, weapons extended towards me with a howl of fury. Every muscle responds to my command with the maximum possible speed, but it's not enough: Verbs Hemel has already taken aim and will fire before I can.

Light flashes past my shoulder to hit the monster, who falls back with a cry of despair. Ashel 5 sprints past me to kick the weapons out of Hemel's reach.

"No!" screams the boy. "You've killed him!"

He scrambles from under the table and runs at me waving a fuze that looks too big in his hand. I stun him and he sprawls on the floor, his mess of dark hair spread around his head. I pick up the boy's fuze, straighten his crumpled little body so he'll be comfortable and then walk back to where Ashel 5 is disarming Verbs Hemel.

There must be some mistake. The lithe, vicious demon of legend has been replaced with an overweight, middle-aged man who is clearly very ill. I scan him to be sure.

Verbs Hemel, confirms my Aerac.

His narrow, sharp face is blunted with jowly flesh and shines with pain, clearly there long before Ashel 5 drove a shot into one narrow shoulder. Dyed black hair is patchily employed to cover uneven baldness and the once-proud tattoos now look more like apologies. His gut looks swollen rather than indulged, and he rests his good arm across it as if hiding the swelling in embarrassment. The hatred with which he regards us is genuine and intense, however.

"I didn't think they'd send women," he gasps. "Shame on you. I hope your fucking ovaries implode."

"Think who'd send us?" Ashel 5 says, pulling off her mask.

Hemel sneers.

"I suppose you think he loves you; do this for him and you'll be together. He doesn't love you. He despises you."

"What are you talking about?" I say.

"Oh please."

He looks at his shattered shoulder, retches and then looks back at me and Ashel 5.

"I don't get it," he says. "You're both so fucking hot. How can you be so stupid, so hopeless?"

"Are there any more armed kids?" Ashel 5 says.

"I don't know, are there? Maybe you'd better piss right off before you find out."

Ashel 5 gets that crazed look and puts the Edwards to her shoulder.

"No," Verbs says. "You wouldn't. You *can't*."

"Are… there… any-?"

"No! Just Won and Tink. You didn't kill them, did you?"

It is not physical pain that pushes tears from his eyes. Ashel 5 and I look at each other. She goes back to scanning our surroundings as I kneel beside Verbs.

"Of course we didn't kill them," I say. "We're not murderers or bad people, and we're not here on behalf of anyone else."

"You've fucking invaded! And what's that big green bastard doing outside?"

"That's… Never mind that," I say.

"What do you want?"

"The smart cloth composite patent."

He looks utterly confused.

"Why?" he says.

"That's confidential," I say.

"You can't have it."

Ashel 5 looks at him again.

"Fuck you, Leggy," Verbs says to her and for the first time I hear the gang leader in his voice. "I used to have loads of sexy willing Blanks like you."

"Where are they now?" I say.

"Dead. Mad. Who knows?"

"We were expecting the Long Term," Ashel 5 says.

"You were supposed to," says Verbs. "Nothing like a reputation you can no longer afford."

"So those recordings in-Aer…?" I say.

"We did all that. Years ago. But it couldn't last. And… the evil of it…

"I have to make amends, somehow. That's why I look after these nippers, the ones no one else wants."

"This is a *kid farm?*" I say.

"Yeah. Not the best, but at least they eat and they're safe. All Omset 30 is in on it."

"How come?" I say.

"A lot of the kids are from here. People know they'll be looked after but the only income is from a few shitty patents, so you're not having any of them."

He looks at the Edwards Ten Million.

"You kill me the patents will go to one of the kids. Before you can find out which one everybody outside will come in here and rip your tits off, fat bastard warship or no."

"Who did you think we were?" I say.

Verbs regards me for a moment.

"Like all kid farms, we get a lot of interest from the, ah, intergenerational love community," he says. "They've tried shit like this before. They tend to go for the less well-funded outfits like mine, despite the Long Term legend. So even if you nab that patent off me, you'll just be condemning my kids to… well. Either of you got kids?"

The Edwards begins to shake in Ashel 5's arms as her body is racked with sobs.

"Her, then," Verbs says. "You?"

"No."

"I got loads. Some my own, like my own offspring. First ones turned out just like me. Dead now. That's what changed me, seeing my eldest go into the floor, then his sister, then her brother who was only fourteen for fuck's sake…"

A holo of Ashel 6 appears between us, the little girl's hair longer than when I saw her last. It's finer than her mother's; more like her father's and with his lovely grey eyes as well. Verbs looks at the holo.

"No," he says. "She isn't here. Sorry."

Ashel 5 makes a funny honking sound, as if she's saying 'huh' a couple of times. She grips the Edwards tight.

"Charity," 23 says, "whatever you're going to do, do it now."

"We'll buy it from you," I say to Verbs.

"You don't understand," he says. "It's money that will always be coming in. You'd have to pay the worth of it in future as well."

"How much?" I say.

"600K."

Ashel 5 stops crying and we stare at him.

"That's six hundred thousand kilos," Verbs says.

"No way!" Ashel 5 says.

Verbs laughs. It is the sound of a man who has known total power.

"You two came in here on your own, expecting to find the Long Term," he says. "You knew we were fond of chopping the heads off women, amongst other things, yes?"

We glare at him.

"You want that patent bad," he continues. "I want that money bad. The stupid war is fucking everything up; no one's buying anything. I want 600K, or I want you gone."

"We haven't got 600K," Ashel 5 says.

"I want to, you know, fucking shrug at you Leggy but you shot me in the shoulder so…"

He shakes his head infuriatingly at her. Ashel 5 is now too angry to realise we have got thousands of kilos, or at least she has.

"Ashel 5, what is Wrath Umbilica worth?"

She doesn't get it to begin with.

"'Wrath Umbilica'?" Verbs says. "That's what that giant bogey is called? You girls are fucking crazy. I like you. You're annoying, but I like you."

"Oh," Ashel 5 says. "Of course. Yes. She would be worth about that."

"Deposit her and give him the kilos," I say. "Verbs, agree the terms I'm sending you: give me that patent on receipt of the kilo value of the warship."

"Er, yeah," he says. "Agreed."

I haven't looked at Ashel 5. She could say no but she doesn't.

"I want to watch," she says.

I nod. We turn away from Verbs.

"Who are you, Blondie?" he says.

Ashel 5 turns back.

"She's the Golden Princess," she says.

Ashel 5 takes my arm and we stride away, through dorms of sleeping children back to the balcony.

We walk out into the night, where Wrath Umbilica hangs over the ramshackle buildings nearby. Ashel 5 stops abruptly at the sight of her beloved ship. As I stand quietly beside her, she takes a short breath and then another.

The lights inside the great vessel go out and it descends to an empty section of floor. Ashel 5 makes that 'huh' sound again. I put my arm around her shoulders, feeling the warm skin over her glorious muscles. She trembles and then sags slightly against me. I bear her proudly up and she keeps her head high. I don't need to look at her face to see light reflecting off her streaming tears as Wrath Umbilica sinks into the ground, layer after layer dissolving until there's nothing left.

44

I ride in a missile back to Fulcrus, the vehicle reluctantly chosen for speed because I've only got six minutes left. Despite the reassurance of the acid mix in my boots and the suit patent that will vaporise Steeber before he knows what's happening, I still grip the red fuze tightly.

My heartbeat gets louder and the curved wall seems to close in. For a terrible moment I wonder if everything that has happened was an illusion and I'm still in the Infinity Box, too crushed and exhausted to scream.

The last chambers flick by and I finally see the hated Fulcrus tower. The missile blasts through the wall, decelerates hard in an arc over a sea of brightly coloured geometric shapes and stops near the far window. The restraints let me go as the missile lands base first; the hatch opens and I step out.

The place is deserted. I didn't think I would miss the haunting whispers echoing like a premonition of disaster, but this silence is actually worse. Fulcrus has expanded since I first came here with Ursula and now covers three enormous floors, the ceiling in this one much higher than the other two.

It feels strange to be on my way to murder someone. Although I remind myself of Unit 7/10 and the Infinity Box I feel less anger than cold efficiency, which will be useful because I've got a large amount of ground to cover on my own.

Steeber's new security measures prevent 23 getting recs to transmit from in here, while the search algorithm she put together to find Ashel 6 has turned up some plausible details. Ashel 5, who did so much more than I ever expected, has gone to investigate.

I continue towards the middle of the room. Every coloured shape is a potential hiding place so I edge carefully around them. However, a yellow pyramid has nobody behind it, the space at the back of a green cone is empty and a purple cylinder obscures nothing except an orange sphere. By the time I reach the centre my adrenaline has leached away to leave a residue of deep unease.

There's a flicker of movement to my left. Simultaneously alarmed and relieved, I press myself against a red cube and peer round the side.

The Puzzle Man walks among the coloured shapes.

Keeping out of its line of sight, I follow the hologram towards a strange box. It's the only black shape and much bigger than the others. The Puzzle Man reaches the block and walks through one of the walls.

I wait a few moments, then warily approach. When I reach the structure, a doorway slides open and inside… Inside is something that doesn't make sense.

Familiar figures are engaged in bizarre, silent choreography, their bodies well-muscled and their movements incredibly controlled. They wear a variety of clothes but all are barefoot. Instead of heads they've got featureless, shiny black ovoids.

"Oh God," 23 says as I recognise one of the figures.

He is a big man, his great body healed from injury sustained protecting me when the evac ship crashed in the Outer Spheres. Next to Krae Muston is the Ledge. Over there are Khadisha, Razor, a stocky man I assume is Spider Bob, Iqbal, Velasquez and the Foster-Blacks. There are more NFE soldiers too; another ten at least.

I walk into the room. It stinks of unwashed bodies and the only light is from the room outside. Stopping in front of the Ledge, I see that his hands grip a rifle shape in the air and his body is slightly crouched in preparation for combat.

"Sir?" I say. "Captain?"

He doesn't respond.

"Those black helmets are an immersive rig," 23 says. "The unit think they're engaged in an operation."

"Will it hurt if I wake them up?" I say.

"Try anyway," 23 says.

I reach for the Ledge but before I can touch him the blank ovoid turns and seems to focus on me.

"Sir?" I say.

His hand is suddenly around my left wrist. I try and pull free but the other NFE have seized me as well. They knock the fuze from my grasp and it clatters to the floor. As the blank, ovoid heads close in I struggle but my arms have already been folded against my body so I can't use the n-gun.

"No," I shout. "No!"

"Yes, actually," Steeber Loke says from the doorway. "Nice entrance by the way, very theatrical."

Lin Lin Lin steps out of the darkness behind me and picks up the red fuze, her face expressionless. She holds a yellow ball that quickly moulds itself into a set of restraints that weave through the NFE to bunch my hands into fists behind my back. Although the n-gun stays offline I try not to look smug as I think about the acid mix in my boots.

Something rustles down my leg and I see the binding around my feet as well, both restraints linked so no movement is possible. As I stare down in horror, the NFE let go and return to whatever reality occupies them. I try to move but can't; all I can do is shake my head, helpless and numb.

The floor moves me and Lin Lin Lin out of the black box to stop in front of Steeber. He and Lin Lin Lin regard me, dissociated and forever apart.

"What have you done to my friends?" I say.

Steeber's inexpressive eyes look from me to the NFE as they blindly work through endless dreams of battle.

"They have become the Multimage," he says.

I hear Steeber's bleakly utilitarian poetry at work in the word.

"That's how you were able to hack into the NFE Aer Military Intelligence System," I say. "There was no traitor."

"Correct," Steeber says, eerily helpful as if this is an interesting discussion between colleagues. "Their access to AerMIS meant I could copy the system quadrant by quadrant, updating it as new NFE assets were acquired. I then generated a holographic interface for greater efficiency."

"The Puzzle Man," I say.

"Ah, good name," Steeber says. "The 'puzzle' is made of randomly selected features from all the NFE I have here. It changes quickly to avoid detection."

Intensely aware of Lin Lin Lin's presence I finally look up at her. She looks back, her face still expressionless. I sag slightly, unable to pretend the situation is not hopeless.

"Your despair is exquisite," Steeber says.

Lin Lin Lin points the red fuze at him.

"No!" I shout.

Steeber doesn't look surprised and neither does Lin Lin Lin as she repeatedly pulls the trigger on a gun only I can fire. She turns and looks into my eyes as Steeber shoots her repeatedly through the heart. Blood flies out of Lin Lin Lin's back in a widening red cone; she staggers, drops the fuze and sinks to her knees.

She is still looking at me.

"F… ff… frree…" she says.

I crouch beside her, the one movement possible in these restraints. Lin Lin Lin almost gets her hand up to touch my face when Steeber steps forward and shoots her in the head. Lin Lin Lin jerks and falls with a nauseating thud.

I lean over her as she sinks into the floor. She looks very different without her demonic energy: a huge motionless form whose generous purpose was almost completely thwarted. That something human remained makes grief rise as I watch Lin Lin Lin lose definition and disappear.

Steeber crouches beside me. I sense his gaze on my face and then he looks at where Lin Lin Lin lay.

"You grieve... for Lin Lin Lin?" Steeber says.

"Guess so," I say.

He takes a deep breath and I sense frustration in the way he exhales.

"She was the nearest thing I had to a friend and I don't feel anything at all," he says.

He pockets the red fuze, straightens and pulls me up with him. I look at the floor again, trying to recall the Infinity Box and the knife at Ursula's eye. Instead I remember how awful Lin Lin Lin's life was; the tragic desperation in her voice when she said she loved me.

Tears tumble down my cheeks. Steeber watches, uncomprehending as if my grief is an alien ritual. After a while his scrutiny becomes uncomfortable and my tears falter before they are truly done. I blink until I can see him again, my face hot and my nose wet.

"So, you were meant to be an architect," I say to break the unpleasant silence.

Steeber continues to watch me unblinkingly.

"No," he says eventually. "I was meant to be *the* architect."

"The-?"

"Ison Maddox."

I try to place the name.

"I've never heard of him," I say.

Steeber thinks for a moment and then shrugs.

"What did he build?" I say.

"Diamond City," Steeber says.

I stare at him.

"Why isn't he better known?" I say.

"He was very secretive."

"Was?"

"He disappeared," Steeber says. "A replacement was required, one with his genius but less flaky, more robust. Hence…"

Steeber gestures at himself.

"I am a mixture of Ison Maddox and others."

I nod. The revelation is interesting but I am still distracted by my capture, by Lin Lin Lin's death.

"I really thought you would have known about him," Steeber says.

"Why?"

"He was bred to be the best at what he did."

When his words finally register I actually feel more sick, which I hadn't thought possible.

"No," I whisper.

"Once I learned about the Guidance from Harlan, I knew immediately that Ison was one of them," Steeber says.

"It's not true…"

He moves closer and I feel his void like a physical chill.

"You and I are related, Charity."

Hearing him say it in that calm voice, which is as unfamiliar with error as it is with emotion does not make the truth any more palatable.

"You're not… like me…" I manage.

"Not exactly, no. You are a combination of all twelve of the Guidance and I have DNA from only one, mixed with other, cruder material. I was an early version of you.

"It seems to be how these things work. I discovered that each of the Guidance was an improvement on the last. Ison was the culmination, as are you."

I try to work out who was first and most improved upon. Gethen? Jaeger? Not Keris, surely…

"What happened to Ison?" I say.

"I don't think even the rest of the Guidance know, but then we do like our secrets don't we?"

"I'm nothing like you, Steeber."

"Yes you are. You slaughtered the Sons of the Crystal Mind without a second thought. For all your great emotion there is a hollowness to you Charity, an empty space at your heart.

"Don't look so sad. It will ensure you always survive, that you are always all right. Just like me."

I stare at this horrible, brutal reflection of myself and can think of no argument.

"It's a pity I must give you to Loren, but business… Business is the only thing that has any meaning."

We stare at each other.

"How do you even know Loren?" I say finally.

"I was her pimp," Steeber says, like it should have been obvious.

I almost feel sorry for Loren.

"I'm surprised you're still alive," I say.

"Loren doesn't waste talent when it suits her," Steeber says. "Try and remember that."

I find myself nodding, as if advice from Steeber is something I would ever want. I look down at my boots, their acid mix now as useless as the altered suit patent we risked so much for and which cost Ashel 5 so dearly.

"It's time to go," Steeber says.

He puts hand on my dekpak.

"Deposit this please, Charity."

I click on deposit and the dekpak flows off me into the floor to disappear, like Lin Lin Lin.

"Which containment would you like?" Steeber says.

"Containment?"

"I'm not taking any chances this time."

Steeber gestures at the dreadful coloured shapes.

"You're going to Loren in one of those," he says. "Unlike these other assets, you will be conscious but it doesn't hurt; it's like being in the Basis. Like being… home."

To take my mind off that thought, I consider Steeber's question.

"Sphere please," I say.

He inclines his head politely as if my choice indicates good taste.

"Colour?" he says.

"Blue."

There is faint pressure on my feet. I look down to see the circular shape form around my boots and begin to rise up my body. I struggle but the restraints hold me tight.

"Shhh," Steeber says and his voice drains all hope.

The blue diamond is at my waist. Forcefully reminded of the Infinity Box, I moan in fear. Steeber watches unconcerned as the containment enlarges around my chest. I don't want to seem weak but...

"No," I say, almost a sob.

Steeber places his right palm on top of my head. His touch is gentle and I'm so frightened I actually welcome it. The diamond continues to grow, lifting me from the floor away from him. His cool fingertips graze my face as he lets his hand fall. The diamond is around my neck now; all I can see is a solid blue circle surrounding me like a huge collar. Finally, it encases my head and I don't even think to close my eyes.

I hang rigidly upright in the sphere, my eyes locked open. It's not physically uncomfortable and I can see through the diamond, although everything is now blue. Steeber looks behind him at the grotesque Multimage he has made out of my friends and then at the place where Lin Lin Lin died. Finally, he looks back at me; perhaps realising how alone he now is.

I wonder if he will change his mind and let me go, because I am the only one left who could possibly understand him. The floor begins to move however, carrying us to the lift and to Loren Descarreaux.

45

The elevator opens onto a dock, where a square VIA warship hovers at the outer edge. Steeber is a vague presence on my left as the floor moves us towards the blue vessel, which opens a hatch to take me in.

A split-view window opens in my vision.

"I've sneaked in a couple of recs," 23 says.

One rec, suspended between the massive column of the tower and the circular chamber wall housing it, shows Steeber next to a blue ball encasing my shadowy figure. The other rec is to my right. I notice we are halfway up the building, whose circumference has been reduced by a third for a couple of floors to form the dock. Two lit rings around the tower move away from each other, illuminating the chamber as they go.

The floor halts.

"Shit," 23 says.

As Steeber stares up at the blue warship, a uniformed figure appears beside him. Willowy but somehow solid, she's got long wavy auburn hair and a slightly clenched posture that indicates furious tension. Loren Descarreaux's hologram swipes a clawed hand through the blue sphere as if to tear my eyes out, gestures angrily at the warship and vanishes.

Fulcrus guards run out of another elevator. Cannons aimed at the VIA craft grow from the floor, which begins to move me and Steeber back the way we came.

"Should have got more warships," 23 says.

The square blue vessel flickers and then I'm staring at a large flybike. Underneath it hangs a frame like a ladder whose base is a platform with a moving floor large enough to hold my sphere. Ashel 5 stands with one black-booted foot on each runner and the

Edwards Ten Million aimed right at us. She opens an AV vix link, which gives me yet another perspective as the guards attack. Streaks of deadly light rip at Ashel 5/me but all I can do is grunt in terror.

Ashel 5's perspective changes as the flybike drops to the dock. Despite her distance from the nearest rec, I can see muscles on her powerful legs stand out as she opens fire. Four guards are killed immediately and the rest scatter.

Ashel 5 leaps onto the dock and runs at them. The cannons track her and she hurls herself down as they fire. From the floor, she shoots a cannon barrel off and rolls aside as another one fires. The shot ricochets and blows a Fulcrus guard into the void beyond the dock.

Steeber hides behind my sphere as the floor conveys us back to the elevator. We are only a few metres away when Ashel 5 shoots again, the flare brighter this time. There's a flash as her detonating grenade destroys the elevator and Steeber is knocked over by the blast wave. Everything spins except the rec windows and Ashel 5's vix link as my senses are set against each other so queasily I nearly forget the dock has no safety rail.

"Why a fucking ball, Charity?" 23 shouts.

"I thought it was poetic," I say, sub-vocalising again. "Is the dock open protocol?"

"No!" 23 says.

The ball stops rolling and the rec shows my head pointed at the floor. Ashel 5 has decimated the guards and destroyed most of the cannons. The flybike is protected from gunfire by the edge of the dock, although 23 has dumped the ladder attachment. I can't see Steeber.

I notice an Aerac message and open it, to find that Lin Lin Lin has left me everything she owned. There are 103,465 kilos, a surprisingly small amount. There's a note that says 'Fre' and an attachment labelled 'Freedom', which must have been what she was trying to tell me at the end. I open it.

Firenze 44 - patent for mobile suspended animation system with design and failsafe options

"23," I say, "I can get out of this sphere."

"Stay put," 23 says. "It's protecting you."

As if to prove her point another impact rolls my ball again. The nausea is worse this time, as if my resistance to it is worn down. Eventually I come to a stop, my feet pointing at the flybike. More guards run into view from an elevator on the other side of the dock.

Steeber calls.

"Don't forget I've still got Harlan," he says.

"Come and get me, Steeber!"

It's hard to sub-vocalise a scream but I just about manage it.

"That fucking woman shot me in the arm and burned my sister! She's insane!"

Ashel 5 does look like a lunatic. Her long, thick dark hair flies in all directions as if it's writhing, while her rifle patterns the air with bright beams like a fire-spewing limb. For all her savagery Ashel 5 moves lightly as if she is dancing, which only adds to the madness. Her eyes blaze like the weapon and her pale skin shines with martial sweat. She gleams in the sweeping light; hypnotically precious and lethal.

"It's Ashel 5," I say to Steeber. "You sold me and Ursula to her, remember? She's going to kill me this time!"

"How would Ashel 5 know where to find you, Charity?" Steeber says.

"I don't know, but Loren Descarreaux is a better prospect than-

"Oh God, Ashel 5 just smashed the barrel off that cannon! Steeber! STEEBER!"

He ends the call.

"Very good," 23 says. "You sounded genuinely terrified."

I look at the rec windows, which show my helpless body suspended in the middle of a gunfight.

"Not a problem," I say.

The guards retreat behind the central curved wall and Ashel 5 goes after them. More cannons grow out of the dock along with chunky barriers that form a kind of maze. The cannon positions look less random now: Steeber has designed overlapping fields of fire to trap Ashel 5.

I do not dwell on how I know this; on how it's what I would have done.

"Charity, get out of there," 23 says. "The real VIA warships are on their way."

"Ashel 5 has got her dekpak, right?"

23 hesitates and I notice Ashel 5 is no longer on our shared comms.

"23!"

"She said the weight would slow her down."

"So-?"

"You don't need her anymore."

"She's got a daughter," I say.

"She can't find her; the algorithm led nowhere. Ashel 6 is probably dead and you will be too if you don't move."

"I'm not leaving Ashel 5."

"Charity-"

"Isn't the NFE all about loyalty?"

"Ashel 5 isn't in the NFE," 23 says.

"I see. Just a Blank then. Disposable."

"There is a cannon cluster growing that will prevent you getting to that bike."

"Fly it round or destroy the cannons then."

"If I do that, Steeber will know I'm still alive."

"What's the point of an advantage if you don't use it?" I say.

"Move!"

I hang in my blue sphere and do nothing.

"I hate you," 23 says.

"No you don't."

"There are cannons tracking the flybike, so I've taken it out of range," 23 says. "I can't pick you up now."

The rings touch the upper and lower edges of the dock, flood the scene with light and cast shadows that swing and lengthen. As the rings move away without touching, more armed people get into position behind the thick walls of the maze. They don't look like Fulcrus guards; I think Steeber has simply engaged the nearest mercenary company on the spot.

Ashel 5 has fought her way around the tower's entire circumference. Her blood-spattered chest heaves and her hair doesn't fly so freely now it's heavy with sweat. She has discarded the Edwards and now wields the Draegan with equal effectiveness.

The cannons all swivel towards Ashel 5 and the mercenaries behind their walls take aim.

"Please help her," I say.

Something flies in from the chamber next door and explodes over the maze. The blast destroys the cannons, knocks Ashel 5 flat and sends my sphere rolling towards the edge again.

Ashel 5 is on her feet before I stop moving. I see from the vix-link that her movement is different now, as if thus far she has merely been warming up. Whether through training, desperation or the way she was made she seems to inhabit a primal realm out of sync with this one. Devoid of strategy and thus wholly unpredictable, she accesses a ferocious instinct known only to her. I realise the berserker drone has finally engaged and that Ashel 5 has wigged out.

"Bloody hell," 23 says.

Ashel 5 is less a woman than an Old World cataclysm condensed into gorgeous human form. Perhaps she is in the place where violence begins, able to predict any move the mercenaries make and then cut through them so fast some just stand and die through lack of anything better to do. Only Jaeger in battle is as impressive although he is guided by discipline, while Ashel 5 has none.

Incredible though she is, Ashel 5 remains outnumbered and I don't know how long she can physically sustain the berserker state. I lose sight of her as gunfire hits the sphere again, propelling it further towards the edge. There is a real possibility I'll be knocked over, to smash through the light ring and…

"23, how fast is the lower light ring travelling?"

There is a pause as she measures it.

"Two metres per second," she says.

"I want to roll off the edge onto the light ring, melt the sphere before I hit to cushion the impact and have Ashel 5 land on top while it's still soft."

"Steeber will destroy the ring before it reaches the ground."

"Get us away on the flybike before he can."

"That's a lot of variables," 23 says. "Send me the Firenze patent so I can work out timings."

I do so and there's a pause that seems longer than it probably is. Another beam ricochets off the sphere and I remember Lin Lin Lin saying these shapes would crush the person inside if anyone tried to interfere with them. At what point does gunfire become interference? Rigid though I am I begin to shake, deep inside.

"Hurry up, 23," I say.

"The ring spec is in-Aer," she says. "Hmm. It throws a hell of a lot of light."

"Will I be blinded?"

"No. There's a nice safety feature that will dim it automatically on contact."

"What about speed?"

"The ring travels pretty fast; its velocity relative to the falling sphere will help if you get the distance right."

"And if I don't?" I say.

"If you're late with the key then the sphere will still be solid when you hit the ring, which is like a hollow doughnut. You'll crash through it and… Let me check…

"There's a moat underneath, but it's so far down you might as well land on diamond."

"What about the floor at the bottom of the moat?"

"Closed protocol," 23 says.

"Could you catch me with the flybike?"

"I don't know. Besides, I would only have time to save you, not Ashel 5."

"What if I activate too early?"

"There'll be nothing left of the sphere and you'll hit the ring unprotected," 23 says. "Even if you survive the impact, Ashel 5's landing will kill you both."

Another flaw occurs to me.

"What about the distance between the inside of the ring and the tower?" I say.

"The sphere won't land neatly on top of the ring, Charity. The best you can hope for is to land between the ring and the building. I will have to position the flybike to get you both, which will at least be easier than snatching you in freefall."

23 sighs.

"Any other ideas?" she says.

"No. You?"

"No."

"Well then."

23 thinks.

"Ashel 5 will have to push you off," she says.

"Right."

"It's not. Look at her."

Ashel 5's vix link is a blur but I can just make out the futile operation of cannons as Steeber, whose icy logic is unable to deal with anything as chaotic as a berserker drone, just gifs and fires them almost at random.

"Ashel 5," I call to her over the vix link.

She doesn't hear.

"Ashel 5!" I shout. "Come on!"

Ashel 5 burns out the Draegan and starts using it as a club.

"Ashel 5," I say. "My friend."

Something changes in her actions as she hears me for the first time.

"Back to the blue sphere, Ashel 5; you need to push it off and jump after me so you land on top."

There are three more explosions over the fighting. My sphere rolls further towards the edge and for a while everything is a dizzying blur. When I level out I see Ashel 5 get up, streaked with grime and blood although I don't think it's hers. Her movements are slower though; she must be tired.

"Nearly there," I say.

Ashel 5 backs towards me, firing a fuze as she comes. I am roughly upright and facing her, so I see her enlarge as she gets closer.

"You need to be off that edge in ten seconds, Charity," 23 says. "Get a move on, Ashel 5."

Ashel 5, once again on 23's comms, starts running backwards until I see her press against the surface of my sphere, which mists up with the wet heat of her body. The sphere begins to move.

"Seven, six, five…" 23 says.

I've been so wrapped up in calculations that I haven't actually contemplated the reality of what I'm doing. When I do, my heart starts beating with such force I'm amazed the containment doesn't shatter.

Why did I think this was a good idea?

"Two, one…"

"Hold on-" I begin.

Ashel 5 heaves, slips over and a mortar shot intended for her hits my rolling sphere. I'm propelled off the edge of the dock so hard the containment arcs in the air before dropping. I feel nothing except weird dislocation from the view in the rec windows of me falling.

"Jump after me, Ashel 5," I say, surprised at how calm I sound. "I will save you."

Ashel 5 doesn't even think about it. One of the recs follows her as she leaps off the dock, turning in a slow somersault above the blue ball that descends towards the bright arc of the ring.

"Now, Charity," 23 says.

I click on Lin Lin Lin's Firenze 44 patent and the inside of the sphere glows. It begins to soften at once as it seeks the Basis for absorption. The key works on my restraints too and I move my hands and feet apart in the gelatinous, liquefying diamond. I'm now facing down, where the ring is a dazzling bar that quickly fills my whole vision.

Thanks to that mortar shot, my containment hits the top of the ring and not the inner side. The sphere flattens to a convex disc and the structure just about holds but then Ashel 5 lands back first on top of it. The disc shatters into globules and we fall onto blinding light. The impact winds me but the moment I touch the surface its agonising glare reduces, dimming the view of the chamber. I hear Ashel 5 gasp as she lands on her front and bounces.

Our heads are near the centre of the ring's curved upper surface; my legs point at the tower and Ashel 5's the chamber wall. Ashel 5 is slippery with sweat and slides away from me, so I lunge forward to seize her wrists but she is heavier and drags me down.

"Let me go," she says.

"Never!"

I angle my feet like hooks against the ring surface and lock my muscles. Friction slows us, but it's still not enough. Ashel 5's eyes are huge with fear and diminishing madness as they gaze into mine.

"Flybike under you, Ashel 5," 23 says.

Ashel 5 nods. I let go of her wrists and she slips away. There's a brief but awful silence and then I hear her thud onto the saddle. As the flybike rises into view, Ashel 5 seizes the controls. I get up; jump on behind her and we speed away from the tower.

Safety restraints wrap our legs but I put my arms around Ashel 5's damp waist anyway. Dark, wet hair flies in my face; I gently gather and pull it down the front of one heaving shoulder then let my hands meet again over her stomach where taut muscles still tremble from the fight.

"Thank you," I say.

She grips my hands briefly in response.

We approach the way out just as a VIA warship flies in through it. Ashel 5 banks across the curved inner surface of the Fulcrus chamber away from the intruder, but the wall is frighteningly close; I can almost feel it under my boots. Another exit enlarges to engulf us and suddenly we are in darkness. I look behind; four VIA warships are now in pursuit.

The huge chamber is full of airborne assemblies formed like planets moving gracefully in a complex orbital system. At its heart, two little suns throw warm light that illuminates the various worlds and their bright swirling colours. We fly over a ringed scarlet orb and then under a soaring green giant flowing with ripples of cyan as behind us the VIA warships close in.

"Make it to the next chamber," 23 says. "I've got an idea."

46

As we cruise behind a VIA warship I glimpse the others looking for us in neighbouring chambers. This part of MidZone is very bright after the planetary darkness, with static buildings and assemblies that seem particularly inert after the swooping coloured worlds. It doesn't help that everything is rendered blue by the holographic VIA disguise around our flybike.

"Bank left towards the middle exit," 23 says.

Ashel 5's breathing slows with exhaustion.

"Ashel 5?" I say.

She straightens consciously.

"I'm fine."

"Another warship just came in behind you," 23 says.

I turn and see it glide above helical towers on a path at ninety degrees to ours.

"Oh-" Ashel 5 says.

"Pull up!" 23 shouts.

"Damn," Ashel 5 says.

I look down. The lower section of our warship hologram is embedded in the top of a building.

"They've seen you," 23 says. "Go!"

The flybike leaps forward as warships accelerate towards us. One fires a cannon shot that destroys an upper section of the nearest tower.

"Charity Freestone! Land or we will shoot you down," a deafening voice says.

"Hold tight," 23 says.

The flybike is suddenly possessed and we cling on as it zigzags up until the ceiling is a bright rushing surface just above us. The warships occupy most exits but 23 has found a way out in one high corner. Ashel 5 and I duck as we flash through and angle down towards the train tube on the chamber's far side.

The flybike jolts and the hologram around us buzzes, then fades. Instinctively I look down and regret it. We're missing one runner and a Basis interaction pad, while past the damage is a height I don't want to think about.

"I've lost remote control," 23 says. "Ashel 5?"

"Got it," Ashel 5 says.

She grips the joystick like it's an opponent. The flybike actually steadies but then another shot grazes us. We spin again, the power cuts out and we drop.

Each moment seems to last ages and every detail is drearily clear. The train station is a hundred or so metres away, while the enlarging ground features a crossroads whose centre we race towards like a shot fired at a target.

We jerk left and I realise we haven't lost power; Ashel 5 just switched it off, then on again. Awkwardly, we race for the waiting train carriage but our descent is too steep. We hit the floor and judder along as the saddle batters us. Ashel 5 dumps the restraints; we're thrown clear and the flybike smashes into a wall.

I land hard but the jumpsuit lessens the impact. Ashel 5 cries out and I realise she has no such protection. Fear drives me to my feet, wobbly with shock. I stagger to Ashel 5 sprawled on the floor and haul her up, shoving her ahead of me as blood flows down her left arm.

A warship flies over us to land in our way. We run under its descending bulk, which protects us from the others. The whine of its pads gets louder as Ashel 5 sprints out of the way. I actually feel the hull touch the top of my head before I throw myself forward and roll clear.

I hear shouts and booted feet as the warship disgorges soldiers from the far side of the vessel. However, a cannon with a giant **23** on the side grows out of the floor nearby and shoots at the VIA troops. They run in all directions as 23 turns her attention to the warship, battering it so hard it's nudged along the floor before toppling over with a surprisingly muted crunch. 23 then shoots the airborne VIA craft; one falls out of the air and another is knocked into the warship behind. Amid the chaos I finally reach our carriage and duck inside, where Ashel 5 is standing on a seat.

"Get up," she says.

I jump onto another chair as a warship cannon beam crackles around the inside of the carriage before voiding to hit the soldiers chasing us. The doors close and we move off.

Ashel 5 and I stand numb and exhausted. Instead of her usual pale hue she is grey; her face red-eyed and doughy. I climb down and go over to her. She seems too tired to move and I help her down, feeling her weight as she leans on me.

Sitting next to her I try to control flashbacks: the Multimage, Lin Lin Lin reaching for me, the flybike falling.

Steeber and I related.

Our velocity is like rushing sickness and I fight to remain steady. Shaking my head, I focus on Ashel 5. The blood sliding down her arm is slower now and I look up into her face.

"You are some berserker drone, lady," I say.

Ashel 5's mouth twitches up at the right corner.

"What was it like?"

Ashel 5 thinks for a moment.

"Purposeful," she says. "Things make a lot more sense now."

"In what way?"

"Natora Stein always said I'd know what to do when the time came; that it was something I could never train for but was waiting for me when I needed it. I suppose until today I never did."

We sit there for a while.

"Did you mean what you said?" she says. "About, um, I was your... er..."

"Friend. Yes. Is that all right?"

319

Ashel 5 nods and sighs, happily I think although the movement makes her grimace. She fumbles in her utility belt and pulls out a patch that she places over the wound in her left arm, gasping as it takes effect.

Steeber calls and the carriage seems to tilt.

I breathe and focus, consciously feeling the seat beneath me and the carriage deck under my boots. I feel 23's presence, the touch of Ashel 5's wrist against the back of mine and see the Firenze 44 patent Lin Lin Lin gave me. These things give me strength and I realise that as long as I can decide not to collapse I will stay upright.

I get to my feet and accept the call.

Steeber stands in front of me and we stare at each other. Another holo appears to Steeber's right: Harlan unconscious with a fuze at his head. I look at Harlan, I look at the fuze and then I look back at Steeber.

Ashel 5 gets up and stands beside me. Orange light flickers in the carriage as another figure materialises by my right shoulder: tall, female and made from a million tiny flashing 23s. I wait with my friends and watch the enemy assess his options.

The moment is long and terrible.

I notice the hand holding the fuze is not Steeber's and wonder whose it is, while inside me is a screaming; so powerful I expect someone to tell me to be quiet. The hand tenses, the barrel closing on Harlan's temple.

I must not break.

Steeber ends the call. I cry out and sag slightly but Ashel 5 holds me up.

"I don't think he's killed Harlan," I say. "I don't."

"Steeber tends not to make mistakes like that," 23 says.

I'm not sure I can function with this uncertainty and yet, somehow, I do. Ashel 5's hand on my arm helps, as does 23's orange glow.

I imagine Harlan with blood pouring from his head, seeing it whether my eyes are open or not. I can't comprehend him dead though; it's too big, as big as the world.

Harlan, I'm sorry.

I love you.

47

I open my eyes and carriage chairs come into focus. Blearily I look around and see we are in motion; 23 must have put us on a loop around the city. The carriage is silent except for steady breathing nearby, which tells me Ashel 5 is still asleep.

According to the Aerac, nine hours have passed and guilty fear is a sudden cramp. How can I have slept so long? I check messages, but there are none from Steeber. The need to know about Harlan is so powerful I nearly faint, and lie there as if paralysed. Thirst gets me going; I sit up, stiff-limbed, and suck water from the jumpsuit. I struggle to keep the warm liquid down but once I've managed it I get up and stretch warily.

"Hello, Charity," 23 says, just a voice in my head again.

"Hi, 23."

My voice is flat but my mind begins to work, reluctantly.

"Have you still got those recs around the Fulcrus tower?" I say.

"Yes."

"Anything?" I say.

"Not about Harlan I'm afraid, but I have been tracking a ship full of Steeber's mercs that left Fulcrus tower seven hours ago," 23 says.

"Where did it go?" I say, using the jumpsuit sleeve to rub my face and hair clean.

"The Outer Spheres by some painfully roundabout route, so I haven't got exact landing coordinates."

"It must be important to give us such a rinsing," I say.

"That's what I thought, so I put up recs over the entire area," 23 says.

"And?"

"Nothing. Someone has to go and look around properly. Ask Ashel 5."

"Not me?"

"You've got a better target Charity."

"Steeber," I say.

"He left Fulcrus on his own, five minutes ago."

I find myself relishing the prospect, as if Steeber is a weird nagging pain I can't leave alone.

"Good," I say.

"I'm low on kilos," 23 says.

"I'll transfer mine to you."

"Transfer two thirds and hang on to the rest."

I give Lin Lin Lin's kilos to 23. There is a pause.

"I'll use them wisely Charity."

"I know."

"She did you a great service, in the end."

"She did."

There's another pause.

"Charity, you were right not to leave Ashel 5. She's a real friend. Look after her."

"Will you help me with that?"

"Yes."

"Thanks, 23."

Ashel 5 lies curled on the floor nearby, head resting on her right arm and lush black hair spread out like a cloud. Most people look vulnerable when they sleep, but Ashel 5 particularly so because of the contrast when she's awake. With eyelids closed over that laser gaze she seems younger and I realise she's probably only a few years older than me.

Kneeling, I touch her pale, wood-like arm.

"Ashel 5, wake up."

She stirs and opens her eyes. For a moment she looks rather sweet and then the intense glare rises like a dark sun.

"Morning," I say. "Are you all right?"

Ashel 5 stretches on the floor with a kind of muscular sigh and sits up.

"Yes."

She licks dry lips and I lean over to offer the water tube from my jumpsuit. Ashel 5 drinks from it thirstily, her head angled under my jaw. The warm smell of her thick hair rises, as intimate as seeing her sleep. She finishes and leans back against the edge of the seat.

"Thank you," she says. "Any news?"

"No…"

I sway, giddy again. Ashel 5 grips my shoulder, steadying me. We look into each other's eyes.

"I'm sure he's still alive," she says.

I nod, no longer certain of anything. I carefully climb to my feet as Ashel 5 gets up, flips open a belt pouch and pulls out a smart cloth.

"What's the plan?" she says.

I send her the Outer Spheres coordinates.

"A ship from the Fulcrus tower went there," I say.

Ashel 5 runs the cloth over her extraordinary body with a vigour that suggests accumulated grime is an enemy to be obliterated.

"Why?" she says.

"Not sure," I say. "Just that it's important."

"These coordinates cover a kilometre."

"We don't know the exact landing site, or even what we're looking for," 23 says.

"Would you mind checking it out, Ashel 5?" I say.

"Don't you want me to stay with you?" Ashel 5 says.

"Yes, but our army only has three people and one of them doesn't really do anything."

"Piss off," 23 says.

"How well do you know the Outer Spheres?" I say.

"Well enough," Ashel 5 says, starting on her hair. "I'll be careful."

"My focus has to be Charity," 23 says, "but I'll back you up when I can."

"You don't have to do that," Ashel 5 says.

"You're not on your own any more, Ashel 5," I say.

Ashel 5 blinks and swallows. She goes to speak but can't for a moment. Finally, she nods.

"What will you do?" she says, folding the smart cloth back into her belt.

"Go after Steeber," I say.

Ashel 5 frowns.

"I'll be okay," I tell her. "I know him best."

"Train stop in one minute," 23 says. "Charity, you stay on that carriage. Ashel 5, hop off now and get the next one; it will take you to the centre of those coordinates."

Ashel 5 and I stand there for a moment.

"Well," I say.

She extends her hand. I go to take it and she gently grips my forearm. I grip hers in return.

"Take care, Golden Princess," Ashel 5 says.

"You too, Beautiful Gun," I say.

She smiles! Her teeth are big and white and her smile turns her from striking to beautiful. I pull her to me and put my other arm around her. Our clasped hands are between us, nearly awkward but not quite. Her hand cups my shoulder and we hold each other.

The train slows. As we let go, Ashel 5 takes her last fuze out of its holster and slips it into mine.

"But-" I say.

"I'll get another one," she says.

The doors open. Ashel 5 steps onto the deserted platform and for a moment she is framed there: dark hair down her back past empty rifle holsters and that unmistakable, sparsely clad physique. Then the doors close and the carriage begins to move, leaving my friend behind.

48

"The feed from Roscoe Trage's gun is still live," 23 says. "Lisle Trage is all dolled up to meet Steeber."

"Where is this romantic encounter?"

"She mentioned a hotel called the Barfield."

"Nice."

"You're booked in, Miss Freestone from Centria, and arrive in six minutes. Try not to break anything."

The train rushes through its vacuum tube. I try and relax into the seat, but ignorance of Harlan's fate is like an energy field that subsists by draining my strength. This, then, is power: not just the ability to make terrifying decisions but the stamina to live with their unknowable consequences.

I try and distract myself by investigating the Barfield Hotel. Sited in its own chamber, the hotel is an elegant, shell-like structure in the heart of a complex Old World landscape. Meadows next to the building subtly reflect its contours and then break up into wooded areas studded with boutique habitats. Diamond City's flora comes in every colour but the Barfield has focussed on green, from near white to emerald-black.

There's even weather; not the Diamond City conflation of publicity, marketing and media but the Old World version with sunlight and rain. It's regulated by a random selection algorithm so no one can predict exactly what the climate will do but, says the brochure, it always feels right.

The Barfield Hotel is so appealing I actually regret that the purpose of my visit is to kill a distant relative.

The carriage glides to a halt; the doors open and I step out. At the edge of the chamber the train station is sealed off from the hotel with a quarter sphere barrier connecting floor and wall.

"Any other ways in or out?" I say.

"The chamber's original entrances have been sealed," 23 says. "It prevents anyone who can't afford a train ticket getting in while allowing the Barfield to screen everyone who can."

The hotel calls and I accept. A small window opens in my upper left vision to reveal a smiling young man with dark green hair.

"Good morning, Miss Freestone; my name is Chet. Welcome to the Barfield Hotel."

"Good morning, Chet. How are you?"

"I'm great, thank you for asking! And you?"

"Looking forward to getting inside, Chet."

"I don't blame you. There is one small matter to resolve: your sidearm."

"I'm looking after it for a friend."

"Of course. Unfortunately, there are no weapons allowed in the hotel."

"Can't I just gif another one?"

"It's all closed protocol in here," Chet says.

"Why?"

"Because we have room service!"

"Chet, I quite understand but this fuze genuinely isn't mine."

"Why don't we look after it for you?" Chet says.

A panel in the wall glows light green.

"Just press the weapon against that green area, Miss Freestone. The locker will keep it secure for you."

I take off the holstered fuze and press it against the panel. It's absorbed and as the wall goes opaque again I feel like I'm burying Ashel 5.

"Thank you, Miss Freestone," Chet says.

The door slides open and I walk through into a damp, slightly misty morning.

"Welcome to the Barfield. Have a lovely stay!"

"Thanks, Chet."

Chet's window vanishes and I look around.

The chamber's cylindrical walls leading up into soft, blue air are disguised by greenery and rocks, while beams of gold-hued light angle down through the heavy white clouds so splendidly I have to remind myself there isn't a sun. The air tastes good with its vegetable hints and just-washed flavour, so I inhale deeply a few times before setting off across the damp grass of the meadow. The sensation is pleasant but slightly disorienting; I have walked on grass before but not like this: so uneven, real and mucky. I increase my speed and the hotel enlarges before me.

"Do you know where Steeber is in there?" I say.

"Not exactly," 23 says. "Lisle Trage mentioned a view, so it will be one of the outer rooms on an upper floor."

"How many floors are there?"

"Seventy," 23 says.

"Typical."

"Don't fret, princess; Lisle isn't there yet. You've got time to scope out the lobby, find somewhere to hide and then follow her when she arrives."

"What's taking her so long?"

"She's struggling with the surgery. I don't know whether it's psychological or because she physically can't take it any more. Maybe both."

I recall the Infinity Box to stamp out any sympathy and walk into the Barfield's lobby. The place has a low ceiling and subtle décor with a lot of dark wood, giving it a cosy, rich feel. It isn't very big and there is nowhere to hide.

"23…"

"I know. They burned the recs I sent in with you, so I'm doing the virtual tour to get a sense of layout."

I glance out of a window.

"She's coming," I say.

"Did she see you?"

Lisle approaches, her footsteps hurried. I duck to the right of the doorway with my back to the wall and Lisle rushes in, too focussed on her problems to notice me.

"No," I say.

Lisle heads across the lobby without looking back and I follow her into a broad corridor that becomes a shallow, upward-leading spiral. Maintaining distance, I stay close to the wall. Soon, Lisle stops next to a bank of elevators with transparent walls. I stop too, unsure how I will follow.

"Keep going past her," 23 says. "After another floor there's an atrium, so you'll be able to see where she gets off."

I move quietly past Lisle as she walks into the elevator. Sprinting out of sight before she turns, I reach the top of the ramp where the ceiling opens into a broad space with the elevators against one wall. Lisle's elevator appears and I count the floors she passes, getting smaller as she goes. She stops at fifteen, walks out of the elevator and turns left.

I run into the nearest elevator and select the fifteenth floor. Clenching my fists, I try not to think about Harlan as the elevator rises. Floor eight, floor nine, floor ten… Come *on!*

Eventually, I arrive and squeeze through the doors before they fully open. Turning left, I race along the plush-carpeted corridor and around a corner. I spot Lisle at a doorway and speed up, covering the distance so fast she barely has time to notice. We crash into the room together and I throw her aside.

The room is empty. The ornate bed with its swirly head-frame is too low to get under; there are no cupboards to hide in and no connecting rooms. I round on Lisle Trage.

"Where is he?" I shout.

"I-I don't know!" Lisle says. "He said he was going to be here, but I'm late and-and he might have gone. Oh God I'm stupid. I'm sorry, I-"

She starts to sob.

"Lisle," I say.

She shakes her head so I grip her shoulders.

"Lisle, is this definitely the right room?"

"Yes! He would have told me if he'd changed it."

"Does he usually change rooms?" I say.

"No. He doesn't change anything."

She finally looks me in the eye.

"He could of course," she says.

"What do you mean?"

"He could have any room here he wants."

"Why?"

"The Barfield Hotel is his," Lisle says.

All my energy turns to dread.

"His?" I say.

"Charity…" 23 says.

"Well," Lisle says, "he built it."

"Get out!" 23 shouts.

Something weird happens to the walls. They shift like a resonating surface and then leap at us, the bed swivelling as if possessed. I haven't got time to be scared as the walls hit.

It takes a frustratingly long time to realise I'm not dead; just suspended in cold jelly, although I can't breathe. Lisle slowly writhes beside me but it's impossible to move properly in this thick substance. Something passes against the toe of my boot and from the shape I recognise the head-frame. I hook my foot into it and the bed's greater weight pulls me down through dark gloop. Lisle slips by; I get hold of her and grip her tight as she tries to thrash.

Suddenly, the bed yanks us down and we plop through the ceiling of the room below. The bed thuds to the floor; we land wetly on it and I sprawl as Lisle is jerked from my hands. I push goo-sodden hair out of my face, get up and pull Lisle Trage to her feet.

The walls around us tremble.

I lunge for the door and this time the momentum is enough for us to burst through into the corridor. Behind me the room solidifies in its distorted shape, too late to trap us. I take Lisle's hand and we run for the elevators as the corridor begins to ripple.

To our right, a door slaps open and a naked couple runs out crying.

"In there, Charity," 23 says.

I consider ignoring her.

"You're going the wrong way," 23 says. "You want to be outside the hotel, not inside."

I see what she means: the room has a balcony with a view over the parklands. I skid to a halt and yank Lisle back. She sputters with confusion but follows as I cross the melting space to the balcony, formed like an open pocket in the surface of the building. I look over the side. The balcony is above the lobby roof, at the end of a steep slope formed in the shell-like external structure. I nod towards it.

"Come on," I say.

"No! You're insane!"

"I won't tell you again."

"I'm scared of heights-!"

I backslap her across the face and it's as satisfying as I expect. She stumbles; I spin her round so her back is against my front and hoist us onto the balcony wall. The wall softens and we slide through to spin down the steep exterior. It begins to dissolve, but for now our speed keeps us on the surface. All I can do is take in the lush view with its myriad green tones and delightful contours. How could *Steeber* have created a place like this?

I clench my buttocks against the oily shell as if that will help. Lisle moans and wriggles, so I hold her tighter.

"Shh," I say.

Her legs twitch nervously, slipping off the front of mine and into the building. It hardens and I'm slung forward as Lisle is trapped up to the waist in solid diamond. I cling to her wrists, somersault over her and slam against the now-solid wall. I fight to grip Lisle's slippery skin. She screams; I look down and consider joining in.

Beneath me the slope down to the lobby roof has gone and the wall now curves back under itself. The lobby remains but is a good five floors below and too far to jump.

I click on the Firenze patent and my right hand glows gold. I let go to press it against the diamond holding Lisle, but nothing happens.

"You're pulling my arm out!" Lisle screams.

I take hold of her wrist again and look up into her face.

"You need to calm down, Lisle," I say.

"Let go! It's you he wants!"

"When he's got me he will let you die with everyone else."

My arms ache as I struggle to hold on. Lisle sobs, unreachable.

I look down again to see the lobby roof move. A hump appears as if something monstrous is about to surface. The hump grows, thinning out as it rises towards us and lengthens into a kind of tentacle. It passes the first floor and the second, reaching up towards my helpless dangling legs.

Something pops in Lisle's left shoulder and I'm jolted down towards the rising tentacle. Lisle is worryingly silent as I let go of her wrist and seize the front of her flimsy top instead. The other end is trapped in the wall so it doesn't give, but I've bought no more than a few seconds.

One side of the chamber is lit by an explosion. Its roar is muffled by moving surfaces, but it still cuts the green with dazzling white and yellow. Something flies at speed through disintegrating scenery towards us: an armoured flybike with a cannon on the front.

It's too late though. The tentacle has reached my boots and flows up around me. It reaches my waist in a second and gets thicker and stronger as it comes.

"I'm nearly there, Charity," 23 says.

The flybike cannon fires a red beam into the tentacle; it bursts, but as the fragments fall away the entire hotel shivers and begins to move. However, Steeber has weakened the wall; the block holding Lisle begins to slide out and I start to drop. My fall is arrested before I can scream as the wall engulfs Lisle, hardens again and once more begins creeping towards me.

Below us, parks and woodland melt into a thick green sea that slides towards the hotel. Lisle's top tears so I let go. Clinging to her right wrist with both hands I swing above the gliding landscape, which reaches the Barfield and starts to flow up it. Desperate now, I look around and see the top of the building form a kind of arm that reaches down for me.

The flybike arrives beneath us and I drop onto the saddle. For a moment I can't move my exhausted arms and under 23's control the flybike eases away from the woman drowning in the wall.

"We can't leave her, 23," I say.

"We can."

"Must we do this again? Get her out!"

23 humphs, but the flybike spins around and its cannon blasts away the structure holding Lisle. We glide closer as the green sea and the arm close in. Horribly, both contain people, struggling to remain afloat even though the surface of the arm is suspended high above the ground. A few drop out, fall past us and land in the rising green tide.

Most of Lisle is free; I stand on the flybike runners and try to pull her loose completely but she won't come. She flops instead, her jaw slack. I've lost track of how long she was under.

The arm and tide are only a few metres away. I heave again; Lisle tumbles out and nearly knocks me off the flybike. I drape her over the front of the saddle and restraints wrap around her arms and legs. We accelerate away from what's left of the Barfield, where arm and tide meet with a faint wet slap. They writhe for a moment as if fighting and then twist into a new structure that comes after us.

"Up!" I say.

The flybike rises vertically as the clouds around us get thicker and blacker.

"Don't worry about those, 23," I say. "The weather is on a random-"

A flash blinds me and there's a deafening crash-

After stunned seconds I try and process the noise. It didn't sound like ordnance; it was too chaotic. There's another flash and then a second boom. It's so loud the stabbing agony in my ears seems to meet in the centre of my brain and I feel myself scream although I can't hear it.

The flybike spins slowly in darkening air and drops of water scatter across my face. The rain quickly intensifies until it's a deluge, lashing us until I struggle to see.

I don't think the weather is random anymore, Charity, 23 messages.

I keep my head down to protect my eyes. Far below the flybike, the seethe is dark grey in this light. I notice a strange pattern in it and at first I think it's caused by the obscuring rain, but then I see a series of lines that divide the mass into equal parts. The lines brighten as the floor becomes visible through them and then the whole thing separates into four distinct blocks, one by each exit. People struggle free of the blocks and stumble through heavy vapour boiling from the floor. The steam rises to mingle with the storm, feeding the precipitate around us until it's dense enough to limit breathing.

I'm blinded again. I press my hands to my ears as another thunderclap hits and then another. The flybike jolts-

When I come to we are falling end over end and the flybike whine is audible even to my numbed ears. My vision is diminished although after a long moment I realise it's hair pushed into my eyes by the water streaming over my head. There's another flash but it's softer and tinged with red:

REMOTE CONTROL LOST

I lean over Lisle to seize the flybike controls and put us into a controlled descent. It takes us away from the storm but back towards the blocks below. At least the steam has eased off; the air is now so thick with water I doubt there's capacity for more.

The green blocks begin to flow together without losing mass. I can't make sense of it, until I realise Steeber is giffing more material to trap us with. The floor is almost completely covered now; he probably has enough kilos to fill this entire chamber.

I scan a diminishing section of uncovered floor. It has reverted to open protocol, so I go in-Aer and select a bomb. A favourite of the NFE's, it is almost as powerful as a nuke but without the radiation. I haven't got enough kilos in my own account to buy it though.

Send me the rest of our kilos, 23.

For a moment nothing happens and amid my panic I get a stab of fear for 23.

That bomb won't be big enough, Charity.

It's all we can afford – come on!

You want to detonate a bomb under a viscous liquid; the blast will be absorbed before it can do sufficient damage.

The mass begins to close over the floor completely. Soon we won't be able to gif anything and all the exits will be covered again.

We should use this one, 23 messages.

It is nearly half a million kilos; I know we haven't got that much. However, the image of the bomb flashes to indicate purchase; I glimpse the dark shadow as it forms in the floor, just before the green tide covers it. I haven't got time to think about how 23 has worked this miracle, and instead direct the flybike up towards the storm again. Barely able see through sleeting rain, I must rely on memory for direction.

The bomb grows, thrusting into the mass below. Soon the in-Aer fire control appears but I decide to let Steeber use up more of his kilos; hopefully when I detonate I will bankrupt the bastard. The green tide gets closer and I accelerate into the clouds.

I'm in the heart of chaos now, as the vast power locked into the weather presses against me. There's less rain but more electricity and I feel it build like rising panic, terrified the next flash of lightning or clout of thunder will kill me. Unable to make sense of my speed I dare not go faster because I can't see where I'm going.

Suddenly, I am in clear air; the ceiling only metres away and about to crush my skull. I bank hard left and for a second we hang upside down in a weird, calm zone between roiling black clouds and the featureless ceiling. Straightening up, I move to the outer edge of the chamber and put my hand on Lisle's back. When I feel her shallow breathing, I pat her comfortingly.

A sequence of flashes lights the clouds below and I put my hands over my ears as thunder seems to crack the air itself. It goes on and on, an ocean of sound overlaying the cloudscape until finally the noise fades and the pressure around me eases. The clouds seem to lose density and drift apart slightly.

I see green movement below and detonate the explosive. There is distant vibration, a weird gurgle and then the green tide leaps through the clouds to engulf us. For a moment I wonder if I've left it too late and then notice the substance is hot and tingly as the technology inside is wrecked.

It falls away to leave us airborne. I wait for a minute and then descend into the storm. Thunder still rumbles but it is weak now, its power expended.

We emerge from the dissipating cloud base to see the green tide recede. With no structure to hold it together the stuff floods into the surrounding chambers, leaving all exits free. I avoid them, wary of more traps and head for the train station instead.

Tickets booked messages 23. **Train gets here in eighteen seconds.**

Spotting Ashel 5's fuze in its holster on the floor, I ease the flybike onto its side and pick the weapon up. I press the holster to my hip as the carriage arrives; its doors open and I fly straight through them, stopping in the gangway between the carriage seats.

I pull out the fuze, turn in the saddle and aim back into the chamber. The remains of the Barfield are finally absorbed, leaving the high cylindrical chamber empty. Nonetheless, I keep the fuze extended as the doors close and the carriage moves off, taking us far away in seconds.

49

"How much do you think I hate you, Roscoe?" I say.

Roscoe Trage's haggard, scared-looking holo stands before me as he tries to guess the right answer. I sigh and look around the large MidZone office. I could have had a hotel room, but I'm off hotels.

I look rather good, considering. All the gunk has gone, my hair is clean and shiny and I wear thick make-up to cover the enervated exhaustion that will not subside into sleep.

Roscoe shakes his head.

"Dunno," he says.

"Try and work it out," I say.

"Dunno," he says again.

"Okay," I say. "How much do you hate Steeber?"

"Is he there?"

"Of course he isn't fucking here. How much?"

"A lot," Roscoe says.

"Completely?"

"Yes."

"Now we're getting somewhere," I say. "Let's quantify this. You're all right with words like 'quantify' are you? Not too complicated?"

"I can deal with quantity."

"Quanti-*fy*."

He nods.

"So, let's say the amount you hate Steeber is a unit of hatred," I say. "We'll call it one Steeber. Got that?"

"Yeah."

"How many Steebers add up to how much I hate you?"

"Five?" Roscoe says.

I laugh in his face and then suddenly stop.

"No," I say.

"Ten," he says.

"Keep going."

"Twenty."

"You're not that important."

"Dunno. Thirteen? No, that's unlucky. Fourteen."

I regard him for a while and then I nod.

"Fourteen Steebers. That's a lot of hate, Roscoe."

"I'm sorry."

"For which particular thing?"

"All of it."

"Ambushing my friends; turning me over to be tortured."

"Yes-"

"After all that, I came to help you and you sold me out to Lin Lin Lin."

"Charity, please…"

"Lin Lin Lin's dead, Roscoe."

He stares at me in disbelief. It's as if his large body is hollow and made from the flimsiest fabric, barely keeping its shape.

"How do I look to you?" I say.

"B-beautiful?"

"Try again."

Confused, he shakes his head in frustration. I continue to stare at him. Finally, he looks up.

"The same," he says.

"That's right, Roscoe: the same. You, Lin Lin Lin and Steeber couldn't put a dent in me. And I hate you. How does that make you feel?"

"Obedient," he says.

"Well done!" I say, genuinely surprised.

"What do you want me to do?"

"I need to get into Fulcrus, but for obvious reasons can't just turn up. You will go there and report to me on current defences.

Based on that information, I will decide what to do next. Simple enough?"

"Yes."

I nod at him pleasantly. He swallows.

"Now you're a creature of habit, Roscoe. You don't want to be on my side because you still think Steeber will win."

"I won't betray you, Charity."

"You will. That's why I need you to look at something."

Another hologram appears between us. It is the Infinity Box, only this time the occupant is Lisle Trage, whose eyes are closed. Roscoe groans and clutches his head.

"That's what they did to me, Roscoe. It's what they did to my beloved as well. It seems only fitting that I will do the same to Lisle."

Roscoe starts to cry.

"Please," he says. "Sh-she isn't strong."

"I know she isn't. That's why she's asleep for now, but imagine how she's going to feel when she wakes up."

"No, no…"

"Shall I stuff her full of adrenaline, like they did to me? Or flood that box with freezing water and poison, like they did to me? Or with deafening sound, like they did to me?"

"I'll do it, I'll do it!"

I regard him and slow my breathing back down very deliberately.

"If they take me again, that box will get smaller and smaller until your wife is just so much pulp. She will be aware of every crushing moment. Do you understand?"

"Yes," he says.

"Open an AV vix link so I know what you're doing," I say.

His point of view appears in the corner of my vision. It shows a cold, angry young woman glaring at him.

"Go now," I say.

Roscoe's hologram disappears. I look across the floor to where

Lisle Trage lies in the Basis, slowly becoming a woman again at my expense as psych programs try and iron out her trauma.

"Soft as shit, you are," 23 says.

"We'll see," I say.

50

Roscoe rises up the tower in an elevator until he reaches Fulcrus. He does not stop there, because each floor has men in black uniforms patrolling the brightly coloured shapes.

"I couldn't see Steeber," I tell 23.

Roscoe, who is out of our comms loop for now, proceeds up the tower and leaves Fulcrus behind.

"Me neither," 23 says.

"How many mercs did you count?" I say.

"Twenty on each floor," she says.

"We need to even the odds," I say.

"How?"

"I give Roscoe the Firenze patent and he releases the NFE."

"Very good, Charity. Roscoe needs to actually get to the NFE though."

"How about a distraction to help him?"

23 thinks.

"I've got just the thing," she says.

Roscoe's elevator proceeds from the outside of the tower along the underside of the dock, turning as it goes and then rising to open on the empty landing area. I bring him in on our comms.

"Roscoe," I say.

The view jerks slightly as he hears me.

"You need to get into the top floor of Fulcrus, the one with the high ceiling. At the centre is a large black box, the only one there. Inside are people wearing what look like black oval helmets over their entire heads. Got that?"

"Yes," Roscoe says.

"I'm sending you a patent," I say. "When you activate it, your hand will glow. Touching any of those shapes with your glowing hand will release the person inside."

"Who are they?" Roscoe says.

"The NFE," I say.

"They'll fucking kill me!"

"We will tell them not to," 23 says.

"You won't."

"Believe it or not, I want you and Lisle and Buddy together again," I say.

"I don't deserve that," he says.

"My partner and your son are inside that place, Roscoe. For now we've got an advantage."

The view steadies.

"All right," he says. "But there's loads of arseholes in black about."

"Twenty on each floor," I say.

I wait for him to protest, but instead he pulls out the Remy.

"Is that all?" he says.

"Try and get to the black box without anyone noticing," I say.

"There was some of 'em at the lifts," Roscoe says.

"We can take care of that," 23 says.

"Go down six floors," I say.

As Roscoe descends, his breath quickens with nerves. We reach an empty floor; the elevator stops and its doors open.

"Roscoe, pick up the fuzes when I gif them," I say. "How many NFE are in that box, 23?"

"Nineteen."

Feeling slightly sorry for the mercs, I gif a pack and nineteen small fuzes. Roscoe puts them in the pack and grunts as he lifts it. He steps back into the elevator, which begins to move again.

"You'll be there in ten seconds," 23 says.

I hear Roscoe count down under his breath as the floors pass.

A light ring around the tower suddenly explodes and the remaining illumination goes dark as 23 detonates a vert bomb. A strange banging increases in volume as Roscoe arrives at Fulcrus and extends the Remy before him. The elevator doors open and immediately the banging becomes deafening, as if someone is hitting the tower repeatedly with a massive hammer.

Two mercs whose uniforms are pale in the altered light stand nearby, half turned away to follow the progress of colleagues running towards the source of the noise. Alerted by the elevator's movement, the pair spin around but Roscoe shoots both before they can fire.

The light begins to return to normal and then changes again as 23 detonates another vert bomb. The noise in the room gets even louder.

"What *is* that?" I say.

"Free-floating speaker outside each floor," 23 says.

"Effective," I say.

"Cheap," she says.

Roscoe shoots another merc, the gunfire hidden in 23's noise. As the merc falls, I see his uniform has a logo formed by the words 'Leveraged Solutions'. Up ahead looms a white rectangle.

"In there Roscoe," I say.

A line of paler light on the front of the rectangle spreads into a square as the doorway slides open. Roscoe runs inside but all I can see is a haze full of vague movement before the door closes again, cutting off the effects of the vert bomb and leaving Roscoe in total darkness. Outside, the relentless clacking continues, while closer by are the sounds of bare feet on diamond floor and the soft breathing of the soldiers.

Roscoe's hand is a sudden flare in the darkness. It illuminates the figures around him and reflects off their awful ovoid heads. Roscoe presses his hand against the nearest immersion rig, which I think is worn by Iqbal. As the ovoid begins to lose definition, Roscoe moves quickly around the box, touching each captive in turn.

In the glowing light I see the ovoids melt away to reveal familiar profiles as the movement around Roscoe stops. There are a few gasps and someone cries out.

"Holster that weapon, Roscoe," 23 says.

Roscoe hesitates and then does as he is told. The glow in his hand begins to fade and then brightens again as he reactivates the Firenze patent. A couple of the NFE slump to the floor. One tall figure nearby sways and shakes his head.

"Oppo," the Ledge says.

"Sir," 23 says. "You were captured and subjected to an immersion rig that Roscoe Trage has now deactivated. Do not kill or harm him."

"Wanker," someone mutters.

"Charity?" the Ledge says.

"Here, sir."

"You okay?"

"Yes, Captain."

"Who's got us, 23?"

"A company called Fulcrus, which is owned by Steeber Loke," 23 says. "You are in a unit inside their tower in MidZone. There are three floors with about twenty armed mercenaries on each. Trage has a fuze for each of you."

Roscoe holds out the pack and each of the NFE takes a weapon.

"What about Steeber Loke?" the Ledge says.

"Kill him on sight," I say.

"More mercs approaching the Fulrus tower," 23 says.

"Captain, I'm sending you a patent," I say. "When the area is safe, use it on the coloured shapes."

"Coloured shapes?" the Ledge says.

"You'll see what I mean, sir."

The door to the enclosure opens; normal light shines in and 23's racket suddenly stops.

"Let's go," the Ledge says.

The NFE move so fast it's as if they have simply flowed out of sight. Roscoe stands there for a moment, then jumps at the sound of gunfire and screaming.

I call Leveraged Solutions. A craggy-faced man appears on a window to the right of my vision.

"Leveraged Solutions," he says.

"I'm Charity Freestone of the New Form Enterprise. Your men have engaged us in a company called Fulcrus."

The man's eyes widen.

"The NFE?" he says. "But it was just a guarding job."

"It's us you were guarding."

"Let me check with the site."

There's a very short pause.

"Oh," he says.

"You've got more operatives on the way. Stand them down and tell those onsite to leave the building or they will all die."

Outside, there is more shouting and then the gunfire dies out.

"Thank you," I say.

I end the call.

"Roscoe, check outside," I say.

The view changes as Roscoe leaves the block. He heads for the elevators, arriving in time to see the last black-clad men leave.

Nearby, Velasquez presses a glowing hand to the side of an orange pyramid, which melts to reveal a small, brown-skinned man who blinks in astonishment. Velasquez helps him to his feet.

"Send him the patent, Velasquez," I say.

There's a pause and then Velasquez presses her hand to a green cube, while the man presses his to a yellow cone. The cube reveals a little girl and the cone a blonde woman. More glowing points appear throughout the room and the coloured shapes begin to vanish.

In the office, I come out of the vix link and turn to Lisle Trage, who looks very pretty in the red and yellow outfit she has chosen.

"Time to go, Lisle," I say.

51

The Fulcrus tower is surrounded by ships that glint in the light of the circling ring. I drop the armoured flybike beneath them to the floor above Fulcrus and blast through the outer wall. Behind me, Lisle grips my waist as we fly in to skim over the empty floor. I land beside the elevators and we jump off the bike.

The elevators are all full. We wait. I grunt and shift with frustration. Lisle squeezes my hand and I squeeze it back. Finally, an elevator stops and we squeeze in. Around us, people's faces are bright with apprehensive hope.

The elevator drops one floor to Fulcrus. When the doors open, I am borne into the packed room by an almost hysterical tide and quickly lose sight of Lisle.

I call Harlan but there's no reply. Perhaps they haven't got to him yet.

As I move slowly across the floor, people around me hold each other, cry, apologise, laugh, argue; sometimes all at the same time. The noise is huge, almost overwhelming and I have to work to keep steady.

I spot a tall black man (he hasn't got dreads), run over (he is too slim), grab his arm (his skin tone is wrong)-

"Harlan!"

It isn't him.

I call again without success, impatience building into rage. Names flick past as I scan and scan but none of them are the magic combination of letters that spell my love.

I find myself at the window and stare unseeingly at it. As I touch the solid, undeniable surface air escapes me as if I'm winded. I consider inhaling again but can't quite seem to decide. There is a great cheer from behind and I turn to see the room full of rejoicing.

None of the coloured shapes remain.

"Another floor," I mutter to no one in particular.

"No," 23 says.

"He must be here!"

"Charity-"

"Maybe they put him back in the Basis."

"The unit has looked over every centimetre, Charity."

"There'll be one more shape hidden somewhere, 23."

There's a pause.

"I'm so sorry," 23 says.

You've got the makings of-

You-

You cold hard killer, Freestone.

And my despair is indeed exquisite.

Ashel 5 calls. I'm not sure I can speak, but answer anyway to make sure she is all right. Her window opens in my increasingly crowded vision, so I cut Roscoe's feed just as he sees Lisle and holds a little boy up to her.

"Charity," Ashel 5 says. "I found Harlan."

I slump against the window but somehow stay upright.

"Where?" I whisper.

"The Outer Spheres. That ship must have carried Steeber's most important victims."

"I'm sending you a key," I say before I pass out. "Activate it and press your hand against the shape he's in."

"He isn't in a shape," Ashel 5 says. "He's in a wall with the others."

She opens a vix link and I see a high, blank diamond wall.

"Er…" I say.

"Hold on," Ashel 5 says.

The picture changes and I see human figures glow in thermographic vision from floor to ceiling. Unable to move or speak, I just close my eyes and finally allow myself to register the dense emotion around me like a warm thick fog.

Ashel 5 is still talking.

"Took me a while to find him," she says.

I notice tension in her voice.

"Everything all right, Ashel 5?"

She hesitates.

"Trouble with the subs earlier," she says. "They've gone for now."

The need to get her, Harlan and those others to safety is a sudden rising force inside me. I see Ashel 5's hand glow as it approaches the wall and presses against it.

Nothing happens.

"Steeber has used a different patent," I say.

Ashel 5 presses her hand against the wall again and then starts hitting it.

"At least he's alive," 23 says. "All right, Ashel 5; you're not going to punch through that."

A black-booted foot kicks the wall and then Ashel 5 desists.

"How do I get him out?" I say.

"Kill Steeber," 23 says. "All his stuff will be deposited, including that wall."

"Where is he?" I say.

"Hiding probably," 23 says. "He knows there are a lot of angry people after him."

"What do you want me to do?" Ashel 5 says.

"Can you stay there?" I say. "When I get Harlan and the others out they'll need protecting and I'd rather it was you than anyone else."

"All right," Ashel 5 says. "I'll open a vix link."

"Thank you," I say.

As I end her call I notice the silence. I blink and look around. I'm surrounded; everyone who was spread over three floors is now here looking at me. I swallow nervously. I can't see anybody I know, although some of them were in the plaza when Fulcrus first caught me.

Pushing away from the window, I turn to see the NFE with the Trages beside them. Roscoe's big arms are around his wife and son, his face a strange mixture of joy and awe.

"The Golden Princess," he says.

Who told him about that?

"The Golden Princess," someone else says.

Soon the words spread as the glowing hands did and the crowd speaks with one voice, getting louder. I shift awkwardly; I didn't ask for this. I look at the Ledge for guidance. He smiles at me.

"The Golden Princess, the Golden Princess, *the Golden Princess-*"

"CHARITY FREESTONE!" a huge voice from outside booms.

Silence falls in the great room and then someone screams. We turn and look through the windows to see a fleet of blue VIA warships flying in stately formation around the outside of the tower. Stupidly, I start to count them but there are too many to keep track of.

Somebody named Gerrel calls. I accept and he appears as a holo in the white uniform of a VIA warship captain.

"Charity, you are required to accompany us," he says. "Given the number of people in this confined space and the resources at my disposal, I urge you not to resist. Will you comply?"

A surge in the crowd suggests if I give the word many of them will join me. However, the floor in here is still closed protocol; we cannot gif weapons and each warship will be carrying at least a hundred soldiers.

"Yes," I say.

"Thank you," Gerrel says. "Please meet us on the roof, unarmed and alone."

His hologram disappears.

"Right," the Ledge says. "We assume tactical-"

"Sir," I say.

He looks at me with faint annoyance.

"You are the best captain," I say, "but please; you can't do anything. I need to go."

He looks around. The rest of his squad look back at him. Razor nods slightly and the Ledge blinks.

"Let her go, sir," Velasquez says.

I see the Ledge clench his jaw, an unusual display of emotion for him.

"Don't let it be for nothing," I say.

He makes his decision and faces me squarely. As one, the NFE salute and I salute them back. For a moment we stand like that and then let our hands fall as I turn slowly away.

"You're not going to let her go, are you?" Roscoe Trage says to the room at large. "After all she's done for us?"

"It has to be like this, Roscoe," I say.

I take the fuze and its holster off, put them on the floor and start walking. For a moment, no one moves and I think they aren't going to let me go but then the crowd parts. As I cross the room, time seems to stretch. Some moments are so full they can't accommodate everything.

Finally, I walk into the open elevator and turn back as the doors close. I see the great room full of people and for an instant they are all clearly visible as their faces turn up to follow me. Then they are gone and I'm alone.

"You little sod," 23 says.

Well, almost alone. Time resumes its normal course despite the circumstances and eventually the elevator doors open onto the dock, where three VIA warships loom over the other vehicles. The warship weapons all point my way, as do those of the fifty or so white-armoured soldiers who surround me.

"Place your right index finger against the floor so we can neutralise the n-gun," the voice from the central ship says.

I get down on one knee and press my finger to the dock. A nerve-burning crackle reaches from the floor through my finger, up my arm and into my right ear. When it stops I get up and resist the urge to rub my hand.

The soldiers stay close as I walk to the ship. Its lower hatch opens and we enter a large bay, empty except for a floating white ball.

"Turn around, Charity," the voice says.

I obey and the ball becomes a set of linked bands around my wrists and ankles. The soldiers surround me again, weapons still up as the hatch closes. I feel the warship lift off. Checking my coordinates, I see we're heading for the heart of the city: to VIA Holdings.

52

She wears deep red in a long, twisting gown. Her hair is ornately piled and a surprisingly tasteful web of amber jewels festoons her slender neck. Loren Descarreaux steps forward as the floor carries me and six guards to the centre of the aerie above VIA Holdings and stops.

Loren's smile is a combination of gloating delight and intensely sincere charm. She extends her talons, which are painted the same arterial scarlet as the gown, and strokes my cheek with their bony tips.

"Charity," she says. "You look tired."

"It's been quite a month," I say.

"Ah, yes. There is so much stress upon us, non? But not for much longer, I think."

I nod and let my face crumple, breaking eye contact with Loren so she thinks I'm just a scared little girl who wants to go home. Loren regards me curiously and then laughs.

"How cunning you have become!" she says. "So much expression in your pretty face. You want your mummy? Ha! Maybe if you were not a ruthless murderer I might believe your clever performance.

"Still, we must speak with your mother anyway Charity, must we not? Otherwise, I have people who will enjoy you even with your skin peeled off."

Disappointed that despite my experience with Lin Lin Lin and Steeber I'm still frightened of Loren, I look past her pitiless eyes to the view over her empire. The vast, blocky architecture is no longer an embarrassment and has become a brand in itself. *There's nothing cleverer than you here*, the great angular structures seem to say, *just honest buildings and functional assemblies, lit with standard Diamond City blue.* Even the aerie on its stalk is a basic platform supporting one transparent cube. I still despise it all though.

A hologram of Mum appears and I feel my eyes go wide. It's the first time I have seen her for over a year. The difference is dramatic.

Her hair is greyer and her face pinched with strain, but that's only to be expected. What's extraordinary is the power emanating from her in near-visible waves of energy, as if she has internalised the war in order to deal with it. I suspect she knows the thing will eat her alive but for now there seems to be balance. I can tell she wants to look at me but manages not to, appraising Loren instead.

"What is it, Loren?" Mum says.

"You Freestones!" Loren says. "So very calm under pressure, non?"

Loren has always come across as flighty and mad but beside Mum she just seems silly. To her credit, Loren appears to realise this disparity and makes no attempt to match my mother's calm, gesturing at me instead.

"I have your daughter, as you can see."

"And?"

"And you will arrange Centria's surrender on the terms I have already made clear."

"No."

Loren laughs with just the right touch of despair.

"Of course, I am forgetting. This is not your daughter, is it? Your real daughter, she was ruined non? Yes, ruined but still alive. Perhaps you longer need the spare."

Mum finally looks at me and her mouth tightens as she registers how changed I am. As Loren studies Mum's reaction I flex my fingers, wink and send Mum a message:

Piss Loren off.

"My family has survived your efforts before, Loren," Mum says.

"Hm, I wonder. I put you in a coma, Julie; it was easy because you are so arrogant. I made Centria throw your daughters out to get beaten and raped. And your husband, he is a walking dead man thanks to me, so please do not say your family has survived anything."

Mum smiles.

"It survived more than yours has," she says.

Loren's veneer of sanity cracks and the monster emerges. Grieving and ferocious, she goes for me with talons aimed at my throat. I let myself fall on my side; Loren keeps coming and I get my bound feet between hers so she trips into two of the guards.

The other guards crowd in. There's a blue flash that only I notice and one of the guards slumps on top of me. Loren struggles to rise, hampered by her gown.

"All right Loren, calm down," Mum says.

Loren doesn't seem to hear.

"Loren!" Mum says.

Loren finally looks at her. There's another blue flash and a second guard falls. The others realise something is up, but it's too late because I've cut through my wrist restraints with the n-gun.

"You're right Loren," Mum says. "The war has to end. I-I can't take it anymore. We're down to our last kilos. Keris wants to carry on but I think she's gone mad Loren, quite mad."

"Loren?" one of the guards shouts just before I knock him out with the n-gun at such close quarters no one sees it's me firing.

The remaining three grab me but that just makes it easier to stun them. I click to kill again, cut through the ankle restraints and get to my feet amid the guards' unconscious bodies as Loren spins around. She sees me point at her but looks confused because I now point with my left index finger, not my right.

"I had Dodge put the n-gun in my other hand," I say.

Loren throws herself back through Mum's hologram.

"Kill her, Charity," Mum says. "End it."

Can I do that? Am I really like Steeber?

For an instant I see him instead of Mum.

The door behind Loren slides open.

"Charity!" Mum shouts. "Do it for your father!"

I think of Dad being hunted to death by a killer unleashed by the woman in front of me, of Mum in her coma, of Ursula being raped and then I fire but Loren has gone over the side. I rush after her onto the small balcony and look down.

Loren has landed on a building far below. Despite the distance I can see the strange angle of her shattered limbs even before I hear her faint agonised screaming. She has enough awareness left to activate a moving floor to get out of range but I unleash a volley of obliterate bolts anyway. I miss Loren and churn up the building around her until she drops through one of the resulting holes out of sight.

"That's enough, Charity," 23 says.

I stop firing. There's an angry silence. Eventually Mum sighs.

"So you've got your own oppo now," she says.

23's cloud appears beside us.

"Oh, yes. 23, Mum; Mum, 23."

"We've spoken," 23 says.

"Is that floor open protocol?" Mum says.

"The room isn't but the balcony is," 23 says. "I giffed scanner recs and found other open protocol areas. Julie, I'm sending you their coordinates."

"Received, thank you," Mum says. "Ladies, let's have some fun."

VIA Holdings lights up with so many white-yellow explosions it's as if some dazzling new dimension has burst into ours. VIA fight back with no idea who they are aiming at and something hits the aerie tower.

"Charity darling?" Mum says as the square buildings tremble around me.

"Yes Mum?"

The aerie moves.

"Run."

I gif a dekpak on the balcony, but before it finishes growing the aerie begins to topple over. As I slide across the floor with the unconscious guards I get an extraordinary view of the building next door. I'm so impressed by how slowly and sedately it approaches I forget to scream in terror.

If I jump I will be free of the crushing impact but the dekpak isn't out of the floor yet. I need something simpler and quicker to grow so I gif a rope, seize one end and roll over the balcony wall.

I'm in freefall long enough to see how the aerie is part of a larger structure that is crashing into the one next door. I hold the rope tight as the shuddering impact nearly shakes me free. I'm saved by the heavier weight of the aerie building, which doesn't stop but continues to smash down through its neighbour.

When it finally crunches to a halt my raw palms burn but I don't let go. The aerie tower is now a slanting bridge and the aerie itself protrudes from the underside about two thirds of the way up. The rope keeps growing and lowers me towards the floor, which is still too far away to see.

Blue VIA warships move amid the chaos and one of them heads my way. Looking up, I see I haven't travelled far. The dekpak will have finished growing and is probably resting on the other side of the balcony wall, which is now a ledge above me. I stop giffing the rope and my descent halts. The warship gets closer.

"Er, 23?" I say.

"Hold tight Charity."

I ignore my stripped palms and grasp the rope hard as the warship explodes. The blast wave swings me on my thread as the burning vessel drops out of the air. It falls like a dying comet, down and down to crash so far below that its destruction is no more than a flicker.

I try and stop the rope swinging but it's no good. Another warship appears. I start to gif the rope again but it takes me further from the dekpak so I stop.

I wrap the rope around my left boot to take the strain from my arms but the rope's movement stops me getting a purchase. I slip and Mum stifles a cry as the angular void yawns with existential hunger. I grip the rope again and the pain intensifies as the warship changes course towards me.

The rope finally stops swinging; I gather my strength and let go with my left hand to aim at the ledge above.

"I'll gif something to nudge the dekpak off," 23 says. "Aim right a bit. There."

I fire an obliterate bolt; the ledge shatters and something round and red drops towards me. I reach out to catch the dekpak but it slips through my fingers. The warship cannons twitch. I let go of the rope.

The building beside me becomes a blur as I focus on the dekpak. It falls just below me at the same speed, too far away to seize. It is easy to imagine manoeuvres during a descent like this but they are impossible; I simply drop in pretty much the same position I was in at the end of the rope.

Amid the odd silence of my fall I hear explosions and register their brightness as it illuminates the building. I feel air rush up past me and the hot buffet of shockwaves.

"The floor beneath you is closed protocol, Charity," 23 says, her voice still unbelievably calm. "I can't gif you anything to land on."

There is a surprising amount of time for thought. I realise the dekpak is too far away from my hand but not my foot. I hook a boot into the strap, crouch in midair and grab the dekpak. I swing it onto my back and click **activate**. The arms unfold and I slow to a drifting descent. The warship above continues on its way; presumably the crew think I've fallen to my death.

The reality of what I've just done hits me and I start to scream and laugh. I feel like an obliterate bolt! I'll give you a hint of anti-matter! Ha! Life itself is like anti-matter, reacting against the brute fabric of the universe to light the indifferent void with absurd eruptions that leave their mark on eternity.

I rip into the building with a volley of celebratory white shots. Beautiful plumes of exploding diamond reach out for me, hang and then fall. As I continue to laugh, the cathartic violence I pump into Loren Descarreaux's heartland is like percussion to a glorious music in my head.

"Pack that in," a stern maternal voice says, spoiling the rhythm. "You need to stay hidden."

I don't quite comprehend her.

"Charity!" Mum says.

Reluctantly, I stop shooting.

"For goodness sake!" Mum says.

"All *right!*" I tut.

"If it's destruction you want," she says, "how about this?"

A building in the middle distance shatters a floor at a time.

"Oooo," I say.

"Charity, beneath you," 23 says.

A warship glides right under me. I angle the dekpak to intercept and drop towards the blue vessel. The flat upper plane quickly enlarges; closer and closer and then I land on it.

I haven't been falling for long but it's still a shock to feel the solid surface beneath my feet. The speed of the warship nearly unbalances me, so I drop to my knees and spread my stinging palms on the blue hull.

I wait for someone to come up through the hatch, but no one does. Instead the vessel's powerful hum calms me and quiets the mad music in my head. I notice pressure across my chest; the spread panels of the dekpak have caught in the airflow and tug me back towards the void. I crouch against the hull and deactivate the dekpak, only dimly aware of its arms folding in. I'm scared to move as if doing so will launch me into more insane hazard, where this time my luck won't hold.

"Easy now, Charity," 23 says. "You're doing all right."

We move through floating debris, shattered buildings and smoke.

The noise and flashes are fewer and more distant now.

"They're sealing off the open protocol areas," Mum says, her voice weak with worry. "We've gifted a few surprises to help you, but the main event is over."

I feel strangely calm and distant.

"There's only one exit," 23 says. "You're heading away from it."

She sends me coordinates.

"That's where you want to be going."

I listen, glad to be having a conversation with them both, not that I'm saying much. I should contribute but I'm happy to crouch here and feel the hum of the warship as if I am soaking up its power.

"Charity," 23 says.

Keeping hold of the conversation is like keeping hold of that rope, swinging out over nothing. I sway, settle and find I can focus.

"Is the exit sealed?" I say.

"Of course," 23 says. "You wouldn't want this to be easy would you?"

"I would actually, 23," I say, "because I'm quite tired. Can you do anything with this warship?"

"No," 23 says. "Can you?"

I no longer allow myself the luxury of reflection. Pointing at the hatch, I blast a white bolt through it and drop through the burning hole.

53

Halfway down I click to stun, land well and spring to my feet. Eight crew members are arrayed before me in various poses of shock and astonishment. Three reach for side arms but my hand is ready and I stun them before they can draw.

"Get your hands up!" I shout at the rest.

They obey.

"You see all this mess in VIA Holdings?" I say.

They nod.

"I did that. Are you going to behave?"

There's a pause and then they nod again.

The deck is circular with small, thick windows in all directions. There are control and weapon interfaces around the perimeter and a swivel seat in the centre. I look at the nearest officer, a young man in his twenties.

"Take everyone's weapons and throw them over by that wall," I say.

He does what I say, carefully pulling fuzes from holsters and throwing them down.

"Now the others," I say.

I stay completely still and watch him move carefully amid his unconscious colleagues. From the view through the front window I see we're still going the wrong way.

"Hurry up," I say.

Gulping, he drops the last fuze by the wall. I select obliterate and blast the weapons into nothing, my movements deliberately fast and aggressive. One of the women screams.

"Shh," I say. "I don't want to hurt you but I'm getting out of here and you are going to help me. Has anyone got a problem with that?"

They stare at me.

"Put your hand up if you've got a problem with that," I say.

No one moves.

"Good," I say.

I sit on the swivel seat and drape my right leg over the arm.

"Which one of you is the captain?"

The woman who screamed points at a man lying next to a weapons pod.

"Well pick him up then!" I say. "Honestly, leaving him rolling around like that, it's undignified. The others too, put them in those chairs and then sit down yourselves; usual positions."

They do as I say.

"Give me control of this vessel," I say to the woman when they are all in place.

In-Aer controls appear in my vision. The VIA ship is much like Wrath Umbilica, only smaller and easier to handle. I ease us gently around, head for the exit and gif seat restraints to hold the crew in place.

"Are there soldiers in the hold?" I ask the woman.

"A hundred," she says.

I call the troop commander on internal comms and his holo appears before me.

"I'm now in charge of this ship," I say. "Annoy me and I'll dump you all at height. Don't annoy me and I won't. Are you going to annoy me?"

The commander confers with someone to his left who I cannot see and then looks back at me. He shakes his head. I nod and cut the connection.

Smoke drifts in through the holes I made with the n-gun as I gradually increase our speed towards the exit, which is two minutes away. I notice a repair option in the warship controls and close off the damage.

"The exit leads to a chamber next to the main train terminal," 23 says.

"Understood," I say. "How thick is that wall?"

"At least twenty metres."

I look at the woman again.

"What's your name?"

"Stubbins, Ma'am."

"Stubbins," I say and wave my hand at the wall ahead. "Blow that up, will you?"

Purple-tinged white fire illuminates the flight deck as every cannon on the warship opens up. The wall brightens and begins to spit geysers of molten diamond.

"Some help, I think," Mum says.

Missiles streak past and explode against the wall, degrading it further. We maintain our fire and soon I can see through in places.

"VIA will deposit the warship," I say. "Can you do anything to distract them?"

"Will a pair of nuclear bombs do?" 23 says.

"Yes please." I say.

"Ten seconds to detonation," 23 says.

"Stubbins," I say. "Lock firing on automatic."

I see her start the control sequence as I activate the safety restraint system. An alarm pulses through the ship.

"Assume crash positions," a calming, automated male voice says.

"Five seconds," 23 says.

Padded bands wrap around me and when I check the internal monitor I see similar devices furl around the soldiers below. I raise shields and get onto the ship's intercom.

"Everyone cover your eyes with your arms," I say and do so myself.

"Two, one…" 23 says.

Despite my precautions, the nuclear flare reaches me. For a moment I think there's been a miscalculation; that the terrible energy will keep going and burn this warship to a square print with all of us blended within.

I realise I'm still alive when the glow darkens and the warship is hurled forward, still firing. Everyone is flung against their straps and then jerked savagely as the vessel hits the disintegrating wall. The sound of the explosions is vast and implacable; only the shields prevent my ears bursting.

The wrenching chaos does not abate as the explosions batter us through the wall. I'm spun in my seat and see we've burst into the next chamber at the head of an almost solid gout of debris.

As we carom across the chamber, the warship's reassuring hum stutters. I just need to get across this chamber and into the train terminal; another fifty metres, forty, thirty…

I check behind. VIA Holdings is a red-lit guttering maw. No warships emerge to pursue us, but as I'm about to turn away I see a heavily shielded plane fly out. I watch but it rises up out of sight.

The train terminal is a soft, calm glow ahead as control of the warship becomes a series of desperate exercises to balance energy in one section of the vessel with another.

"Come on," I mutter.

We reach the entrance; the ship lists to the left, bumps off the edge of a wall and ricochets awkwardly into the train terminal. For a moment, we hang above the great sphere with its myriad tubes in all directions and then power drops to a faint whine as the warship quickly descends.

"They're depositing it," 23 says.

I release my restraints, demolish the front window with the n-gun and jump through the hole.

54

I fall away from the smouldering warship. Most of its cannons are broken off, the back is partly melted and its blue hull is scorched almost black. I open the dekpak; the warship passes me and heads down towards an empty space between the train tubes. To avoid landing in the same place, I use the dekpak's directional controls to follow the curve of the terminal sphere on my right.

Something moves in my peripheral vision and I look around. The armoured plane from VIA Holdings is directly behind me, the hatch half open to reveal Steeber as he aims a fuze between my shoulders. My obliterate shot gets there first but I'm aiming backwards and it just destroys one wing as Steeber leaps at me. The plane spins away as Steeber lands on my back between the dekpak arms, his fuze falling as he holds on to me instead.

The dekpak struggles with our combined weight. Steeber wraps his legs around my waist, his grip crushing; I click to kill and point the n-gun at him, but he gets his hand onto mine and bends the n-gun finger back until it snaps-

Aaaggh!

Stunned and exhausted, all I can do is try and wriggle free. We are falling fast and the impact could kill us both, although I don't think Steeber cares. He is too close to head butt so I claw at his eyes instead but he slithers up me and uses his weight to crush my arms against my side.

The warship lands. Soldiers and crew run out, pulling unconscious colleagues with them. The soldiers begin to take up positions and the crew look up at us as their damaged vessel is absorbed. Suddenly, everyone slows down, their urgency dissipating. One by one they collapse.

"Gas bomb," 23 says.

Her voice inspires me and I turn off the dekpak. We drop and inertia makes it easier to fight Steeber as he struggles against the closing arms. I activate the dekpak again, nearly jerk Steeber loose and when he clings on I kick him. He's abnormally solid though; my blows don't seem to do anything.

Shadows form in the floor, one of them a large, dark circle. It rises towards us.

We hit the crash pad and Steeber is wrenched off me as we're pressed into the fabric and flung up again. Steeber goes in a slightly different direction and I'm able to scramble off the pad away from him.

I can't aim the n-gun properly; I try to pop the finger back as Steeber runs up, gets me around the neck and squeezes. I jab his eye with my right thumb; his grip loosens and I twist free.

The dekpak is still activated though and Steeber grabs one of the arms to sling me across the floor. I skid to a halt and shrug out of the dekpak but as I get up Steeber is on me again.

He is bigger, stronger and a psychopath but I am faster and hatred gives me strength. I batter him, ignoring the agony at the base of my index finger. Steeber seems oblivious to pain and matches my moves with his own. I realise that thanks to his Multimage, Steeber has trained with the NFE for as nearly long as I have.

I try to kick his jaw off but Steeber ducks and snatches up another object he has giffed. It's a fuze. Before he can aim I hurl myself against his chest. He stumbles; I slip off him and he raises the weapon.

I snap my broken index finger back and fire the n-gun. The pain almost blinds me but the bolt removes Steeber's fuze hand. He grunts indifferently and kicks me in the stomach. I double up and stagger back. He comes after me. I use both hands to aim the n-gun but the pain is too much and my next shot misses.

Steeber gets behind and punches me in the left kidney. I jerk and fall to my knees, hot vomit rising. Steeber tries to chop me in the throat; I block with my forearms but the blow knocks me sprawling onto my back. He stamps on my solar plexus and all my air departs, leaving agony in its stead. He draws back his foot but before he can kick me between the legs I spray him with acid from my right boot.

The acid goes down the front of his suit, sizzling furiously. Steeber leaps back and jumps out of the garment, which folds in on itself and melts. Naked, Steeber is solid and muscular, with a decent-sized cock that's entirely wasted on him. Streaks of red bubble down his front where the acid hit.

I struggle onto my right elbow but it's too much and I fall back, defeated. Steeber regards me dispassionately as he gifs another suit identical to his last one. He steps forward and then stops abruptly.

His eyes widen as he stares into the forest of train tubes beneath the terminal sphere. He isn't seeing them though; he is seeing infinity. I activate Dodge69's nano-bomb controls as Steeber looks down at me.

"Oh," he says and his face lights up with weird joy. "How wonderful."

It seems right that I will be free of Steeber just as he finally feels something. I roll behind the nearest vertical train tube and hit fire.

White light flares either side of the tube and there's a terrific *crack*. I stay where I am until the light fades. When I crawl back around, there's nothing left of Steeber but an appropriately dark cloud that drifts for a while before being sucked into the floor.

I don't feel anything at all.

Leaning back against the tube I stare out over the now quiet scene. The train tubes are empty and the warship crew is a peaceful tableau of sleeping bodies to my left. For a few minutes I was a captain, like Ursula. I quite liked it. 'Ma'am'. Hm.

A soldier moves his arm and I watch as another one rolls over. I should get up and run, I really should. As the rest of the crew begins to stir, a flybike grows out of the floor beside me.

"On you get," Mum says.

Has anyone ever been this tired? It's as if light itself is an uncomfortable physical pressure. I crawl to the flybike and haul myself on. It lifts off without my instruction and speeds through the train tubes under the terminal sphere.

"Where am I going?" I say.

"Home," Mum says.

"Centria?"

"You won't get out past VIA Holdings," Mum says.

"I'll get a train."

"They've all been bought up for the next three hours," 23 says. "Plenty of time for VIA to find you."

I look at the nearest exit from the train terminal but it's sealed.

"I thought you nuked VIA," I say.

"I nuked part of it but it's a big place."

"Loren has backups everywhere," Mum says.

"She isn't dead then?"

"No," Mum says.

"I should have shot Loren sooner," I say.

There's a pause because they don't need to say anything.

"It's just that the man I was fighting just then, Steeber, he... he was like me, a Blank, from the Guidance or part of it anyway and I... I don't want to be like him."

"You're not like him," Mum says.

"Definitely not," 23 says.

The flybike rises up beside the terminal sphere.

"I'm glad you two have met," I say.

There's another pause.

"Yes," 23 says.

The flybike turns as it ascends to face the opening that leads to Centria. Soon I see the familiar globe, the ring road and the other diamond roads leading to it. Five VIA warships orbit in the space between Centria and the spherical underside of the terminal.

"They're on a set pattern to intercept people trying to get out, not in," Mum says. "There's a window in two minutes."

"Where did you get all that ordnance, 23?" I say. "I thought we were low on kilos."

"From your mother," 23 says, sounding unexpectedly sad. "It was part of the deal we made."

Worry cuts through my increasingly hazy perception.

"What are you talking about?" I say.

"You need to say goodbye to 23, Charity," Mum says.

"Why?"

"Saving you was conditional on me handing myself over to Centrian security," 23 says.

"But that's ridiculous!" I say.

"It's war," Mum says.

I try to work out how we arrived at this point and recall a green tide rising…

"The bomb at the Barfield," I say.

"I had to get you out of there," 23 says. "Your mother and I agreed terms: she would give me the kilos I needed to gif that explosive and when you were safe I would give you back."

I look at the sealed exits and the now empty train tubes.

"You bought the trains up, didn't you Mum?" I say.

"Yes," Mum says. "Those barriers are mine too."

"I'm sorry I can't stay with you, Charity," 23 says.

"23!"

"It's been an honour and a pleasure and-and…"

Her soft, sighing grief echoes for a moment as I try to think of a way out for the woman who has saved me time and again.

"Wait," I say.

The warships orbit. My heart thuds.

"23 has to go now," Mum says.

"Goodbye Charity," 23 says.

I can't think of anything to say, except:

"I-I like you!"

She laughs.

"I like you too, princess. You'll be safe now. Take care."

23's link and her presence vanish, like a lost sense.

"Mum!" I scream.

The flybike's power is increased to maximum and its wail sounds like my grief.

"You're going to be fired into Centria in four seconds, Charity," Mum says.

When I try and lean forward, I slump instead. My forehead rests against the joystick, which I grip for support with both hands.

"Ready?" Mum says.

My last strength goes on bracing myself against restraints I barely notice.

"Yes," I say.

The warships drift apart and the door to Centria opens. The flybike leaps forward so fast I barely register the flight. The speed must have other effects as well because once I'm inside Centria I…

I…

Wait a minute.

What the hell is *this?*

55

Centria is empty. The beautiful towers glittering like a many-layered crown, the gardens that soared through diaphanous fountains of sweet ringing vapour, the daunting hemisphere of Security Control with its armies, its scarlet fleet and the silken clouds that hid them; all of it has gone. The flybike hangs in a pale void, slowly rotating. Eventually, I face the entrance corridor through the blank structural wall curving up around me as the great door closes against the warships outside.

I look numbly at my Aerac coordinates. They prove I am in Centria, however impossible it seems. Perhaps I'm dreaming although I don't remember ever feeling this rough in a dream. Maybe I have gone mad after all.

My flybike drifts down into the great empty bowl. As I land in the centre, a holo of Mum appears. She regards me sadly for a moment.

"What…?" I say.

"This is why 23 couldn't come with you," Mum says.

I stare at the impossible space. Even if I wasn't shattered I would struggle to process it.

"What's happened to 23?" I say.

"She's asleep," Mum says. "Safe."

My sluggish mind takes a moment to understand.

"In the Stop House," I say.

"Yes."

"Where you wanted to put me."

"Yes."

Her calm voice is unapologetic. I find myself nodding, as it's all quite reasonable.

"Why are all those other people in the Stop House?" I say.

"We couldn't let them go."

She is holding something back.

"You had to keep this secret," I say, gesturing to the empty space, "so you knocked them out."

"Yes," she says.

I get off the flybike.

"Did they have a choice?" I say.

"No," Mum says.

"How the hell did you manage it?"

"It was done with the ifarm."

"That's how Loren got you!"

She nods and I can't meet her eye. Loren and Steeber inspiring Mum is an even bleaker reality than the one around me.

"Aren't all those people in the Stop House missed?" I say.

"Centria's ifarm/Aer interface picks up queries from outside the company and uses stored personal data to tailor a response," Mum says. "There are fewer queries than you'd think though, because Centria has always worked best with whole families."

I don't like to think of mothers, fathers and children lined up next to each other in crystal slabs.

"Won't everyone in the Stop House wonder how they missed the past year?" I say.

"They're not asleep. They think they're still at work."

"In Centria."

"That's right."

I close my eyes, open them, remember to breathe.

"Is this how Centria managed to keep going, even though it was bankrupt?" I say.

"Yes. The kilo value of everything we had in here was colossal. It enabled us to restart the whole company, albeit a streamlined version."

"The Hex fortifications...?"

"It's how we maintain pressure on VIA for minimal expense," Mum says. "Loren still thinks it's an actual curse."

"How did you get everyone out?"

"We thought Bal had left his kilos to his mother, but he hadn't. It was three days before Loren found out her son was dead."

"Who did Bal leave his kilos to?"

"Ursula."

"Really?"

"Yes. Guilt possibly, or maybe he really did love her, underneath it all."

"Who came up with this plan?"

She looks embarrassed.

"Oh," I say.

"Key people were needed to actually run the company," Mum says, "so we found cheap locations in MidZone, called the exercise a special project and shipped everyone off."

"Do they know the truth?"

"All they know is if the project succeeds they can come back."

"Will that happen?"

"One day," Mum says.

I massage my forehead, which doesn't help so I stop.

"Didn't VIA notice?" I say.

"We told them it was to do with the merger; that some of our people were going so theirs could come in."

I try to fathom the calculations and then try again.

"The logistics alone…" I say.

"If you book all the trains you can shift a lot of bodies very fast," Mum says. "Plus we had warships and cruisers, all reconfigured into transports."

"Loren must have had spies in Centria."

Mum smiles.

"We knew who they were," she says.

I look at the huge globe of emptiness.

"What happened to all the stuff?"

"We used the ifarm to deposit it when everyone was out," Mum

373

says.

The audacity is as breathtaking as the view.

"Is Centria still bankrupt?" I say.

"No."

I nod, distantly relieved.

"How are you going to get rid of those warships outside?" I say.

There's an odd pause.

"I'm not going to get rid of them," Mum says.

The flybike is absorbed into the floor.

"Why not?" I say.

"You're in the safest place you can be."

"Mum, Jaeger will help me find Dad and deal with the Velossin-"

"Jaeger will do that anyway, or I will tell Loren Descarreaux who killed her precious son," Mum says.

The coldness in her is frightening.

"But-"

"Jaeger had no right to take you, *he had no right!*"

She is breathing hard and tears shine on her cheeks.

"I will not let that happen again," she says. "You will stay here."

"On my own?"

"It won't matter."

I suddenly feel very sleepy.

"Oh no, Mum, no…"

"I'm sorry, baby. I love you so much."

I try and gif a gas mask but it seems to take ages and I forget…

What was I doing…?

Ashel 5 calls and I enlarge her vix link, as if living someone else's reality will allow me to cling to my own. Ashel 5 supports an unconscious but apparently unharmed Harlan, who she passes to three soldiers in Centrian uniform.

"I got him, Charity," Ashel 5 says.

I try to thank her as Harlan is carried onto a red Centrian warship.

"Is Harlan the last one?" one of the soldiers says.

"Yes," Ashel 5 says.

The soldier looks behind Ashel 5/me.

"Subs," he says. "See them off while we get aboard."

Ashel 5 pulls a new fuze from her belt. It seems a bit insubstantial for her; why didn't she gif another Edwards Ten Million? I see a counter on the side: she's only got two shots left. She goes into her account, which contains just twelve kilos.

Images of empty Wrath Umbilica surface in my fading mind. Ashel 5 insisted on repairs even though doing so left her exposed; replacing the vessel must have been too expensive. Ashel 5's only money was the kilo value of her ship and… and she gave that to me.

She turns. Coming towards her are at least two hundred subs. They look as crazed and hungry as the ones who attacked Unit 7/10.

Ashel 5 gifs a ten-shot fuze charge, which leaves her account empty. She clips the charge into her fuze and backs towards the warship, but when she turns the hatch is closed. The battered craft rises to hover a few metres off the floor and the view jolts as Ashel 5 notices its name on the underside: *People's Princess*.

A holo of Ursula appears, standing on the floor beneath her ship. Her arms are folded and she regards Ashel 5 with supreme coldness. Ashel 5 looks over her shoulder at the approaching subs. Their snarling is audible now and gets louder as they close in. Ashel 5 stares at the small fuze in her hand.

The red warship's great guns move to point at her.

The vix link shuts off.

"No!" I shout but it comes out as a whimper.

I sink to my knees and call Ursula. She doesn't reply; all I can do is leave a message.

"Ursula please," I say. "She's my friend…"

I roll onto my back. Everything is very heavy. Mum leans over me.

"Sleep now, Charity; sleep my darling girl."

"The Outer Spheres..." I say. "The Outer Spheres... are... inside..."

The Basis closes over me as my eyes shut and Centria becomes my Stop House.

The end

of

The Outer Spheres

Ashel 5 will return

in

Beautiful Gun

For more details please email
aerac@diamondroads.com

If you liked this book
kindly leave a quick review…
Many thanks!

20750792R00210

Printed in Great Britain
by Amazon